Praise for Kem Nunn's *Chance*

'*Chance* takes place in the twilit world of noir, where people
and things are never what they seem… for all the mayhem
in *Chance,* its conclusion is delicately funny'
– *The New York Times Book Review*

'Sentence by sentence Nunn achieves a muscular eloquence
– I almost wrote elegance – unusual in what at first appears
to be a genre novel. There hasn't been fiction this good
about a San Francisco medical professional gone off
the rails over a woman since Frank Norris's deluded
dentist in the 1899 novel *McTeague*'
– Alan Cheuse, *San Francisco Chronicle*

'Is it too much to compare Kem Nunn to Raymond
Chandler?… like Chandler, Nunn's great subject is what
lies beneath the surface, the desolation that infuses us at
every turn… The power of this disturbing and provocative
novel is that it leaves us unmoored among the signposts of a
morally ambiguous universe in which, even after
we have finished reading, it is uncertain who has
been feeding whom'
– *Los Angeles Times*

'The book could be considered a pulp masterpiece. It has
everything from a femme fatale to a dystopian setting
where the California sun is blotted out by a black-ash fog
from wildfires burning around the Bay. Chance is the kind
of everyman whose bad choices are noir staples. But calling
it pulp would undersell the sheer genius of the writing,
which uses the convention of mystery-thrillers to create
a psychological allegory of Freud's construct, id, ego, and
superego at war with themselves'
– *The Arizona Republic*

CHANCE

Titles by Kem Nunn

Tapping the Source
Unassigned Territory
Pomona Queen
The Dogs of Winter
Tijuana Straits
Chance

CHANCE
KEM NUNN

NO EXIT PRESS

This edition published in 2017 by No Exit Press,
an imprint of Oldcastle Books Ltd, PO Box 394
Harpenden, AL5 1X
noexit.co.uk

ISBN
978-0-85730-162-8 (print)
978-0-85730-163-5 (epub)
978-0-85730-164-2 (kindle)
978-0-85730-165-9 (pdf)

2 4 6 8 10 9 7 5 3 1

Typeset in 12pt Minion Pro
by Avocet Typeset, Somerton, Somerset, TA11 6RT
Printed and bound in Denmark by Nørhaven, Viborg

For more information about Crime Fiction go to crimetime.co.uk /
@crimetimeuk

This one is for Ulrike, my only Uli

Chance 1. *The absence of any cause or series of causes of events as they actually happen that can be predicted, understood, or controlled. Sometimes granted agency, as in:* **Chance** *governs all.*

Chance and the summer of love

Early on, before it had become apparent just how acrimonious, costly, and downright mean spirited the divorce would become, Chance had thought to find a place in or near the Presidio, a small house perhaps, with a view of the water, the proximity of redwood and cedar. The fantasy was short lived. The good places were expensive and hard to come by though nothing in the city was cheap anymore, that other Summer of Love a long time gone.

He'd settled finally for a modest one-bedroom apartment with a shared basement garage at the edge of the Sunset from whose front-most windows he might on occasion glimpse the sea. The streets in his new neighborhood, though raked at a slight angle to run downward in the general direction of the Pacific Ocean, were uniformly flat and treeless, bordered by long lines of gaily painted stucco and wooden structures. On sunny days he found these streets infused with such light as he'd come to associate with the deserts of the Southwest, their hopeful pastels bleached of meaningful distinctions. On foggy days the colors were made impotent as well, barely distinguishable from the damp concrete sidewalks, the asphalt streets, or the pale, slate gray sky. Analogies he might have drawn with his own life appeared tiresome even to him.

What he'd taken as the decline of things in general had coincided with a particularly disturbing case. It was not a complicated case. There were no legal or medical puzzles to be solved. There were only the facts, which he had summarized as follows:

At the time of my evaluation Mariella Franko was 34 months post a head-on motor vehicle accident in which her 68-year-old father was killed in gruesome fashion. (In an effort to avoid a wayward dairy cow that had wandered into his lane, her father had collided with an oncoming delivery truck. He was decapitated. His head rested in the rear seat. Mariella remained trapped next to her father's body till freed by the Jaws of Life. She remembers shouting 'Daddy!' many times while in the car.)

Review of emergency medical services indicates her Glasgow Coma Scale was 15 at the time of their arrival. Her chief complaint was listed as 'My daddy… I want my daddy!' She was medicated with intravenous fentanyl and transferred by ambulance to a CalStar helicopter that carried her to Stanford. Upon arrival, she was crying and asking for her father. No fractures or internal injuries were found. She was monitored overnight and sent home with plans for follow-up by a primary care physician.

A psychiatric evaluation done one month later describes anxiety, depression, startle reactions, spells of tachycardia, tachypnea, and perspiration together with intrusive thoughts of her father. It was noted that she had spent three months off work and attempted to distract herself by trying to watch television. Her social life had become very constricted, with severe withdrawal and isolation. She described a predominant state of hopelessness and lack of motivation. Ms Franko was found to be suffering from chronic post-traumatic stress disorder and major depression. A course of psychotherapy together with antidepressant medication was recommended.

Unfortunately, Ms Franko went on to receive neither psychotherapy nor pharmacotherapy and remained, at the time of my evaluation, anxious, depressed, and struggling to avoid any such thoughts, mental images, or feelings as might return her to the night of the accident. I agree that Ms Franko suffers from chronic post-traumatic stress disorder. She faced a life-threatening situation, believed she was going to die, was present at her father's death, and was trapped in a vehicle with him under gruesome circumstances. The photographs I have been shown speak for themselves. It is unfortunate that a second psychiatric consultation was not obtained until more than 2 years had passed following the accident. And while her avoidance of mental health care professionals is understandable, it is exactly this avoidance to which health care providers should have responded...

Eldon J. Chance, MD
Associate Clinical Professor
Department of Psychiatry
UCSF School of Medicine

There was more to the report but that was the gist of the thing. Someone's insurance company had retained him to evaluate the nature and severity of her psychological trauma. Chance was a forensic neuropsychiatrist and made the better part of his living explaining often complicated neurological conditions to juries and or attorneys who would soon be standing in front of juries, in cases ranging from personal injury to elder abuse to undue influence. He was sometimes asked for evaluations by other doctors and sometimes retained by family members or estates. It was not the practice he'd once imagined but it was the practice he had. He rarely saw someone more than once or twice and rarely worked with them as patients.

And so it had been with Mariella Franko. He had seen her only once, at the time of his evaluation. He did not know what had become of her, how her case had come out, or whether or not she had received any of the recommended therapies or medications. Nor, it no doubt goes without saying, was she the only patient he saw that summer. It was a season in which any number of cases might have occupied his thoughts.

J.C. is a 36-year-old, right-handed white woman with a long and complicated medical history. The product of an attempted abortion (born prematurely at 7 months) she suffers a mild form of mental retardation, the result of oxygen deprivation at the time of the botched procedure and premature birth. The patient admits to a long-standing incestuous relationship with her father and after seven miscarriages gave birth to a son with numerous congenital anomalies…

M.J. is a 42-year-old, right-handed black woman with several years of college education. The patient relates that at the age of 36, while walking from her job in a bookstore to her home in the Mission District, she was assaulted by an Hispanic male standing over six feet tall and weighing more than two hundred pounds. She has only partial recollections of the assault but remembers having her head struck repeatedly against a fire hydrant after trying to run from her attacker. M.J. states that over the next year she was extremely depressed and spent 12 months watching television or staying drunk. During this time she acquired a handgun and would occasionally discharge it in frustration and rage. Her closest friend was a pet rat, which she says would come over and put its paw on her hand to console her. M.J. currently lives alone in low-budget housing for the homeless and mentally disabled in San Francisco…

L.S. is a 46-year-old woman who grew up with an abusive alcoholic mother. The identity of her father has never been made known to her. L.S. is at pains to present herself as an individual with learning disabilities. She states that as a young child she seemed to learn everything 'backward.' She would read not only individual words but also pages backward. If she is forced to read a book beginning at the front, she seems to have little sense of the story until she is able to read it again from the end to the front. Although the bulk of L.S.'s time is spent caring for the 104 exotic birds she owns, her second greatest passion is reading about mental *illness and learning disabilities. The patient states that for as long as she can remember she has felt depressed, empty, and uncertain as to who she is...*

D.K. is a 30-year-old right-handed white male last employed as a graphic artist in San Jose, now four years status post a pedestrian vs. truck injury at the Port of Oakland with resulting head injury. The patient states that while he is unaware of changes in his personality, he is also aware that others, including his wife, say that his personality has changed completely. His wife further states the patient has confided to her that he believes he will someday play a major role in a battle between Satan, Yahweh, and Jesus. Six months ago, in the context of believing it necessary to cleanse his body in preparation for the coming conflict, the patient ingested a range of household cleaners, including Hexol and Clorox...

Still, it was Mariella Franko who came along for the ride on those first dreary days of an unusually hot and early summer, hunting apartments in the City by the Bay, fielding papers from opposing attorneys, seeing patients, writing reports, watching as the money melted away like a late snow, departing with a good deal more rapidity and in greater amounts than it had ever arrived, watching as the life he'd so carefully arranged for himself, his wife, and daughter broke apart upon the rocks of a heretofore scarcely imagined reality.

His soon-to-be ex-wife, an aspiring photographer, was not self-supporting. Sales of her work could not be counted upon even for the rent of her studio. Her lover, with whom she had so recently taken up, a dyslexic personal trainer ten years her junior, worked only part time at a gym in Sausalito, and there would be little in the way of financial support from that quarter. Her attorney had already acquired a writ from a judge. Chance would be paying for both attorneys, his *and* hers. The house would be going on the market in the worst of markets. His daughter's much beloved private school with its Monterey pines and views of the bay was appearing less likely by the day. The public school nearest their current home was the stuff of nightmare.

As for Ms Franko in this time of drought and ash – the skies were so often thick with it of late, the result of fires sparked by some mishap in the Richmond refinery east of the bay, complicated by the unseasonable weather and dry, accompanying winds – she lived with her eighty-nine-year-old paternal grandmother in an apartment building on the south end of Palo Alto. At one point in his evaluation he had inquired as to how her grandmother had responded to the death of her only son. Mariella had said that her grandmother was very sad. She said her grandmother took medication on a daily basis but did not recall its name. She did not know if the older woman shared any of her recurring nightmares or intrusive recollections of the event that had claimed the life of their father and son.

Oddly enough it was Chance who had experienced a number of recurring nightmares together with intrusive memories and vivid recollections of the photographs he'd been asked to look at and these accompanied by the image of this shy and diminutive creature, alone in those still-dark hours, inquiring of the now speechless effigy at her side. Off this, he would move to imagining her out there in the apartment in Palo Alto, alone in some no doubt terminally banal setting, attempting to 'distract herself by watching television'. What would she watch? he wondered. What could she possibly find that would not lead to the gouging out of one's own eyes? The image suggested Lear and unaccommodated man, the thing itself. Job at least had God in the whirlwind. Mariella got police procedurals and vampire bloodletting. And that was just the news. He seemed to recall that she worked full time as a packager for Granny Goose potato chips in San Jose and that prior to the accident her interests had included painting, drawing, and collecting small statues of frogs.

There came a night, alone in his new apartment, half in the bag, he had actually gone so far as to imagine his driving the forty-five minutes it might take to reach her. She was not unattractive. In his report, he had described her as follows:

A petite 39-year-old woman of Italian descent with black hair that is pulled back tightly into a bun. She has straight, almost classical, features and large brown eyes. Her fingers are well manicured and she wears no nail polish. She wears a leather coat over a tan pin-striped suit and brown leather high-heeled lace-up boots. Her general manner, while pleasant, is marked by a total absence of spontaneity. The interview proceeded in a series of questions followed by unelaborated answers.

What he had thought but not recorded, what set her apart from so many of the others, was that she had about her some aspect of the caged bird, of a life un-lived. And it was just *that,* he thought, the horror of the life un-lived, that had found him out, in the midst of his own decline, wherein each day seemed at risk of being even more dimly lit than the one before it.

He held to the belief, possibly illusory, that there are times in a person's life, moments really, when the right word or motion, when a single touch might wound or heal. It was to this end that he imagined the drive. It was not about some sexual conquest. He might just as easily have enlisted the aid of another had another arrived. It was the *striking through* that he envisioned, the freeing of the caged heart. He knew better, of course. He could see all of this for what it was, the half-mad quixotic gesture better dreamt than executed because well… because that was what life was like in the end. It was an image in a glass darkly. It was all just half lived. There would be no drives and no interventions. The workings of the world would not permit them. In lieu of these he opted for additional wine. But my God, he thought a moment later, refilling a glass, imagining for the simple sake of imagining it, his arriving unannounced upon her doorstep, what *would* she think? He heard the night made horrible with her screams.

He dozed thinking of Blake: '*Every night and every morn / Some to misery are born… Every morn and every night / Some are born to sweet delight. / Some are born to sweet delight, / Some are born to endless night.*' He woke later in the still dark to the waves of Ocean Beach through the walls of his room. Rising, he was treated by way of a bathroom window to a strange orange light upon the eastern sky – what he was willing to take as evidence that in the hills above the Richmond oil refinery, the fires continued to rage.

The Printz collection

THE FURNITURE was French Art Deco from the late thirties, the work of a well-known designer by the name of Eugene Printz. The set comprised a desk, a bookshelf, and two chairs. It was made of palm wood and oxidized brass, and worth a considerable amount of money. It would have been worth even more but some of the brass was missing from the bookshelf and desk, several strips that should have run along the bottom edges of each. He'd gotten it that way and had paid accordingly. Still, it was a beautiful set and he'd always enjoyed how it looked in the big house he'd shared with his wife and daughter. Viewed now, in the confines of the small apartment, the stuff seemed sad and out of place, if not outright ridiculous. Over time it had come to irritate him and he'd begun to consider selling it. There was a dealer who specialized in such stuff, a black gentleman of perhaps seventy or more, down on Market Street. Chance couldn't recall the man's name but he could remember the location of his store, which was within walking distance of his office, and resolved to go there at his earliest convenience. An opportunity presented itself within the week, a cancellation butting up against his lunch hour, and he set out on foot for the dealer's showroom.

* * *

Generally speaking, a walk in the city was something he enjoyed. On the day in question he could not shake the feeling that he was being shown the future. It was something less than what one might have hoped for. The flames had died in the East Bay hills but what felt to be the entire Bay Area remained covered in ash. Cars were made to appear uniform in color. It lay thick in the corners of things like drifts of dirty snow. A trio of young Asian women he took as college students passed along the sidewalk wearing surgical masks. This is how it will look, he thought, moving past the women. It will look like this, and then it will look worse.

There had come a point in the evacuation of the East Bay hills, their narrow streets jammed with cars, when the firefighters had called for the distraught residents to abandon their vehicles, to flee on foot. The fires of Richmond had moved east and south at alarming speeds. The Berkeley Hills were suddenly ablaze, the night sky raining sparks. The citizenry had declined the directive, preferring to ram one another in their flaming cars. College professors and accountants, dot-commers or whatever it was they called themselves, the writers and artists, the academics and doctors of the Berkeley Hills… They had driven over one another in the black smoke like insects gone mad, like blindworms, for God's sake. He'd watched it all on the late-night newscasts from the relative safety of his apartment. What was it to horde or sell? What did his fancy French furniture amount to when already the birds of prey were increasing their number?

It was in a state of just such apocalyptic fervor, brow damp and lungs burning, that he reached the building, an old brick warehouse from before the war situated on a narrow, well-kept alley just off Market Street. Entering, he could hear at once a man's voice, a bright falsetto animated with rage. 'Are you his bitch, then…? Is that how it's going to be?' The voice broke off at the sound of the bell that signaled the front door and Chance soon spied the owner of both business and voice in conversation with a young man of some apparently Latino extraction in a black skintight T-shirt, skintight black leather jeans, and pointy-toed black leather boots that rose to just above his ankles. The older man was as Chance remembered him, well over six feet tall, dramatically thin and flamingly gay. He was even dressed as Chance remembered, in favor of rings and things, ascots, and loud sport jackets. If anything, he was older than Chance had recalled, closer to eighty than seventy. A guy that age, Chance thought, black and gay? One could imagine that he'd seen some things.

The old man cut short his rant. 'Young man,' he said, addressing Chance while turning from the other as if he'd suddenly ceased to exist, his voice no longer shrill but rising pleasantly to float among the rafters. 'What news of the Printz collection?'

'Jesus. You remembered.'

'Of course. But let me see… there was a desk and chair.' He paused. 'And a cabinet!'

'Bookcase and two chairs, but that's not bad. When was it that I was here… two, three years ago?'

The old man's hands fluttered in the muted light. 'Who keeps track of such things? But there was something missing…'

'Some bits of brass.'

'Ah, yes. A shame.'

As Chance and the old man spoke the leather boy drifted away, disappearing into some dim recess of the old building. It was the musty, cavernous feel of the place that had drawn Chance on his initial visit. He had been new to the neighborhood then, out exploring. Surely, he'd thought, this was a place where treasures lay in wait, gathering dust in the shadows.

'I'm sure you told me your name,' Chance said. He put out his hand.

'Carl,' the old man told him. They shook. 'And you… are a doctor, as I recall.'

'A neuropsychiatrist. Eldon Chance.'

The old man laughed. 'Of course, Dr Chance. How does one forget that? I remember furniture but lose names. To what do I owe the honor?' He went on without waiting a reply. 'I have recently acquired a cabinet that might just go with that set of yours…'

Chance held up his hands. 'I wish. I'm thinking of selling what I have.'

Carl raised his eyebrows.

'I'm in the midst of a divorce,' Chance said. He was still not quite used to saying it out loud. 'House is up for sale. I'm living in an apartment.'

'Say no more,' Carl told him. 'I'm sorry, sorry to hear that.'

'Me too.' Chance had taken photographs of the furniture and put them on his laptop, slung now by way of a canvas travel case over one shoulder. He lifted the case. 'I have pictures,' he said.

Carl led the way to a large table where they looked at the pictures. The old man studied them at some length. 'Beautiful,' he said. 'The size of that desk makes it unusual. It's a wonderful piece, as are the others. What do you hope to get for them?'

'I was hoping you might tell me.'

The old man studied the pictures a moment longer. 'Without that metalwork… fifty, sixty thousand, maybe.'

'What about with the metalwork? Just to make me feel bad.'

'Twice that.'

'Christ, just for some brass?'

'It's the difference between selling to someone in the market for a nice grouping and a serious collector. Do you know what the set looked like originally?'

'I've seen pictures, in books.'

'Then you know. The strips were substantial, etched with acid, quite lovely, really. You have one piece of it left here, in the bookshelf.' He pointed to one of the photographs.

Chance nodded. 'Yeah, I know. Guess the way to look at it… the set had been complete I would never have gotten it for what I did. Still…'

'It's a big swing.'

'In a tough time, let me tell you.' Chance spent his days listening to the woes of others. Rarely did he air his own, particularly of late, in the absence of wife or family, or even, when he thought about it, of a close friend. 'Didn't imagine I'd ever want to sell,' he said, indulging now in the perception that Carl was in fact the type of guy one might tell one's troubles to. 'Always entertained the fantasy that someday I'd be poking around in a place like this, and there it would be, a pile of brass runners gathering dust on top of somebody's armoire or something.' He smiled and shrugged it off. 'How might we proceed?' he asked. 'If I wanted to go for the sixty?'

Carl tugged at a short goatee that was almost completely white and neatly trimmed. A moment passed. 'Let me show you something,' he said.

They left Chance's computer on the table and walked toward the rear of the store. There was a hole cut in a wall back there to make a window with a little counter on it. There was what appeared to be a workroom on the other side. The window did not allow for much of a view. What Carl wanted him to look at was the cabinet he had spoken of. It was indeed a wonderful piece, made also of palm wood with brass trimming.

'Beautiful,' Chance said.

The old man nodded. 'Brass work is not *exactly* the same as what should have been on yours but not so dissimilar either. *And,* as yours is missing…' He let his voice trail away. 'Let's just say I thought of you. Odd you should stop by when you did.'

'Yes, well, were I buying instead of selling…' His eyes clocked to the cabinet. 'Probably out of my price range even then.'

'Oh, it's not original,' Carl put in almost before Chance could finish.

Chance just looked at him.

'The piece was in very bad shape when I found it. No brass

at all. It's not even by Printz, or at least it's not signed by him, but I could see there were possibilities.'

Chance looked more closely at the metalwork. 'I looked into having mine replaced once. None of the samples I was shown were anything like what I'd seen in the photographs. And nothing like this.' He faced the old man.

'It was all in the process,' Carl told him. 'For one thing, they used natural sponges to get the patterns. No one uses those anymore. There were other materials involved too, acids and dyes… Suffice it to say, it is a process lost to time. Part of what adds to its value.'

Chance looked once more at the cabinet. 'And this, then?' His hand brushed the metalwork. 'Do you know who did it?'

The old man smiled. He went to the little window and called for someone he referred to as D. Whether this was Dee as in a given name or simply the letter *D* as the shortened form of some longer name, the old man didn't say. In another moment or two a very large man, which is to say a man built roughly along the lines of a refrigerator, appeared on the other side of the window. The man rested a formidable forearm on the little counter and bent to look out. The act allowed for a pair of observations, both in regard to the man's head, which was large and round, though not disproportionally so given the size of the arm resting on the counter. The first of these was that the man had no hair, neither on his face nor his scalp. There was none. Chance took him as suffering from alopecia universalis, an extremely rare condition by which every last bit of body hair is lost. The causes were not well understood. And while on certain even more rare occasions the hair might at some point return, as rapidly and mysteriously as it left, the condition was generally thought to be permanent. The second thing one noticed, which one could in no way avoid noticing, was the large black widow spider maybe half again as big as a silver dollar tattooed dead center on the great expanse of otherwise unmarked flesh that covered the big man's skull.

The big man didn't say anything but looked from the window with flat dark eyes, from Chance to Carl and back again. Given the man's size in relation to the window, the effect was that of making eye contact with a caged beast.

'Come on out here,' Carl said, careful, Chance thought, to be overtly cheerful in making the request. A door soon opened and D appeared. Chance guessed him to be well over three hundred pounds, though not much taller than Chance himself, who was five nine but thin as a rail. He wore a khaki-colored military-looking jacket and military cargo-style pants well soiled with a variety of paints and stains above black combat boots equally tarnished. The boots, Chance noticed, were worn without recourse to laces. The jacket was worn open over a black T-shirt with some red writing across the chest that Chance was unable to quite make out. There was an Army Rangers patch on the sleeve of the jacket. It was difficult, given the man's size, his smooth, hairless face and head, to be precise about his age. Chance was willing to put him somewhere in his early to mid-thirties. He was an unusual-looking person to say the least but in no way misshapen or ugly. His features in fact were almost fine, organized by way of straight, well-ordered lines above a powerful jaw and thick neck and within only a moment or two of making the initial observations regarding size and lack of hair, one could not quite imagine, or even wish upon him, save perhaps for the unfortunate tattoo, any other look than the look he had, that of a heavyweight Mr Clean in black and tan.

Carl introduced them and D smiled a bit at hearing Chance's name. 'Dr Chance,' he repeated.

'That's what I told him.'

D looked to the old man. 'Great minds, huh?'

The three stood for a moment or two in silence.

'The doc brought pictures,' Carl said.

They returned to the table and Chance's pictures. Carl pointed to the bit of brass on the bookshelf. 'Look familiar?'

D nodded.

'So what do you think?'

'Sure. He's not in a big hurry.'

D looked once more at Chance, then turned and walked away.

'A man of few words,' Carl said.

'You're telling me what, exactly?' Chance asked. 'D can make this look like the original?' He waved at the photographs still on display.

'He's good,' Carl said. 'As you have seen.'

'Yes he is, and then what? You would put it on sale, as an original?'

Carl just looked at him.

'There wouldn't be ways... of checking...'

Carl shrugged.

Chance stood in the muted light of the big room. He was trying to formulate his next question. 'What are the odds?' he asked at length.

'That furniture is signed, as I recall.'

Chance nodded.

'That's generally enough. Did you buy from a dealer or a private party?'

'Private party.'

'Are they still alive?'

'It was an estate sale, some guy, selling off stuff that had belonged to his mother. I've forgotten his name.'

'That's a plus. If it had been a dealer, if the set were to show up at some later time and the dealer were to see it and recognized it and so on and so forth... that kind of thing.' He waved his hands. 'Private parties are good,' he said.

'Still...'

The old man nodded. 'Yes, there's always a chance.'

The two men looked at each other.

'How about that?' Carl asked him.

Chance went out as he had come in, by way of the door fronting on Market Street, his head spinning with possibility. He found the sunlight blinding after the darkness of the building. Turning north in the direction of his office, he noted the boy in black across the street. The youth appeared to be smoking something in a glass pipe with a pair of look-alike companions. Chance took it for crack, or perhaps some form of methamphetamine. The boy looked in Chance's direction before inclining toward his friends in a manner that might only have been taken for conspiratorial so that in heading up Market Chance was aware of all three looking in his direction, and averted his gaze. Still, in rounding a corner at the end of the block, he was afforded a last glimpse of the youth as he crossed through traffic to reenter the old man's place of business.

Jaclyn

Jaclyn Blackstone is an ambidextrous 36-year-old woman living in Berkeley. She has a college education and a teaching credential. She is employed as a substitute teacher for middle school classes in the Oakland School District, where she also works as a private tutor for students in algebra and geometry.

The patient is referred for evaluation from the Stanford Neurology Clinic for complaints of intermittent memory loss and periods of poor concentration. As a child and young adult, Mrs Blackstone reports that she was a 'sleepwalker,' often waking in strange places without any memory or knowledge of how she had arrived. She describes her recent episodes of memory loss as 'like that,' in reference to these earlier sleepwalking episodes. A full set of laboratory studies (including SMA-20, CBC with diff. and thyroid function tests, vitamin B-12 levels, heavy metal screen, and serum ceruloplasmin) were completely normal. An MRI head scan was within normal limits. Her neurologic examination was normal and no evidence was found to suggest an organic basis for her cognitive disturbances.

The patient states that she has recently become aware of a 'second personality,' whom she calls 'Jackie Black.' She states that Jackie is daring and extroverted, a person who comes out at times of particular distress. In particular, it is Jackie who continues to have a sexual relationship with her estranged husband, even though she, Jaclyn, does not approve of this. Mrs Blackstone states that she hates being called by the name of Jackie and the only person who uses

*that name is her husband, a homicide detective in the
Oakland Police Department. The patient states that while
prior to her discovery of Jackie Black there were no other
known alternative personalities, there have been 'periods of
time' for which she has no specific recall. As to whether or
not these 'blank spaces' may also be associated with other
personalities, the patient is unwilling to speculate. The
patient further states that at one point she acquired a gun
as a means of killing herself if things became intolerable.
She says now that the gun has been sold to a pawnshop
dealer in downtown Oakland.*

IT SEEMED straightforward enough, really. Mrs Blackstone's
memory problems were clearly secondary to psychiatric
distress, engendered most directly from her continuing
to see the abusive husband from whom she is ostensibly
seeking a divorce. *'The development of secondary or multiple
personalities occurs most frequently in the context of physical,
sexual, or psychological abuse,'* Chance had written. *'I think
it is important for this warded-off aspect of her personality to
be addressed and, ideally, integrated into her basic persona.
However, as long as she continues to have a relationship with a
person whom she both despises and fears, there is little reason
to believe that her underlying anxiety can be successfully
treated with pharmacologic approaches.'*

By way of treatment, he had recommended that
Mrs Blackstone consider psychotherapy. He had also
recommended that she work with a female therapist and had
offered a name, Janice Silver, a therapist in the East Bay he
believed to be particularly good.

In most cases that would have been the end of it, and
there was nothing about this case to suggest that Jaclyn
Blackstone was the type of patient he would ever see
more than once. Nor was it likely she would have replaced
Mariella as the object of his obsession. She would have
faded back into that great gray array of the lost and lonely,
the neurasthenic and terminally distraught, the walking

wounded he saw by the score day in and day out. But then two things happened.

* * *

The first was a chance meeting with Jaclyn Blackstone on the streets of Berkeley. It was quite unplanned and took place in a trendy little shopping district at the northwest side of town. He was still trying to figure out what to do about his furniture and Carl's offer and Big D and all of that and was poking about in the Art and Architecture store on Fourth Street, looking through a book on French Art Nouveau furniture, when he caught sight of Jaclyn Blackstone among the aisles. It was scarcely two months since she'd visited his office yet he was struck by how different she looked. At the time of his evaluation she had worn a shapeless sweater over an old-fashioned blue print dress, her hair pulled loosely back, held by the kind of small white combs a little girl might use. She had looked all of her thirty-six years and then some, matronly, he had thought at the time. In the store she wore jeans and running shoes and a leather jacket over a yellow T-shirt and was anything but matronly. Her hair was different too, shorter, trendier. The fact was, she had caught his eye and it was only upon closer scrutiny that he realized who it was. The recognition was followed rather quickly by the thought that maybe this was not Jaclyn at all, but Jackie, and he wondered if she would see him and if she did, would there be any sign of recognition, though he also understood that even as Jaclyn she might not be so eager to say hello given the circumstances of their original meeting. He was therefore a bit surprised when, as their eyes met and after only a momentary delay, she favored him with a rather shy smile and a little wave of the hand.

Their paths crossed at the end of the aisle. They were both holding books. 'Don't you love this store?' she asked.

'I do. What are *you* reading?'

She held up a rather small book with a picture of two

wooden chairs on the cover. 'I like to find old pieces of furniture that I can strip and redo.'

'Antiques?'

'Nooo. Junk.' She produced an iPhone, pulled up her photographs, then scrolled around a bit before finding something for him to look at, half a dozen straight-back wooden chairs that had not only been rather gaily painted with pastel washes but bore as well the likeness of movie stars reminiscent of Andy Warhol's silk-screened portraits.

'Madonna and Marilyn,' she told him. 'I call them my icon chairs.'

'These are quite good,' he said. 'I mean it.'

'Yeah?' She found two other chairs that had pictures of dogs on them. 'I like dogs too,' she said.

'Me too. Do you have one?'

She looked away. 'I did. But I lost him,' she said. Her smile of only moments before had given way to a look of profound distress.

'I'm so sorry. It's sad to lose a pet.'

She nodded. 'I have a cat.' Her eyes clocked to his book. 'What do *you* have?'

He showed her the book on French furniture.

'Well, see…' she said. 'Yours is fancier than mine. But then you're the doctor.' It was the first reference either had made as to why they were even standing here talking.

'Yes, well… I have some furniture kind of like this that I'm thinking of selling.'

'Well don't think too long,' she told him.

He laughed. 'Now why would you say that?' he asked.

She shrugged. 'I don't know. It seemed like good all-purpose advice. One could say it about so many things.'

It was almost as if she were flirting with him. He was even beginning to wonder if she'd lied. Maybe there were more than two of her. He was also enjoying her company and in a short while discovered that he had moved with her into the checkout line at the register where he felt somehow obliged to buy the book he carried even though it was more money than he'd wanted to spend if for no other reason than to prolong the pleasures of the moment.

Minutes later, on the sidewalk in front of the store, the absurdity of it all descended on him for the first time. In the twenty years of his marriage he'd been faithful to his wife, raising his daughter, building a practice. He'd seen no one since the separation. That he was suddenly standing here, amped like some schoolboy in the presence of an attractive woman he just happened to have seen as a patient, that he just happened to know was possessed of at least one secondary personality willing to engage in rough sex with an estranged spouse, by all accounts a dangerous psychopath, was enough to render him at least momentarily speechless. The really disturbing part was that he was also trying to decide if he should invite her to coffee as there was one of those upscale little East Bay coffee joints almost directly across the street from where they stood. Mercifully, she spoke first and thereby, he would conclude later, saving him from God only knew what horrors. 'I just want you to know that I'm seeing the therapist you recommended,' she said. 'It's changed everything.' When next he spoke it was as what he was, a doctor addressing a patient on the occasion of a chance meeting in a public place. 'I'm so glad to hear that,' he said. 'And you're feeling better?' He might have added that she looked like a million bucks but decided against it.

'I am,' she said. 'I'm feeling better than I have in a long while.'

They stood for a moment with this.

'Well…' Chance said.

'Sometimes I use numbers,' she told him.

Chance just looked at her.

'On the furniture,' she added. 'Formulas, sometimes, or geometric shapes. But sometimes just numbers.'

'Ah.' He recalled that she was also a teacher.

'I substitute,' she corrected. 'I started doing it again, after the separation…' She allowed her voice to trail away, as if from the subject.

'You're looking well,' Chance said, acting suddenly on his earlier impulse. If he'd hoped to put the smile back on her face he was successful.

'Am I?' she asked, and in doing so managed somehow to shift the tone of their meeting ever so slightly once more.

Was it him, he wondered, or did she really know how to play it so well? Or perhaps he was not according her the benefit of the doubt. He'd seen therapy turn people around. Why not Jaclyn Blackstone? 'You are,' he said finally. 'I almost didn't recognize you there in the store.'

'Well,' she said, and she offered him a hand. 'I am glad we ran into each other just now.'

He took her hand. 'So am I. And I wish you the best.'

She seemed to take this as his way of saying goodbye, and perhaps it was. It certainly should have been. Still, in letting go of her hand he experienced a pang of remorse.

'Well...' she said once more. And he really did feel that they were both reluctant to break it off. 'Enjoy your book. And good luck with your furniture, whatever you decide.'

He smiled and nodded and like that she was gone, or so it seemed. So conflicted had he been at just that moment in trying to decide if he should not have added something more, that in thinking back on it later, he could not quite recall if they'd even said goodbye. He concluded they had not. He had nodded. She had smiled. He had been left to stand there as she moved off down the sidewalk, pausing at the window of some store half a block away before moving on and out of sight, for good as far as he knew, so that what he was left with in the end was that very particular ache he had not felt in many years, the exultation of wanting in combination with a certain knowing, that the object of such desire is forever unavailable, that and the wonderful curvature of her spine as she posed like a dancer before a shop window, the afternoon light on her ash-blond hair.

Any such feelings of romantic ambiguity as may have washed over him in the immediate aftermath of this meeting were, in the days that followed, replaced by a profound relief that he had not succumbed to the absurd temptation to involve himself further in her affairs and he had returned to the contemplation of what to do about his furniture. He felt no great sense of urgency in this regard. It was his nature to view a thing from as many angles as possible, to imagine any and all worst-case scenarios. His wife and daughter had often accused him of being overly cautious in such matters, ganging up on him without mercy as Chance spent days on end lost in the evaluation of some apparently trivial decision or purchase, but then Chance was a believer in caution. He supposed such traits were drummed into him by his father, provost at a small Bible-based college on the outskirts of Springfield, Missouri, who, like the Master for whom the school had been named, was a lover of parables. His father had favored those in which some youthful indiscretion leads inexorably to a life of pain and deprivation. And while Chance declined entrance to his father's school, he could not say the old man's words had failed to dog his tracks. Nor had his own work as a doctor served to make him any less wary. He'd spent far too many days with people for whom everything had changed in the time it took to draw a breath… because they'd turned left instead of right, failed to see the light or hear the horn, or those like Jaclyn Blackstone, guilty of little else save the kind of poor judgment that would place the heart above the head, now at Mercy General Hospital in downtown Oakland with an orbital blowout fracture on the right side of her face awaiting surgery to relieve pressure on an entrapped inferior rectus muscle, and that was the second thing that happened.

He'd heard the news from Janice Silver. She'd called because Jaclyn had come to her by way of Chance and she thought he would want to know. She was also angry and wanted someone to vent to and lastly, as Jaclyn was without insurance and in a county hospital, she was wondering if Chance might be willing to look in on her, to evaluate the extent of her injuries himself.

Chance said that he would. He was seated in his office, the very book he had purchased in Jaclyn's presence open on the desk before him, the buildings outside his window losing definition to a creeping afternoon fog. 'This is the work of the ex?' he asked.

'I can't believe it's not.'

'But you don't know for sure?'

'She's not saying.'

Chance watched the fog. He heard Janice sigh, the anger in her voice. 'She had been doing so well,' she told him. 'You know this bastard had been coming to see her once a week. She'd begun to say no. It was working. Jackie was staying out of the picture. It *had* to be him.'

'What does she say?'

'She says she surprised an intruder on the patio of her condominium.'

'I suppose that's possible.'

'Oh, absolutely,' Janice echoed, 'anything is possible. Let's not rule out alien abductions.'

He went the following day. He did not visit her straightaway but spoke instead to her attending physician. She'd received a concussion but there was no evidence of bleeding into or structural damage of her brain. The surgery required to relieve the entrapped muscle was straightforward enough and he felt satisfied that she was in good hands. As to the nature of the incident, she had yet to claim additional knowledge. There was only the bit about having surprised someone at the rear of her condo and that was all.

He considered leaving it there as the course of prudent behavior then caved to the impulse to stop by her room. He found the door open and a man seated in a chair at the side of her bed. The man wore a gray suit. He was broad shouldered with thick dark hair. He had his back to the door and was leaning forward a bit, holding on to one of Jaclyn's hands, speaking to her in a low voice. Chance heard little more than a name… *Jackie*… before retreating to a nurses' station to make conversation with one of the nurses, while waiting to see if the man would leave anytime soon, and where, having identified himself as a doctor, he inquired further regarding the patient in room 141.

'She's been in quite a lot of pain,' the nurse told him. 'Complaining of double vision. She's scheduled for the surgery this afternoon.'

'Has she had many visitors?'

'Just the husband,' the nurse told him, and excused herself to check on a patient.

Chance was still at the station when the man came out of the room. He was, as Chance had noted, a lean, broad-shouldered man of medium height, a handsome enough man, Chance thought, and fit, certainly capable of doing some damage with his fists.

Chance had expected him to walk on by and was surprised when he stopped before him. 'You one of her doctors?' the man asked. The man's eyes were black and direct. Chance of course recalled that he was a homicide detective for the city of Oakland and he had that about him, whatever *that* was, some air of authority, some hint of the bully. Chance had no difficulty in believing he was a cop. He had no difficulty in believing he was a bad cop. 'I'm a neuropsychiatrist,' Chance told him. 'I was asked by her therapist to look in on her.'

'You were in her room just now, why didn't you look in?'

'I saw she had a visitor. There was no rush.'

'No rush? Not like the doctors *I* know.'

Chance thought that perhaps the man would smile but he didn't. Chance just looked at him. The man looked back, a moment longer, before moving off toward the elevators at the end of the hall. Chance waited till the man was gone before returning to Jaclyn's room.

She looked about as he had expected given the nature and severity of her injuries. One side of her face was badly swollen and bruised. She turned her head a bit on the pillow at his approach and he could see that she had been crying.

'Jaclyn...' he began. 'I'm so sorry...'

'Please,' she said. 'You should go.' She spoke through clenched teeth, turning to the wall, where a small dirty window looked out upon the city of Oakland.

Chance put his hand on the forearm that was on the outside of her blanket. 'You're going to be fine,' he said, feeling both moved and impotent, reduced to cliché. 'You will feel better when they free up that muscle and you can stop seeing two of everything.'

He'd hoped to joke a little but she wasn't having any. Her hand opened and closed, holding to the sky blue blanket that covered her bed. He gave her arm a gentle squeeze before releasing her. He would have held her in his arms if he could have, so delicate and wounded did she seem just then, lying there in that sterile room with its plastic curtains and hospital blankets, its dismal view of the city. He recalled their conversation in the bookstore in Berkeley not two weeks prior, the business about the chairs, her expression in recalling the loss of her dog, her beguiling smile as they had waited in line to buy their books. She was a gentle soul, he thought, a kind spirit. She declined to look at him and she declined to be comforted. And of course the truth was that while surgery might free the trapped muscle, it would not free her from the man Chance had seen in her room just now, bending over her like some B movie vampire, her hand in his, the same that had beaten her. For now that Chance had looked into the man's face he had no doubt that Janice had been right. There'd been no intruder in the back of the condominium. It was the man he had seen, the bad cop, hunting his whore, angered at her sudden disappearance.

Beyond the walls of the hospital, which were dull and gray and rather more like a prison than a place of healing, a pall had settled. Even those views of the city by way of the Richmond-San Rafael Bridge that had almost never failed to cheer seemed veiled in gloom. He spent the rest of the day in the small, overly warm kitchen of a retired dentist. He'd been retained by a distant relative on suspicion of elder abuse and asked to make an assessment with regard to vulnerability to undue influence. The man, William Fry, though he preferred to be addressed as Doc Billy, was ninety-two years old. He sported dual hearing aids and was attached to an oxygen tank. The requisite cognitive and psychiatric testing had dragged on for hours. By the time Chance reentered the day, as claustrophobic as Doc Billy's kitchenette, the afternoon had given way to darkness, the sidewalks made wet by a roiling fog he might once have found romantic. Returning to his apartment, he was alerted by way of a letter that the IRS had just put a lien on any profits realized from the sale of his house.

Though well into the dinner hour, he was able to get his attorney on the phone. The situation was explained as follows: The government's interest had been piqued as a result of an audit of his soon-to-be ex-wife's business, a small photographic studio. There'd been a couple of years there when he'd pumped some money into the enterprise in an effort to help her get it off the ground. It seemed now that the money had not been properly accounted for. On his end were unsubstantiated expenses, on hers unreported income. Being married, the two had filed jointly, leaving both now tarred with the same brush. The only difference between them was that he *had* money, albeit in dwindling sums, while she had none. The government was looking for back taxes and penalties in excess of two hundred thousand dollars. There would of course be further bills from the requisite attorneys. He thanked his attorney and hung up.

He sat holding the letter from the IRS, fingers trembling with rage or stress, or fear, unable to shake the feeling that his former spouse and confidante, the mother of his child, had ratted him out. 'It never fucking rains…' he said to no one, realizing almost at once and with a lasting chagrin it was exactly the kind of thing his mother might have said. And how he would have hated her for it, she with her platitudes and clichés, her grating homilies. But then he guessed that was how it was… you stuck around long enough… your reward was to become the very person you'd spent the better part of your life holding in contempt.

He took a three-dollar bottle of Trader Joe's wine from the cabinet above his refrigerator, found something to drink it from, and seated himself in his own kitchenette, only slightly larger and less confining than Dr Fry's, and began his report:

> William Fry is a 92-year-old right-handed dentist who has been retired for 30 years. He is single, has never been married, and has resided for the past 55 years in a second-floor apartment in the Castro District of San Francisco. Questions have been raised regarding the possibility of elder abuse by a female in-home care provider to whom Mr Fry has apparently given more than $1,000,000 in the form of a series of checks from a money market fund…

That was as far as he got. He hadn't the heart for it. Not tonight. He turned instead to the wine, sipping from a ridiculously large glass container that had once housed a drink called a Hurricane from a bar in New Orleans and was the only clean bit of glassware he'd been able to find after a thorough search of his apartment. He thought about his wife ratting him out. He thought about Jaclyn Blackstone with her fractured face. He thought about the darkness in the hearts of men. He recalled something Doc Billy had said to him in the course of their long afternoon: 'You can't imagine how it feels… ninety-two fucking years old and feeling loved for the first time. Money just doesn't matter that much anymore.'

Chance believed he could imagine all too well how it might feel being ninety-two fucking years old. Unhappily, this did not serve to make him any less anxious about his own difficulties and his eye fell upon the slick French furniture crammed into a corner of his tiny living room and he resolved to sell it forthwith, for as much money as he possibly could. The consequences could go fuck themselves.

It was, for Chance, an unusually rash call. Later he would blame it on the cheap wine, this in concert with the simple fact that he had been unable to find a suitably clean smaller glass.

D

THE FOLLOWING day was Saturday and he made his way to Allan's Antiques upon rising. He found the building even more dimly lit than on previous visits and so quiet as to appear deserted, although the front door was open to the sidewalk off Market as always. He went in. He did not hear Carl's voice nor could he find him. He'd half expected to see the crack-smoking leather boy around somewhere but he was absent as well. He went to the big table where they'd looked at the computer images of his furniture, called a tentative hello to no response, then moved on to the back of the building.

A flickering blue light came from the hole in the wall that led to Big D's work area. Approaching this and looking in, he was able to see Big D himself at work with some kind of handheld torch on a shining piece of metal. Chance waited for a bit, watching as D worked. The scene had about it some archetypal aspect Chance found satisfying to observe and was reluctant to disturb, the big man at work amid the tools of his trade, intent upon the task before him. There was something in the absolute physicality of it. It spoke, Chance thought, of another more rudimentary and therefore, perhaps, simpler time. Though it occurred to him as well that simpler times were surely more a function of longing than of history, that life on planet Earth had never been all that simple.

Chance waited till D had paused in his labors then knocked on the wall to get his attention. D placed the thing he was working on atop a bench and came to the window, using a heavily gloved hand to push a darkened pair of safety glasses to his forehead as he walked. 'Doc Chance,' he said. His face was flushed from the labor and the sweat ran from his cheeks but his voice was flat and matter-of-fact, as though Chance's being there was of little or no surprise.

'Hello, D,' Chance replied. He was hoping to sound upbeat. 'Is Carl around?'

'Stayed home today.'

'Is he well?'

'Little under the weather,' D replied.

The big man was dressed as he had been the day they'd met, minus the jacket, allowing for the observation that the sleeves had been cut from the shirt to make way for arms the size of Chance's legs. The shirt's lettering was now legible as well – *The art of the blade,* in bloodred script.

'Ah.' Chance hesitated, thinking it over. 'Well, I guess maybe you're the guy I'd probably need to talk to anyway, at least to get things started. You remember the furniture we looked at?'

'I do. You decide you want to make it right?'

Chance smiled at the big man's phrasing. 'I guess that'd be one way of putting it. I'd need to know what it would cost, if I'd have to pay up front or if there would be a way of settling when the stuff was sold.'

'Payment, you'd have to talk to Carl.'

'Of course. Do you think he'll be back anytime soon? Not serious, I hope, what's wrong with him?'

'He'll be okay. I'd expect him back in a day or two.'

'I guess what I'm wondering,' Chance said, 'is if I shouldn't take steps… Just get the stuff down here. I'm sure we'll be able to work something out.' Now that he'd been confronted with some minor obstacle, it came to him just how badly he wanted to sell. 'I'd need help moving it,' he added. 'Carl must have someone he uses for that kind of thing.'

'He's kind of between those people right now.'

'Does he keep a truck of some sort, here maybe, at the warehouse?'

'He did.'

Chance nodded. He could see that D was not one to elaborate on the mundane.

'I'll tell you what,' D said after a moment or two had passed. 'Go to the U-Haul or someplace. Rent yourself a truck big enough so that we can do it in one trip. I can help you get the stuff down here.'

'Really?'

'Do it today, you find a truck.'

Chance gave it a beat. 'Shit,' he said. He felt compelled to make a show of patting himself down. 'Phone's in my apartment. Is there one here I can use?'

D nodded to the door.

Chance made his way into the workroom.

The place was quite expansive once inside, with lots of benches and blocks and vises and tools. There was also a cot in a far corner with a wooden crate placed on one end to form a kind of nightstand with some personal items arranged neatly on the top. There were a number of books scattered about the floor at the cot's foot and some cardboard boxes stacked neatly along one wall. A large mirror set into a freestanding wooden frame, almost certainly borrowed from Carl's collection, appeared as part of this arrangement, as did a large piece of plywood affixed to the brick wall upon which someone had drawn a more or less life-sized outline of a human torso in black ink with numbers drawn on it to indicate what Chance could only imagine to be targets. The overall impression of the place was such that Chance was willing to take it for D's living quarters as well as his workplace.

As Chance studied his surroundings, D dug a well-worn San Francisco directory out of an aging school desk from which a good deal of the finish had been scraped away before pointing him to an ancient black telephone mounted on a wall. 'Knock yourself out,' he said, and went back to doing whatever it was he had been doing when Chance showed up.

There was a U-Haul place in Noe Valley. It was not the closest but they had a truck ready for that afternoon. Chance told them he would take it then called for a cab and joined D at his workbench.

'We good?' D asked.

'Cab'll be here in fifteen, or so they say. I'll be back with the truck. I appreciate your doing this.'

D nodded. He was once more at work on the piece of steel but had traded the torch for a small hammer with which he was tapping at the edge of the thing.

'Mind if I ask what that is?'

'You can ask.'

Chance smiled. Big D, apparently not without a sense of humor, held the article up for him to see. Chance asked if it was a hatchet.

'Tomahawk,' D told him.

'I didn't know there was a difference.'

'Hatchet's a tool. Tomahawk's a weapon.'

'In this day and age?'

'You'd be surprised,' D told him.

'Is it for you?'

'Buddy of mine… Keeps going back to Afghanistan.'

Chance recalled their first meeting, the military jacket with the Army Rangers insignia. 'Is that where you were?'

D nodded. 'What I was doing here, when you came in, was using the torch to temper the blade, same as you would with a knife. You want it thin enough to cut, hard but not brittle.' He held up the tomahawk once more. 'I've been working out a design with this guy for his past two tours. He lets me know how it works, how he thinks it might work better. I modify it accordingly.'

Chance was a moment in imagining what the particulars of such an exchange might actually be like. 'I better go out and meet that cab,' he said.

It all took longer than expected and the truck a piece of shit with blown shocks and springs poking through vinyl seat covers and the late light drawing out the shadows in Chance's neighborhood by the time he and D came finally bouncing up from the Great Highway in the ancient rig, one of many as the afternoon rush hour he'd been hoping to beat lurched into full swing with lines of cars at each and every intersection and jaywalking children with backpacks and cell phones and Chinese workmen unloading fish trucks at competing corner groceries and tattooed teenagers with funny hats on clattering skateboards. There was even a guy carrying a surfboard, headed in the general direction of Ocean Beach but looking a trifle lost, when, as if on cue, the old truck backfired by way of announcing their arrival.

Big D started as if he'd been shot at and Chance laughed. He couldn't quite help himself. 'It's like the Joads,' he said.

'Fuck are the Joads?'

'*The Grapes of Wrath?*'

D just looked at him.

'The great novel of the Great Depression; wasn't a bad movie either. John Ford, Henry Fonda. Joad was the name of the family, farmers fleeing the Dust Bowl for California, everything they owned strapped to the back of an old truck. I drive around in a rig like this, that's what I think of, the Joads.'

'That's just great,' D said, but he didn't sound all that happy about it.

There was of course no suitable street parking left anywhere near Chance's apartment. Nor was there, given the truck's height and width, any chance of gaining access to the small basement garage he shared with his downstairs neighbors. He nosed the truck into the apartment's scrawny driveway as far as he was able, set the brake and hazard lights as a warning to such traffic as would now be forced to evasive maneuvering, and got out.

He could hear D behind him, huffing and puffing, as

they made their way up the narrow stairs. By the time they reached the apartment to stand looking at the furniture, the big man was once again red faced and sweating as he had been in his workroom, and Chance was beginning to worry that the stairs in concert with the heavy lifting might prove too much, that given the man's weight and apparent lack of conditioning, his rush to get all of this taken care of today may have been a mistake. A hypertensive stroke did not seem out of the question. 'Would you like a glass of water?' he asked. He was thinking the guy might like to sit for a moment, that and trying to recall the last time he'd been called upon to administer CPR.

'Forget about it,' D told him, 'you get that.' He nodded toward a chair while advancing upon the desk, the largest and heaviest piece in the set and which, without waiting a reply from Chance, he tilted against his thighs, found his grip, brought the entire piece flat to his chest as though it were of no more consequence than a fold-up card table, and headed for the exit. Chance followed, watching as D wrestled the big desk down the difficult staircase, turning it first one way and then the other, at one point, in exiting the building, going so far as to heft the entire thing above his head. When he'd gotten it into the back of the truck he turned to Chance, still in possession of his chair. 'You want to get this shit wrapped and strapped, I'll get the rest.'

And that was how they did it. By the time Chance had wrapped the desk in a mover's blanket and secured it to a wall of the truck with a canvas strap, D was back with the bookcase. By the time he was done with that, D was back with the remaining chair, no more winded and no less so than when they had begun.

At some point, while Chance was still in the truck, some guy had started honking. The traffic was always slow here and the position of the truck was making it more so, effectively squeezing what was usually a two-lane, two-way street into a single lane as motorists were forced to take turns getting around the rear corner of the truck. This was not an unusual occurrence for anyone used to the neighborhood. But horns were not so unusual either, and one guy in particular seemed intent upon taking umbrage at the situation. He was driving a gunmetal-gray BMW, one of the big ones with tinted glass, and he started honking about three car lengths back from the truck. What he hoped to gain by all of this was unclear, but there he was, honking away. The honking inspired two or three other malcontents to join in.

Chance went once to the rear of the truck, where he and the driver of the BMW, a capable-looking young man in a white shirt with the sleeves rolled above his wrists, were able to make eye contact. Chance held up his hands, palms out and up, as though to ask, 'What do you expect me to do? This is what it's like here.' It was that kind of gesture. The driver responded by flipping him off. Chance went back to wrapping furniture.

The BMW had drawn almost even with the rear of the truck, its driver now taking to punctuating his honks with the occasional shouted epithet by the time D returned with the last chair. D set the chair in the back of the truck and, as the driver's turn had finally come and he was about to move around the truck, stepped very matter-of-factly into the street in front of him, effectively blocking the BMW's path. The car came to an abrupt stop. The driver honked and gesticulated and worked his jaw. D just stood there staring at him. At some point the guy seemed to get the picture. A profound silence settled upon the street. The driver sat waiting as several cars in the opposing lane went on by, then tried backing up as far as the fifteen other cars behind him would allow and cranking his wheels as if a wider turn into the street would somehow effect his escape. D responded by taking one step toward the car and one to his right. The driver's position was by now painfully and wonderfully obvious. His options were roughly three in number. He could run over the man in front of him, undoubtedly the dictate of his heart, but this was impractical as there were witnesses and really, given the traffic, no way to go very far very fast. He could of course get out of his car. Or, finally, he could sit there and shut up till it had been made manifest to any and all concerned just how thoroughly he'd been made a cunt of. Not surprisingly, he opted for door number three. After some seemingly appropriate amount of time had passed, D moved and the guy went quietly on, hands atop his wheel, eyes dead ahead.

Chance had by now finished with the furniture. He went up the stairs once more to take a last look around and locked the door. D was waiting in the passenger seat of the truck when he came back down. Chance got in behind the wheel. They drove for a block without speaking.

'That was pretty good,' Chance said finally. He was referring to what had happened in the street. The fact was, he was having some difficulty in repressing a deep sense of exhilaration.

D nodded, resting his head against the metal grate behind his seat, and closed his eyes. 'Shit like that makes my day.'

A fool for love

IN THE days that followed, Big D ostensibly at work on Chance's furniture, Carl yet in absentia for reasons still unknown, Chance went about his business. He continued his work with Doc Billy. On the Beck Depression Inventory, Billy endorsed the following items:

- *I feel sad much of the time.*
- *I feel more discouraged about my future than I used to.*
- *I have failed more than I should have.*
- *I don't enjoy things as much as I used to.*
- *I feel I may be punished.*
- *I cry more than I used to.*
- *I have lost most of my interest in other people or things.*
- *I don't consider myself as worthwhile and useful as I used to.*
- *I sleep a lot more than usual.*
- *I get tired or fatigued more easily than usual.*
- *I am less interested in sex than I used to be.*

Chance noted the Doc's score as 13/63 and consistent with a mild level of depression. He might have said the same for himself but he was trying not to go there. He'd been drinking more of late and this worried him. He'd been considering Lexapro but had thus far rejected the option as some form of capitulation to despair, a position he would not have shared with the many patients for whom he would no doubt continue to prescribe the drug. With regard to Doc Billy, he was in no less of a quandary. His sympathies were with the old man but professional considerations were proving difficult to ignore. His livelihood was, at this point in the game, more or less dependent upon maintaining his reputation as an expert witness in just such cases as Dr Billy's, and the Beck Depression Inventory was only one of the many tests he had thus far administered. Cumulative scores suggested it would be mistaken to say Dr Fry's problems with attention, concentration, and memory were primarily or exclusively the result of emotional issues, i.e., the intrusion into his personal life on the part of a relative he believed to be quite distant and interested only in his money. Cognitively speaking, the old boy was most definitely on a downward slope.

The other player in all of this, the caregiver and prime suspect, was Lorena Sanchez, formerly of Oaxaca, Mexico, a devout Catholic who prayed often in Billy's presence. When asked for a description, the doc had described her as five feet tall and chunky. They were seated in the dreaded kitchenette, Dr Chance and Dr Billy, windows shut and shuttered, blinds drawn, stove at three-fifty for 'extra heat.' The elder doc was sporting the hearing aids he described alternately as 'Jap work' and 'not worth shit.' The green oxygen tank was at his side, emitting a series of soft clicking sounds, as if extremely small and perhaps alien visitors were trapped inside, attempting communication with the outside world of which Chance himself was more or less a part. 'The thing is,' Billy told him, 'when she gets dressed up…' He shook his hand, as though shaking water from the tips of his fingers, eyebrows raised. Chance got the picture. 'First time I saw her like that… we were at the Bagel House on Lombard and I told her, too, I told her how beautiful she was.'

'And how did she respond?' Chance asked.

The old man was a moment in thought. 'She took me by the hand,' he said softly, his eyes tearing. '"I never had anyone like you," she said to me.' He paused and looked at Chance. 'She meant it, too. I can tell you that. She wanted us to get married. Still does. Can you believe it? In case there are ever problems, financially speaking, she says.' Billy slapped his leg with the flat of his hand. 'We fell in love with each other,' he said. 'And yeah, I know there's probably some ulterior fucking motus. I'm ninety-two years old, for Christ's sake. She's fifty-three. But this other… that's the long and the short of it. If she's not the real deal, the real deal does not exist, not in this life.'

By 'this other' Chance had taken him to mean the part about falling in love, upon which subject and about half drunk, Doc the Younger was inclined to wax philosophical:

> The philosopher Nietzsche asserted that 'In the end, one loves one's desire and not the desired object.' Viewed in this somewhat detached framework, one might say that by virtue of his relationship with Lorena, William felt safe, protected, and valued. He also experienced for the first time the euphoria of being in love. To his great credit, he is able to acknowledge that at some level he knows, and has known, that he has been manipulated. Nevertheless, he comes back ultimately to the question, 'What value is money without love?'

Chance polished off yet another bottle of wine as he worked, attempting to conclude his assessment of Doc Billy, with whom he had been just that day another four and a half hours in the small saunalike apartment. He sat now in his own, depressingly similar to Billy's save for the heat. Billy had been in his for fifty-five years, alone and unloved. Little wonder he'd fallen for the wondrous Lorena, short and chunky notwithstanding. 'While acknowledging that there appears to be compelling evidence of elder abuse in this case…' Chance went on, casting about, ever more desperately, it would seem, for some favorable comment on which to end, anything really that might stave off such humiliations as time, the world, and the Oregonian relatives were almost certain to inflict, '… one needs to be open to the possibility that at some level William Fry recruited Lorena for his own *purposes, that he retained her, as it were, to subject himself to undue influence, that is, he wanted to experience the combined feelings of love, safety, and pleasure in her companionship. I believe that William, in fact, remembers somewhat more than he admits to knowing. In essence, he has been a partner in a cover-up, a co-conspirator who now wishes to protect Lorena from the legal consequences of her actions...'* Feeling that this was somehow unsatisfactory, he paused and tried again. *'Still, and in spite of his evident physical limitations... and rather obvious need for the appointment of a financial watchdog... Dr Fry retains considerable dignity, awareness, and insight into his predicament...'*

In the end, he sighed and put the thing aside. There was, after all, only so much that a man in his position might be expected to do. What would be would be and the best he supposed that one might hope for would be that the old boy at least find some way to go out with his boots on, some doomed yet heroic last stand... all but bedridden at ninety-two, oxygen tank in tow, at long last at one with his brothers, a fool for love.

When he tried to imagine what the doc's last stand might look like, however, he found that he could not, and his thoughts turned, as they so often did of late, to Jaclyn Blackstone. In fact, she was in danger of replacing Mariella as the object of the season's obsession. Was she, too, for perhaps darker and more twisted reasons than Doc Billy's, the partner in a cover-up, a co-conspirator now wishing to protect her former lover from the legal consequences of his actions? He had no sooner put the question to himself than he thought less of himself for doing so. He thought of the driver Big D had stared down in the street. The fact was, he could not escape the feeling *he* had been made a cunt of there in the hospital, impotent in the face of Jaclyn's tormentor. What, he wondered, would Big D have done with that, knowing what Chance knew, and allowed himself the rather lengthy indulgence of a variety of school yard fantasies. The fantasies were remarkable for their clarity and sheer amount of bloodletting. This Blackstone did not just drive away. He did not get off with any benign stare down. He was alternately beaten toothless, disemboweled, garroted, emasculated, and murdered outright. Chance went to inquire after his furniture at noon on the following day.

As on all other visits, he found the front door open, the building dark and void of customers. Finding no sign of Carl, he moved directly to the back of the building. The light was on in D's workroom but the big man did not answer his call. Bending to look through the narrow window by which he and D had first been introduced, he could see that a rear door had been left open to the alley, a slant of yellow light spilling in. Chance took the liberty of letting himself into D's space and making for the light. Along the way he noted his furniture, piled rather unceremoniously, it seemed to him, in a corner of the big room. If D was at work on the trim and general restoration, it was not yet in evidence.

He found the big man outside in the alley, seated on an overturned crate, a bag from some local fast food joint at his side, a large Diet Coke in one hand and a copy of *The Grapes of Wrath* in the other. He looked up as Chance moved to join him. 'I'll be all around in the dark,' D said by way of greeting. He did not consult the book. 'Wherever there's a cop beatin' up a guy, I'll be there. I'll be in the way guys yell when they're mad. I'll be in the way kids laugh when they're hungry an' they know supper's ready. An' when the people are eatin' the stuff they raise, and livin' in the houses they built... I'll be there too.' He paused. 'I may have left out a couple,' he said. He looked at the book.

'That's about the way I remember it,' Chance said. 'That's very good.'

'Somebody mentions something I don't know, a book or something... sounds interesting, I'll track it down, try to see what it is.'

'An admirable trait,' Chance said. He seated himself on a concrete step near D's crate.

D closed the book and looked at him. 'Sup, Big Dog?' he asked. 'You got more furniture to move?'

'Hardly. But I can think of a few more assholes you might give the treatment to, like that guy in the street.' It flattered Chance to believe this was something they had shared, a kind of male bonding, as it were. As for the myriad fantasies the incident had inspired... he'd keep that to himself. The joke about a few more assholes was about as far as he would permit himself to go but D was all over it. 'Who?' he asked, and Chance did not get the feeling that D was joking around. He came this close to saying something about Jaclyn Blackstone and her predatory husband, the bad cop, before sound judgment got the better of him. The guy was an Oakland homicide detective, for Christ's sake. He had an expensive suit, a gun, and a badge. He was, as Chance saw it, a man at home in the world, a man who knew how things worked, and how they didn't. He would crush a person like D, not physically perhaps, not in a fight, but he would crush him all the same, and Chance along with him, grind them both beneath his shoe and never break stride. 'Half the city,' Chance said finally, making light. 'How's it with the brass?'

D seemed a bit disappointed and when he spoke again it was with considerably less enthusiasm. 'Take a little time for me to get what I need,' he said. ''Nother day or two, I'll be able to start. Should take me about a week.'

At which point Carl Allan appeared. 'Is there a doctor in the house?' he asked. He was standing in the doorway that led back into D's workroom, puffy in the face with a still swollen nose and dark half-moons beneath his eyes, a jaunty straw hat in the style of certain fifties hipsters placed well back on his head to accommodate the white bandaging that peeked out beneath it. He was leaning on a wooden cane with an ornate silver handle. 'Thought I heard your voice,' the old man said. He was looking at Chance and doing his best to smile.

Chance rose at once. 'My God,' he asked. 'What happened?'

Carl waved it off. 'A minor mishap,' he said. 'I'll be right as rain in no time at all.' He went on before Chance could say more. 'I was pleased to see you brought your pieces in. I've already spoken to two buyers who may be interested.'

Interested in what, Chance wondered, copies or originals? Were the buyers in question private parties or dealers? Perhaps he should inquire. But then he *had* brought the stuff in. A course had been charted, and looking about him there in the alley, he felt himself, for what must have been the first time in a life noteworthy for its adherence to convention, a partner in crime. There followed a momentary, unaccountable elation and he looked once more to his co-conspirators, the one the size of Texas just now making gurgling noises with his straw as he sucked down the last of an enormous Diet Coke, the other rail thin in a plaid sharkskin jacket, head wrapped in gauze – desperadoes beneath the eaves.

'You're done out here,' Carl said, interrupting his reverie, 'come inside. I need you to fill out a couple of papers.'

'Papers?' Chance asked. He was not sure he cared for the sound of it.

'We'll want to document the pieces,' Carl told him. 'We'll want your signature.'

The idea of actually attaching his signature to something was sufficient to stifle his momentary elation. Signing papers evoked the specter of attorneys and courts of law, the stuff of life, as opposed to fantasy. D chose this moment to repeat the gurgling sound with his straw. My God, Chance thought suddenly, what have I done? Surely this was the very kind of poor judgment his father had so often warned of. The deal would sour. It was so written. He would be found out. Additional lawsuits would be added to those in which he was already mired. His life would turn to shit.

'You youngsters keep right on talking,' Carl said. 'I'll be here when you're ready.' He turned unsteadily in the doorway. Chance watched as he walked away, leaning heavily on the cane. 'The hell happened?' he asked of D, not quite able to mask his own sense of desperation.

'Kid took him off.'

'That kid I saw in here? Leather pants and pointed boots?'

'I guess.'

'There's more than one?'

D laughed. 'The old man has a weakness, I guess you could say, but yeah, it was probably that one you saw, flavor of the fucking month. Kid wanted money. Carl said no. Kid came in here with two of his pals, beat him up pretty good and stole some shit.'

'Christ.' Chance seated himself once more on the step. 'What did they take?' He supposed he was imagining how it would have been had his furniture been here a week earlier, and how it might be if they came back wanting more.

'Couple of antique chairs, some money was in that desk up front...'

'Did he go to the police?'

'He came to me. What pisses me off, I wasn't here when they came around but I guess that's how they planned it. Little prick knew his routine. Knew mine too, I suppose. You gotta watch it with that shit.'

'What shit would that be?' Chance asked. 'I'm not sure I follow.'

D just looked at him. 'Having a *routine*,' he said. 'Same place, same time every day? Like walking around with a fucking target on your back.'

D was, Chance thought, beginning to sound uncomfortably like certain of his patients, the ones with delusional paranoia. He kept the observation to himself and nodded, as if to confirm the position's fundamental soundness.

D waved toward the building at his back. 'Stuff's all back in there, is what I was about to say.'

'The stuff that was stolen?'

D nodded.

'You got it back?'

'That and then some.'

Chance waited.

'I needed to make it worth my while.'

Chance shook his head, imagining what that might mean. 'You make it sound easy,' he said.

'Pretty easy.'

'They weren't armed? They didn't want to fight you for it?'

D shrugged. 'The kid knew me.' He pulled the plastic top off his Diet Coke and examined the inside of the cup, apparently wanting to be sure that he'd gotten the last of it. 'One of his pals thought he'd try his luck with a baseball bat.'

Chance laughed out loud. He was thinking about the BMW driver in the street, that and Detective Blackstone, entertaining his fantasies.

'Not a good idea, you're telling me.'

'He should've stuck to baseballs.'

'So what then?'

D got to his feet, tossing his trash into a nearby Dumpster. 'Then he went away,' D said, as matter-of-factly as ever.

Chance gave it a moment to see if D would say more, but D seemed done and was now peering into the Dumpster as if he'd found something there to interest him. 'When you say he went away…' Chance started but let it drop. He was thinking maybe it was one of those 'don't ask, don't tell' kind of things. And what, after all, did *he* know?

In the end, Chance signed his papers and left. Funny, he thought, once more in the street, preternaturally quiet, it seemed to him now, striking for its absence of loitering youth, how these little trips to the old furniture store could put a new slant on one's day. He returned by way of city streets to his office to find Jaclyn Blackstone in his waiting room, staring pensively at the clouds beyond the window, a silver splint on her nose, bruises not unlike the old antiques dealer's fading beneath her eyes, which for the first time, he noted, were a rather beautiful shade of golden brown, almost yellow, he thought, like those of a cat.

The office visit

CHANCE SHARED the suite of offices on Polk Street with three other doctors, Salk, Marks, and Haig. Jacob Salk was a psychiatrist, an authority on mind control, cults, brainwashing, and vulnerability to undue influence. David Marks was a neuropsychologist Chance knew from his days at UCSF. Like Chance, he was married and a father. Unlike Chance, he was *still* married. And finally there was Leonard Haig. At forty-five, Haig was already the most dramatically prosperous of the group, a neurologist of private means who'd managed a specialty out of defense work for the big insurance companies. He had recently purchased a house in the South of France. He was said to be an exceptionally fine tennis player and successful womanizer. If not crossing paths as dueling expert witnesses in a court of law, as had happened on a number of occasions, Chance and Haig rarely spoke. Yet it was Haig who alerted him to the presence of Jaclyn Blackstone in the building.

'I have just directed a patient to your waiting room,' Haig told him. They were standing in the hallway before a black-and-white photograph of a clearly deranged elderly woman seated in a tiny windowless room. The room was bare as a prison cell save for a string of paper dollies by some means suspended above the woman's nearly hairless head.

Chance did little more than lift his eyebrows. It seemed to him highly irregular that Haig should find the directing of anyone anywhere as anything other than a task beneath his station.

'She was in mine by mistake,' Haig told him. 'I thought

of keeping her, but what the hell. She wanted you.'

'Well… I guess I should thank you then,' Chance said.

'Or at least return the favor.' Haig inclined toward the demented woman Chance recognized as the work of the building's chief parking attendant, Jean-Baptiste Marceau.

Formerly of Paris, France, Jean-Baptiste had once been a student of anthropology and medicine. A head injury at twenty-four with resultant scarring along the motor strip near the back portion of the frontal lobe had made of him an epileptic, subject to partial as well as complex or frontal lobe seizures in the manner of Saint Paul and in the wake of which he had abandoned his formal studies for paths less traveled. One of his interests was photography and he had, in the forty-odd years since the accident, amassed an impressive collection of prideful, demented individuals in various states of physical and mental decline and from which he occasionally sought to decorate the walls of the building.

'He's at it again,' Haig said in reference to the picture. 'I'm thinking this time… maybe *you* can talk to him.'

Of the artist's work, Chance was of two minds. On the one hand, the stuff intrigued him for reasons he could not entirely fathom. On the other, it made him want to hang himself. Of Jean-Baptiste he was not at all conflicted but considered him one of the city's hidden treasures, a kind of peripatetic holy man sworn to the pursuit of subjects not yet identified. He lived alone in the building's tiny basement apartment, procured along with his job by way of some connection to the landlord, an ancient Chinese woman of immense wealth, that was not altogether clear, though Chance suspected some form of very beneath-the-boards type treatment/therapy as perhaps part of the equation given that Jean-Baptiste, while lacking in appropriate credentials, had been known to see people now and again as patients, especially in such cases as were inclined toward astro travel and talks with the dead. But whatever the arrangement, and clandestine therapy was pure conjecture on Chance's part, attempts by certain of the building's tenants to dislodge him had ended badly. The Frenchman was protected from on high.

But that was only part of it. The other thing about Jean-Baptiste was that when it came to parking cars he made no distinction between the late-model Porsches, Beamers, Mercedes, Range Rovers, and Audis that filled the underground lot and Chance's 1989 Oldsmobile Cutlass. (His wife in possession of the Lexus, he'd found the Olds on craigslist.) Where other attendants were almost uniformly inclined to hide the creaking wreck, Jean-Baptiste was given to placing it among the building's most desirable spaces, an act of charity that had led some, Haig among them, to believe the two in some special alliance.

'He's taken this Diane Arbus routine to new heights, or lows,' Haig went on. 'We'll have patients going out the windows.'

Chance studied the demented woman. While it was true that in the months since Jean-Baptiste's arrival in the building's basement, and particularly in the wake of his own divorce, Chance had come to rather enjoy the other's exuberant disinhibition – to the point of imparting certain confidences he would not have shared with his more professional colleagues – it was also true that Jean-Baptiste was a thing unto himself, as subject to influence as the weather, but pleasures had been few of late and Chance would take them where he could. 'I don't know,' he said, his eyes on those of the woman. 'I kind of like this one.'

Haig just looked at him.

'Something about those dollies. I mean, think about it.' He had started once more for his office.

'Fuck you then,' Haig called after him. 'She comes in here again… I'm keeping her for myself.'

Chance gave him a little wave. 'Perhaps you should meet Big D,' he said, too distant to be heard but indulging his latest fantasy. 'On a dark night in a dark alley. Oh, and bring your bat.'

* * *

He caught sight of *her* from the back, through one of the rectangular glass panels that flanked his door. She wore boots and jeans and a long gray sweater. She was staring out a window and he was taken, as he had been in the bookstore, by her length and line. Funny how well she'd hidden it on the occasion of her first visit, in the flat shoes and dowdy dress, the lackluster arrangement of her hair.

She turned as he entered, showing him her splint and bruises. As he started toward her, he became aware of Lucy, the young woman he'd hired to manage his office, giving him the evil eye from her place behind the counter. She was the perfect height for it at five feet even. Sometimes all you could see from across the room was the top of her head down to her eyes. She had red hair and the kind of horn-rimmed glasses once favored by Buddy Holly. Her skin was milk white, pure as the driven snow save for the full-sleeve tattoo decorating one arm, extreme perhaps but beautifully done, the work of some latter-day Dali, all melting clocks and serpents in the garden. He didn't know what else. The tattoos disappeared into her clothing but presumably went on from there. There was a small silver stud in her face just beneath her lower lip. She favored dresses from retro secondhand stores and Converse sneakers but she knew how to put it all together. Before reinventing herself as a psych major at UC-Berkeley she had studied art at Hunter College in New York City. She was really quite sexy in a druggy, artistic sort of way when you got right down to it. Probably why he hired her. Not that this was anything he would ever have acted upon. But he did like seeing her there, behind the big, curved counter, greeting patients, moving about the office. It was why people kept exotic birds. Her colors filled the room.

'The Jenkinses are waiting,' Lucy said. She affected a somewhat breathless delivery, one eye on the wounded Jaclyn. 'I told Mrs Blackstone she would have to make another appointment…'

'It's all right,' Chance told her. 'I'll handle it.'

'The Jenkinses have been waiting for half an hour.'

'Please tell them that I will be with them momentarily.'

Lucy looked at him just long enough to punctuate her disapproval then did as she was asked.

Chance crossed to where Jaclyn stood waiting, blue circles beneath her yellow cat's eyes. 'I *do* have someone,' he said.

'Should I go?'

'It may be awhile, is what I'm saying.'

She looked to the window as if to master her emotions.

The Jenkinses were a married couple with two small children. Ralf Jenkins was thirty-nine years old. He was two years post a second craniotomy and following radiation therapy for a malignant brain tumor. Since the second surgery he'd been experiencing word-finding difficulty and fine-motor problems with his right hand. Chance had recommended both a speech pathologist with regard to his language problems and a psychotherapist for assistance with the psychological effects of his brain cancer. That had been at the first of the year. Last week they had scheduled a return visit for reasons he might anticipate but had yet to be certain of. He imagined the appointment would take anywhere from one to two hours. Since moving into private practice, Chance had always tried to make large allowances of time for the patients who came to see him. Their conditions were often grave. They were often confused, frightened, angry. The universe was already rushing them. They didn't need it from him. 'How much time do you have?' he asked of Jaclyn. He was aware of Lucy, watching from her post in the reception area.

'I have the afternoon. I'm sorry to just show up like this...'

He raised a hand. 'It's okay. It's dull waiting up here. There's a little café just downstairs at the end of the block. Why don't you go down there and wait, have a cup of coffee.' He looked to a table in his waiting room. 'Take a magazine. I should be able to join you in an hour or so.' He looked at his watch. It was just after one. 'I have to pick up my daughter by four, but we should have some time to talk.'

Her eyes found his. 'That would be very kind of you,' she said. Her fingers fiddled with the buttons on her sweater. He could see that her thumbs were raw around the nails where she picked or chewed at them. 'I have a cell phone,' she told him. 'If I have to leave, I'll call your office. But I'll try to wait.'

'That'll be fine.'

'Thank you,' she said. 'I don't know...' She started off on some new train of thought then reined herself in. 'I'm sorry. Really. But thank you.' She moved away, ignoring the magazines and exiting the office.

'Don't even go there,' he said to Lucy on his way to the Jenkinses. 'You don't know what she's been through.'

'Maybe not, but she strikes me as someone who knows how to get what she wants. You should've seen her little-girl-lost routine with your buddy Dr Haig.'

'He's hardly my buddy.'

'And she was hardly lost. I mean, she's been here before.'

'And sustained a pretty good concussion *since* that time. How come you're so tough all of a sudden?'

Lucy ignored the question. 'Meeting in the café,' she said. 'Is that like a freebie, then?'

'Believe me,' Chance told her. 'It's the least I can do.'

His meeting with the Jenkinses lasted for more than an hour but Jaclyn was waiting in the café, nearly empty at this time of day. To enter was to descend a short flight of tiled steps by which the café's windows were brought nearly even with the sidewalk, the wheels of passing cars. Jaclyn had chosen a table well back in the room and away from the windows. Chance ordered coffee on his way in and joined her in the shadows.

'How was your patient?' she asked.

He told her about Ralf.

'He's dying then?'

'He has six months, maybe.'

'Jesus. What do you tell them?'

'The truth. I suggest counseling, support groups, hospice care.' A cable car rattled past in the street. 'It's not always as grim as you might think,' he said. 'What you see... sometimes, with some people... is the bullshit falling away. They see what's important, and what isn't. You get the feeling... with some, that they actually begin to live for the first time.' It pleased him to believe this was so.

Jaclyn nodded but didn't say anything.

'A blast occurs outside that window, the white light of some nuclear holocaust. You've got five seconds. Now what do you do?'

Jaclyn looked to the street. There was only the muted light of a foggy afternoon. 'I don't know,' she said. She looked to Chance. 'Do you?'

He reached across the table and took her hand. 'This. Maybe this is all there is. They find people like that, you know, everywhere from Pompeii to the World Trade Center.' He let go her hand. 'We all die,' he told her. 'It's what we do with the time we have that matters.'

Her eyes filled with tears. 'You're a good doctor,' she said.

'People want miracles. Sometimes the only miracle is, I take your hand. That's the miracle.'

A moment elapsed. She regained her composure.

'What do I do?' she asked him.

'I'd think you have to start with the truth.'

'He'd kill me. He's said he would and I believe him.'

'We're talking about your husband now, not some intruder? Just to be clear.'

She nodded that this was so.

'It was your husband who beat you.'

She smiled in a way that seemed to suggest the naiveté of his question. 'He wouldn't. He wouldn't be the one to get his hands dirty.'

'He *had* it done? Is that what you're telling me? It's important for us to be clear about this.'

She shrugged and looked away.

'Have you ever talked to an attorney? Another cop? There

are attorneys who specialize in cases where people are threatened...'

'I'm talking to you.'

'But now, that you've actually been hurt...'

'You think this is the first time? Look, I *know* the drill... What you don't know, what nobody knows... is how smart he is. He knows the law. He's also crazy. He would get me in the end. It's what he's like.

'He knows people. He could be in jail and still have it done.' Her voice broke for the first time. 'He knows how to do things,' she whispered. 'He would know how to make Jaclyn disappear.'

'You just referred to yourself in the third person,' Chance said. 'Is this Jackie I'm speaking to now?'

'No. I don't know. I don't care about Jackie.' She gave it a beat. 'I have a daughter,' she said.

Chance was stunned. There had been no mention of a child in any of the paperwork pertaining to her case. Nor had the subject come up at the time of his initial interview. He studied her for some time in the muted light.

Jaclyn Blackstone studied her hands.

'The child is his?'

She shook her head. 'I was seventeen. Her father and I were never married.' She hesitated and went on. 'I gave her up for adoption. We reconnected two years ago. She's in school at Chico State. Raymond pays her tuition.'

'Raymond is your husband?' He believed it was the first time he'd heard her say his name. She indicated that such was the case. 'Why didn't you mention any of this when you came to my office?'

'I guess... what I was most afraid of just then... was that these symptoms I'd been experiencing were neurological.'

His first inclination was to mention that he was in fact board certified as both a neurologist and as a psychiatrist, that any proper evaluation of her particular symptoms would require his being privy to any and all pertinent information.

Upon reflection this struck him as needlessly argumentative, given the circumstances, and he chose to let it go, at least for the time being. 'I take it,' he said finally, 'that you believe your daughter to be at risk as well.'

'He's said as much.'

Chance imagined himself no stranger to the machinations by which people went about establishing the architecture of their own imprisonment, the citadels from whose basement windows one might on occasion hear their cries. Like Houdini, we construct the machinery of our entrapment from which we must finally escape or die. Mired in the legal and financial difficulties following in the wake of his divorce, he did not find in himself any particular exception to this rule, though in comparison to Jaclyn Blackstone, his chances of death were certainly more figurative than literal. 'Beyond trying to find *legal* help,' Chance said. He was at the end of another long pause. 'I don't know what to say. Will you continue with Janice?'

'He's forbidden it. This was a big deal, me coming here. This is dangerous for me.' Her eyes searched the room. 'It could be dangerous for you too. I could be putting you at risk. I had to think about that.'

He was for the second time that afternoon aware of the day's fresh slant. 'There is,' he said, 'quite often a difference in what people threaten and what they will actually do.' But noted that his pulse had quickened.

'Right,' she said.

'Look,' he said. 'This is not easy. I get that. What do you risk to get your life back? Do you risk losing it? And it's not just you. There is your daughter to consider. I can't tell you what to do. I still think some kind of discreet conversation with someone more versed in the law... I'm often called to testify in court as an expert witness. These are rarely criminal cases, but I do know a number of attorneys. I could make inquiries... Beyond that...'

She reached suddenly across the table to take his hand. 'Maybe it's like you said,' she told him. 'Maybe there's just this. Maybe this was why I came.'

The move caught him. He sat with his hand in hers, studying her in the late light. Christ, he thought, you could land a plane on those cheekbones, and wondered how at their first meeting he could have missed so much. She pulled his hand toward her, clasping it between her own, the wedding ring she still wore sharp against his fingers. He imagined himself outside looking in. He imagined the picture they might make at just this moment. He imagined the bad cop looking on. One should really be more mindful of appearances, he thought, in the manner of his father, one should be more cautious, but his hand remained where it was. He was aware of the pulse in her wrist, warm against the heel of his palm. He was aware of his desire, taking him by the throat.

The interventionist

ONCE MORE they had parted on a city sidewalk, and once more he had watched her walk away, but the bit in the café had left him unsettled. He was vulnerable to certain things just now, he thought, even more so than usual, what with his personal and financial life in such total and utter disarray, in the absence of female companionship. Stress was not conducive to clear thinking and one needed to remain cognizant. It was, he concluded, like walking around with a fucking target on one's fucking back and he arrived ten minutes late at the entrance to his daughter's school.

The school was located near the marina with a view of the bay. He found the wind coming up hard and crisp beneath the span of the Golden Gate Bridge as he pulled in before the coral-colored buildings, the bay littered with whitecaps, Alcatraz in the distance. The sight of the old prison conjured images of law enforcement gone awry, the steely gray eyes of Detective Blackstone.

His daughter, Nicole, was waiting alone beneath a tree. When she saw his car she marched toward him in the manner of the condemned, a notebook held to her chest with folded arms. He was given to understand that his wife had broken the news about the schools. He could only imagine the delivery. Nicole opened the car's door and got in. He could see that she had been crying. They sat for a moment in the street, cars passing, wind off the bay casting a fine mist across the windshield. Clearly she was determined upon stoicism. 'I'm sorry, Nicky,' Chance said finally. 'If there had been any other way…'

'How about you just stay with Mom.'

Chance sighed. He considered it bad form to say it was Mom's idea and thereby assign blame, though in point of fact it had been Carla's idea. He wondered if it was possible that Nicole still did not know about the dyslexic personal trainer. Anything, he supposed, was possible. 'It's complicated, Nicole. You may not know all the details, but you do know that it's complicated.'

His daughter bit at her lip and stared out the window.

'I know how much you liked Havenwood. But there *are* other good schools…'

'Marina South blows.'

Marina South was the name of the public school in whose district their old house had been. 'Yes,' Chance said. 'Marina South does blow. I've done my homework and I know that. What I was about to say was that there are good schools across the bay, in Berkeley.'

'Berkeley's not where we live.'

'It's not where we live now. But I've been looking into it. If I were to get an apartment over there…'

'You just got an apartment over here.'

She appeared intent upon making each of these pronouncements to the trees beyond her window, having been very careful not to look at Chance directly since seating herself in his car. Chance covered her hand with his. 'Nicole,' he said, then waited until she looked at him. 'This is difficult. It's difficult for all of us. But that's what life is sometimes. What I want you to know is that I'm doing the best I can for you and I always will. I love you very much.'

Her eyes got watery once more and she looked away. 'I know,' she said, her voice faint. Theatrically so, one might have said but he knew her to be sincere, in both her pain and her stoicism.

'We'll get through this,' he told her. 'It will all work out. You will see.'

She nodded. Chance gave her hand a little squeeze. She squeezed back. 'I know,' she said once more, even fainter than before. Chance let go her hand and put his car into gear. His heart went out to her. The world she'd known was being broken apart. He'd read somewhere that the family is an instrument of grief and there were times when it seemed to be so and he looked once more to the old prison, ghostlike upon its windswept rock.

He dropped his daughter off at his former house before which a realtor's placard flapped forlornly in the afternoon wind from a corner of the property, and watched her inside. From there he drove directly back to his office. The building was closed for the day. He went along its familiar steps and corridors, letting himself into his own suite then rummaging in his files till he'd found Jaclyn Blackstone's. Some of what it contained were the questionnaires she had filled out at the time of her initial visit that would be certain to contain both her current address and phone number. He left in possession of the document, exchanging pleasantries with the night watchman in the lobby and feeling for all the world as if he were getting away with something.

He sat that night alone in his apartment. It was becoming routine. He'd thought to finish with his evaluation of Doc Billy, as the relative in Oregon was pressing for action and the case was expected to go to trial by summer's end, but he could not quite summon the required resources. He sat instead with his by now customary bottle of wine, watching as the fog rolled up the sidewalks outside his window, and considered instead the problem of Jaclyn Blackstone.

If, in the fullness of her paranoia, she was to be believed, the thing was a conundrum in which one felt blocked at every turn. He could not help noting in his initial report her use of a neuroleptic medication – somehow she had been started on Trilafon, and had remarked at the time, '*She may be experiencing akathisia as a side effect of her dopamine-*

blocking medication, perphenazine.' He considered this anew. It had been his concern that a worsening akathisia be misperceived as a worsening anxiety, to be treated with still higher doses of dopamine blockers and so further aggravating the situation, at least with regard to her anxiety and paranoia, exacerbating the very fears she would have to overcome if she were to free herself from her predator. But then he had visited her in the hospital. The concussion was no fantasy. Nor were the broken bones or the entrapped muscle. She might well have sustained permanent damage. He saw such people every day of his life, broken creatures aboard a carousel of cognitive and pharmacology therapies, beset by memory loss and hallucination. They were, after all, his stock-in-trade. He looked once more over the file from his office, rereading yet again what he had written at their initial meeting. *'I believe,'* he had said, *'it is important for this warded-off aspect of her personality to be addressed and, ideally, integrated into her basic persona.'* And so she had tried to do, following his advice, and gotten for her troubles a berth in the trauma center at Mercy General, medical bills that would stalk her for years to come.

There was one other bit that caught his eye: *'One cannot rule out masochistic features in her ongoing relationship with her husband.'* That might have been true. But she had moved to end the relationship after only weeks of therapy. The husband was the sick one. Chance had confronted the monster himself and been found wanting. He thought once more of how she had appeared to him at the time of their first meeting, her somewhat affectless description of the split in her personality. Rarely, he concluded, had life pitched him such a curve. Suffice it to say that what most of the people he saw in the course of his practice had in common was that they had already reached a place of no return. What set Jaclyn apart, what she shared with Mariella Franko, as far as that went, and very few others, was her ability to provoke in him the belief that there was still time, that some form of intervention was not yet beyond the pale. And while that was generally where such feelings ended, save but once, this Jaclyn Blackstone was carrying him into deeper waters. Perhaps it was no more than her coming to his office, her pulse on his palm, because the thing was... the usual reservations notwithstanding, an actual, even somewhat realistic, plan of action had begun to form. He considered sleeping on it just to be sure but then he was a little drunk and eager to share. He was also in possession of her number. She answered on the second ring. 'Can you talk?' he asked.

The Jollys

Bernard Jolly is a nineteen-year-old right-handed white male who, until his recent arrest and incarceration, has lived in the home of his maternal aunt, Amanda Jolly of South San Francisco. His father and mother were never married and he claims never to have known his father. His mother deserted him when he was six years old, at which time he went to live with his mother's sister, a woman he now describes as an obese crazy person. He was, at the time of my initial interview, three years into a postconcussive syndrome following basilar skull fracture and intracerebral hematoma following a bicycle-automobile accident in which he was riding the bicycle. He reports the accident as occurring at the corner of Judah and Sunset and relates that his last memory was seeing a red pickup truck he would eventually learn to have been driven by a Mexican gardener approach him on the left side. He was found unresponsive at the scene and transferred to UCSF Emergency Room, where on examination he was awake but confused.

During hospitalization his hematocrit fell from 45 to the low 20s and a retroperitoneal hematoma was detected. He was stabilized with two units of packed cells. Repeat CT scan revealed decreased brain edema, a left temporal intraparenchymal hemorrhage, and a small right hemisphere epidural hemorrhage.

Because he remained febrile, the patient was started on Vancomycin and Ceftizoxime for presumed bacterial meningitis. The temperature fell and by the 14th hospital day he was afebrile and able to cooperate with examinations. He was discharged two days later.

Since the time of his discharge, the patient admits to both visual and olfactory hallucinations. Visual hallucinations consist most often of seeing the Mexican gardener who struck him, even though he has been informed that this man has since left the country. He has on several occasions prior to his recent arrest chased and accosted strangers he believed to be the gardener. The most serious of these occurred when, at the wheel of his own car, he intentionally struck a pedestrian that he believed to be the Mexican gardener who had struck him. The pedestrian survived but not without serious injury. Mr Jolly, arrested at the scene, spent a period of four months in a state mental hospital. Olfactory hallucinations include hay, incense, marijuana, and the 'smell of different beings.'

THE JOLLYS had not come to him by way of the usual channels. The fact was, he had gone to them. What was needed in the case of Jaclyn Blackstone, he had concluded, was at least one well-positioned friend. It was to this end that he had called the Oakland DA's office and volunteered to do a psychiatric evaluation or two pro bono. It would be an effort to insinuate himself in the department. While not wholly convinced by Jaclyn of her husband's near omniscience, the beating followed by his own encounter with the man were enough to warrant caution. One could not just wade in making charges. There was too much at stake. He'd spoken to an attorney he knew who handled cases involving threats and abuse. The story was always the same. One filed complaints. One got restraining orders. A determined or insane predator was apt to have his prey. The law would have him only after, when the deed was done. And then there was Jaclyn's claim that Raymond was not the type to dirty his own hands... that he could *have* things done. 'He's corrupt then?' Chance had asked. To which she'd laughed softly as if to some private joke. 'He's everything,' she told him.

Well, maybe so, and maybe that was the key. If Chance could make a friend in the department, maybe there would be a way of putting them onto the bad cop in their midst. Maybe that was how to get Raymond Blackstone, the best possible way really, for something else he had done, Jaclyn and her daughter not even in the picture because if he was bad on one count he would be bad on two. It was like getting Al Capone on tax evasion. Putting him away was the thing. It scarcely mattered how. What seemed equally important, as this was likely to be an ongoing project, was for Jaclyn to have some way of continuing with therapy. It was to this end that he had broken from his written report on Bernie Jolly, now a petty criminal on trial for the rape of a twelve-year-old girl, and set out on foot to meet Janice Silver for coffee at a café on Market Street, not far from Allan's Antiques and Chance's furniture.

The air had improved somewhat since his last stroll in this part of the city, though here and there the occasional surgical mask was yet in evidence. He seemed of late to be counting them for no good reason he could think of. He found Janice at an outdoor table beneath a small sycamore.

'I've taken you for my ally,' he said, sitting opposite.

'So I see,' Janice told him. She was a slight middle-aged woman with the dress and manner of many Bay Area lesbians, though in point of fact her sexual orientation was, even after all the time they'd known one another, something of a mystery. They'd met while both were on staff in the teaching hospital at UCSF and had remained friends. She had over the years become something of a de facto therapist and one of the few people to whom he had confided with regard to certain aspects of his past.

Their talk on the phone had been brief. He'd done little more than announce the subject of their meeting. She brushed at some ash that had fallen near a plate of cookies. A masked cyclist passed in the street.

'Was this stupid, us meeting here?' The question was his.

'I don't know. Was it?'

'Being outside, I mean. It's been weeks already.'

'Yes, I know, and I have no idea. Avoid strenuous exercise, they say. I don't think this counts.' She looked to the sky. 'We're waiting for the rains. Now tell me about this plan of yours. You were quite mysterious on the phone.'

Chance watched as the cyclist vanished in the haze, ordered iced tea from the waitress, and turned his attention to the woman before him, noting that the amount of gray in her hair seemed to have increased since their last meeting. Well, he thought, she's like me. Time flies when you're having fun. 'She's got no chance,' Chance said finally. 'Not with that man in her life.'

'And yet she stays, here, in *his* city.'

'She says that if she left he would find her.'

'And you believe that?'

'We've seen what he's capable of.'

'Yes,' she said. 'We have seen that.'

'Nor should she *have* to run. Her life is here. Did you know she has a daughter?'

'Yes, she told me.'

Chance took this as a good sign, allaying at least some of the apprehension generated by her confession in the café. Janice was waiting for him to go on. 'She needs two things,' Chance said.

'Only two?'

'She should continue with some form of therapy and she needs a friend.'

'Sounds like she has one.'

'Hey, now… I thought we were on the same side.'

'If you mean thinking this guy she's hooked up with is a monster and that she ought to have the chance to work through her shit, then yes, we're on the same side. But I'm thinking there's more to it. Let me rephrase. I'm afraid there might be more to it. Assuage my fears, why don't you?'

He told her about his attempt to ingratiate himself with the Oakland DA, his theory of well-positioned friends.

She was longer than he would have liked in getting back

to him. 'Are you kidding me?' she asked finally. 'I mean… if he's everything she says… how is he not going to get hip to you poking around?'

'It's a big department. I will be dealing directly with the DA's office. Blackstone can't have his finger on every little thing that happens over there. Plus, he's a homicide detective. What they're going to want from me are profiles, judgments regarding testamentary capacity. Cases should be all over the map. Might not be a homicide in the bunch.'

'You've already begun then?'

'A phone call was all that took, a little back-and-forth online, a couple hours. It's not like they're drowning in expertise over there.' He went on to tell her about the first case he'd been asked to evaluate, that of Bernard Jolly.

'Poor boy,' she said.

He took her to mean Bernard and not himself.

'Well…' she said finally. 'Whatever. Just don't say I never warned you. What's more concerning to *me* is the degree to which you are *involving* yourself in all of this. I just can't see that it's the best thing, for either of you.'

She was not one to mince words and he liked that about her, yet he inclined toward the combative. 'Of course,' he said. '*Involving* is such a dirty word. Implying as it does the getting off of one's ass.'

'That's not what I'm talking about and you know it.'

'Janice… We do something or we don't, it's that simple.'

A moment passed. Janice looked to the street. 'So… you're going to find her a friend. That's one thing.'

'She tutors kids in math, kids Nicky's age. I'm thinking I could have her come to my apartment. You could meet her there, continue therapy.'

'Did she tell you how she found her daughter?'

Chance was surprised by the question. 'She said only that they had reconnected.'

'The husband found her. Excuse me, the cop.'

Chance waited.

'It was a closed case, meaning that when she signed the

papers to put the child up, she agreed never to attempt contact.'

'She was seventeen years old.'

'Yes, and those types of closed cases were more common then than now. Still... Do you know how she met her cop? She was being stalked by some guy, someone she'd gone out with, apparently. She called the police. Guess who showed up?'

'She wouldn't be the first to trade one abusive man for another.'

'Or maybe it's more about finding one man to save her from another. Maybe it's what she does, consciously or unconsciously...'

'Maybe that's where Jackie Black comes in.'

'If you're willing to go there. Have you ever met her, this Jackie Black?'

'Not that I know of.'

'That's a lame answer, but neither have I, and some would say you don't diagnose a true dissociative identity disorder without having actually made contact with at least one alter.'

'You doubt her whole story then?'

'I don't know yet. She's complicated. Her story is atypical... late in life for the development of a secondary personality, if that's what this is. And of course, if you really are willing to go down that particular rabbit hole it's possible there are others... personalities *she* is not even aware of, earlier patterns of abuse not yet brought to light.'

'Well... however many of her there are, or aren't, I can't imagine that any of them would want to go on getting beaten.'

'I guess that would depend on how sick she is.'

Chance said nothing.

Janice softened a little. 'I am on her side, Eldon. You know that. I like her. I think she's a bright woman who may someday be whole. Or not. She has a difficult past and she's developed what I'd call a dangerous strategy by way of coping. But I felt we were making progress. I was angry when this happened, as you know, being the one I called to vent. And of course I thought it would be good for you to look in on her, make sure they weren't missing anything at that zoo they call a hospital. But I would never have asked you to involve yourself in this way.' She gave it a beat. 'There,' she said. 'I used it again, your dirty word. But I would still say it's appropriate here. I would not have asked that of anyone and especially not you. You were right the first time, sending her to a therapist. You were right to choose a woman.'

Chance watched as the sun moved from behind one of the high-rise buildings to the east, still enough ash in the sky to shift its light toward the red end of the spectrum, allowing for the apocalyptic hues he had not only come to expect, but rather to enjoy. 'I met the husband. Did I tell you that?'

'No, you didn't. What was that like?'

'Creepy, is what it was like. It would be hard to abandon her to him.'

'Yes,' she said. 'I imagine it would. I'd imagine something else too. I'd imagine that's what she's counting on.'

'She won't be seeing me. She'll be seeing you.'

'In your apartment.'

'We don't have to provide the student and it doesn't have to be in my apartment. The point would be to set up some cover by which you and she could continue to meet. How about this? How about I put it to her? Maybe she will know someone.'

'I don't know, Eldon. I really don't. I will have to think about it.'

'We're back to our two choices,' Chance told her. 'We take some extraordinary measures in an extraordinary case. We intervene or we do nothing and hope for the best. I think we both know how that ends.'

Janice sighed and looked to the street.

'Would that be a yes or a no?' Chance asked.

The check and the frozen lake

I T WAS a yes finally, with reservations, but who didn't have those. And they would definitely pass on his apartment. 'I'll ask her today,' Chance told her.

'I'm sure you will,' she said, then added upon rising that as a general rule she was opposed to subterfuge.

'Aren't we all?' Chance asked.

She left without saying more.

Chance made the call from his cell phone, still seated in the restaurant.

'This isn't a good number,' Jaclyn Blackstone told him. 'Give me five, I'll call you back.' His phone rang in ten.

'Okay,' he said. 'I think I've got something.' They'd spoken only briefly the night he'd called. He'd mentioned a plan but stopped short of details, asking that she give him a couple of days. 'Is this a good time?'

'You mean now?'

'Now, later, whenever would be convenient for you.'

There was silence on the line, the clatter of something in the background, music from a distant radio. 'I'm at work right now,' she said. The radio was turned off. 'There's a lecture tonight on the campus. I was planning to go. It's in the math department. One of the graduate students is lecturing on "The Axiom of Choice."' Another moment passed. 'If you'd like to come?' she said without quite finishing.

Her quality of voice along with the way she'd formulated the invitation gave the impression that her doing so had not come without cost and he was reminded of her vulnerability, recalling at just that moment the delicate architecture of the hand that had opened and closed on the sky blue blanket as he'd sat by her side in the dismal room, the city draped in gloom upon a far horizon. 'I'm afraid it would all be lost on me,' Chance said and not without some cost to himself. He had not counted on her asking to meet. She didn't say anything right away and Chance waited, the phone to his ear. Traffic passed in the street. 'There is a little Thai place on Shattuck not far from the campus,' he said suddenly. 'Do you know it?' It was an oddly fractured moment in which he seemed to be both speaking and listening at the same time.

'We could meet there after.' Her voice had dropped to something scarcely above a whisper.

'We could.'

'At seven?'

'Seven it is.'

They hung up.

Chance paid his bill and headed down Market Street, elation at war with apprehension; nothing like a clandestine meeting to put a new slant on the day. He thought about her and he thought about the lecture she had invited him to, 'The Axiom of Choice.' What could be more fitting than that? He imagined visiting his furniture as a way of calming his nerves.

He could hear Carl on the phone as he entered. The old man, in a dark brown suit and brilliant yellow scarf, was pacing between an armoire of the late French Modernists and a sculptural coffee table of Japanese design. The one-sided conversation was indistinct but animated, the still bandaged old man turning upon his toe in the manner of some brightly plumed fowl, his free hand in conduction of an invisible orchestra. Taking note of Chance's presence, he paused just long enough and with such hand movements and facial gestures as might indicate to Chance that he was to proceed on his own to the rear of the building. Or so Chance was willing to interpret the elaborate combination of head feints, grins, and fluttering eyebrows. In passing, it seemed to him that the old man was just giddy enough with excitement to suggest a new leather boy had entered his life, this or the use of stimulants.

Chance went on through the store. He paused at D's work window but was unable to lay eyes on his furniture. A noise from outside led him to the rear door and a view of the alley where D was wrestling what appeared to be a new radiator into a 1950 Studebaker, a Starlight coupe, to be exact.

'What's with Carl?' Chance asked, moving outside. 'New boyfriend?'

'How'd you guess?'

'The look of love, as they say.'

D nodded and heaved. The radiator dropped into place. He snatched up a rag, set about wiping his hands. 'Ever heard of the Frozen Lake?'

'I'm not sure what you mean.'

'Then you haven't heard of it. It's the thing you want so badly you'll go to the center of a frozen lake to reach it.'

'Where the ice is thinnest.'

'But you won't think about that. Everyone else will, just not you. I learned it in the Teams. Let's say I'm rolling with my guys and someone says to me, "You're on your frozen lake, bro." What that means is… I need to stop and think, *what*ever it is that I'm doing… I need to stop 'cause he sees something I don't. May even be we're stateside, may be I've got eyes for my buddy's wife and he picks up on it. Whatever. Everybody has his frozen lake. In conflict… you discover your opponent's, you're one up. The old man likes his leather boys.'

'You point that out to *him*, about the frozen lake?'

D's sigh was one of resignation. 'About a thousand times. What are you going to do? Fucker's as old as the hills.'

Chance smiled but he was thinking about frozen lakes and not the old man's. He studied the coupe, a brilliant lemon yellow. The vehicle was pointed fore and aft in the manner of a boat. 'That's a Starlight coupe,' Chance said. 'My grandmother had one just like it.'

'No shit?' D was either interested or he was fucking with him a little. Chance suspected the latter but chose to indulge himself. The car was a time machine. 'I was little, I thought they looked like flying saucers. What my grandmother and I did, we went to the army surplus and bought an old gas mask. Then she would prop the trunk open with a stick and drive around while I rode back there wearing the mask and shooting at things with a plastic gun.'

'Lucky she didn't get rear-ended.'

'She was about four and a half feet high; barely see over the wheel. The car was covered in dents. It was like Destruction Derby.'

'And you got back there.'

'With great enthusiasm,' Chance said.

D had taken to tightening bolts on radiator mounts. 'He's no good either.' He nodded at the back of the store. 'You've seen that bumper sticker: "I Brake for Hallucinations"?'

'This is his then?' He meant the Studebaker.

'Picked it up at some estate sale. I'm restoring it for him. Ought to be good for something.' The comment served to remind Chance about why he'd come, to inquire after his furniture.

'It's gone,' D said.

Chance was not certain that he'd heard correctly. 'Gone?' he asked.

'Yesterday. Figured that was why you were here.'

It was at just this moment that the old man appeared at the rear of the building. Bandages still peeked from beneath the brim of his hat although the swelling about his eyes had gone down. The yellow scarf draped about his neck was a dead-on match for the Starlight coupe.

'Young man!' Carl intoned. He was looking straight at Chance, a golden tooth prominent in his smile. 'Would a check in the amount of eighty thousand dollars brighten your day?'

In the Little Thai Hut

CARL HAD photographed the furniture before it left the building, mounting the pictures on black paper then arranging them in a black cardboard folder that Chance now carried. He'd thought, after visiting the warehouse, to get back to his office and Bernie Jolly. His report was due by week's end and there was still the matter of arranging for an interview. But the sale of his furniture had put him off stride and late afternoon found him having a beer on the waterfront, Oakland across the bay. He'd placed the eighty-thousand-dollar cashier's check from Allan's Antiques in a safe-deposit box at his bank. Given his troubles with the IRS, it seemed prudent to consult with his attorney before actually depositing the money. But that was only the half of it and did not account for the intermittent waves of vertigo, palpitations, and excessive perspiration the check had inspired. The furniture had been sold as a set of originals.

'But I thought it was what we had agreed upon,' Carl had said, surprised by Chance's initial reluctance to accept the check. 'It *was* why we did the work.' And so it had been, but hadn't he also imagined some final opportunity to rethink his position when the time came and the buyer at hand? The set had gone to a Mr Vladimir of San Francisco for the sum of one hundred thousand dollars with Carl holding back twenty for D's work and his own commission. 'And that's a deal,' Carl had added. 'D likes you. So do I. And we know what you're going through.'

D's work was of course not the issue. He was welcome to

whatever was fair, as was Carl. It was the other side of the thing that bothered him, what for lack of a better term he was coming to think of as the dark side.

'I thought you'd be happier,' Carl had said.

What was left but thank you and goodbye?

That done, he'd returned to the office just long enough to give Lucy the afternoon off. He'd imagined leaving the folder but found the pictures required looking at now and again as some means of reassurance, that the pieces really did look like other pieces, in other books, the ones with all their parts intact.

'Vladimir?' Chance had asked, his final query before vacating the warehouse. 'He's a Russian then?' The thing was complicating by the second. He was thinking of an article he'd read in the *Chronicle* on the presence of the Russian mob in San Francisco. But Carl had only clucked and shaken his head. 'The stuff looked terrific, my young friend. Mr Vladimir is very rich. And now he's very happy. The set will probably be in his family for the next hundred years. You should be happy too.'

Chance had agreed to try. He placed the folder on the bar before him and sat looking at it yet again by the pale light of the room's high windows with their views of the Bay Bridge and the Oakland hills but the happiness continued to elude him. The water separating the cities appeared gray and forbidding, lashed by a late wind and a good deal of the charred hills lost to a thick haze that lay across the entire region as might the gauze upon a weeping wound, but he knew what lay beneath, the treeless summits, the skeletal remains. He knew the score, as would the Russians, should his cover ever get blown, in which case it was hard to imagine them taking it well.

The haze had turned to a light mist by the time he left the bar for yet one more questionable destination. He supposed it not too late to phone, call the whole thing off. He held Carl's folder containing his photographs flat against his leg in hopes of protecting it from the damp air. The evening seemed unusually charged, the citizenry agitated. It might have been him. Walking to a BART station near Powell Street, Chance was made witness to a homeless woman defecating in a phone booth. She was a woman of color and hopelessly obese. It was a booth of the old-fashioned sort that till that moment he might have thought extinct. This one seemed to have been restored, the gleaming artifact of an age gone by and yet absent the grotesque display he might well have passed without notice. As it was, the unfortunate woman filled it completely, her tremendous buttocks flattening upon the glass where they appeared to contend in the manner of bull seals or perhaps the phantoms of H. P. Lovecraft as she made to hike a crimson dress above ample hips. One could see what was coming. People averted their eyes, quickened their step. Some appeared to actually run. It was all too terrible. Chance was no exception. *That,* the exception, was to be found at the entrance to the station, propped against a tiled wall, a stick-thin man of indiscernible age, his scrawny arms tattooed like a sailor's, if not homeless then surely the denizen of some Tenderloin flophouse, as in making for the underground Chance was brought close enough to see that till the moment when the man's eyes met his they had been fixed with great interest on the horrid spectacle in the booth. Finding himself now eye to eye with Chance, the man favored him with the bright, sun-blasted grin of the long-haul drinker.

'Boy that's rough,' the man said. He inclined toward the booth.

'History is coming for the empire,' Chance told him.

The man offered to high-five him but Chance went on by. Leprosy was not unheard of in the city, nor were the new, antibiotic-resistant strains of tuberculosis, a product some said, in their most virulent form, of the Russian prison system.

* * *

For Chance, fearing earthquakes, the passage beneath the bay was unpleasant as always, made more so by some brief but irritating delay getting out of the Powell Street station. Lights flickered and went out then came on again. Passengers exchanged glances. A garbled announcement issued from the train's sound system, impossible to understand. Chance, always a bit claustrophobic, reacted accordingly. The essential feature of a panic attack, as outlined in the *Diagnostic and Statistical Manual of Mental Disorders,* is a discrete period of intense fear in the absence of real danger that is accompanied by at least four of thirteen somatic or cognitive symptoms. Given that the Bay Area was the meeting place of at least three major fault lines and dozens of minor ones and years past due for a seismic event of catastrophic proportions, Chance was willing to categorize the current episode as at least marginally situational, this accompanied by two somatic and one cognitive symptom for a total of three and therefore short of a clinically diagnosable event. He was nevertheless, by the time of his arrival in Rockridge, not feeling altogether well.

It was Chance's inclination to believe in problems surrendering themselves to reason, if one could only come at them with a clear eye and open heart. It pained him to see a soul in torment. It pleased him to imagine that he'd found a way out. To be frank, it had pleased him to imagine himself Jaclyn Blackstone's knight, though he was aware, as Janice Silver would have been quick to point out and in fact had, that this was dangerous ground, even for a man without Chance's particular history and predilections.

The fact was, the sale of the furniture, the finality of it, had forced a new perspective on certain recent behavior. He was suddenly less certain of himself than he had been only hours ago, leaving his office for his meeting with Janice. Perhaps, he thought, it was not too late to set things right, to return them to their natural order. The very idea seemed to lift his spirits and he resolved to do just that. *Every*thing up to now, in his dealings with both Jaclyn and Allan's Antiques, had been a kind of aberration. But the veil had been lifted. The coming meeting would be brief and to the point. He would not imbibe. And that was only the beginning. He began to think about clearing things with the Russian as well. The money after all had not been spent. He would not put anything off on Carl or D. He would explain that it was all on him. The furniture was as the Russian had bought it when Chance brought it to the store. He, Chance, was the one who knew its secret history and he alone. But *now* that the set had actually been sold, he was just not feeling right about it. Or, and here he was willing to hedge a bit, he might claim *himself* as victim. It had only now come to his attention that the furniture was not as he had thought. They had *all* been deceived. News had reached him by way of some anonymous tip or some other fucking thing… whatever, really. The point was, he would offer the Russian his money back, or at least some portion of it, should the man still choose to purchase the set. He would go to Carl in the morning. He would make it plain. He would be equally clear with Jaclyn. He was sorry but his plan with the DA's office was simply not working out. Janice was willing to make herself available but Jaclyn would have to manage the rest on her own. Chance had done what he could to put things into motion, but that was as far, ethically speaking, as he was prepared to go.

One might have imagined such waffling accompanied by guilt, or at least some slight twinge thereof, given the recklessness with which he was apparently willing to abandon all previously held plans and positions. And while he would not have ruled such feelings out of his future, what he really felt just now, exiting the train for Market Hall and Highwire Coffee – one of their blends being a particular weakness and his reason for choosing the Pittsburg/Bay Point train over and above the more direct Richmond train – was a great weight lifted from his shoulders. He could after all *live* with guilt. What else was new?

Having completed his purchases, coffee beans and a number of breakfast buns he intended to share with his daughter, he entered a cab near the station, continuing his journey in the company of a wizened black man of perhaps eighty, his driver. Chance took him for a man of Haitian descent, in part as he was listening to a strange religious program that smacked of Santeria, though how and where such a program would and could exist was a mystery. Perhaps it was a tape or CD, the recorded program from someplace more exotic than the present. But then these were strange times, the skies parting at day's end, allowing by the last long rays of light for the occasional glimpse of the blackened hillsides, of burnt structures like ruined teeth, as nearing the campus, he became aware that the old man at the wheel had begun to chant softly in concert with the radio, beneath his breath in a foreign tongue.

The restaurant was as he remembered it, small and dark, outfitted in bamboo and party lights. He was a bit early. There were only a handful of customers, students mostly, seated at windows with a view of the tree-lined street, the campus beyond. Chance moved to the back of the room, seated himself in a booth that was finished in dark red vinyl, and ordered hot tea. He was still composing imaginary conversations regarding both his future and his furniture when a man entered the room. Chance did not at once take his full measure. When he did, he saw that it was Raymond Blackstone.

The detective stood for a moment framed by the doorway that opened onto the street. When he spotted Chance in the booth he waved off a hostess and crossed to where Chance sat. To Chance's great surprise Detective Blackstone said nothing by way of greeting but moved to sit opposite him in the booth, taking occupancy of the very place where Chance had thought to find Jaclyn. The detective didn't say anything right away and neither did Chance. There was a place setting on that side of the table and a second cup. The party lights strung gaily upon a wire above their heads bathed them in a rosy glow, as outside the evening had grown dark with a light mist falling once more.

'Expecting someone?' Raymond asked. He looked to the unused place setting and then, before Chance could respond, 'Dr Chance, isn't it?' He spoke in a pleasant, conversational tone.

Chance nodded, not immediately willing to trust his voice.

'We met in the hospital,' Raymond went on in his pleasant manner. 'You were looking in on my wife.'

'Yes,' Chance said. 'That's correct. I remember you now.'

'Now. As opposed to when you saw me walk in?' He made no adjustment in tone for the bullying nature of the question.

'You looked familiar. I meet a lot of people in the course of a day. That was some time back, as I recall.'

'Uhm,' was all Detective Blackstone had to say. He turned over the cup before him and reached for the pitcher. 'Do you mind?' he asked. He poured without waiting for a reply.

'Please,' Chance said. 'Feel free.'

The detective nodded and poured a bit more for Chance as well. 'Thank you,' Chance said. It was an absurd response. He could not imagine what was next. A waitress approached but Blackstone waved her away. A certain amount of time went by. The folder containing the photographs of Chance's furniture rested on the table between them. Raymond Blackstone took the liberty of turning it toward him and flipping it open. He looked at a number of the pictures. 'Would this be what they call Art Deco?'

'It is. French Art Deco. Probably from the late thirties or early forties. Prewar. These you're looking at happen to be signed by the designer.' Why he felt inclined to add this last bit was at that moment a mystery to him.

Raymond lifted an eyebrow. 'I'm impressed. Yours?'

'It was. I recently sold it.'

'Well,' Blackstone said, 'I hope you got your price.'

'Yes, so do I.'

Raymond smiled a little. He closed the book and looked at

Chance. 'So… what brings you to our side of the bay, Doc?'

'I sometimes see patients here. I enjoy being on campus now and then. It reminds me of my student days.'

The detective nodded. 'Are you on staff at any of the hospitals here?'

'I was asked by Jaclyn's therapist to look in on her. She was worried about possible trauma to the brain. She wanted to make sure they weren't missing anything. So I came, but I'm not on staff.'

Chance was aware of the detective's hands on the table, one of which seemed to remain in more or less constant motion, opening and closing as Chance spoke. Raymond Blackstone was not a small man. Chance took him to be about six feet in height, with the lean, rawboned build of a light heavyweight fighter. Even so, the hands at play on the table seemed unusually large and powerful, the veins prominent across their backs. They were also, Chance noted, quite well groomed, manicured even, if he was any judge. There was a plain white gold wedding band on his left hand, an expensive-looking watch on his wrist. 'Well,' Raymond said at length. 'I shouldn't intrude. I saw you sitting here and thought I'd come over and say hello.' He paused for just a beat. 'You did say you were meeting someone?'

To Chance's great displeasure, he was aware of the perspiration beginning upon his brow. He'd be damned, he thought, if he was going to sit here and sweat in front of this man. As far as that went, he was damned if he was going to continue to sit here. 'Actually,' Chance told him, 'I *didn't* say that. Not at all.' Exit strategies were much on his mind. A cup of tea, that was all, a walk down memory lane, the lines by which he might excuse himself and be gone. Unhappily, it was at just this moment that Jaclyn Blackstone walked in from the night, shaking the rain from her ash-blond hair.

Jackie Black

'WELL, WELL,' Detective Blackstone said. 'Look at this.' He made a show of waving her over. She came without a word and sat next to her husband. Chance found her expression impossible to read.

'Look who I found,' Raymond said. He was at this point addressing Jaclyn. 'Dr Chance.'

'Hi,' she said. She was looking straight at Chance. It was kind of through him, really.

'Dr Chance was just about to tell me who he was waiting for.'

'You must have misunderstood,' Chance told him. 'I was just telling you I wasn't waiting for anyone.'

'Ah, yes,' Raymond said. 'So you were.'

Jaclyn moved to push back a strand of hair that had fallen to touch her eyebrow. She was dressed for jogging in black leggings and running shoes, a light, pale blue Windbreaker that had a sporty look to it. She was far and away, Chance thought, the prettiest woman in the room and that would include the ones half her age.

'A coincidence then,' Raymond went on. 'You'd be amazed how many coincidences I hear about in my line of work. You'd be equally amazed at how often they turn out to not be coincidences at all. I'm getting to a point where I'm not even sure that I believe in such things.'

Jaclyn studied the tabletop before her. Some music began in the background. Chance took it for the recorded songs of whales. They were after all east of the bridge. He willed himself to meet Raymond Blackstone eye to eye. 'A coincidence is simply the condition of coinciding,' he said. 'Any number of people and or objects occupying the same space at the same point in time. I will give you an example. A workman installs a light fixture in the lobby of an upscale hotel. For some reason the job is improperly completed. Screws are left out of the assembly. Sometime later, a woman enters to join friends at the hotel bar. As she does, a large truck turns into the street approaching the hotel. To reach the bar, the woman must cross the lobby. The truck is now passing directly in front of the hotel. The lobby experiences some slight vibration, but it is enough to dislodge the fixture that falls at the exact instant she is passing beneath it, striking her on top of her head. In the case I have just described the blow led to a subarachnoid hemorrhage with a resulting global aphasia. The woman's life has never been the same. But it is a horribly wonderful study in geometry. Short of recourse to some machination of the gods, it is a case of two objects meeting by pure chance in time and place, a pure coincidence. I see it all the time. I see lives changed, irrevocably. I sometimes imagine it is by such geometries that our lives are *our* lives, these random meetings in time and space.'

Detective Blackstone just looked at him, a long beat before turning to his wife. 'And they call him Dr Chance,' he said.

Jaclyn managed a smile.

'Not responsible for our actions then, is the point?' Raymond asked. ''Cause I've heard that one a few times too.'

'Yes, I imagine you have. Someone once asked William James if he believed in free will. He said, "Of course, what choice do I have?"'

'*That's* good,' Raymond said. He looked at his wife. 'He's all right. How was your lecture?'

'It was good,' Jaclyn told him.

'That's it?'

Jaclyn smiled a little once more, affecting the demeanor of a bright but shy child called upon in class. 'It was on the Banach-Tarski paradox,' she said. 'And don't ask me to repeat it.' When no one said anything right away she sighed and went on. 'It's a counterintuitive theorem stating that a solid ball in three-dimensional space can be split into a finite number of nonoverlapping pieces, which can then be put back together so as to yield two identical copies of the original ball. And that's all I'm going to say.'

'Fuck me,' Raymond said. He looked at Chance, a twinkle in his eye.

'The balls are theoretical,' Jaclyn added, her voice dropping. 'An infinite scattering of points.'

If Chance had been party to a stranger conversation it had not been in a good long while. He was beginning to believe that he had entered a minefield without end, an infinite scattering of points, theoretical and otherwise. Well, he thought, it was what you got, crossing the big water on a fool's errand. He heard Raymond ask Jaclyn if she was hungry.

'I came for takeout,' she said. 'I need to get home and shower. There are papers I have to read for tomorrow.'

The jogging clothes were good then, Chance thought. They lent credence to her story and he found himself wondering if this might possibly have factored into her wearing them in the first place, the possibility of something just like this.

Raymond studied her for a moment or two in silence. 'Well then,' he said. 'Why don't you go over and get your order in?' He looked to the cash register. 'I'll be there in a minute to pay.'

'That isn't necessary,' she said.

'Forget about it,' he told her.

Jaclyn got to her feet. 'It was nice to see you again,' she said, looking at Chance. They didn't shake hands.

Raymond watched as she crossed the room. 'We've been living separately,' he said. 'But then you probably knew that.'

'I'm not a therapist. I saw Jaclyn to determine the extent of her neurological injuries. Speaking of which, did they ever find the person responsible?'

Blackstone ignored the question. 'Whatever you're having here, I want to pick it up. My treat.'

'I can't let you do that.'

'Of course you can. You were kind enough to look in on my wife. And no, we have not yet found the person responsible. But we will. You can go to the bank on that.' Raymond Blackstone now slid from the booth and stood looking down on Chance. 'Tell me, Doctor, are you a married man?'

'I'm divorcing,' Chance said, after a brief hesitation.

Blackstone nodded. 'Children?'

'I have a daughter.'

Blackstone nodded once more. He gave it a moment, then... 'I don't envy you that.'

Chance just looked at him.

Blackstone took a business card from the inside pocket of his coat and placed it on the table. 'It's rough out there, is all I'm trying to say. We're a predatory species, Doctor.' He smiled a little but it was not an altogether pleasant one. 'Not what they teach in the hallowed halls across the way there I'm sure. And not, if you're a cop, what you'd ever say to the press, not in *this* town. But that's the truth. And that's the world *I* deal with, every day.' The man was looking directly at him and it was, Chance thought, about as dark a look as he'd ever gotten from another human being. 'Ever vigilant,' the detective said finally. 'That's all.' He turned as if to go, then stopped and turned back. 'Enjoy your meal, Doc Chance. Next time... us coinciding like this... It's on you, my man.' It was at just this point that he noticed the bright red bag from Market Hall, till now hidden on the seat at Chance's side. 'Look at you. French furniture. Market Hall. Must be nice.' He went so far as to lift the bag and look inside – a pure act of aggression Chance did nothing to stop but sat listening, his face on fire, as the detective read aloud the name of his chosen blend, 'Conscientious Objector.'

This done, Blackstone returned the bag and looked once more at Chance. 'There's some shit you can't make up,' he said.

Chance watched as Raymond stopped at the register where Jaclyn stood waiting for her food. The detective spoke to a hostess, who ran his card. When this was done he signed the receipt and left the building. He never looked back. Nor did Jaclyn. When she had her food, she was gone too and Chance was left to imagine what the evening might hold, for them all. He quit on the tea, drank three glasses of white wine, and left without eating, the detective's card in his wallet. *The City of Oakland,* it read. *Raymond Blackstone. Detective. Homicide. Police.*

It was still relatively early and he called his daughter upon reaching his apartment. 'What's wrong, Daddy?' she asked. 'Nothing,' he assured her. 'I just wanted to hear your voice.' The declaration seemed to place her at a loss. 'You should know I was in Oakland today,' he added. 'Came home with a few of those breakfast buns for you and mom.' She said, 'Cool.' Chance told her he loved her and said good night. In lieu of sleep, he opted for additional wine, Wikipedia, and Banach-Tarski.

The surprising and counterintuitive results of the paradox were not possible, Chance read, without recourse to the axiom of choice. While not mentioning this in the restaurant, it *was,* he recalled, the phrase she had used in inviting him to the lecture. He found it to be an axiom of set theory allowing for the construction of nonmeasurable sets, collections of points without volume in the ordinary sense. And yet why *should* they be, he thought suddenly. He was by now, in the continuing absence of food and well into the wine, more than a little drunk. Why should any fucking thing be ordinary? The very idea stopped him cold, stirring him to a mindless rage. It was more than one could bear. 'It cannot be borne,' Chance intoned to an empty apartment lit only by the light of his computer and a small bulb above the stove.

Without the requisite mathematical understanding of what he read, it was for Chance the simple arrangement of words that held his attention, this and his desire to make sense of the day's insults and inanities in some new and heretofore unexamined way and to that end the experiment was not without merit as there really was *some*thing in all of this, as if in this little matrix of words the whole of the human condition might indeed be found. We might well bleed upon Nietzsche's secret sacrificial altars, but are we not also impaled upon the axiom of choice? The formulation pleased him as sufficient unto the day. Add to it the day's other new concept, Big D's theory of the frozen lake, and you were really getting someplace. His phone rang at two o'clock. 'I'm downstairs,' she said.

The creature he found there, in the brick-lined entrance to his building, was as alive as any he had ever encountered and so purely sexual as to have emerged fully formed from depths both Freudian and fever driven. Her eyes were on fire with it. She pulled herself into him without hesitation, her body flush against his own, her face turned toward his. 'You're my knight,' she whispered, her voice just audible.

Under any set of circumstances more ordinary than the present this might have struck him as laughable but Chance was far from laughing. She wore the athletic gear she'd worn to the restaurant and he could feel the heat from her body through the sleek, tight-fitting fabric, her thigh moving between his. It was, for the love of Christ, an exceptionally bad time to be drunk. The thought occurred even as his hand rose to her ash-blond hair, stroking it from her face, cradling the back of her head in his palm. The light from the street was slanting in just so, across the bones of her cheeks, the white tips of her teeth between parted lips. 'I want to make love to you with my mouth,' she said, more clearly this time and in a voice not entirely her own.

Freud and Fliess

IT WAS good, he would think later, that she had spoken as and when she had. For he knew just then it was not Jaclyn Blackstone in his arms at the door of his building. The stress of the evening, the coinciding of such bodies in space and time, in such ways as have been heretofore noted, the intensity of such repercussions as one might only imagine had very clearly served to call forth Jackie Black and my God was she something. Any man not wanting to fuck her blind should go hang himself. Chance fell to wrestling with her.

She was strong. Chance was drunk. She was intent on having his dick in her hand. In the almost certain knowledge this might prove his undoing, Chance fought to prevent it. He *contended,* like Jacob with the angel, though for opposite ends. Where the former had hoped to secure a blessing, Chance meant to avoid one. Their struggles carried them about the brick-lined entrance. Chance's shoulder slammed against the building's intercom system, no doubt ringing his downstairs neighbors. From here they twirled away as if in dance, across the sidewalk, stumbling with enough force into a plastic trash container to knock it over and into the street. It was the container filled with empty wine bottles from Chance's apartment. Several tumbled from the sidewalk to the street and went skittering along the asphalt. One broke upon an iron grate leading to a storm drain. A light appeared in the window of the downstairs apartment fronting the street. A small dog began to bark.

Cumulatively, these distractions proved enough to break

the witch's spell. He felt the strength go out of her arms. She pulled back from the light to a corner of the entry where she sank to her haunches, circled her knees with her arms, and began to cry. Situated just so, she was once more the Jaclyn Blackstone of the Oakland hospital, alone in her bed, the bird with the broken wing.

Chance looked up to find one of his downstairs neighbors, a balding, potbellied computer programmer he had on more than one occasion heard either in heated argument or violent lovemaking with some live-in female partner Chance had yet to lay eyes on, standing at the doorway of his apartment.

The man, having opened the inside door, was still somewhat obscured by the heavy metal screened door that opened to the entry where Chance and Jackie Black had vied for Chance's member. Chance supposed that the programmer had positioned himself just so in the assumption that the steel mesh of the door would provide at least some modicum of protection should things go badly in the street. 'Everything all right?' the man asked, his voice pitched at a higher octave than any Chance had yet to hear him use.

'Yes,' Chance told him. 'Sorry. Sorry for the disturbance.'

The man remained at the door.

'It's all good,' Chance said.

The programmer peered for a moment longer into the dimly illuminated scene, the darkness beyond, no doubt hoping for a look at Chance's invisible opponent, if only to make his story complete. Failing this, the man glanced once more at Chance, nodded, and went back inside.

Chance moved to where Jaclyn still cowered in the shadows. 'I don't know how I got here,' she said. 'I don't know what just happened.'

Chance bent to take her hands in his own. 'Are you all right?' he asked. She appeared to be so.

Her eyes searched his face. 'Was it Jackie?' she asked.

'She didn't tell me her name, but yes, I believe it was.'

'That's never happened,' she said. 'Only with him.'

He let her use the apartment to make herself presentable while waiting for a cab. 'This is where you live?' she asked. She had expected something on a grander scale. He told her about the divorce. She washed her face. He made coffee. He was curious as to how Jackie had gotten his address. 'I guess you'll have to ask her,' she told him.

'You don't know?'

'I don't always remember. There are blank spots.' She saw his laptop in the kitchenette, open on the table. 'You were still up,' she said.

'That little bit at the restaurant… sleep didn't feel like an option. What happened after you left? What did he say?'

'Nothing.'

'Nothing?'

'He can be like that. He's a control freak. He likes to keep people off balance. He likes suspense and high drama. I haven't seen him since we left the restaurant. At least that's how I remember it.' She touched a key and woke his computer. 'The axiom of choice,' she said, and the shadow of a smile played across her face, half flirtatious, like she'd been that day in the bookstore. If only she had not been so alluring. It would all have been so much easier.

'Mathematically speaking,' Chance told her, 'an axiom is a proposition that is assumed without proof for the sake of studying the consequences that follow from it. You *could* say that's how we live. Life presents us with choices. We're defined by the choices we make yet we make them in uncertainty. In hindsight our choices will often seem arbitrary.'

She appeared to give this some thought. 'I'm not sure what a mathematician would say,' she said, her face clouding. He had the feeling she was not altogether comfortable with his take on the matter. 'I mean,' she went on, 'they sometimes have different meanings for words; like *arbitrary*.' She seemed to be posing this as if it were a question.

'Certainly. There's a language of mathematics and I am not conversant. Words are what I have and it's the words as words that interest me.'

'It's words as words I like to escape now and then,' Jaclyn Blackstone told him.

Chance could hear his neighbors in the apartment below. Gratefully, they were neither arguing nor making love. The voices were low and indistinct, probably, he thought, still talking about what had happened outside their door, and for a short time that was all he and Jaclyn had to listen to, the distant murmuring of other voices in unseen rooms.

'I didn't know he was violent,' Jaclyn said. He assumed it was Raymond Blackstone they were about to discuss. She told him about the stalker, Raymond's response to her call for help. That was how it had started. Eventually he'd asked her out. It was only *after* the marriage that she saw the violent streak. There was another time lag between her seeing it and his directing it at her. That had come one afternoon amid the rolling hills of West Marin. They'd gone for a drive in the country, out to the coast to see the lighthouse at Point Reyes. Coming back there had been a flat tire. They'd both gotten out of the car. He had set about exchanging the flat for the spare. It was true they'd both been tired, the sky darkening at the end of a long day. On the bluff overlooking the lighthouse they had shared a bottle of wine. He had lifted the car on the jack without first loosening the lug nuts, which meant only that he would have to lower it again in order to do so. It was a minor mistake, of little consequence. But she'd said something, a joke perhaps? It was lost to her now. He'd struck her in the face with the jack handle. Just like that. 'Like being struck by lightning,' she said. 'Out of nowhere on a cloudless day.' Later he'd apologized. He invented a story for the emergency room doctors, but afterward, driving her home from the hospital when it was clear that she was no longer responding to his words, he had pulled the car to the side of the road and he had let her know how it was, how it would be, if she ever told anyone, if she ever tried to leave. Incongruously, it had seemed to her at the time, he had wanted sex when they got home.

He liked seeing her beaten up, she guessed. He'd gotten off on it. It was at some point in and around that time that Jackie Black had made her first appearance.

For some reason, and one could not rule out the elevated levels of alcohol in his bloodstream, he elected to disclose his plans for infiltrating the Oakland DA's office, for making a friend in the department. Feeling himself on a roll, he went so far as to tell her about the Jollys.

She stared at him aghast. It was hardly the reaction he had anticipated.

'What?' Chance said.

The downstairs neighbors had ceased their murmurings. A hush had fallen over the apartment. Jaclyn had begun to pace. 'You haven't heard anything I've said. It wouldn't make any difference if he *were* in jail. They could put him away for the rest of his life…'

'Jaclyn… He's not omnipotent. He's not God. There *are* limits.'

'It won't stop,' she told him. 'Not till he's dead, him or me.'

He just looked at her. 'But I told you on the phone that I had come up with something that might work, with a plan… Why did you agree to hear it if that's what you think?'

'I wanted to see you,' she said.

When it was clear she was not going to say more, Chance went on. 'I am not willing to accept this as a problem that cannot be solved.' It was no more than a rehashing of the plan he'd already so much as abandoned, but then her presence did seem to warp things. She was possessed of her own gravitational field, he thought, like some stellar phenomenon, capable of bending the light. 'Nor…' Chance rambled, rather like an empty boxcar on a downhill run, 'do I think making a friend in the DA's office is such a bad idea. This is a dirty cop we're talking about. If he's dirty in one way, he will be dirty in two. He doesn't have to get caught for what he's done to you. That's the beauty of the thing.'

'Of your plan.'

'It's like Al Capone,' he said. 'They didn't get him for all the people he murdered. They got him for tax evasion.'

'Umm.'

A car stopped in the street.

'Probably your ride,' Chance said. He went to the window.

A car from the East Bay Cab Company had indeed pulled up in front of the apartment. He turned to find that she had risen from her chair. 'You can't lose faith,' he said. He was overcome by the desire to tell her something. He wanted to take her in his arms is what he wanted to do. She was, in her own way, as seductive as Jackie, if not as dangerous. Or maybe she was. The conventional goal of therapy in treating dissociative disorders was to integrate the personalities into a unified whole, and he found himself, in his still somewhat inebriated state, giving way to a brief meditation on just what an integrated Jaclyn/Jackie might be like. 'We will find a way,' he told her.

She nodded slightly.

'And what if there was a way for you to continue with Janice? It wouldn't be in her office. We'd find a cover, someone you could visit as a math tutor. Janice could meet you there...'

'You're my knight,' she said suddenly.

'That's what *she* said,' Chance told her.

She was only momentarily put off.

'You should probably go down.'

'She was right then.' It took him a moment to realize she too was talking about Jackie Black. 'You *do* know that... that you should think of all these things... that you stood up to him in the restaurant.'

'I hardly "stood up to him."'

'Oh yes you did.' She let a moment pass. 'And don't think he didn't notice. You'll be on his radar now.'

His phone began to ring. 'That's got to be your cab,' he said. 'Will you think about Janice?' He lifted the phone, told the driver they would be down shortly, and hung up without waiting for a reply. He looked once more at Jaclyn Blackstone.

'Are they really the Jollys?' she asked.

* * *

It was on her way out that she noticed the cabinet Chance kept stocked with perfume bottles. She paused to look. 'My God,' she said. 'What's all this?' There was something playful in the way she'd said it, like when she'd asked about the Jollys, not quite Jackie Black but not quite the other one either, the huddled creature from the street.

'I'm interested in the connection between our sense of smell and our recollection of past events. It's a little hobby of mine. At least it used to be.'

'That's a relief,' she said. 'I was thinking that maybe I should check your closet before I leave.'

'Nothing there,' he assured her. 'No evening gowns or spiked heels. I envisioned once a kind of olfactory Rorschach test that might be particularly useful in helping individuals with certain types of amnesia.'

'But you don't anymore?' she asked, reaching for a vial.

'I don't know. Maybe. I haven't thought about it for a while, you want the truth. We really should go down,' he said, but she'd already dabbed a bit on the back of her hand and he looked to see what she had chosen, a male scent from France. 'What do you think?' he asked.

'The desert, after a rain. It's nice. Can I try one more?' She pointed to a particularly ornate bottle.

It was, he saw, another of the male scents. He took it from the cabinet. 'Try it like this.' He took one of his smell strips from a drawer beneath the perfumes, dabbed it with the scent, and passed it to her.

She tried it then made a face and pushed it away. 'Too much,' she said.

'Too much in what way?'

'It's right on top of you.' She returned the stick, the fingers of one hand pressed to the hollow of her throat. 'It's like the funeral home, when they close the lid.'

He might have asked about funeral homes and past associations. He chose instead to talk about smell's direct access to the limbic system. 'All other pathways run through the thalamus. Cognition modulates sensation. Olfactory input has one less filter. Sensation influences cognition. Which is why visceral, emotional reactions to scent can be so immediate and powerful in ways that other forms of sensory input cannot. Most people in my business tend to ignore this.' He stopped and looked at her. 'Boring?'

'Are you joking? For me you read about the axiom of choice.' She was holding his eyes with her own. In the dim light of his apartment he could feel her heat in the air between them. 'Why?' she asked. 'Why do they ignore it?'

'It all has to do with Freud's relationship with a guy named Wilhelm Fliess, an ear, nose, and throat specialist who fucked with Freud's nose somewhere in about 1895.'

'Oh come on, you can't stop with that.'

'There *is* a car downstairs.'

'How long can it take?'

In fact, he thought, there was something kind of fun in this little game she had started. It felt safer than what had gone before. With a car waiting, how far could they really go?

'Well then…' he said at length. He was still just drunk enough to play along. 'Okay. The salient points… In the 1880s, as Freud was formulating his thoughts on the role of sexual trauma, real and imagined, in the development of hysterical symptoms, he was for a time quite interested in the role of smell. He said that he had often suspected an *organic* element in repression involving the abandonment of what he called the "ancient sexual zones" linked to the changed role of olfactory sensations, meaning that the importance of smell in shaping behavior changed when we began to walk around on two legs instead of four. Formerly *interesting* sensations emanating from the ground became repulsive.

Those were *his* words. And he went further. *Memory,* he said, now gives off the same stench as an actual object. Just as we avert our sense organ from stinking objects, so the preconscious and our conscious apprehension turn away from painful or unpleasant memories. This is what we call repression. *But,* and this is where it gets interesting...'

'I think you're interesting,' she told him. 'I like it when you talk like a doctor.'

Christ, he thought, she really could get away with things. He reminded himself that she was about to go and carried on. 'He never systematically explored the sense of smell in relationship to hysteria, the neuroses or the psychoses. And the *reason* for that... was Fliess, who for years lectured and wrote about what *he* considered to be a physiologic relationship between the nose and the female genitals. He *conceptualized* a number of somatic ailments as *nasal reflex neuroses.* To treat these *neuroses* Fliess either applied cocaine to, or cauterized, the nasal mucosa *or* surgically removed portions of the nasal turbinate bones.'

'My God. Talk about the Dark Ages.'

'Now Freud fell in with this guy. And he also, at the time, just happened to be suffering from recurrent nasal infections. Fliess prescribed cocaine and operated, on two separate occasions, on Freud's nose. And finally, at Freud's request, Fliess traveled to Vienna to operate on one of Freud's patients, a woman suffering from certain ailments that Freud was willing to interpret as the kind of nasal reflex neuroses Fliess had imagined. Fliess operated and went home. The patient developed a severe postoperative infection and nearly died. It was later discovered Fliess had left packing gauze in her nose.'

'I hope she found him and cut his throat,' Jaclyn said. She seemed quite serious about it.

'Nothing so dramatic. But she did survive. Remarkably, Freud even came to view the woman's postoperative hemorrhaging as an hysterical symptom.'

'Now you know why I like numbers.'

'I do, and one might speculate here on Freud's own unconscious goals... The real point, however, in all of this, in *my* opinion, is that Freud's interactions with Fliess traumatized him. He was burned both literally and figuratively, and as a result, the uncharted, intensely private and nonverbal sphere mediated by our olfactory organ was to remain off-limits to Freud's followers for the next hundred years or so.'

It was at this moment that the driver from the East Bay Cab Company sounded his horn from the street below – a bit more fodder for the neighbor's mill. Jaclyn seemed intent upon ignoring it. 'That's quite a story,' she told him. 'Now let me try one more, *please*. You pick. Give me something nice to go out on. I don't want to have to keep thinking about that woman and her poor nose.'

He picked one he was quite sure she would like. It was a woman's scent from a boutique maker in the south of Italy and one of the most expensive he had. He dabbed some on a stick and passed it to her.

The change in her countenance was immediate and profound. The huddled creature from the street returned. The stick dropped from her hand. She said nothing but the look on her face was one of pure terror. No more jokes about the Jollys and no more games. No more anything. She turned and was gone.

Chance stood where she had left him, her footsteps upon the stairs. It was necessary to close the door behind her. From there he went once more to the window. She was just getting into the cab on the street below and he could see the yellow streetlights in her yellow hair, and she was there on the street and there beside him as well, a palpable presence. Any one of her might have had him. Jackie Black had come within a heartbeat and already he was wishing her back. He made the unsettling observation it was an impossible longing he now shared with Raymond Blackstone, and he noted for the first time the car parked opposite his apartment, the kind

of gray, featureless Crown Victoria favored by the police.
He could not see clearly enough to be sure but it appeared
there was someone seated behind the wheel, no more from
Chance's vantage point than a shape in the darkness, and
even though his apartment was still dimly lit he took an
instinctive step back and away from the glass. In another
moment this seemed a somewhat foolish if not cowardly
precaution and he moved to the window once more, in time
to see the unmarked car make a U-turn in the street and
drive off in the same direction as the cab. The thing he was
left to consider was whether or not the anonymous caller
he'd so recently spoken to had in fact been the person he'd
imagined it to be.

Chance and the perfect sign

T HERE WAS, he found, no end to the considering of it. It was bottomless, like the axiom of choice or the book of Job. He rose late from a fitful sleep. What had passed in the night seemed at first light the stuff of dreams. There were no hanged cats at his door or unmarked cars waiting at the end of the block. He inspected the building's entry for signs of the night's struggle but there were none to be had. He had righted his trash can before retiring. The wooden and stucco houses with their muted colors, the treeless street and parked cars... it was all quite void of mystery, flat as a two-by-four in the morning's tepid light.

As a general rule he avoided the city's mass transit systems, but on the morning in question he hadn't the energy for much else. Still, the bus was a mistake. He saw it at once. The thing was filled to capacity. The air was close. But this was only the half of it. Save for a handful of unruly teenagers carving graffiti into one of the plastic seats with a box cutter, or this at least was what they *appeared* to be doing – he was reluctant to look too closely lest he be beaten before breakfast – the morning's other riders might well have been on their way to his office for evaluation.

Chance took it as a great irony, and not a happy one, that if he'd spent the first half of his life trying to remember, stuffing his head with all manner of data and detail, he would surely spend the second and final half consumed by a desire to forget. With certain notable exceptions, Mariella Franko, Jaclyn Blackstone, Doc Billy... his patients and their afflictions were not the baggage he wished to carry. There were over nine hundred entries in the *Diagnostic and Statistical Manual of Mental Disorders*. In the time it took to traverse a city block, he was able to diagnose any number of neurological and psychiatric disorders, including tardive dyskinesia, Parkinsonian gait, one cervical dystonia together with an impressive display of what were no doubt substance-induced and quite possibly hallucinatory states of both agitation and elation, and that was just inside the bus. The list might have gone on but he fled several blocks before his intended stop, only to be greeted by a man hardly older than himself. The man was both legless and homeless, rather clearly in the final stages of chronic obstructive pulmonary disease, positioned in a ratty wheelchair reinforced with plywood before the Wells Fargo bank at Van Ness and California, holding in his lap a battered piece of cardboard upon which he had printed in black ink the words YOU ARE PERFECT! The sign was framed in painted wood roughly assembled and rested on what Chance took to be a well-worn copy of Gideon's Bible.

The man held his message aloft as the bus lurched from the curb, as though to spare it the roiling exhaust, or perhaps that it might be more clearly read by the very people with whom Chance had just shared the morning's ride and who were certainly in need of some reassurance. He put a dollar bill in the can at the man's side and hurried away. Walking east on California Street, he became aware that the man in the wheelchair had begun to read aloud from the Bible in his lap. At least he imagined it to be the man, without actually turning to look. The man was reading from the Revelation according to John in a loud and surprisingly mellifluous voice.

* * *

Lucy was at her post, eyes running to the clock on the wall as Chance entered. 'Am I fired?' he asked. He was mildly perplexed by her powers of intimidation.

She watched as he fumbled for the key that would allow for the relative safety of his office. 'Why should I care if you're late?' she asked. 'It's that.' She was pointing at the wall where it appeared that Jean-Baptiste had taken the liberty of hanging yet one more of his disturbing photographs – one more elderly woman, this time stark naked save for what might be taken as the elaborate headgear of an American Indian. 'Did you *say* he could do that?' Lucy asked.

Chance moved for a better viewing. 'Not exactly. He asked. I didn't exactly say that he couldn't, either.'

'Think maybe you could say so now? Since I'm the one who has to look at it.'

Chance's nod was noncommittal, Lucy's stare not so much. 'The Footes will be here in half an hour,' she told him. 'You want their file?'

Chance was still looking at the picture. 'This one is a bit extreme, I'll give you that.'

'Thanks. Does that mean you'll ask him to take it down?'

'He's dying,' Chance said.

'Thaddeus Foote?'

'Jean-Baptiste. I'm not really supposed to tell anyone, but I'm telling you.'

'Are you sure?'

Upon reflection Chance supposed it true that Jean-Baptiste, a self-acknowledged confabulator, had been dying for quite some time now, but it was also true that he *had* been a patient in the bone clinic at the Stanford teaching hospital. 'I spoke once to one of his doctors,' Chance told her. 'It's something rare, that no one's been quite able to figure out.' The doctor had not said that Jean-Baptiste was dying exactly, but Chance had been willing to take it as implied.

'That puts a new slant on things, I guess. How do you suppose knowing what he knows relates to the photographs he takes?'

'Have you ever talked to him, about the photographs?'

'No.'

'Maybe you should sometime. He's a smart guy, eccentric

but smart. You can't let on that I told you he was dying but you could ask why he takes the pictures. I'd be interested in what he tells you.'

'Have you ever asked him?'

'I haven't. But I think it might be better… coming from you.'

'Why?'

'I'm not sure. I just do.'

'Well,' she said. 'I knew he was smart… just seemed a little pushy… hanging those things everywhere…'

'They *are* an acquired taste.'

'I guess I should be nicer to him.'

'Be nicer,' Chance said. He turned once more toward his office.

'Thaddeus Foote. You want the file?'

'What I'd like you to do is cancel their appointment.'

She gave it a beat. 'You're kidding me, right?'

'I don't think I am.'

They regarded one another from across the room.

'They're probably on their way.'

'Then maybe you can catch them.'

'You're serious.'

Thaddeus Foote was a tall, morbidly obese, schizophrenic young man of twenty-nine almost certain to be brought in by his mother. Taken together they formed about as dull and depressing a duo as one was likely to find. 'Do you remember,' Chance asked, 'how Mrs Foote described her son's condition on our questionnaire? One word, *psychological*.'

Lucy actually smiled at him. 'They're a little slow.'

'And life is a little short.'

She gave him a look. 'Rough night?'

'I wouldn't know where to start.'

Lucy nodded, in the manner of someone who'd had a few rough nights of her own. 'What should I tell the Footes?' she asked. 'About his meds? There's no way she's not going to ask.'

'Amitriptyline. Twenty-five milligrams twice a day.'

As Lucy reached for the phone, Chance made good his escape.

Psychological indeed. The youth so described had sustained a concussion, a basilar skull fracture, and an intracerebral bleed as the results of an automobile accident on the Shoreline Highway. The accident, his third in as many years, had resulted in the death of a twenty-three-year-old blind woman riding in the car Thaddeus had hit. Formerly the valedictorian of her senior class, she was a college student at the time of her death, home for the winter break, in the company of friends and headed for oysters on the Tomales Bay when struck by Thaddeus who, acting on instructions from his car's radio, had driven the 1953 Buick Roadmaster belonging to his mother, an ungainly beast scarcely fit for the street, across the double yellow line on the Shoreline Highway and into oncoming traffic. The blind girl's father, a landscape architect by trade who'd raised her as a single parent after her mother's death, had since turned to drink and lost his business. Insurance companies had begun protracted wrangling over fault in light of the boy's colorful past and questionable capacities. Assorted insurers, Mrs Foote, and even the Department of Motor Vehicles had all been implicated. Chance could not, without consulting his records, remember exactly who among them was paying for Thaddeus's visits, nor could he imagine that any amount of wrangling, however it all came out, would make much difference to the girl's father.

It was the primary concern of the chubby duo that Thaddeus not lose his license to operate a motor vehicle as his mother was counting on him, primarily for rides to and from the store where she liked to purchase her movie star magazines, newspapers, and cigarettes with food stamps provided by the state. As to any concerns the couple might have shared over future instructions from the car's radio and their effect upon young Thaddeus, both were at pains to state, in a manner that might only have been taken for upbeat, that, *in general*, Thaddeus was quite able to say no to such suggestions.

Chance's great and single contribution to this tale of woe had been, by way of a series of letters and phone calls, to keep the dim-witted fat-ass from regaining his place behind the wheel under threat of house arrest. Mind-boggling that no one had done this previously but there it was, your tax dollars at work. Needless to say this had not sat well with mother and son who now used every opportunity to lobby hard for the immediate reinstatement of Thaddeus's privileges and would no doubt have continued to do so on the day in question had Chance consented to give them a hearing.

Lucy put her head in a short while later to say that she had pushed the appointment to the following week. 'Excellent,' Chance told her. 'And thank you. The day's visit was not to be borne.'

She stood a moment longer in the doorway to his office. 'Are you *sure* you're all right?' She actually looked worried. Chance assured her that he was. She took a last long look around, as if expecting to find something he'd hidden there, Jaclyn Blackstone perhaps, and left him alone. Sometime after lunch, which he also skipped, he put in a call to Carl Allan of Allan's Antiques but the old man was out. He left a long, possibly incoherent, message on the business's answering machine and hung up.

There were a number of incoming calls throughout the remainder of the day but Chance declined to take them. Lucy came on two separate occasions to check in on him. He continued to assure her that everything was A-OK, finally sending her home early at just before three o'clock.

When she was gone he continued to sit at his desk, which, like the pieces so recently sold, was an antique of similar vintage but worth considerably less, housing at one of its corners the small bust of Nietzsche he had acquired as a student abroad, a trip undertaken as a break from the study of medicine, the latter being not so much the dictate of the heart as a thing that had been required of him by his father.

Well, he thought now, watching the golden light and late wind play havoc with the clouds above the rooftops, he had been the good son, at least to a point. Twenty-odd years in the practice of medicine and it had gotten him here, to something very much resembling the oft-cited life of quiet desperation, unfulfilled in his work, divorced and indebted, half in love with an impossible woman, a potentially malignant blip on another man's radar. If that wasn't the shits he didn't know what was.

While doing nothing to advance the workings of his office, he did feel inclined to call Janice Silver. He was still operating on the assumption that, whatever else happened or didn't, they would find a way for her to continue with Jaclyn, and he wanted her to know about the perfume.

'Do you mind my asking what she was doing in your apartment?'

He told her about the meeting in the restaurant and Jackie Black. This was followed by a moment of silence. A trolley rattled past on the street below.

'I don't know, Eldon,' Janice said at length. 'I don't think this sounds so good.'

'I saw a soul in distress. I made a decision to help.'

'I guess we both did. And now we may be finding out firsthand why they warn against it. My God, what are you going to do when this man… the husband, comes looking for you?'

'It's not my intention to start *see*ing her,' Chance said. 'Socially *or* professionally. I was hoping to *arrange* something, find a way for her to continue therapy while I look for this guy's Achilles' heel.'

'And how are we coming with all of that?'

'To be honest with you, I'm not sure.'

There was another lengthy pause. 'It's a dangerous game you're playing here,' Janice said at length. 'On two counts. There's her and now there's him. I say this as your friend. As far as therapy is concerned, I'll go along with this to a point.

I've a friend whose daughter is having trouble with her algebra. So we can try that. But as you know, any progress she may make is pretty much dependent upon her getting out from under the relationship that has given rise to her problems.'

'This is true. But what I'm also thinking... this guy may not be the alpha and omega of her problems. Has she ever said anything that would have suggested abuse from an earlier time?'

'She thinks her childhood was wonderful.'

'Her thinking it might not make it so.'

'And one needs, as you well know, in the current climate, to be cautious in suggesting that.'

'Both parents are dead, as I recall, limiting their ability to bring suit. There was something in her reaction to that scent that is simply hard for me to ignore. It suggests something buried, something she has yet to speak of, maybe even to become aware of herself... She fled immediately. There was already a cab waiting in the street. It was hardly something I could pursue but I think you might. I'd be happy to provide the perfume.'

'That's your domain, Eldon, but let me think about it.'

'It's interesting that the scent in question was a woman's scent. You would think, given what we know of her history, that if anything was going to elicit that kind of flight response, it would be a man's scent.'

To which Janice only sighed before going on. 'She and I met exactly six times. Most of the work we did was along behavioral lines... strategies by which she might say no to her husband. *My* point being... there is very little that we actually *know* about her history.'

'Maybe that's something we could work on.'

Janice sighed once more. 'Yes, Eldon, maybe it is. But right now... I have a patient waiting.'

When they'd hung up, Chance went back to his initial report on Jaclyn Blackstone and read it one more time. The thing ran for a mere six pages. She had been referred by the Stanford Neurology Clinic for complaints of intermittent memory loss and difficulties in concentration. Biographical information was scant. Born in Virginia Beach, Virginia, graduated from high school in San Jose, California, with high marks, college in San Diego, where she had majored in applied mathematics, both parents deceased, married three years to Raymond Blackstone. There were no children, at least none she had admitted to in the report, although she did claim to have been pregnant once at the age of thirty-two. The pregnancy had ended in miscarriage. Chance had of course seen all this before, but that was back in the day. Jackie Black had upped the stakes.

In the wake of the miscarriage, she had seen a therapist, a Myra Cohen, for a period of one year, at which time Dr Cohen had died suddenly. There was no more to it, at least not here, meaning she had volunteered nothing more at the time of their initial meeting and he had not asked. Still, it was in reading about Dr Cohen that he saw something he had until now overlooked.

He had always assumed her seeing the therapist was in response to depression following the loss of her child. What he saw now was that this was not exactly the case. Depression had been a factor but there was more to it. Buried in her talk of depression and the loss of her child were also 'vague paranoid feelings' as might, he concluded, be expected in someone beset by repressed memories.

Jaclyn had claimed Jackie Black as a response to Raymond Blackstone. This was, as Janice had pointed out, atypical. Dissociative disorders of the type thus far in evidence were generally thought to arise out of *childhood* abuse and were often associated with repressed memories. Coupled with this were a number of interesting if not disturbing questions. How had Detective Blackstone known to come to the restaurant? Had he intercepted a message, overheard a conversation, or was it a game Jaclyn played, an unconscious game but a game nonetheless, the pitting of one man against another, the new knight against the old?

The control mastery theory of psychotherapy is predicated on the idea that all people do through life is try, in unconscious ways, to master early trauma, that all relationships take on meaning in reference to feelings of shame and helplessness versus control and domination. Life itself becomes an expression of the will to power, to do to others what was done to you. Locked into such a pattern, the victim may become a predator out to ensnare predators from whom to be rescued, preferably by yet one more predator. Could that be the dance and Jaclyn the caller? If Jackie Black had found him once she would find him again. Distancing himself might not be so easy as he'd once imagined. The lives of certain very fucked-up types were like that after all. It was a blood in and blood out kind of thing. One exit strategy might be to go at it head-on, to seek out the earlier trauma in the hopes of effecting a cure, to bring the hidden patterns of behavior out into the light and so end the dance once and for all. It was to this end, he concluded, that it might be of interest to look into the death of Dr Cohen, surely a matter of public record. Perhaps, if they were lucky, there would be medical records as well, maybe even the doctor's notes. Might any of these have survived? Might one track them down? Would he entrust this to Janice Silver or engage in the hunt himself?

There were, of course, any number of things with which one might engage. Effort would be required, a 'heave of the will' worthy of William James. Jaclyn Blackstone was after all only one of his troubles. There was also the matter of Carl Allan. One really *ought* to go see the old bird face-to-face. One *ought* to do something about a certain check in a certain safe-deposit box not a block from where he sat. Awash in the day's complexities, Chance remained at his desk, the six pages of Jaclyn Blackstone scattered across its surface, his beloved Mahler on the sound system, staring across city rooftops made faintly luminous in the afternoon light.

At exactly five thirty-five, the late light growing ever longer and Chance still at his desk, there was a call on his personal line. He saw that it was from his soon-to-be ex-wife. He did not like seeing this and, not liking it, took the call.

'Is Nicky with *you*?' Carla asked.

He heard the fear in her voice, as in answering to the negative he could feel it in his own.

A predatory species

WITHIN AN hour he was at the house. It was the first time he'd actually been inside since moving out and he was shocked to find the place in such disarray. Boxes filled the living room. Closet doors opened upon empty spaces, gutted and boned. Nothing was as it had been. Carla had apparently made the decision that while continuing to look for buyers, the house should be leased. 'We can't afford to live here,' she told him, in response to his taking the place in, her manner accusatory.

A mountain bike, its tires caked in dried mud, sat in the nook off the living room that had once housed his piano. He took this for the dyslexic personal trainer's but found little point in going there. Nicky had been expected more than three hours ago. She had been seen at the school talking to some friends, none of whom seemed able to say when exactly she was last seen or where she was. Calls to friends' houses had proven fruitless. And of course there had been no calls in on the part of Nicky. Carla, never a model of restraint, had called both Nicky's school and the San Francisco Police Department to file a missing persons report.

Chance was at a loss. There was a voice at one shoulder saying surely there was some simple explanation for all of this. They would learn it at any moment. The phone would ring. Nicky would check in. The call to the police was certainly an overreaction on the part of his ever over-reacting soon-to-be ex-wife. The voice at his other shoulder said things he didn't want to hear, the stuff of any parent's darkest imaginings, and that was only the beginning as the voice of bad tidings morphed into that of Raymond Blackstone, looming above him in the restaurant, lit by party lights. 'A predatory species,' Raymond Blackstone had said, and said again now in the ruins of Chance's former house that was like visiting the scene of a wreck on the high seas, the water swirling with the flotsam and jetsam of a life come to ruin. He had never felt more impotent or more driven by murderous unfixed rage. 'What did the police say?' he asked.

'Who was the last to see her? The names of friends... They wanted to know if she had a boyfriend. They wanted to know if she uses drugs.' Carla began to cry. She was a slight, energetic woman, in one former incarnation an aspiring yoga instructor before abandoning that to become an aspiring marriage counselor and then on to the aspiring photographer that, to the best of Chance's knowledge, she was today.

He circled her with an arm. She leaned briefly into him then pulled away, her eyes puffy, ringed in red, her face framed in the light brown curls Chance had once found so attractive. 'Do we even *know*?' he asked. 'Who was the last to see her?'

'Shawn. But all Shawn said was that she had seen her walking near the marina, that she was by herself and that she assumed she was on her way home.'

'Do we have Shawn's number?'

'I already called. So did the police.'

'Then we *do* have a number.'

'Are you even listening to anything I'm saying?' Carla asked.

'Yes, but I'm not going to just sit here. I can't. If there's someone to talk to I want to talk to them.'

She was looking for the number when the call came in. It was Nicky. She was alive, less than a mile from home, but she was also in tears, in need of a ride. Someone had punched her in the face and taken her purse.

Chance went. Carla stayed to make the appropriate calls. He found her at a gas station on Lombard. She had no money. The owner, a Pakistani gentleman of perhaps fifty with scant English, had let her use the station's phone. She was seated just outside the office in a metal folding chair, looking fairly stoic as Chance drove up. It was a moment or two before she spotted his car and him getting out, walking to meet her. At which point she more or less broke down. She'd fallen to sobbing in the time it took for Chance to reach her.

He pulled her to his chest then held her at arm's length to look at her face. There was some redness on one side, the beginning of a slight bruise at the edge of her right eye. Her pupils were round and symmetrical. 'How are you feeling?' he asked.

'How do I look?'

'Like someone slapped you. Do you have any pain, is what I'm asking.' He raised his hand. 'Follow my finger.'

'Daddy...'

'Indulge me for one second.'

She made a point of looking away. 'Can we just *go*? Please.'

He was aware of the owner watching them from the open doorway. 'Thank you,' Chance said. 'Thank you for letting her use your phone.'

The man nodded and raised a hand, as if to say it was nothing.

'Okay,' Chance said. 'We will *assume* your pupils are reactive.' They started toward the car. 'I *will* look more closely at home.'

'I'm fine,' she said. She'd stopped crying, exasperation and what she seemed now to have taken for some public humiliation at the hands of her father having apparently trumped whatever else she'd been feeling when he drove up.

They were by now on their way home, passing among the trees of Golden Gate Park – the route she had always favored. 'Will you tell me about it?' he asked.

'Some asshole hit me and took my purse.'

'With his fist or an open hand?'

'Open hand,' she said, her voice reduced to the point of being nearly inaudible.

'Where did this happen?'

'I was on my way to the yogurt place.'

'On Chestnut Street?'

She nodded. 'Do we have to talk about all of this right now?'

'We have to talk about it at some point, Nicky. We need to know what happened. You were three hours late.'

No response.

'Your mother was calling all over, the school, the police…'

He could hear her groan. 'How are you feeling?' he asked. 'I want to know that at least.'

A moment passed. She reached to touch his arm. 'I'm fine, Daddy. Really. Thanks for coming.' They rode another two blocks in silence. 'It's just so gross,' she said.

'What?' Chance asked.

'Everything.'

They found on arrival a disturbing number of cars parked before the house, including one black-and-white patrol car, the words SAN FRANCISCO POLICE DEPARTMENT in gold lettering across its door. 'Jesus Christ,' Nicky said, with a weariness that cut to the bone. It was, given the enormity of the world's sorrow, a small thing, yet it cut him all the same. If the Almighty could note a sparrow's fall, why should not a father lament the signs of a child's passage from innocence, however incremental? They parked half a block down and trudged back up the hill together.

The police wanted a signed report on the mugging. As Nicole and Carla sat down at the dining room table to give them one, Chance moved to the front porch in hopes of being alone. He very much needed to collect his thoughts. What he got was Holly Stein, the principal of Havenwood, rushing to join him.

Holly Stein was an impeccable woman of perhaps fifty with the air of a Berkeley professor. 'I'm wondering,' she said, 'if we might have a moment alone.'

It felt to him that they were already alone but Holly Stein seemed to have other ideas, indicating by way of a head nod toward the open doorway, toward his wife and daughter seated at the table with a uniformed officer, that some further removal was yet required.

'We can use the study,' Chance told her.

The study was, like the house, full of ghosts and cardboard boxes but missing furniture. 'It's been a while since I was called before the principal,' Chance said, closing the door behind them. The missing furniture in this particular room was that sold to the Russian under false pretexts.

'You'd be surprised how often I hear that one,' she said.

'Not original, you're telling me.'

Holly smiled. 'We're concerned about Nicole,' she said.

'Yes, it's been a rough day. Thank you for being here.'

'It *has* been rough. I'm so sorry. How is she?'

'Shaken. I think she'll be fine.'

'Who wouldn't be shaken? My God.'

They stood for a moment in silence, during which time Chance noted a number of what appeared to be exercise books piled along one wall, those and a rather sleek gym bag, half open. The fucker's taken my study, Chance thought. He nearly said it aloud.

'There is another matter we need to discuss,' Holly said. 'I'm sorry it has to be now, but maybe now is as good a time as any.'

Chance was only half listening. He was still thinking about the dyslexic personal trainer prowling about the premises. The word *marijuana* caught his attention.

'It was only a stem. In her art box…'

'Someone was going through her things?' The question was more or less reflexive.

The principal of Havenwood stiffened noticeably. 'She left it in her last-period classroom,' she told him. 'Under the circumstances…'

Chance nodded. He'd taken to chewing on the inside of his lip.

'As you know, the school's policy is zero tolerance when it comes to drugs of any kind.'

'I am aware of it,' Chance said.

Holly nodded. A moment passed.

'I guess I'm not quite sure what you're saying,' Chance said. 'Are you telling me this because you wanted me to know? Or are you telling me she's being kicked out of school?'

'Zero tolerance is just that,' Holly said. 'We're still talking about it, but yes, expulsion is a very real possibility.'

They stood with that, the very real possibility of things.

'And of *course* I wanted you to know. Whatever happens with the school… you need to know what's what.'

Chance nodded. He was thinking about what was what.

She affected a look of deep concern. 'All of this that's going on…' she added, treading lightly but treading nonetheless, '… it can be very hard on a child…'

'The divorce.'

'Yes. And I'm sure I'm not telling you anything you don't already know. But we may see things from our end not so obvious at home, especially when there are *two* homes. You may not be aware that Nicole's grades have dropped. Classes she was getting A's and B's in last year… If things continue apace, she's on track for C's and in one case something less.'

'I'm sorry. I was *not* aware of that.'

She allowed herself a deep breath. 'What I'm seeing is that there may be a pattern developing – falling grades, signs of drug use…'

'I would hardly call a stem in her art box "signs of drug use."'

She went on as if he hadn't spoken. 'There hasn't been time for us to talk to her yet about where the marijuana came from… but we're thinking this today…'

Chance just looked at her.

'The marijuana had to come from somewhere. Did she get it from someone on campus, and if not, then where? Might that have been where she was today, after school? Could there have been more in her purse? Might someone have known about it? Might *that* have been what the thief was after?' She paused once more. 'I don't know the answers to these questions and I'm not accusing her of anything save what we already know. I also know this has been a rough day... and I am so glad she is okay. But I felt that you needed to hear this. And I wanted to say it to *you*. Not them.' She looked to the closed door of his office, allowing him to guess that the 'them' in question was the uniformed officer now at his dining room table. Who would have thought?

He questioned Nicky himself, later that night. The report had been filed. The police were gone. They were seated on the front step of the porch, a place where they had often sat together when she was very young, in another age of the world.

'What difference does it make if my grades are shitty?' Her starting position. 'I'm not going to be there anyway.'

'I'm guessing you're not serious.'

Nicky looked to the darkness at the foot of the hill.

'You just got smacked and your purse stolen. So let me be blunt. Was there marijuana in your purse? Was there money to buy it? Is that what you were up to?'

She looked at him as if he'd been the one to strike her. 'I was on my way to get yogurt. This guy just came at me, out of nowhere.'

'I'm sorry, Nicky, but I had to ask that.'

'Is that what *she* thinks, Ms Fatass?'

'Be happy she said it to me and not the cops. That's called cutting you a break. Where did you get it?'

'At school. Everybody has it.' She wiped at her eyes with the back of her hands. 'This is such bullshit.'

'To a point, yes, but it's the bullshit we all have to live with. Better to learn how than to rail against it.'

She said nothing and they sat for some time in the soft light of the porch. The night had taken on the salt smell of the ocean. 'You know what I remember, sitting here?' Chance asked. He was tired and looking for some happier note on which to end. 'I remember the day… you must've been about three, and we were sitting here and you said the words *outer space* out of the blue. Do you remember that?'

Nicky nodded. 'Yeah, sort of. I said it was down there.' She pointed toward the end of the street.

Chance laughed. 'Yes. I thought it was so strange and funny that you would just come up with a phrase like that, something I'd never heard you say, and when I asked you where outer space was, you pointed down the hill and you said it was down there.' A moment passed. 'I remember that like it was yesterday.'

'I guess that's where I thought it was,' she told him.

He'd pushed her no further on the subject of the stem in her art box. Her final position was the one she'd begun with, that she'd gotten it from someone at school, but would not say whom. 'Now or ever.' He was inclined to believe her. Which left the guy coming out of nowhere to slap her and take her purse, either as a random act of violence or because someone had put him up to it, someone who never got his own hands dirty but who got things done. Talk about a fucked-up twenty-four. On the sleepless night that lay before him there could be no consolation in the axiom of choice. The very *idea* that Raymond Blackstone had reached into his life and touched what was most precious ruled that out, that and pretty much all other consolations as well.

One more letter from the IRS was waiting when he returned to his apartment. And why not? It had been that kind of day. He tossed it unopened upon a small pile of other unopened mail he knew to contain bills from attorneys. There had been times of late, and this was one, when he felt himself to be in the midst of some profound disintegration, as if the mental construct that had been Eldon Chance, cheap trick to begin with, was about to disappear altogether, nothing in its wake but the faint odor of a spoiled egg. He felt the need to confide in someone, to lay bare his fears, to talk about what, if anything at all, could possibly be next, but he had no idea who would want to hear it. Nor could he imagine anyone he knew having anything worthwhile to say on the subject. As far as that went, he had no *real* idea about who would even take his call at such an hour without thinking him delusional; a pathetic enough admission but there it was. Dwell too long on that, there might well be brains on the ceiling by first light, a brief notice in the *Chronicle*. Fearing the worst, he broke from his room near midnight and set out by car in the general direction of Allan's Antiques.

Of feeders and receivers
and brave volunteers

THE FRONT of the old warehouse was dark and Chance went round to the alley where a pale light could be found issuing from the storage door he knew to be D's and knocked softly. He soon heard the tumble of locks, the door rolling on its iron rail, enough for D to look out. The big man was fully dressed, clearly awake and not at all, it would seem, surprised to find Chance at his door in the dead of night. 'I was in the neighborhood,' Chance told him.

A pair of black leather Eames chairs complete with footrests had been arranged sociably enough in D's space and they seated themselves in these. 'Nice,' Chance said. He slapped an armrest with the flat of his hand. He guessed them fresh from the showroom floor.

'Sup?' D asked. They were just like two regular guys, Chance thought. 'Hell if I know,' he said, and he didn't. But he proceeded to talk. He talked about many things, his divorce, his wife and daughter, the IRS, the practice of medicine, the inequities of a broken system. He may even have mentioned Bernard Jolly, Mariella Franko, and/or Doc Billy for all he could remember about it later on. Eventually of course he got to the reason he was there, Jaclyn Blackstone, a.k.a. Jackie Black, and her former husband, the homicidal homicide detective Raymond Blackstone.

D proved a good listener. He listened right up to the part where Chance had gone to the restaurant expecting Jaclyn and getting Raymond. At which point D stopped him.

'This was an arranged meeting?'

'Yes, I'd planned to meet this woman.'

'And this guy shows up?'

'Indeed he did.'

'How do you think he knew about it?'

'I've given that some thought. He overheard something, found a note. One cannot rule out the possibility she tipped him off in some way…'

'She would do that?'

'Depends on how sick she is,' Chance said, echoing Janice.

'Well,' D said. 'Big picture… it doesn't really make any difference how he found out. Just being there is a threat. *Unless*… it's some kind of game the *two* of them play and they're setting you up for something. You've thought of that?'

'Yes, but what I think more likely is that he just found out, or that if she did in some way *allow* him to find out, it was an unconscious thing.'

'You're the doctor,' D said. 'Anyway… there he is… in the restaurant. What I would do now… I'm him… I'd be very fucking friendly. That's how you scare someone. Was he friendly?'

'To a point. She came in. It got a little weird.'

'Define "weird."'

'Good. Okay. Tense. Let's just say it was tense.'

'But he never made any overt threats?'

'He got into this weird bit about my daughter, how it was tough being a parent in a predatory world. Something to that effect.'

'That's not so good.'

'No. And he gave me his card.'

'You still have it?'

Chance produced it.

D sat looking at it. 'And now you wonder if he was behind this thing… with Nicole.'

'It's what I wonder.'

'Could be some trouble she's gotten into on her own.'

'It could be.'

'But you don't think so.'

'I think it was *him*, making a point about coincidence. Letting me know what I have to look forward to if I don't back off.'

'He's smart then.'

'He's half a gangster, you hear her tell it. Never gets his hands dirty but he gets things done.'

'Like putting this woman in the hospital.'

'Like that.'

'Like this, with your daughter.'

'It's what worries me.'

D returned the card. 'Sounds like you've gotten yourself into something, Doc.'

'That's a terrible way of putting it. But I think you may be right.'

'There's no right or wrong about how you put it. It is what it is. A guy like this can be a problem.'

'He knows how to game the system.'

'He *is* the system.'

A moment passed during which the big man, who had till now treated pretty much everything with a rather Buddha-like equanimity, became suddenly more animated. It was the mention of *the system* that seemed to have done it. His face colored. The hand that lay upon the armrest nearest Chance rolled itself into a fist the size of a lunch pail. 'This is bullshit,' D said finally. 'This cheap fuck… gun and a badge… tough guy. I'd like to see him meet *me* someplace.'

'There's one other thing,' Chance said.

'What's that?'

'Last night… after the restaurant… she came to my apartment. He *may* have followed her.' He told D about the unmarked Crown Vic.

'Let's walk,' D said.

It wasn't exactly the response Chance was expecting. But then it wasn't really a question, either. Chance didn't ask where and D didn't say. Given the strangeness of the past forty-eight, the idea of going for a walk with Big D at two in the morning seemed to make about as much sense as anything else.

They went out by way of the alley where the night smelled of garbage and there was a slight chill on the noxious air, winter waiting in the wings. D wore the old Army Rangers jacket over jeans and a black T-shirt. One of his heavy black combat boots was patched with duct tape. Chance was still dressed in the clothes he'd put on that morning, dark slacks, a pale yellow sweater, and brown loafers. Only thing needed to make the oddness of their pairing complete, he concluded, was the white doctor's coat with his name on it that hung more or less as a prop from his office door, that he sometimes wore in front of those patients for whom he thought such outward signs of competency might help in allaying their fears.

For the most part they walked in silence. D set a good enough pace that Chance actually had to work to keep up. They went east on Market and then north. It was neither the hour nor direction Chance would have chosen. 'Not the best part of town,' was how he voiced his concern. D grunted and kept walking.

Lights failed briefly nearing the Tenderloin, though here and there some bit of neon hung frosted in the dank air. Figures half realized rustled among the shadows as might insects disturbed by their passing. In time they came to a street where the tawdry neon was more prevalent. There were hookers on corners now and dimly lit bars, men with bottles on the stoops of flophouses, their liquor in brown paper bags. There was also the occasional flare of a butane lighter beneath the bowl of a glass pipe and small bands of prowling youth.

Chance found that he'd broken a sweat. It beaded up on his hairline in the chill of the improbable night, made ever more improbable with each step, whereupon something new, equally improbable, and profoundly disturbing began to occur. Big D began to limp. He began to do something else as well. He began to hold his right arm up, bent at the elbow, his left hand bunched at his side in the manner of a stroke victim so that his entire body might be seen to participate in the ruse, if ruse it was. Chance's first instinct was to indulge in the luxury of doubting his observation. It was after all the night on the heels of the day in the wake of the previous night. He was short on sleep, nerves wrung to the breaking point. Unhappily D continued to limp, possibly even to refine his limp, till Chance could doubt it no more. 'Are you all right?' he asked. He was a little afraid of the answer but D only nodded and turned forthwith into a brightly lit liquor store at the heart of the broad way, still dragging a leg and favoring an arm.

The store was as shabby and inherently threatening as any Chance had been in for some time. A large, surly man with the well-muscled, heavily tattooed arms of an aging gangbanger noted their entrance from behind the safety of what Chance could only interpret as bulletproof glass, the latter heavily pitted and scratched, as was the wooden counter beneath. The glass had a hole cut from it by which the tattooed man might exchange pleasantries with his customers, of whom there were several milling about in the aisles, locals one and all, or so it appeared. Chance was aware of their eyes on him. The next thing he was aware of was Big D turning to face him. 'Got a money card?' D asked.

Chance was not immediately certain as to what was meant. 'Excuse me?' he said.

D looked toward an ATM machine squeezed between a rack of pornographic magazines and a sweating cooler jammed with beer. The money machine was anchored to the floor by way of a chain one might only have described as maritime.

By the harsh light of the store Chance was able to regard his companion anew then wished at once that he hadn't.

Exercise and the night air had served to further redden D's face. Sweat beaded up on his naked, tattooed dome. The military jacket was threadbare and tattered, and for the first time Chance noticed what appeared to be a nearly empty half-pint bottle of Jim Beam Kentucky bourbon protruding from the side pocket of the ragged coat. And then there was the boot patched in tape, the same that the big man had taken to dragging along the pavement behind him. Was it Chance's imagination or had he also, in asking about the card, begun to slur his words?

'Excuse me?' Chance said again. It was apparently the best he could do.

'ATM card,' D repeated, only slightly testy. He was, Chance thought, definitely slurring his words. 'Are we buying something?' he asked.

'That'd be one way of putting it.'

Chance looked to the sorry machine. 'You know... if you need something in here... I've got cash.' He was trying to keep his voice down, still aware of being watched.

'Just use the machine, brother.'

My God, Chance thought, they were through the looking glass. A pair of mutually exclusive propositions seemed possible. D was consciously establishing them as targets or he had brought Chance here to rob him, the former only slightly less disturbing than the latter. As to the factualness of either, he absolutely could not say. The thing was opaque.

They might, he supposed, have continued to stand there, discussing at such lengths the use of Chance's card and whether or not he was being held up till they had come to resemble the characters of a Beckett play with no shortage of spectators. A small, or perhaps not so small, group had collected at the end of an aisle near the tattooed man and his bulletproof glass.

Faced with the situation's mounting complexities, Chance remained as he was, rather like a rabbit in the headlights, as D gimped off in the direction of the machine. As for what the locals might be making of Chance, or of the two of them together, he could only guess: father and prodigal, huckster and mark, or maybe something a bit more on the kinky side. He supposed they were in a part of town where everything went, where from behind the shelter of his worried glass their tattooed host had, as the saying went, seen it all.

Aside from his being caught away in the clouds or beamed directly back to the mother ship, Chance was where he was. It was not likely he would attempt escape. Good luck finding a cab. In the end, he opted for the course of least resistance. 'Any particular amount?' he asked, having followed D to the machine. The question seemed to emanate from his throat as little more than a croak.

'Go big or go home,' D told him.

Chance pulled out three hundred dollars in crisp new twenties.

'My man,' D said. He took the bills from Chance's hand and counted them back to him, an absurd and attenuated exercise given D's recently acquired physical limitations. 'Machines'll shortchange you now and then,' he added. 'But you're okay.' He kept twenty for himself and made his way to the bulletproof glass. He bought a pack of smokes and a short dog of Silver Satin. He managed all of this with his left hand, the occasional assist of a right elbow. Exiting, however, in some apparent attempt to replace the bourbon with the short dog, he succeeded only in dropping the former. It broke upon impact, the scent of cheap bourbon filling the night. The man behind the glass shouted, his words indistinct. Chance was not about to seek clarification. They went on another half block before it occurred to him that a lanky black kid of indeterminate age but certainly no older than thirty had come with them from the store and was now trailing them along the sidewalk.

'There's a guy back there,' Chance said when they'd gone another block and the guy was still with them. D nodded, attempting to open a pack of smokes with his teeth, leading them ever deeper into the heart of the slum, another block and a half, at which point the young man ducked into a strip joint and was gone.

Chance's relief was immense. He'd given up trying to diagnose the man at his side. He would leave him to his Jim Beam and his Silver Satin. Not since moving into the new apartment had his quarters seemed so thoroughly inviting as they did just now. His euphoria lasted for perhaps one more block whereupon he was made aware not only of the lanky man's return, but of the fact that he had done so in the company of reinforcements, three men of roughly his own size, age, and bearing, two black and one white. Three of the men wore jeans and work boots and loose flannel shirts in the manner of gang members. One wore a blue bandanna around his head. The man from the liquor store wore a leather jacket, his hands thrust deep into the pockets. All four looked mean and thuggish, intent on their prey.

Chance's stomach performed several intricate and delicate maneuvers. He looked to the man at his side. 'Do you see what I see?' he asked. 'Man's got a friend.'

'He's got three friends,' D said. He stuffed the cigarettes, still unopened, back into his coat.

'I don't like this, D. I'm not happy with this. This is not good.'

'For somebody.'

They came to an alley.

'Down here,' D said.

'Jesus Christ,' Chance said.

The alley was rank and narrow. It ran for only a few yards before angling off to the right. Chance hesitated at its mouth. D, who had already started down it, stopped and looked back. 'Stay here if you want to, but I wouldn't recommend it.' His speech, Chance realized, had come full circle; nothing there he failed to understand now. D turned and moved on. Chance went with him. He saw that the big man had lost his limp and was moving at a good clip toward that place where the alley turned and the light failed.

The others followed a beat or two behind, apparently what D had wanted but Chance's throat had gone dry as a bone. Up ahead, past where it had angled off, the alley ended in a shallow turnaround lined with Dumpsters and ancient bricks, the backs of warehouses. Both arms swung loosely now at D's sides, and as they came to the end of the alley he stopped abruptly to rest both hands on Chance's shoulders, steering him between a pair of Dumpsters, putting his back to a wall. 'Anybody starts shooting,' D said, 'duck. Other than *that*, don't fucking move.' D gave him a last look then stepped into the alley where the four men were coming to meet him.

Chance heard a soft clicking sound and saw that the man from the liquor store had drawn a switchblade from the pocket of his coat. He felt a weird tingling sensation along the inside of one thigh he was willing to take as an early indicator that he was about to piss himself. What happened next was both very fast and very slow, and ultimately did *not* include pissing himself. What it did include would have been more difficult to define.

It became clear almost at once that the would-be muggers were put off their game by the big man moving to face them, for surely this is what he had intended all along. It had been his call and here they were. There followed a moment's hesitation among their ranks. Their line buckled. The guy with the knife stepped forward but even he seemed suddenly more tentative. 'We need to borrow some money,' he said.

The psychological dimensions of the thing were quite something. Had D shown fear, they would have been on him in a heartbeat. Chance was certain of it. Numbers favored the attackers and yet they were the ones showing weakness, the evident bravery of the one calling forth the cowardice of the mob. It probably didn't hurt that the one in question was the size of a small house. Still, it was the word *borrow* that seemed to do them in. Someone should have tipped them to the philosophy of Big D. Go big or go home. They would have done better to run. They stayed. The lanky man, still a bit forward of the others and seemingly aware of his position as their leader, turned his hand as if to display the knife, as though D had not seen it already, as if this show of weaponry would prove somehow the final arbiter of the action, and in a sense this was so.

D closed the distance faster than Chance would have thought possible. He reached the man's knife hand even before the other could bring the blade to bear, turned it with his own, and drove it back toward its owner, burying the instrument in the man's midline below the abdomen, in the general vicinity of the abdominal aorta. The man staggered back, clutching at his wound with both hands, at last removing the blade and dropping it to the asphalt amid a torrent of blood as D now went straight at the remaining muggers.

The men had made their original approach four abreast with the obvious intent of encircling their prey, and while clearly taken aback by the loss of their leader, the remaining three had not given up on the strategy. D prevented it by moving to the outside shoulder of the man on his far left, striking to the throat with an open hand, effectively depriving the man of breath while at the same time forcing him into the path of the man nearest him. The net effect of D's movement was to keep the attackers lined up in front of him, one behind the other with himself at their head.

And so it went. The big man proved impossible to flank. Perhaps if there had been more of them – another five or ten, let's say – but this was all happening very fast and none of the attackers seemed to be quite getting it, so that as the one guy staggered back gasping for air, D was already on the outside shoulder of the next, striking to the eyes, and then there was one.

The would-be muggers never had a chance. The stabbed man had managed an escape of sorts, limping from the alley, spraying blood. The others were not so lucky, but Chance's elation at D's prowess was short-lived as he was suddenly and at close quarters made witness to the sheer volume of the big man's violence and it was unlike anything he had ever seen. D would not be content with escape or even victory as in sport. This was Sherman's march to the sea, the United States Army at Wounded Knee. It was three men beaten beyond recognition, the most extreme not four feet from where Chance stood watching as D drove the man's face into a corner edge of the Dumpster till there was no face left to drive, teeth broken at the gum lines, lips sheared away, reduced in seconds to a thing both bloody and skeletal, left to fall among the others, so much refuse upon the alley's floor. And then they were gone, just the two of them now, running like schoolboys from the scene of a prank, D snatching him from the wall, propelling him headlong in the direction from which they had come, one or two lifetimes ago and the streets exactly as they had left them, neither augmented nor diminished. Stars had not fallen nor had the moon turned to blood and the fog rolling in as the fog was wont to do with the regularity of the darkness itself and this in concert with the rather fecund scent of the city's beaches while Chance for his part would, on the day that followed and many more besides, search the local papers front to back, going so far as to return on two separate occasions by car, looking for some word or sign… crime tape at the mouth of the alley… a wreath perhaps, like what you might see at the side of a road where some fatal accident has occurred… anything really to give indication of what had transpired here, that might say something about what had become of the men who'd hoped to rob them, possibly to beat them, maybe even to murder them and he would remind himself about that, that it was *they* who had come after *them*, but there was nothing in the papers and nothing in the street nor would there ever be, and definitely no colored bouquets at the mouth of the alley where it was hard to believe that one or more of the men had not died.

'There's two things,' D told him. It was the first either had spoken since running from the alley and they were back where they had begun behind the warehouse and Big D calm once more, unusually so one might think, given the magnitude of their ordeal. Though perhaps, Chance thought, it had only been an ordeal for him, him and the ones they had left behind. 'The old man says you were asking after that guy who bought your stuff, rethinking the sale,' Big D said. 'I wouldn't go there, brother.'

'Go where?' Chance asked. It was taking him a moment to get his bearings.

D went on as if he hadn't spoken. 'Might reflect on Carl in a negative way. Might reflect on me too, as far as that goes.' He took an oversized manila envelope from the inside pocket of his jacket and passed it to Chance. 'Here's your money,' he said. 'You might want to count it.'

'I'm not sure I understand,' Chance said.

'What's to understand? That's eighty thousand dollars. Message you left got the boss a little spooked. Canceled the check and pulled it out in cash.'

Chance stood holding the envelope. 'I have any say in this?'

'You did.'

'And you had this on you… the whole time?'

'Fucking A,' D told him.

'My God,' Chance said. 'Is that what all this was about?' by which he meant the beating in the alley. 'You scaring me?'

Big D just looked at him. 'That was about me getting right,' he said. 'What you do with it is up to you.'

Chance was at a momentary loss. He really could not decide which was more distressing, what it took for D to get right, his being forced to take money against his will, or that Big D had been so willing to put the entire amount at risk in a Tenderloin alley. 'You said there were *two* things,' was what he finally got to. 'What's the other?'

'It's this cop, Blackstone. There's ways of handling guys like that.' Now that he'd gotten his fix, D was back to the matter-of-fact way he had. ''Cause right now, he's the feeder.'

'I don't know what that means.'

'That's a problem,' D said. He gave it a moment's thought. 'That shit in the alley… How did I work that?'

'I don't know.'

'You watched it, bro.'

'It was very fast and very violent.'

D gave him a look, as might an adult called upon to explain some simple fact to a rather dull child. 'I made sure *they* were reacting to *me*. People talk about self-defense. Self-defense is bullshit. I'm defending, I'm losing. I want the other guy defending while I attack. Doesn't make any difference how many people I'm fighting, I want them all defending because that means I'm dictating the action. I'm the feeder. As long as I'm the feeder, I win. I don't care if it's a dozen. Right now, this cop is the feeder. You're the receiver. You need to turn that around.'

'And how would I do that?' Chance posed the question more or less in spite of himself. Half an hour ago he'd been ready to piss himself. Then he'd been ready to puke, then he'd been ready to never see the big man again, and now he was asking advice, the thing he had come for.

'First thing,' D said, 'is to collect intel on this prick. She says he's dirty. What does that mean? It's not that hard to kill a clean cop. They put themselves in dangerous situations all the time. Any one of them could go wrong. But a guy that's dirty? His whole life is a dangerous situation. You just need to pay attention. Where does he go? Who does he see? When is he most vulnerable?'

'The idea, I think, would be to see him arrested.'

'Why?'

'Let's just say I'd feel better about it that way.'

'Play by the rules?'

Chance shrugged.

'You think that's how he feels?'

'I don't know. I don't know how he feels. But let's say I

like the idea of getting something on him…'

'That's fucked up, but all right.'

'I can't just start following him around. He knows what I look like.'

'You might hire it done.'

'You?'

'We could talk about it.'

'And how expensive might this become?'

'I know you've got eighty large.'

It was not always easy to tell when the big man was fucking around. He was, as Chance had learned, not without a sense of humor, of sorts anyway. 'I guess I'd have to think about that one.'

'Absolutely. But as long as *you* think, *he's* the feeder. So think about that.'

Chance was thinking about it when headlights appeared at the far end of the alley. His first impulse was to believe they had been followed or found out. He imagined the rotating red light that would momentarily explode like a ruptured artery on the alley's narrow way. What they got was the lemon yellow Starlight coupe that in time drew even with them.

They were standing at its passenger side. A window dropped. There was a leather boy of no more than twenty on the other side of it. He was looking bored and smoking a joint, his greasy head resting on the seat back. Carl Allan was behind the wheel, dapper in what appeared to be a three-piece brown and yellow pin-striped suit. The sweet scent of marijuana drifted into the night from the car's interior, lit only by the dim illumination of its own dashboard.

'Sup, Big Dog?' D asked of Carl. He bent down a little to look inside.

Carl, meanwhile, was peering out at them, one to the other and then back again, as if the sight of them standing there together in the alley at the rear of his store at four in the morning were cause for neither question nor alarm but rather some secret merriment. 'Boys, boys, boys,' he said. His delivery was that of a headmaster prepared to lecture. The light in his eyes suggested the parody thereof. But that was it. He had nothing more to say. The window went up. D and Chance stepped back. The car drove on, passing from sight at the opposite end of the alley from which it had emerged.

D sighed, watching as the Studebaker's taillights faded into the night. 'What did I tell you?' he said. 'He's at it again.'

'Those guys, in the alley…' Chance said finally. He was beyond sleep deprived. The Blackstone of it would have to wait. 'How could you know they wouldn't *all* be armed? How could you know they wouldn't have guns, that it wouldn't be the two of *us* left for dead?'

D reached down to lift the cuff on one enormous pant leg, far enough for Chance to see some type of handgun at the top of his boot. He didn't say anything, he just showed Chance the gun. The next thing he did was to open his jacket, far enough to permit the exhibit of three simple but lethal-looking blades hung in a row by way of some bit of nylon webbing stitched into the fabric. 'Most fights are over before they begin,' D said. 'Those guys followed us into an alley. What kind of idiot runs into an alley trying to escape? No one. But they didn't *think* about that. They just reacted. Emotion over logic and by which they allowed me to dictate the terms and setting of the encounter.' He gave Chance a moment to consider. 'Think of it like this,' he said. 'There are no victims, only volunteers.'

The patient in question

THERE *WERE* victims for Christ's sake. Chance had spent half his life in the same room with many of them. What was Bernard Jolly if not a victim, bereft of protectors, damaged beyond repair, mentally and physically, to the point that he now too was a predator, not yet old enough to buy a drink and already caught in the jaws of a gorged and lumbering bureaucracy, one more bit of human excrement on his way to the sea?

Perhaps, Chance thought, he was being too literal. It was equally possible his own ruminations on the subject, running to the obsessive in the wake of an evening with Big D, were, on the morning in question, exacerbated by his surroundings. He was, after all, seated between his wife and daughter on a leather couch, lined up like ducks in the proverbial shooting gallery in the principal's office of the Havenwood Academy, and feeling every bit the receiver.

They were all there. Holly Stein, a male vice principal whose name kept escaping him, a favored teacher... The question before them was his daughter's status. They'd been there for the better part of two hours. He supposed some progress, however painful, had been made. But life was short, and at just that point when it had been pretty much concluded that Nicole could stay, albeit on some probationary status, Chance elected to inform them that, in point of fact, she would be leaving. One might have heard a pin drop. What Chance heard was the great foghorn at the mouth of the bay.

'I'm afraid I don't understand,' Holly said when the foghorn had retreated once more into silence.

'What part don't you understand?' Chance asked. He was thinking he might take a run at being the feeder.

'What are you *do*ing?' Carla asked him.

'I'm explaining the thing,' Chance said.

Nicole, he noted, was not even looking at him. Nor, he thought, did she seem particularly interested in the proceedings, which he took as a bad sign. Her eyes were fixed on a window behind the principal's desk by which the masts of boats in the marina might be seen glimmering in the morning light.

'It's really very simple,' Chance told them. He was very pleased she would be able to finish out the semester. Beyond that, it was a question of money. Until the divorce was final and terms set, until the IRS was off his back, money was the deciding factor in his decision. His approach was, for him, uncommonly direct. When it was over he rose and left the room. He was aware of their faces, vacant as the moons of Jupiter, or any of those other planets having more than one, staring after him as he went out into the light.

Carla was livid but she was the easy one. It required little more to shut her up than Chance telling her she was welcome to keep Nicole at Havenwood. All she had to do was pick up the tab. 'Maybe,' he suggested, 'what's-his-name would be able to help.'

Nicole was more difficult, having more in common with Bernard Jolly than the rest of them, a victim of her parents' ineptitude and folly. They walked along a tree-lined strip of grass with views of Marin County, hills green as Ireland, crowned in fog beyond the rust red towers of the Golden Gate Bridge, the city falling way at their backs. From this vantage it was all white light and shimmering surfaces, a sensory beauty. Fucking San Francisco. 'I'm flying down to UCLA to deliver a paper,' Chance told her. 'I get back,

I'm going to find an apartment in Berkeley. The schools are better there.'

'You keep saying that.'

'I just thought of it, Nicole. It will take time but I will make it work. Trust me. In the meantime, I don't want you walking home from school by yourself. Matter of fact, I don't want you going anywhere by yourself. Are you with me on this?'

'Dad… I'm okay.'

He stopped and he made her stop too. He put his hands on her shoulders. 'I'm serious about this, Nicky. We don't know why this thing happened. It may have been random. It probably was, but we don't know.'

'What else *could* it have been?' When he did not answer immediately she went on. 'You still think it was my fault, that I was off somewhere… trying to buy dope?'

'No… I've taken you at your word on that.'

She appeared unconvinced. 'So what then…'

'"*What then*" is just this… I want *you* to trust *me*. I want your word that you will make sure you are with people.'

She sighed with apparent resignation, pierced to the heart by the mere possibility of his doubt, or so she made it seem. She had taken of late to such theatrical displays. 'For how long?' she asked.

'Till I say it's okay.'

She shook her head and looked away.

'Do it for yourself, Nicole. If that's not enough, then do it for me, but I want you to promise. I want your word.'

There had been an implied 'Or what?' in his daughter's look that she had not voiced and for which he was eternally grateful. He left the next day for Los Angeles, where they had him in a large hotel near a shopping mall and the Cedars-Sinai Medical Center. It was an ugly part of the city though much of L.A. was ugly to his eye, the hills above Sunset Boulevard lost to the polluted air. As an apparent precaution against jumpers, the hotel's builders had seen to it that all of the windows were hermetically sealed.

He spoke that night to several dozen people in one of the university's many lecture halls with raked theater seating, where he delivered a PowerPoint presentation on what was intended as a fresh and rapid approach to the assessment of cognitive function. It was also intended as a kind of ad campaign for a method of testing in whose development Chance had played a part at what seemed just now to be some very faint point in a very distant past. His coworkers, a neurologist and neurosurgeon based in Seattle, had deemed the conference at UCLA a good place to revive interest in the project. As San Francisco was a good deal closer to L.A. than Seattle, it had fallen to Chance to make the trip and so he had, and so he was. Though in truth, he was coming to find in the exercise a welcome diversion – the return to a subject that had once interested him, enumerating for the benefit of a not unenthusiastic audience such factors as might contribute to confusional states over and above a true neurogenic dementia and thereby making the latter a good deal more difficult to diagnose than was commonly believed before retiring to his room and dosing himself with Ambien. He awoke hours later from an unsound sleep to find that a large manila envelope had been pushed beneath his door.

The thing had apparently followed him south, having been first delivered to his office on Polk Street. As the packet had been marked as urgent, Lucy had elected to forward it to his hotel. The envelope bore no return address. Chance sat with it, in T-shirt and boxers, still half asleep at the foot of his bed. Inside were copies of certain official documents, an arrest report together with a subsequent restraining order, both filed in the state of Arizona. In addition to these there was also a copy of an admissions report for psychiatric hospitalization, also in Arizona. The documents were years old. Chance had often been asked to look at such material as the starting point in his evaluation of a new patient. In this particular case, however, the patient in question was Eldon Chance, and *his* questions were all about the sender.

A phone call to Lucy revealed zip. The thing had come by way of messenger – some weirdo in a gray jumpsuit, she said. There had been nothing to sign and no receipt, no record anyone had been there save the package itself. There were, to the best of Chance's knowledge, only two people in his current circle who knew of these things. One was Janice Silver. The other was Jean-Baptiste Marceau. He'd concealed it even from his wife. There was also a note asking him to check his computer, which is where he found the kiddie porn. Panic attacks followed, weathered with Valium and drink. It was, he supposed, upon reflection, just as well that the windows of his room had been sealed against jumpers.

It remained, while still in Los Angeles, to survive a final presentation of his material. The thing passed in a blur. The number of attendees together with their level of enthusiasm was immaterial and for that matter unknown, as any such lifting of the head from his notes for the purpose of making eye contact with his audience, a feat he had managed with ease the first time around, was on this night rendered impossible by the certain knowledge that everyone present had his number. There had been talk on the heels of his first presentation of a faculty dinner but that was moot as he fled the lecture hall, the campus, and in fact the city in a boozy sweat, arriving at San Francisco International Airport near midnight and from there making straight for Market Street and Allan's Antiques. One might have thought this choice of destination, given the events stemming from his previous visit, to have been arrived at only after a good deal of soul searching and even then not without a good deal of trepidation, but this would not have taken into account the power of panic to override doubt, that and any other fucking thing.

De Clérambault syndrome

'SUP, BROTHER?' D asked. Not only was the big man always around, he was always up, in the same old cargo-style khakis with all manner of crap stuffed into many pockets, sleeves cut from the black T-shirts he seemed to favor, and the old black military-style boots worn open at the top, most often untied, laces flapping as he walked.

'Do you ever sleep?' Chance asked.

'That why you're here, to find out if I'm asleep? Fucking Wee Willie Winkie. Aren't you supposed to have a little candle or something?'

Not forty-eight hours had passed since Chance's last visit. They were standing now as they had then, one in the warehouse, one in the alley. 'Sorry, man. I need to talk. The shit has hit the fan.'

Not surprisingly, D invited him in.

Too rattled for small talk, Chance went directly to an Eames chair with his laptop computer for a brief display of the kiddie porn before moving on to the incriminating material. D wanted to know if the stuff was legit.

'The kiddie porn? You're asking me if the kiddie porn is legit? I've never looked at such hateful crap in my life.'

'Pull yourself together, Doc. I meant the rest of it. What we looked at just now.'

'Have you ever seen that movie *Blue Angel*?'

'Not really.'

'It's old. With Marlene Dietrich. She's a dancer in a club. The movie is set in Berlin. This aging professor becomes obsessed with her. I won't bore you with the entire plot. Suffice it to say the obsession proves his undoing. It was kind of like that only I wasn't a professor and we weren't in Berlin. We were in Boston. I was doing a residency in psychiatry and I was a bit younger than her. But she was a dancer. She was also a patient...'

'Would this be your way of telling me the arrest report and restraining order are the real deal?'

It was maybe the second time Chance had seen D give evidence of surprise. He went on with his story. 'She came into the psych ER one night when I was on call. She'd gotten hold of some bargain basement ecstasy or something, released on her own recognizance within a couple of hours. But that was all it took. I'd seen something in her, the bird with the broken wing, and I knew where to find her. At first, I just thought I was in love then it got a little more fucked up. There were missed appointments, late papers, failing grades. Family money had been set aside for my education... She was big on gifts. I was big on giving. The thing had me by the throat.

'I drank a little in those days, indulged in a little pharmacological research, no more than what the age appeared to demand. She made it worse, of course. For a while there... I thought maybe that was it, that if I could quit all of that I could quit her too. But it was something else with her and of course I was convinced she felt as I did. It was thought later to be a variant of de Clérambault syndrome, delusional erotomania. Not by me necessarily, but that was the name they hung on it. Everyone feels better when a thing has a name, but I digress. There came a point at which *she* wanted us to go to Arizona, so we did, for *me* at the expense of family, friends, money, education... Unhappily, when the money ran out so did she. Seems there was another man in Arizona that had been there all along, that I'd known nothing about. I didn't take it well, hence the restraining order and arrest. I later experienced what, in the parlance of our time, might be thought of as a nervous breakdown. I've always thought that ultimately... the real casualty of the entire episode, all things considered, was my relationship with my father. He was an educator and a man of the cloth. I'd always looked up to him. I'd always been very careful about what I did… very mindful of how it might reflect on him. We stopped speaking. He died of a heart attack within a year. I blamed myself. Eventually I got myself back on track, came west, opened a practice, but he never knew it. He died thinking I was an incurable fuck-up. As for all of this…' He looked at the paperwork. 'Let's just say I've lied a little now and then. I mean, someone asks if you were ever arrested, and they don't all that often, it's pretty easy to just say no. And of course the more remote a single incident becomes…'

A moment passed in which neither man spoke.

'And now, if all this came to light… What would that look like? You lose your license? They kick you out?'

'No, no… aside from being hugely embarrassed, I'd still be a doctor, but it would change drastically the nature of my practice. The thing now is… the thing I've built… The majority of my work is in court. I'm retained as an expert witness. The people that hire me have agendas, money at stake. They don't want the waters muddied. The mere possibility of the waters being muddied, the slightest *whiff* of impropriety, past or present, and they will hire someone else.' The image of Leonard Haig appeared before him, complete with mocking grin. 'I would have to start over, from scratch, at a time when I'm barely making ends meet as it is. It would not be a pretty sight.'

They sat for a moment in silence.

'And that's not taking into account the porn,' Chance said. 'You add *that* to it, all bets are off. Done deal. Fait accompli.' He might have continued but it was not making him feel any better. He studied his hands on his knees, a pair of found objects, better suited he thought for scuttling across ocean floors.

'That's fucked up,' the big man said.

'Sadly yes. How does this even happen?'

'Time bomb.'

Chance just looked at him.

'You get access to someone's computer, either by hacking or by getting your hands on it and you input information, hide it and rig it to open on a certain date. The day comes… the file opens, populates the computer. You can also rig it to go to email. Everybody you know could wind up with this stuff. It'll look like a mistake of course, but people will think it was *your* mistake. They'll think this is how Doc Chance gets off. And it will be everyone you've ever traded emails with.'

'Jesus Christ,' Chance said. He felt set upon by a new wave of panic.

'You check your Sent box?'

They looked together. There was no indication that this had happened.

'Your laptop always with you? Was it in your car the other night in Berkeley?'

'My car wasn't there. I was on foot.'

'Then I'd say you got hacked. I'm not the expert, but it can be done, the guy is good enough.'

'I'd say the guy was good enough.'

'Blackstone?'

'Who else?'

'How about someone at your office. Someone you pissed off in court. A crazy patient.'

'It's him, D. He's out to crush me. And there's one other thing…' He told him about the Jollys. He'd filed his assessment of Bernard with the DA's office before leaving for Los Angeles.

'Christ, Doc. It's always one other thing with you. You think of that one by yourself?'

Chance admitted that he had.

'Well… if you're right about Blackstone… whatever flipped his switch… he's not out to crush you, he's out to let you know he *can* crush you. There's a difference.' The big man seemed to be warming to the entire mess, a rosy glow lighting his cheeks, the great dome of his head beneath fluorescent bulbs. 'But here's the other thing he's doing… *if* he was behind that shit with your daughter… and now this? That tells you something. It's like fighting. Every time you throw a punch you're open to a counter. Coming at you *this* hard? He may be fucking with you, but he's also creating exposure for himself, and he's not dumb. He might not think you're capable of acting on it but he knows what he's doing. My question would be why?'

'Because he can?'

D shook his head. 'He's the bad boy your lady friend says he is… he could have you hit. End of story. But he's trying to scare you instead. That tells you something. My guess… you're scaring him a little, maybe a lot, but that's what you need to find out. You need to know more. You need to find his frozen lake.'

'Seems I already have.'

A city dump truck passed in the alley, its mechanical arms at work with the Dumpsters, the landslide of city refuse, and then it was gone.

'The other night… You said the guy was outside your apartment.'

'I said I *thought* it was him.'

'Let's say it was. Crown Vic's an easy car to break into. Pop the tail-light with a screwdriver… gives you access to the trunk. Hand drill gets you into the backseat. You'd need to do a little surveillance. Trail him for a few days. He shouldn't be hard to find. You know where he works. Maybe there's a bar he likes. Good to get him on his way from work 'cause he'll probably have his laptop and that's what you want. Take a thumb drive… download his files. He'll never know you were there and maybe you get something on him. You wanted to mess with *his* head a little… you could give him back some of his own, time-bomb the fucker. Give him some kiddie porn. Or how about this? How about some radical Islamic shit? *That'll* go over good, get it on his email? That's not bad. That's pretty good, in fact. That'd probably get him investigated right there.' D was rolling now. God forbid he suggest a walk.

'I don't want to *mess* with him,' Chance said. 'It's not a game. The idea would be to *get* something, pass it on... an anonymous tip... I don't want to go crazy with it.'

He worried for a moment the big man might take offense but D just laughed at him. 'Right,' he said. 'But here's the thing about that. There's a whole bunch of people out there who think the world is some kind of orderly place, that if things get weird they can run to the cops, hire an attorney... *They're* the ones who think it's a game. They even think there are rules. Go to the cops with what you've got right now and see where it gets you. Rules favor the people who make them. Only time you or I mean anything to those fuckers, they're looking for cannon fodder, or a vote. I'm not saying it was ever much different. World's the world. Tour of duty'll put a new slant on things... you want to talk about going crazy. Now there are of course people for whom the fucked-up thing never happens... live their entire lives in that happy bubble we call civilization. But really... what I think... you look at the big picture, it's relatively fucking few. People like you maybe, no offense, doctors, lawyers, and such. I'd say Indian chiefs but I'd guess those fuckers've known the score since pretty much day one.'

Chance had fallen to thinking about his patients and how it was with them – the light they hadn't seen, the horn they hadn't heard, the blind alley, the sleeper wave, the mutating cell – boned beyond all recognition in the blink of an eye, and not a cloud in the sky. He'd never been on a field of battle but he'd seen something about the frailty of things and was willing to concede the big man had a point.

'So then,' D said. He was absently using one hand to pop the knuckles of the other. 'We ready to talk numbers?'

See poor Alice

THE NUMBERS looked like this. Five large bought Blackstone's computer, ten a beating, if for nothing else than the principle of the thing. Twenty made Blackstone go away.

'That would be five thousand we're talking about?' Chance had asked. He was thinking it best not to have even heard about the others.

'It's what you were *trying* to do with that bit about going to the DA, you stop and think about it. Slow boat to China, you want my opinion, but let's say you did get next to someone over there... you'd still have to have something to give them. You didn't, it would be your word against his and you wouldn't want that.'

It was true, Chance thought, he wouldn't. 'I'd like a night to sleep on it,' he said.

'Take ten nights. But here's the deal with that. This guy's shown you what he can do. My take... he's still hoping to back you off. He's probably not going to do anything more till he sees what you do. Which is pretty much one of two things, show him your ass and make sure he sees it, or man up and call his bluff.'

'I've got a little time then, in your opinion?'

'I've got something I'd like to give you.' D went to a bookshelf he'd made of blocks and one-by-sixes. He returned with three books.

Not surprisingly, one was by Friedrich Nietzsche. 'I've read the Zarathustra,' Chance said.

D nodded and put the book aside. 'No one's born a warrior,

and no one a slave. We become what we are.'

'Yes... life as a literary exercise. To what extent do we write our own script or allow it to be written by others? It's an interesting question.'

'Let's face it,' D told him. 'The guy had balls. Go big or go home.'

Chance assumed they were still talking about Nietzsche. 'You'll have the money by noon tomorrow,' he said suddenly. 'The five large.' A no doubt superfluous clarification but he was feeling that he'd just run a mile at altitude.

Somewhere between the warehouse and his apartment a new and somewhat more acceptable way of looking at all of this presented itself. How was hiring D so different from hiring a private detective? While it was true that Chance had never done so himself, it was equally true that others had, and many of *them* professionals like himself, upstanding citizens. And while D was not exactly a *licensed* private investigator he was certainly a capable man, a retired military combatant with training few could match. It was almost, Chance thought, as if he'd chosen the course of prudent behavior after all.

It was shortly thereafter that he reached home amid a fog so dense he'd not seen the Oldsmobile's hood ornament in more than a mile, nosed into the underground, and climbed the stairs to his apartment, where a number of items were lying in wait. One was a small envelope with his name on it taped to the locked steel door that led to his stairs. He opened it on the spot. There was a scrap of paper inside with the words *Scaredy-cat* written on it in what he took to be a feminine hand, this and a small troubling spot it was impossible not to interpret as blood. There could be little doubt as to the identity of its author. His eyes searched the street but there was little to be seen in the hopeless fog. At some distance an invisible homeless person had begun to bang at a steel lamppost with what sounded like a steel pipe. Chance let himself into the stairwell and went up. A second message waited on his answering machine. It was from Carla announcing that Nicole had a boyfriend and had apparently already spent a night with him, away from home and without permission. There was a third message from his tax attorney telling him that the IRS had come up with a number. It was big, the attorney admitted, but at least there was a number. And finally there was a note from Big D sent via email to Chance's computer, the same that contained Raymond Blackstone's lecherous porn.

> Battle is a joyous thing. We love each other so much in battle. If we see that our cause is just and our kinsmen fight boldly, tears come to our eyes. A sweet joy rises in our hearts... This brings such delight that anyone who has not felt it cannot say how wonderful it is. Do you think that someone who feels this is afraid of death?... He is so strengthened, so delighted, that he doesn't know where he is. Truly, he fears nothing in the world. – Jean de Bueil, 1465

'My God,' Chance said to no one in particular, the fleeting sense of euphoria so recently experienced having by now pretty much deserted him altogether. He was staring into the small mirror attached to the medicine cabinet where he'd gone in search of a suitable pharmaceutical cocktail with which to knock himself out. 'See poor Alice.' He was making new friends and they all knew where to find him, as from the fogbound street the invisible homeless person continued to announce his or her presence, authoring their own script no doubt and he guessed that soon enough someone would call the appropriate authorities, and that the appropriate authorities would come, much as they'd come for that other crazy whose cries might yet be heard, even through the mists of time, on the Piazza Carlo Alberto in the city of Turin, because that was the thing about the proper authorities... rightly or wrongly... they were never as far away, or as proper, as one might like.

The plot thickens

OF D's other books, the ones Chance came home with, one was entitled *The Virtues of War*, by Steven Pressfield. It was a novel of Alexander the Great, as told by the great man himself, and Chance saw that D had underlined certain passages. The willingness to die and out of that a sanctification for the willingness to kill scored well, as did any passage celebrating the glory of combat and what the book's author took as the 'seminal imperative of mortal blood.'

The second book, *Ignore Everybody* by Hugh MacLeod, was a collection of cartoon drawings accompanied by aphoristic observations on the nature of creativity, principally on the willingness to carve out one's own path, a celebration of the road less traveled. Somewhere near dawn, Chance put the books aside to sleep fully clothed, albeit fitfully, on his living room couch, his reading lamp still on.

He woke to the din of traffic beyond his window and drove directly to his bank, where he withdrew five thousand dollars in cash, Big D's fee and no second guessing allowed, before arriving late to the office. One might say it was becoming a pattern.

'How did it go?' Lucy asked. 'Any more on who sent you that stuff?'

It took him a moment to realize she was asking about the lecture and the mysterious package she had forwarded to the hotel. He'd been thinking about what he had just done, Big D on the case, this and the *'seminal imperative of mortal blood, as ineradicable within man as in a wolf or a lion, and without which we are nothing.'*

'That bad?' she asked.

It occurred to him that he still had not answered. He was stopped between her desk and his office, in full view of Jean-Baptiste's prideful, demented woman absolutely lost in thought. 'Nothing new on the package,' he told her. 'As for the lecture… let's just say I was feeling a bit distracted.'

'Was?' Lucy asked. He supposed she was alluding to his present condition but chose to ignore the comment. He was thinking about sleep deprivation and wondering if that was how it had started when it started before, so long ago with the red-haired dancer. There *had* been a drug-fueled run to Martha's Vineyard, just the two of them, on the family money, days on the road. He could remember that much. He went to Lucy's desk where he took up a pen and began to write. What he wrote was the name of Jaclyn's former therapist. 'Let's see what we can find out about her,' he said. 'She was in the Bay Area somewhere, now deceased.' With D set to begin surveillance, Chance thought it time to look into the fate of Myra Cohen and the records she was sure to have kept.

Lucy gave him a long look. 'What do you want to know?' she asked.

'Anything you can find. Was she a partner? Are the offices still there? Maybe something about the cause of death.'

Lucy nodded but he could feel her watching him as he crossed to his office, where he passed the morning alternately reading about Alexander the Great and napping at his desk, each instance now accompanied by some intrusive recollection of the Tenderloin, a man's face sheared off at the edge of a city Dumpster. He took this as indicative of post-traumatic stress, the glory of battle eluding him altogether. His first call of the day was to his wife. There was not much to add to her original message. Nicole had a boyfriend and that was all she knew. She'd never met him. She hadn't a name. He was supposedly older and lived somewhere in San

Rafael. She'd learned all of this from Shawn's mother, who'd heard about it from Shawn and thought Carla should know.

'What's Nicole have to say?' he asked.

'She won't talk to me about it. I don't know what to do.'

'Where is she now?'

'At school.'

'And when was this, that she spent a night?'

'The night you left.'

'Where were you?'

'I was here, right here.'

'And you never heard her leave?'

'She's getting sneaky, Eldon. I don't like it.'

'Nor do I. I told her to stay close. She said she would.'

'Well,' Carla told him. 'There you have it.'

Chance said he would talk to her.

'That's just great,' Carla said and hung up. Accusations and words left unsaid – there *was* a reason they were no longer together.

His second call was to Janice Silver. Appointments had been arranged and he was eager to discover how it was all working out, a couple of weeks by now having passed.

The therapist answered at once. 'There's been an incident,' she told him, even before he'd asked, then paused dramatically.

'Really?'

'Yes, really. She stole something.'

'And you were going to wait *how* long to tell me this?'

'I was trying to decide exactly how to break it.'

'You're certain it was her?'

There was a moment of silence. 'No,' she said finally. 'I asked her. She denied it, but all the evidence points her way.' She paused once more. 'We're talking about some cash, which makes it hard to trace, or find. I didn't want to involve the police, for reasons I'm sure you can understand.'

'How much cash are we talking about?'

'Just over two thousand dollars. The girl she was tutoring… her dad's got his own company. He makes a lot of money, and he keeps a lot around, in cash. There was five thousand dollars just lying on a counter in the kitchen. Half of it disappeared. It was noticed just after one of our sessions…'

'And nobody else had access? Maids, friends of the daughter, the daughter herself?'

'House cleaner's been with the family for fifteen years. The girl doesn't have any friends. It was all I could do to keep them from calling the police. I told them I would talk to her. It's lucky the guy is loaded. He'll never miss it but I'm done. No more subterfuge. I should never have let you talk me into it. This case is more complicated than either of us guessed. I think now that we have been irresponsible, to proceed in the way we have.'

'What other way was available?'

'I don't know, Eldon. I can only tell you that this is not going to work.'

'So tell me again… what exactly did Jaclyn say?'

'She says she doesn't know anything about it.'

'Maybe she doesn't.'

'Maybe lots of things, Eldon. Maybe Jaclyn *doesn't* know. Maybe Jackie does. Could be, Jackie doesn't want Jaclyn to get well. Might even be there are a few more out there, waiting in the wings, folks you and I have yet to meet, you're willing to entertain the high drama of multiple personalities. Did you know she cuts herself?'

'I had no idea.' The thought sickened him.

'I went to see her about the money…'

'You went to her condo?'

'I did.'

'A little risky, for you both.'

'Yes, and I'll get to that. I just felt that I had to. I needed to see her face. She was in there painting one of those bits of furniture she likes to paint, working in a T-shirt and jeans, and I saw the scars on her arms. She wasn't expecting me. Some were fresh. Others were not. It's a whole new ball game, my friend.'

'What does she say?'

'That she doesn't always know what happens, that there are periods of time for which she has no memory. Could be you were on to something with your impromptu sniff test… *that* makes you feel any better. But guess what? These kinds of cases are not my forte.' She gave it a beat. 'Nor are they yours. Christ, Eldon, you barely even *see* patients, and certainly not as a therapist.'

'So what else happened? How did it proceed?'

'Like what you might expect in a patient with some form of dissociative identity disorder, with periods of amnesia. *Jaclyn* was extremely upset. She was either extremely upset or she's a very good actor. But then that's always part of it with this stuff, isn't it, and why there are people who specialize?'

'What do you think?'

'Does the term *borderline* ring a bell?'

'As an actual diagnosis or an easy out?'

'That's not fair and you know it.'

There was a moment of silence on the line.

'I think she needs a different therapist and a different type of therapy. I think she needs to get with someone who specializes in difficult cases and is willing to take her on. Why don't we just leave it at that and preserve our friendship?'

'And how do we imagine that she will do this?'

'We don't, Eldon. I'm happy to help her find someone, but she's going to have to want that and be willing to go see the person I come up with. No more of this running around.'

'Kind of gets us back to where we started.'

'There's one other thing,' Janice said. 'You asked about my going to her apartment, whether or not that was dangerous, and I said I'd get back to it. When I left, I found that someone had broken into my car, stolen a camera, and slashed both rear tires.'

'That's disturbing.'

'Disturbing gets you about halfway.'

'A random act or he's having the place watched.'

'Which would seem to be his style.'

'Any idea how it went with *her*, after you left?'

'None at all. I'm sorry, Eldon. Really. We tried. I think that's the best we can do.' When he did not respond right away she went on. 'I use the word *we* advisedly. This is not a person you should be spending time with. Can I be any more direct?'

Chance said he understood. Janice said goodbye.

Lucy came in before leaving for the day. She'd found out something about Dr Cohen. Myra Cohen had not died of natural causes. She had been raped, mutilated, and murdered by an intruder who was never found.

'For Christ's sake,' Chance said.

'Does the plot thicken?'

Chance just looked at her.

'Sorry.' She started to leave then turned back. 'I was friendly to Jean-Baptiste today,' she said, apparently by way of cheering him up. 'I'm letting him bring in some more of those god-awful pictures.'

Chance and the happy hour

Before she was raped, mutilated, and murdered by her unknown assailant, Myra Cohen had worked out of a small group of offices just off San Pablo Avenue in Northwest Berkeley that she had shared with two other doctors. When he drove to the address what he found was a vacant lot. When he spoke to the owner of a nearby house, he was told the place he'd come to see had burnt to the ground almost two years ago to the day. He was able to track down one of the doctors who had been part of the original practice. The man was now working out of an office in South Berkeley near the hospital. Chance called from his car. He got through by announcing himself as Dr Chance for Dr Miller. In the end, however, Dr Miller had little to add. He knew very little of Myra's patients, and no, the name Jaclyn Blackstone did not ring a bell. The circumstances of Dr Cohen's death were indeed tragic. As for any medical records... the old offices had been a complete loss. As to whether or not Myra had kept backup files at another location, he simply could not say. As far as he knew she had lived alone, her home sold shortly after her death. Chance asked if he knew who sold the house, if perhaps there were relatives and if so where. Dr Miller said that he was sorry but that was the best he could do. Chance thanked him and hung up.

At this point he might well have returned to the city. There was after all no lack of things to do. For starters, he had promised Carla that he would speak to Nicole and so he would, though in truth he found the prospect terrifying. She was growing up and the world would have her. What on earth could he offer save words while his own life fell apart and her there to see it? And then of course there was his office, Lucy Brown at her desk, the voluminous amounts of paperwork certain to precede each and every forensic evaluation piling up by the hour and him already behind. This ought to have been cause for alarm yet here he was, still parked before the empty lot, Chet Baker on the stereo, 'Let's get lost' wafting from his open window on the dusty summer air.

The day seemed washed in a brilliant light rendered excessively harsh before the blackened hills that seemed now to dominate the landscape east of the bay. The houses bordering the empty lot were of a type he generally found pleasing, well-kept Spanish-style homes dating to before the war, but on the day in question he found their whitewashed walls difficult to look at in the unpleasant light. Once he dozed. Sleepless at night, he was finding that he could, at any other time, sleep almost anywhere and at any hour, in broad daylight on a busy street... the buzz of activity providing for the anonymity denied him in the dark confines of his apartment. And then, finally, there was the truth of it. If not on the street where she lived, he was at least on *her* side of the bay, near a place she once must have visited with some regularity before... And there, he thought, was the question, before what? Before Raymond Blackstone had gotten wind of it and shut it down, in a way that would pretty well qualify him as some variation on the Prince of Darkness? He could not rule out the possibility but he couldn't quite go there either. It was all just a bit too much, in spite of everything. He supposed that he might ask her, but then one might also ask a delusional patient suffering from schizophrenia if she was being followed. In lieu of anything more productive, he elected to try for what he knew to be happy hour at Spenger's Fresh Fish Grotto.

The restaurant had been there since the turn of the century, a real old-time San Francisco Bay fish house with dark polished wood, the brass accoutrements lifted from ships shimmering in the muted light, and old photographs mounted on walls. The photographs were of boats and docks, the latter spilling over with great glittering mounds of fish and of the men who had caught and killed them – real men, by God, men who no doubt knew a thing or two about the seminal imperative of mortal blood and all of this in stark contrast to the crowd that filled the place just now as Chance drank at the bar, for it was no longer even the student crowd of his first days in San Francisco, but a sad gathering of what seemed to be drunken tourists dressed for whale watching.

He drank martinis as shadows lengthened beyond an open door, finally setting out near sunset for the street where she lived. He found her neighborhood dark and without event. Willing to take Janice's experience as evidence the place was being watched, willing to believe almost anything, really, he parked as far away as he was able while still managing to maintain visual contact and settled in. He was admittedly a little drunk.

His actions, he concluded, while bordering on the patently insane, were not altogether pointless. He was hoping to see her leave, hoping to follow at a distance, long enough at least to ensure that he was alone in doing so and then to find some opportune moment to make good his approach. He felt that they needed to talk, in light of what had transpired at the student's house, in light of what he had learned about Myra Cohen. They needed to talk and it needed to be in private and this was about half of what he was doing there, at the wheel of the old car, at the dark end of the street. It was the half that explained well, or at least better than the other half that ran to the obsessive-compulsive and didn't explain worth shit.

It occurred to him that there had been a time and it was not so long ago when he might well have gambled on the system, gone to the police, laid out his entire case, from the beating of Jaclyn to the death of Myra and everything in between. He was after all a respected member of the medical community. He even managed the short-lived entertainment that such might yet be the case. It died with the last of the light at the feet of ravaged hills. The past he'd thought to hide had found its way into his present. Add to this an acrimonious divorce, his battle with the IRS, his daughter's drug-related school problems... There was even, God help him, his phony French furniture and the boys of Allan's Antiques. His days of respectability were behind him. There was no getting around it and none of his present endeavors were likely to bring them back. A more balanced individual, on the heels of such insights, might have elected to call it a day. Chance stayed where he was. His watch said eight o'clock.

At around eight thirty he saw her leave her apartment. She was in her car, a small gray Honda, ordinary to the point of near invisibility. He followed as far as the campus where she parked and got out and entered the grounds. He parked too. He could find no sign that she had been followed by anyone other than himself and after what felt to be some appropriate amount of time, he left his car and went in after her.

He came upon her at the koi pond in a part of the campus known as the Oriental Garden, alone on a small bridge, looking down into the dark water. She wore jeans and a long-sleeved top. He stood watching her then crossed the garden, lit only by a number of small lanterns hung among the trees, and came onto the bridge. She turned at his approach, eyes widening. He came to her straightaway, taking her hands in his own. His impulse was to turn them palms up, to see the scars for himself. What he did instead was launch into a tortured apology for what had happened with Janice, for his coming upon her unannounced. 'I want you to know I'm not quitting on you,' he said.

'You can't be here,' she told him, surprise giving way to something more like panic. 'He has my daughter...'

'What do you mean by "has"?'

'They can't find her. She hasn't been to classes but I know it's him. He's got her somewhere. Or *they* do.'

'They?'

'The mob, the Romanian mafia. Whatever you want to call

them. I've told you he was dirty, that he has friends, that he can have things done… If he finds out that you're still in the picture…'

'You were at my apartment,' he said.

She ignored this. 'Did you hear anything I just said?'

He squeezed her hands. 'I need you to do one thing for me. I want a letter of consent, allowing me access to Myra Cohen's files.'

The name registered. 'She's dead.'

'I know.'

'It was horrible…'

'I want to try something,' he told her.

'You were trying something before.'

'This is something different. I've never known a therapist who didn't back up their files. I want to find out who sold her property. It was probably a family member. There may be a way…'

She put an end to it by stepping toward him, her cheek coming to rest on his chest, her hair brushing his lips, her scent in his face. 'You're so good,' she said. When she pulled back there were tears in her eyes. 'But there's nothing you can do. I'm his. I know you want to help. You're just not strong enough. No one is.'

'You're better than this,' he told her.

'It's what you want to think.'

'Wanting is where it starts. We can find a way. There's always a way.'

'I guess you know better than that.' There was mostly sadness in her face, that and something like pity that cut to the bone.

'Tell me about Myra Cohen.'

'You already know.'

'I don't know what you talked about. I don't know if he knew. I don't know why she died. I don't know if it was a random act of violence or something else. I'm asking what you think.'

The expression on her face did not change. 'What does it

matter?' she asked. 'You can't fix this, and you can't fix me. I'm too broken.'

'There are no victims, Jaclyn, just volunteers.' The line with which he had so recently quarreled seemed suddenly to fit. She laughed in his face before reining herself in. 'This won't end how you think.' She let go of his hands and stepped back.

He began again but she was already walking away. When he took a step in her direction she seemed to hear it and began to run. There was a part of him that wanted to run after her, to what end was another matter. He went back in the direction from which he had come, this time crossing with a young man who might have been a student. He was of that age. But there was something about him... the lithe athletic physique, the fashionably ragged clothes... so that Chance was seized by the sudden and jealous certainty that what he had really done just now, coming upon her in the way that he had, was to thwart some clandestine and romantic meeting. So strong was the feeling that he actually did turn around and began to run after her. Forget that she was on to him. He went headlong, as if propelled by some force beyond his reckoning, all the way to the koi pond where he found her gone. Nor was there any sight of the man.

The night so ended, he was at Allan's Antiques the following day. It was late afternoon. Nearly two full days had passed since D's hire. One might, in the wake of the disastrous East Bay outing, have thought him discouraged but like the man said, there's a time for everything under heaven. Hypomania no doubt exacerbated by sleep deprivation came to mind but why go there? Half a dozen soporifics came to mind as well but he was eager to see if the big man was getting anywhere. He would not have been surprised to find him out and on the job. He found him in the alley at work on the Starlight coupe.

'Yeah...' D said, giving the word time to breathe when Chance had raised the subject. 'Needed to finish up on a couple of things around here.'

'It's been two days,' Chance said.

D nodded. 'Maybe you could hand me that socket wrench.' He was pointing at a toolbox near Chance's feet.

Chance handed him the wrench. 'I guess I don't understand. I thought you were ready to go on this.'

D examined a spark plug before setting it into the block and giving it a turn with the wrench. 'Start right now if you're up for it?'

'I'm not sure I understand,' Chance said once more. 'I thought we *had* started.'

D just looked at him.

'I've given you the money.'

'Oh yeah… we're cool with that… just a little short on wheels right now and the old man's down with the flu.'

Chance was a moment in assimilating the statement's various and sundry implications. 'Are you telling me you don't drive?'

'I'm not saying that,' D told him. 'I used to drive all over the fucking place. It just didn't go well.'

Down these mean streets a man will go...

I T WAS to this end that Chance's days acquired a new and heretofore unimaginable pattern. As it turned out, D was more than short on wheels. He was without a driver's license as well, having failed to renew the old one since returning from his last tour of duty. Road rage had been a problem, but that was only one of several. And so it began. Chance would work till late afternoon then drive to the Mission to retrieve Big D. From there they would strike out in pursuit of Raymond Blackstone.

On a number of occasions they took the Olds. Once they took the Studebaker. Other times they would rent something so as not to become conspicuous by virtue of repetition. In this and apparently all other matters Chance had given himself almost entirely to the counsel of Big D. Later, usually after a dinner consumed in one of the cheap, high-calorie restaurants favored by his companion, they would return to the old warehouse to discuss the day's discoveries, or lack thereof.

Such discussions might last well into the night, including, as they often did, lengthy digressions on the part of Big D regarding any number of topics, everything from the warrior's mind-set to the origins of such metalwork as had been brought to bear on Chance's furniture, the chemical makeup of a particular acid wash, or the means by which the patterns once made by the natural sponge might in fact be duplicated. These in turn might give way to a twenty-minute dissertation on the proper way to prepare a grilled cheese sandwich.

Carl, once recovered, was often there too, pondering his books, crunching numbers. He'd hear the two come in and be around back in a matter of minutes. It didn't take long for Chance to see that the two had no secrets, though it was usually the old man who, after joining them for a time, was also the first to opt out. 'He can go on all night,' he once said in reference to Big D. 'He doesn't sleep.' And it was true, as near as Chance could tell, he didn't. No mention was ever made about Chance's furniture or the message he'd left on Carl's machine or the old man's response. As far as that went, no mention was ever made about Chance's having taken over what apparently was to have been Carl's job, that of Big D's wheelman, but there were never any weird vibes about any of it either. It was the church of Big D and Chance was just one of the gang.

He'd spoken exactly once to his daughter during this period. He found her contrite but less than forthcoming. Still… there had, according to Carla, been no further incidents. She was attending classes. If she was seeing the guy, she was at least spending her nights at home. Chance's insistence that she never be alone seemed to fall on deaf ears. Trying to have her stay at his place, in light of both recent and potential events, seemed altogether out of the question, though as part of their forays across the bay Chance had taken to scouting neighborhoods in appropriate school districts, sometimes stopping to take down the number of a place for rent then listening as Big D offered his critique. D was big on risk assessment with respect to break-ins and general defensibility in the event of martial law. Nor was the possibility of a full-blown zombie apocalypse to be taken lightly. The big man paid particular attention to window height and door placement together with angles of sight. Fences were of interest, as was the proximity of power lines and trees.

The absurdity of all this was not lost on him, the sheer outrageousness of it. D was cutting him some slack on the bill in return for his willingness to drive. 'You never know what you're capable of till you find out what you're capable of,' the big man was fond of saying. And so it was proving to be. The thing was… he was finding a kind of contentment in his work, not at the office but here, at the wheel of the aging Oldsmobile, Charlie Parker on the stereo, Big D filling up the seat at his side. He felt that he was actually doing something. *What* he was doing was a little sketchy it was true, a little fucked up, possibly dangerous. On the other hand, he was spared the tedium of his own company, spared too from any more disastrous solo outings, and in that regard, Big D, with his talk of feeders, receivers, and frozen lakes, was a kind of stand-in for the tranquilizers he had thus far declined.

It was true that sleep was down to no more than three hours per night but there were benefits in this too. Acuity felt sharpened. He was more aware, more present for the patients who continued to come and go. Mornings passed quickly in anticipation of the afternoons. Afternoons passed in a sepia tone blur, shadows lengthening into night. He could no longer recall if this was what it had been like before, the elevator lift to a full-blown mania worthy of a bipolar 1 diagnosis ending in flames and blood, a suicide watch lasting the better part of a month. But then he no longer gave it much thought. There was no time and those moments of existential dread in which he was seized upon by his own absolute inability to explain himself were growing fewer and farther apart. The thrill of the hunt was upon him, the seminal imperative of mortal blood.

On the third day of the second week, they caught a break. At least D said it was a break. Who was Chance to disagree? His beloved James had been right, it really was all faith or fear. The detective did not go straightaway to the condo where he lived. Nor did he stop at the cop's bar he sometimes frequented near the waterfront where the parking lot was close to the street and always crowded. He drove instead to the outskirts of downtown Oakland in the general direction of the airport, to a land of single-story buildings, strip malls, and gas stations where much of the signage was written in Korean, entering at last among a particularly tawdry collection of storefront operations including one with the incongruous moniker of European Massage printed out in both English and Korean in bold block lettering across blacked-out plate glass. He drove through the lot, passing in front of the buildings before circling round to an alley that ran at their backs.

Believing it unwise to drive into the alley, Chance parked nearby, allowing D to go in on foot. He was back in ten with more good news. 'Fucker parked in back of the massage parlor and went in.' He looked toward the building. 'More to that place than meets the eye,' he said. 'There's a little lot in back, half a dozen cars, all high-end. You'd never guess it, tucked away down here.'

'Maybe that's part of the attraction.'

'Maybe.'

'So Blackstone's either working a case or getting laid.'

'Yep, saw a woman letting him in. He's been there before. I'll say that much. We'll see how long he stays. An hour or more, I'd say he's a customer, which means at some point he'll be back. He does and we're on it. Lot's fucking perfect.'

Detective Blackstone was gone for a full hour and twenty-two minutes. 'Putting a little stink on his johnson,' D said. Chance looked to see if he was smiling but he wasn't. The color had risen in the big man's cheeks. He was staring into the alley with the intensity of a hawk in search of a field mouse, that and cracking his knuckles, first one hand and then the other, though he did not seem conscious of the act.

A day later and Blackstone was back, same time same place. 'Lock and load,' D told him. 'I'm going in.'

Chance let him out a block from the bar, in possession of a screw-driver, a portable power drill, and a blank thumb drive, which he carried in a nondescript nylon backpack, then drove to a large park nearly two miles away and waited.

Little more than an hour had passed when D reappeared. Chance spotted him through the trees on the far side of the park that was maybe a hundred yards across and featured at its center an ornate fountain and pool. It was approaching the dinner hour. In the streets the cars were turning on their lights. Looking east into the Oakland hills one might judge the fire line by where the lights of the houses began and ended. Nearer to where Chance waited, the fountain and pool were particularly well lit, their jets of water thrown skyward in a rush of white light to fall like sparks before a darkening sky.

There had been some discussion about this part of the plan. They had been seated in D's quarters at the rear of the warehouse and Chance had argued for a closer rendezvous point. 'Better like this,' D had told him. 'Something goes wrong, I want time to distance myself from the scene before you and I meet up.'

'Seems like you'd want me closer if something went wrong.' The prospect of something going wrong seemed so unimaginably fucked up it was difficult even to say. The old man had attempted to calm his fears. 'You'd never believe it,' Carl told him. He was looking at D as might a proud father on a favored son. 'Knows how to make himself invisible.'

'Part of my training,' D said by way of acknowledging this improbability. 'I was in the Teams... we used to do these drills... guy gets dropped off in some part of the city, San Diego usually... where I did my basics but it could be anywhere. Whatever... Point is... it's the rest of the team's job to find this guy and what *he* has to do... is make it back to some agreed-upon location without being spotted. You learn how to move, how to use the shadows, play the angles, lines of sight from any given point... Sneak and peek, we called it...'

'You'd never think a guy of his size could pull that off, but I've seen him do it.'

'I take Carl out sometimes, try to show him shit.'

'Got me working on my template of nine.' The old man drew a fixed-blade knife from his pocket and waved it about in the air, appearing to strike at what Chance took to be three different targets. 'So far I'm only up to three, three of nine.' He struck at the invisible targets for a second time. 'Pretty quick, huh?'

Chance had no idea what the old man was talking about but expressed his admiration, asking only if he carried the thing around in his pocket like that, with nothing to cover the blade.

Carl removed a small leather sheath and let Chance look at it. 'See those little wires?' There were four very fine wires, looped to make little prongs, coming out from four different places on the sheath. 'D put those on there. They hang up on the lining in your pocket, hold the sheath so you can draw the knife.' He felt compelled to re-enact the demonstration yet again.

Chance advised him to keep up the good work.

'You bet,' Carl told him.

And that was pretty much the end of it. The point of rendezvous had remained the park, where Chance now waited, still living in hope that all of those sneak-and-peek drills honed by the big man in the course of his training would prove forever unnecessary.

He watched as D ducked into a public restroom where he remained for some time before reappearing to start once more in the direction of the car. The park was a lively enough place at dusk. Joggers made their way around the park's perimeter. A few teenagers had gathered near the fountain, assorted musical devices plugged into their ears, taking pictures with their phones. Here and there were mothers in tandem pushing baby strollers, toddlers in their wake. Many turned to look as D rumbled by. He was not, under normal circumstances – i.e., when not on one of his sneak-and-peek missions – one to go unnoticed, with his massive bulk, his naked dome showing white as he passed beneath the trees. Children and pigeons scattered in his wake.

Chance wondered what the others must make of him. Did they think him homeless? Did they know he never slept? Might they imagine he'd fought for his country in the dark and dangerous places of the world, seeing and experiencing things that few others ever would? Two little black girls seemed to take a particular delight in the spectacle of D. They giggled and waved and skipped along behind him across the weathered grass of a late summer for some distance rather like pilot fish in the shadow of a whale. D paid them no mind. The fallen leaves danced about the cuffs of his cargo pants. His jacket was open and flapped about his ample waist, accentuating his mass.

As D reached the car and heaved himself inside, Chance could see that he'd managed to splash a good deal of water on his shirt and pants. His face, even more reddened than usual, was still wet and dripping. It looked, in what was left of the light, more or less as if the big man had been crying. 'How did it go?' Chance asked. The absurd inquiry seemed to fly from this throat of its own accord, infused with a false gaiety.

'You might want to get us out of here,' D said.

Seated side by side in the front seat of Chance's Olds, the breadth of D's shoulders was such that the two men were nearly touching. It was, Chance thought, like being in the water in a very small boat next to an immense liner. If the big boat went down, it was taking you with it. Perhaps, he thought, this was why he was just now lowering his window, an unconscious desire for escape. 'For Christ's sake,' Chance said. He had yet to start the car.

D's eyes ticked toward the car's ignition. Chance turned the key. The engine came to life. 'What happened?'

'That's a story,' D said. 'But I got you this, you still want it.' He pulled the thumb drive from the nylon backpack and held it up for Chance to see.

Chance was hesitant to take it. 'Why wouldn't I still want it?' he asked. There was something about his continuing in darkness as to the exact nature of its acquisition that had him spooked. D was apparently waiting for him to leave the curb before further disclosures.

Chance put the car into gear. He checked both rear- and side-view mirrors like any other resident of the real world and entered the flow of traffic.

'The mission was compromised,' D said.

Chance imagined that he might be sick. A moment passed. 'But you have his files,' Chance began. A second moment passed. A second thought occurred. 'Or was that why you asked if I still wanted it? There's nothing on it? You didn't have time to download?' A happy enough outcome, he thought, when placed alongside all other possible outcomes in which a mission had been compromised.

'I didn't say the mission was aborted,' D said. 'I said it was compromised. There was collateral damage. It's been taken care of.'

Chance drew as deep a breath as he was able. The road they were on circled the park before intersecting with the street that would take them to the freeway, but the intersection slipped past as Chance continued on around the park, passing once more the spot in which he had waited for Big D. 'What exactly are you telling me?' Chance asked.

'You're driving in fucking circles,' D said.

Chance found it necessary to pull over. They were by now on the opposite side of the park from which they had begun yet still on the circling road. 'What are you saying, D?'

'What about collateral damage and *taken care of* don't you understand, Doc?'

'Any of it, neither in part nor in whole. I don't understand it because you haven't told me.'

D just looked at him.

Had Chance not known what D was capable of, he might have considered punching him in the face. With this off the table, he proceeded as best as he could. 'I need it in plain English, D. I'm part of this. I need to know what happened back there.'

'Actually you don't.'

'Actually I do.'

'The more you know, the more you're in.'

'I'd say I'm in pretty goddamn deep already.'

'Get on the freeway, will you?'

'You're telling me you killed him.'

'If by him you mean Blackstone, no, I didn't kill him. Least I don't think I did. I put one in his chest but it didn't look like a kill shot. Be good to get across the bridge. I'm not saying they'll close it, but you never know... one of their own goes down.'

This time Chance failed to check his mirrors. Talk of a closed bridge had panicked him. He pulled directly into the path of a diminutive gray-haired woman at the helm of a silver Prius, barely tall enough to see over the wheel.

God only knew how much time was consumed by what followed. Chance and the lady, a former high school English teacher for the city of Oakland in the days before movies had sound, exchanged pleasantries and insurance cards. The Oldsmobile was relatively unharmed. The Prius would require a new bumper and fender assembly. 'We'll not worry about my car,' Chance told her. It was all on him, he said. Damned blind spot is what it was, but not to worry. And no need for police reports or insurance companies, what with rate hikes and all of that...

'The newer cars have little cameras in them,' the lady said. She was looking with obvious disdain upon Chance's Cutlass.

'Take your car anywhere you like,' he told her. 'Put whoever does the work in touch with me and I will take care of it.'

'There were blind spots,' she said.

'Yes, I understand. That is absolutely correct. But really... this will all be fine. And you have all of my numbers. I can be reached at any one, at any time.'

She looked once more at the offending Oldsmobile. 'And you really don't think we should call the police?'

Chance guessed her to be well past eighty, in what appeared to be the early stages of Parkinson's disease and probably not long for the road. Report of an accident was probably no more in her interest than it was in his. He'd so far stopped just short of telling her this for fear of depressing her but certainly hoped that it might yet be implied, that she would catch his drift. 'Well,' he said. 'You know the police, and you know the insurance companies.' He mustered his best smile, no small feat given the circumstances.

In the end, she was willing to go along. It might have been that she did in fact catch his drift. It might also have been his business card or the fact that, in her words, he was possessed of an honest face. Writing out the last of his information, he heard sirens and found that his hand had begun to shake. 'There, there…' the woman told him. She went so far as to pat him on the arm. Her name was Delores Flowers, now of Alameda. 'Let's just be thankful no one was hurt.'

He returned to the car. D was seated with his great head tilted back on the headrest, his eyes on the car's headliner in which a small tear had begun near the windshield. 'Good one, Doc.'

While the Bay Bridge would certainly have been the more direct route to Allan's Antiques, they opted for a more circuitous return. To put a finer point on it, D opted for the more circuitous return. For Chance, mileage was the last thing on his mind as eventually the Richmond-San Rafael Bridge was made to appear before them. Thankfully, it appeared to be open. Chance had a FasTrak transponder on his windshield, meaning they would not have to stop and pay the toll but D reached over and took it down. 'Use this, there'll be a record you were here.'

'Could be already, given what just happened and how she handles it.'

'Thought you said she was cool.'

'Just now, she was. Who knows about tomorrow?' They reached the tollbooth where Chance gave a five-dollar bill to an obese woman in a conductor's hat and drove on.

'You're worried about that old lady, say the word,' D said. 'We'll go back and take care of *that* right now. You got her address, I take it.'

Chance hadn't the courage to ask if he was serious. The Richmond–San Rafael Bridge rose before them, a regular stairway to the stars. The city of San Francisco appeared on their left. Chance held to the wheel. Soon they would be within sight of the federal prison at San Quentin. It occurred to him that a guy like Big D might actually find a home there. Given enough time, he might well run the place. Chance figured his own life expectancy in such an establishment at around six and a half minutes. He attempted to force such thoughts from his mind by concentrating on the ribbon of concrete that ran before them, unfurling into the night.

The wolf and the dog

A RED MOON broke from among the clouds to light the bay. San Francisco, made ethereal in the aqueous night, seemed to float somewhere just below it, hovering above the blackened waters, apparently free of the earth and therefore unbound by any of the usual constraints.

As some embodiment of the Crystal City, the place never failed to disappoint. It had been so since Chance first laid eyes on it, twenty years ago, fresh from the east and hoping to put the past behind him... the red-haired dancer, the death of his father, the calamity his life was in danger of becoming. He'd come like so many before him, in flight from history and he'd thought for a good long time that he'd actually managed it. He supposed he should have known. He thought of the note a professor had once attached to an important paper he'd written for a class. It had been toward the end of things, the girl having claimed him, the downward spiral begun. 'It's harder than this,' the man had written.

'The fuck?' Chance said. They had been riding in silence for a good ten minutes.

D draped an arm over the back of the seat and shifted his weight, apparently quite at ease. 'Some asshole came out of the place,' he said finally.

'The massage parlor?'

'No, man, the Mongolian Grill, a midget with takeout.'

A moment went by. They had begun their descent. Chance realized that he had begun to speed and forced his foot from the accelerator. The cops kept an eye on the bridge. Fines for speeding were over the moon.

'Yeah,' D said. 'The massage parlor. Some goon that worked there would be my guess. Guy was all geared up.'

Chance was forced to ask what was meant by 'all geared up.'

'Mace, stun gun. Could've been strapped but I never saw it. Fucker caught me dead to rights getting out of Blackstone's Crown Vic. He might have been another cop but I'm thinking private security, kind of an Eastern European-looking guy. Russians are deep into the whole massage parlor racket. Romanians too. It's all about white slavery. Moving women. It's a dirty business. Whatever this guy was, he knew the car and he knew it wasn't mine; he came right at me. What I'm wondering is, how does he know that? He either works with Blackstone or he works for the joint. Thing that fucking *worries* me is how did he *know* to come out? Could be it was just some random thing, like having a smoke or making his rounds, looking in on that lot because that's what he does. *Or...*' And it was here that D paused. 'They've got some kind of surveillance system. Now if they do, it's gonna have to be pretty fucking high-tech 'cause I looked around and didn't see dick, but that doesn't rule out the possibility.' He looked to the west, a distant sea. 'That would not be good,' the big man said. 'That would be fucked up in the extreme.'

It took another half mile for Chance to inquire as to just how fucked up in the extreme it all might be. The big man held up a hand. On the first finger was a heavy ring Chance was certain had not been there when D had gotten out of the car at the mouth of the alley. The band had no sheen to it in the muted light. It appeared as dull silver and quite wide. It looked big even on D's hand and D's hands were the size of shovels.

Chance watched as best he could while D turned his hand, revealing the ring as part of an exotic-looking blade that lay flat against his palm. A second movement brought the blade into play so that it extended for maybe two inches from the side of a closed fist where it curved like the fang of some predatory animal. 'Called a karambit,' D told him. 'Lots of ways you can use it… hook, stab, slice… great for controlling an opponent.' He made some small movements with his hand in the air between them. 'You can enter a joint, separate vertebrae… It's a very effective weapon, easy to conceal. Almost impossible to disarm a guy who knows how to use one. You want… I'll teach you someday.'

'Thanks,' Chance told him. 'I believe I'll pass.'

'That's a poor attitude, Doc.'

Chance declined a response.

'There are three kinds of people.'

'Here we go.'

'Sheep, wolves, and sheepdogs. The sheep are afraid of the wolves but they don't like the dogs much either. You look at it from the sheep's point of view, the dog is a lot like the wolf. He's got teeth like the wolf. He growls like a wolf. He smells like a wolf. Only time the sheep like the sheepdog is when the wolf comes. *Then* they like him. Rest of the time… they don't even want to have to think about him, much less see him. You catch my drift?'

'A little like the warrior-slave dichotomy.'

'It's not a little like it, it's a lot like it. You learn to use the blade or wait on the dog, and hope the wolf doesn't get there first.'

Chance saw in this the opportunity for a broader discussion of free will but declined to go there.

'Fucker pepper sprayed me,' D said at length.

'Why your eyes were so red. I thought maybe you'd been crying.'

'Oh absolutely. That's what you thought?'

'My attempt at gallows humor.'

'That's good, Doc. You had me fooled.'

'So he pepper sprayed you, then what?'

'Then nothing. Then his problems began. Christ… I was in the Teams. We pepper sprayed each other for laughs.

Shit's for girls, something they can carry in their purses to make them feel safer on blind dates or some fucking thing. Next thing after that is, he pulls a Taser. If he'd pulled a piece and started shooting he might've had a chance, but there he was with his pepper spray and Taser.' D gave it a moment's thought. 'Could be he was just trying to handicap me… thought if he could do that, he could beat the shit out of me and feel tough. He was a big guy.' He paused once more to shake his head. 'Thing about a Taser is, you really need two of them to be effective, and even then you can fight your way out, you know how. These guys have no training. It's pathetic when you stop and think about it. Case of tonight… I used this to cut the line.' He held the blade once more for Chance to see before enclosing it in his fist. 'Got myself close enough to hook him through the ocular cavities and snap his neck.'

'Jesus Christ,' Chance said. It took another moment to recover some semblance of what might pass for his bearings. 'What happened to *controlling* your opponent?'

D ignored him. 'That's when things got *really* interesting,' he said. 'Fucking Blackstone showed up. Guy must have beeped him or something. He pops around a corner of the building, like he'd come out the front then around to the side…'

'My God, he saw you?'

'Don't know, really. He probably saw something. It was dark enough the lights were coming on, both corners of the building. I could see him pretty well but it was still pretty dark where I was. He had something in his hand. Might have been a phone. Might have been a gun. My vision was still a little fucked up from the spray. Only thing I could be sure about at that point was that I didn't want him getting any closer to where I needed to go, which was down that alley. That's when I put the one in his chest I was telling you about and got out.'

'You shot him?'

'I was thirty seconds into a compromised situation, Doc. Last thing I needed was sound. You've seen my throwing blades. I might have tried for a kill shot, but like I said…'

'You couldn't see.'

'I didn't say I couldn't see. I couldn't see… you and I wouldn't be sitting here. I could see who it was, I could see I hit him, and I could see he went down. There wasn't time to close. What I couldn't know was what had transpired between him and this goon… maybe nothing… maybe a call… maybe more help on the way and like I said…'

'You were thirty seconds in.'

'Time to go.'

'My God,' Chance said once more. 'I can't get my head around this… I can't find the terms. A man is dead.'

'It happens. Who do you think this guy was?'

'I have no idea.'

'He was a soldier. He was armed. He had choices. He made a bad one.'

'And there was no other way to end it?'

'You think of one, I'm all ears.'

'Disarm him. Knock him out.'

'You've knocked out a lot of guys in the course of your practice? Disarmed them first, of course?'

Chance said nothing.

'There you go,' D told him.

They came to the freeway and southbound lanes where they drove once more in silence. The passage of time seemed of little consequence and the world changed. They came to the Waldo tunnel and the Golden Gate Bridge. San Francisco lay in the distance, disappearing even as they watched it, lost to a fog bank worthy of John the Revelator so that by the time they had reached the middle spans of the great bridge the thing toward which they pressed was gone and what they entered was no longer the Crystal City but only a vast impenetrable darkness. It was, Chance supposed, thinking now of the origin of things, how it had all begun and how at some point in the perhaps not-too-distant future it would no doubt end. How then to make sense of the evening's progression? What difference would any of it make when all was said and done? When entropy and darkness had had their way? It was admittedly the long view. But then the long view was what he was after, the short one having been fucked up beyond all recognition.

The great ice-cream hunt

THEY HAD by now entered the city though you'd be hard-pressed to know it. The car's wipers swept the windshield, squeaking audibly with each pass while doing little to improve visibility.

'Wasn't that bad, really, when you stop and think about it,' D said. 'I was wearing latex. Cop never had a clean visual and nothing of *mine* left at the scene. All in all I'd say it was a pretty clean op. Not perfect, but still pretty clean. Exit was a little fucked up but that's on you, brother.'

Chance didn't trust himself to speak. He had taken to imagining what it must have looked like, a man hooked through the ocular cavities.

'You know what I'd like?' D said. 'I'd like a fucking malted. The old kind, where they actually put the malt powder in so it's not just milk and ice cream.' A moment passed. 'My mother turned me on to those,' he added. 'There was someplace in the city she used to take me. You know where we can get one?'

It was, Chance thought, the first he'd heard D mention family of any kind, and what's more, that *till* this moment, he might just as well have been willing to believe the man at his side not only without the usual progenitors but sprung fully formed from his own forehead, the product of some mysterious singularity. That said, Chance was *more* than willing to go engage in such an outing and no chore too absurd. In truth, he was grateful that D had come up with something for them to do. Anything short of more bloodletting would have served, anything to spare himself the empty apartment he knew to be lying in wait for him out there somewhere in the fog, rather, he imagined, like the proverbial beast in the jungle, waiting to spring.

The great ice-cream hunt, which is how he came to think of it, began somewhere near Fisherman's Wharf while the night was yet young. It ended at a place called Ruby's at the far end of Ocean Beach, where one had the feeling that a good many other things had ended as well. The air smelled of wet sand and dying kelp. Unseen waves thundered at them from across the Great Highway. A number of drinks calling themselves malteds had by now been purchased and consumed along the way but none were to D's liking. This didn't keep him from pounding them down. Strawberry was his flavor of choice. Chance had pressed on in hopes of finding an actual drink but none had been available till Ruby's.

Ruby's was the real deal, a genuine full-service establishment, all worn plaster and chipped Formica. The linoleum flooring was laid out in old-fashioned checkerboard patterns of green and black. Memorabilia covered the walls – enough to suggest the place had been there since before the Great Flood. A black-faced clock with white hands and the likeness of Mickey Mouse at its center read twelve o'clock straight up when they came through the door that opened to the highway and the beaches beyond. It was half past two when they left. In the interim they sat opposite one another in a red Naugahyde booth like any other pair of nighthawks. Food followed drinks, at least for D, who opted for the bacon-wrapped cheeseburger times two, french fries, and a large Diet Coke. Chance watched, nursing a bottle of Rolling Rock beer. 'My God,' he said finally. It was perhaps D's mention of his mother, this in concert with the fact that Chance was a little drunk, that led to his addressing the big man as if he were just one more of the planet's mortals. 'Do you ever worry about diabetes?' He was looking at the array of food and remnants thereof spread out on the table before them.

'I take medication for that,' D said matter-of-factly.

'Ah. And your cholesterol?'

'Cholesterol is great. Blood pressure is great.' At which point D embarked on an elaborate apology for the use of salt in eliminating fat from the diet. The theory, such as it was, appeared to hinge on the notion that salt had been shown as an effective cleaning agent in removing grease from skillets. The big man went on at some length, all the time adding ever more salt to the food on his plate, but Chance was finding it difficult to follow. Nor did it occur to him to ask if the other was serious. Four years of medical school, an internship, two residencies at prestigious hospitals, credentials up the wazoo... who was he to question anything? He was the guy who'd run away with the schizophrenic dancer, robbed the family money and broken his father's heart, failed husband and father, now wheelman in flight from a murder and botched robbery on the outskirts of Oakland is who he was.

Whatever sleep he was granted that night came behind the wheel of the Oldsmobile in the small garage beneath his apartment where he reclined the seat as far as it would go and covered himself with a jacket. He was afraid to go inside, for any number of reasons.

He was awakened the following morning by the computer programmer come to get his own car from the garage. As to whether or not the programmer had seen him there, asleep at the wheel, he could not say. The two had not spoken since the night of Chance's struggle with Jackie Black and had in fact gone so far as to avoid eye contact at those times when they might otherwise have exchanged pleasantries, though Chance put this more on the programmer than on himself. He was still willing to be friends. When the man had at last managed to extract his Toyota from its hopelessly cramped space and the door swung shut in his wake, Chance went upstairs to shower and shave. Later he rode the bus to his office, where men in suits were awaiting.

Bob Marley

THERE WERE three of them altogether. Chance could not say the sight was unexpected but this did not make it any easier to take. Passing from the hallway and into the outer waiting room of his office, it occurred to him that he was at that very moment in possession of Big D's thumb drive and the files of Detective Raymond Blackstone, lifted from his laptop computer on the day of a murder and he exchanged what must have appeared, at least to her eyes, a look of pure terror with Lucy behind her desk. She responded with a raised eyebrow then stood to make the introductions.

One of the men, the youngest of the three, was a Shorthand Reporter, certified as such by the state of California. The other two men were attorneys. There was a Mr Berg, appearing as counsel on behalf of the plaintiff, in this case a Mr Chad Dorsey of Eugene, Oregon, and Mr Green, counsel for the defense, Dr William Fry, retired. Charges of elder abuse and undue influence were at long last being brought against Lorena Sanchez and the agency that had sent her to Dr Fry. To ensure the future safety of whatever was left in Dr Fry's numerous accounts, Mr Dorsey, a distant nephew, was seeking a ruling by the court that would have Dr Fry declared incompetent with regard to testamentary capacity and thereby grant the power of attorney to his heirs, in this case the aforementioned Mr Dorsey. Dr Fry had chosen to fight. Much to his chagrin, Chance had been asked to appear as an expert witness on behalf of the plaintiff. Things being what they were, the entire proceeding, on the books now for at least two weeks, had slipped his mind.

'Are you all right?' Lucy asked, her voice at a whisper. She was standing at Chance's shoulder. He had just seen the men into his office. The question seemed to have become a standard one of late. Given his current circumstances, any interest in his well-being from any quarter was more than welcome. 'I'm good to go,' he told her. 'But thank you. Thank you for asking.' A moment passed between them. 'You've changed your hair,' he said. 'There's more red in it today.'

'Umm, for about two weeks now.'

'Really? I'm sorry I didn't notice.'

Lucy just looked at him. She seemed torn between laughter and a call to 911.

'I like it. Did I say that?'

'You did, just now.'

Chance nodded.

'Doctor…' She looked toward the room, the waiting men.

'Well,' Chance said. 'It's very pretty.'

Depositions were dreadful enough things, the tedious answering of the same tedious questions that had become his meat and potatoes, the barrier he had erected to save him from the Jaclyn Blackstones of the world. This particular day's proceedings were even more dreadful than most as Chance was soon made witness to an attenuated pissing match between the two attorneys, it being Mr Green's contention that with respect to Dr Chance there was a distinction to be made between a consulting expert and a retained expert. He was no doubt hoping to keep certain of Chance's original comments, made in his original report to the family regarding a possible neurodegenerative condition, out of the courtroom. Mr Berg had never heard of such a ridiculous assertion. Nor would he hear of it now. And so it went. By the three-hour mark Chance was not yet fully deposed. 'I wonder,' he asked, 'if I might take five minutes to use the men's room?'

'Good idea,' said Mr Green, and they all went out together. Chance finished first. He left Mr Berg and Mr Green, along with the state-certified recorder, whose every act, urination included, seemed carried out in complete silence, arguing the merits of some particular golf course somewhere south of the city. The two were apparently old friends.

Chance found Lucy waving him over as he reentered the waiting room and he crossed to her desk. 'She keeps calling,' Lucy said.

'Who?' he asked then realized he had spoken before she'd finished with whatever it was she had to say.

She gave him a look before consulting her pad. 'Delores Flowers. She says it's very important that she talk to you. She says you will know what it's about.'

He could only wonder if his relief was apparent. 'Ah... yes... Ms Flowers. She and I had a little run-in east of the bridge. You must tell her that you are my office manager and that you have my proxy. Anything she wishes to say to me, she can say to you. There is the matter of a bill for some work that will be done to her car.' He gave her his credit card. 'Have her tell the shop or garage or whatever it is to call here. Have them charge this account. That doesn't take care of things, tell her I will call her after work.'

The remainder of the day was spent in the company of Mr Berg and Mr Green. It was, all things considered, the longest, most tedious deposition of them all. The day's only bright spot was that neither attorney seemed privy to any part of Chance's history, so recently unearthed. He was left to imagine that, failing conviction for accessory to murder, his career as an expert witness was yet intact.

When the gang of three had gone and he was at last alone, he lay on the floor at the foot of his desk watching the late light at play among clouds through the wonderful old glass of his office windows. "'Lord, it is time...'" he said aloud then, skipping from the beginning to the end, "'Whoever has no house now, will never have one. Whoever is alone now, will stay alone."' He'd once been able to recite the poem in its entirety, in the language in which it had been penned. "'*Wer jetzt kein Haus hat…*"' His recitation was interrupted by Lucy calling in from the front desk. 'You might want to come out here,' she said.

'Delores Flowers?'

'No, it's something else.'

He went out to find Jaclyn Blackstone in jeans and a red T-shirt with a picture of Bob Marley on the front beneath a black leather jacket. Her hair appeared fashionably tousled, freshly cut. She was deep in conversation with the tragic Jean-Baptiste, who, perhaps emboldened by Lucy's becoming friendlier, had come in broad daylight for the hanging of yet one more of his dreadful photographs, an act that till now might just as well have been carried out by a cat burglar operating in reverse.

Chance moved as quickly as possible to separate them, with apologies to Jean-Baptiste for interrupting a conversation he was loath to even imagine while taking Jaclyn by the elbow and steering her into the hall. He had no idea about where to begin. She saved him by going first. 'Raymond's been hurt,' she said. 'He caught someone trying to break into his car. Last night.' She took a breath. 'The guy threw a knife. He's in the hospital with a collapsed lung. Another man was murdered.'

'A cop?'

'Some kind of bouncer at this place where they were, a massage parlor in Oakland. I think Raymond may have an interest in it.'

'You know that, for a fact?'

'I don't know anything for a fact when it comes to him. No one does. And I wouldn't say that to anyone else. If he even thought I thought it, I would be in trouble.'

'But you *do* think it.'

'I hear things now and then.'

'What do the police know? Are there suspects?'

He was aware of being perhaps too eager and the question hung fire between them. 'They won't really tell me anything but I don't think so.' Another moment passed. 'Anyway, he says he's got it.'

Chance was aware of some movement beneath him, the floor perhaps, tilting beneath his feet. 'Has what?'

'The investigation, revenge… I have no idea. It was all he said. I was with him last night, and then again this morning, before work. At some point I need to go back. He says he's going to handle everything himself, when he gets out.'

'Well…' he began but wasn't sure where to go with it.

She found his hand with her own. 'Come with me,' she whispered.

Chance hesitated.

Her grip tightened.

'Go to the café. Give me twenty minutes.'

Returning somewhat unsteadily to the confines of his office, he passed Lucy on her way out. 'Don't tell me,' she said. 'You sent her to the café.' He might have responded but she was already gone, waving at him over a shoulder with the tips of her fingers, nails of crimson.

Jean-Baptiste was adjusting the new photograph as Chance made his way back into the waiting room. Chance had not actually seen Jean-Baptiste in some time. He heard that his illness had taken a turn. Another man had been filling in, parking cars beneath the building. 'What a remarkable woman,' was how Jean-Baptiste greeted him. 'That one I was talking to just now. Is she a patient?'

Jean-Baptiste was scarcely more than five feet in height, nearly as big around as he was tall. In this respect one might say that he was perfectly proportioned. Chance guessed him to be no more than fifty, putting them at roughly the same age. The Frenchman wore heavy horn-rimmed glasses and was possessed of an imposing head of black hair streaked with gray that he wore pulled back into a ponytail half as long as himself. It was his complexion Chance thought that gave him away, making him look older than his years – the papery quality of the skin, the faint yellowing one might associate with some form of ill health.

'Professionally speaking,' Chance said, 'I saw her one time for an evaluation, then sent her to a therapist, Janice Silver.'

'One time is not so bad.'

'One time is still one time.'

Jean-Baptiste was a moment taking him in. 'Is this *me* you're talking to, or are you now speaking to yourself, one of your enemies from within, perhaps?' The question was followed by a little wink. Of Jean-Baptiste, it was said that he'd cut rather a wide swath with the ladies upon his arrival in the city by the bay.

'Both, would be my guess,' Chance told him. 'I sent her to the café on the corner.'

'Good for you.'

'You're hoping to see me disbarred?'

'Nonsense. A slap on the wrist, and *that's* if someone complains. I'm assuming you didn't make love to her on the floor of your office at the time of your lone evaluation.'

'Hardly.'

'Too bad. That's one attractive woman. She is also smart and sexy. How crazy is she?'

'I don't know. A history of memory lapses, at least one secondary personality...'

'Ah yes,' Jean-Baptiste said. He managed the tone of someone recalling with some fondness another age of the world.

Chance knew him to be a skeptic with regard to convention but he was not looking for a fight. Nor were his own views on the subject entirely clear, even to himself. 'She remains caught in an extremely stressful and abusive relationship,' he said. 'Very debilitating. If she could free herself from that...'

'This other might go away.'

Chance shrugged.

'Or not.'

'Or not,' Chance admitted.

'And you're trying to help.'

'Something like that.'

'Well,' he said. 'It's like Orpheus and Persephone in the cool gray city. And who can blame you? I, for one, am all for it.'

'All for what?'

'Oh, come on. The woman is taken with you. It's as plain as day. And you're taken with her. How long since you've gotten laid?'

With Lucy gone, there were just the two of them there, them and Jean-Baptiste's infamous subjects. The one in the photograph Jean-Baptiste was just now finishing with was a man probably no older than seventy, the apparent victim of Alzheimer's or some other form of dementia. He was dressed in what appeared to be a large cloth diaper with a ribbon about his chest that read CAPTAIN AMERICA in bold letters. The man was standing on a plain wooden chair before a long, empty table as if preparing to hang himself in what looked to be some kind of communal dining room. What made the photograph especially arresting was the gleam in the man's eye, at once unsound yet full of what one might only call a fierce, unyielding light.

'Knowing you're about to die affords certain freedoms from convention,' Jean-Baptiste was saying. Chance remained fixed upon the man on the chair in the new photograph. 'The thing about one's last act… without recourse to an afterlife…'

'I was under the impression that you were not a believer in last acts,' Chance said, cutting him off. 'I thought that was one of your things.'

'I'm giving it to you straight,' Jean-Baptiste told him. 'Without further possibilities to become. There's only what you are. *You* should think in terms of your Nietzsche, the eternal return.'

Chance managed to free his gaze from that of the demented man. 'Janice Silver seems to think she may be borderline.'

'Yes, well… there is always that. And I'm sure she would know. What do you think?'

'I don't know.'

'Of course not. Who ever does? But it's not a bad out.'

Chance just looked at him.

'She *is* borderline, there's nothing you can do, you or anybody else. She is what she is, the product of whatever tragic beginnings and fucked-up set of circumstances she had the great misfortune to be born into. What's Beckett's line? It's a hell of a planet? My advice, make love to her while you still can. Make wild, passionate love and move on, onward and upward as they say, but tell me all about it, will you? Details, please.' When Chance said nothing, Jean-Baptiste continued with this latest train of thought. 'You know how they say getting older means settling for less. It's a good deal more dire than that, my friend, it's staring the gray rat in the eye and refusing to blink.'

Chance looked once more to the man in the diaper, Captain America, aware of a fresh insight into his old friend's work. 'Is that what he's doing?' he asked.

'Oh, there's no doubt about it.'

'It's what you look for… in all of them…' His eye swept to Lucy's favorite, the old lady in her Indian headdress.

'That certain spark, yes… the immediacy of it. Unflinching, I suppose would be another way of saying it.'

'And how do you differentiate unflinching from purely mad?'

'Ah…' Jean-Baptiste said, warming to the subject. 'Therein resides the tale, my friend. But I let the viewer decide about all of that. Frankly that part doesn't interest me all that much. It's the light that I'm after, a moth to the fucking flame, that and a few vicarious forays into the land of the living. It's what remains and I'm counting on you to deliver.'

Chance smiled at him, in spite of everything. He couldn't quite help it. If details were what he was after… Chance had details.

'"Go under young man…"' Jean-Baptiste said. He was

quoting now, from the man whose likeness perched upon Chance's desk, Big D's main man. Christ, Chance thought, there's no escaping the fucker. But Jean-Baptiste's eyes were cast to the heavens, his voice possessed of a theatrical tone in the lower register. "'I love him whose soul is deep, even in being wounded… I love all those who are like heavy drops falling one by one out of the dark cloud that lowers over man: they herald the coming of the lightning and as heralds they perish.'"

'Oh for fuck's sake,' Chance said.

'My point exactly,' Jean-Baptiste told him.

Cool, grey city...

Tho the dark be cold and blind,
Yet her sea-fog's touch is kind...
  – George Sterling, 'The Cool, Grey City of Love'

S HE WAS waiting for him in the little café and she was the
woman she had pretty much always been in his presence,
the one from the bookstore in Berkeley who had so nearly
charmed him into asking her out. The effect was such that
the subject of Raymond Blackstone did not come up again.
He would never have imagined it that way but that's the
way it was; a moment out of time and that was, as Doc Billy
would have said, the long and the short of it. Blackstone was
still in a hospital room in the East Bay and the night was
theirs. Later they walked, an empty bottle of some Napa
Valley cabernet at the table to mark their passing, through
city streets for what must have been half the length of San
Francisco and the entire place made magical by the simple
fact of her being in it, the sky void of stars but shot through
with a grand, seemingly omnipresent luminosity that was
no more than clouds giving back the city's own light.

In places they would stop to window-shop for things they
would never buy and half their sentences began with the
phrase *'If I ever had a ton of dough...'* and then they would
laugh and go on. They found a tiny store off an alley not far
from Allan's Antiques that specialized in extremely high-
end European pianos and Chance managed a somewhat
halting version of a Chopin nocturne on a prewar Bechstein
finished in rosewood and could not believe such a jewel of
a place had escaped his attention until just now but felt too
that perhaps a good many things had escaped his attention
until just now.

Not from weariness but in an ever increasing hurry, they caught finally a city bus that Chance rode without diagnosing a single person save the one he was with, who sat close beside him on the plastic seat, covering his hand with her own, moving it for him to the inside of her thigh, warm through her jeans that seemed to fit her just there as might a second skin, the outside edge of his hand brushing up against the seam where it cut against her sex, as along their descent toward the Great Highway the moon split the clouds with such light as would take your breath and exiting they could hear the surf and smell the air thick with salt and he was dizzy with wanting her. *I love him whose soul is so overfull that he forgets himself, and all things are in him: thus all things become his going under...* Fucking Jean-Baptiste.

He was not sure how it would be, in the heat of the moment when the moment finally came... Jackie Black perhaps with whips and sex toys, some sadomasochistic limit experience worthy of Michel Foucault. It was after all *his* city of love... the place where the great man and fellow Nietzschean had come to conduct his own interrogation of limits by way of transgression and finally to orchestrate his end by way of its bathhouses and leather bars and let's face it... it wasn't exactly like Chance had never gone there with Jackie Black, in the emptiness of his apartment, in the still of the night, in the depths of his obsession, or fantasized that in fucking her he might even play out his own variation of the bad cop, having her because he could, because that was the stuff of fantasy, all power and pain, humiliation and control. But it wasn't like that either, not finally when all was said and done. It wasn't like anything except what it was like. There was really no room for anything else, no vacant spaces and no more quips about him as her knight or how it was when he talked like a doctor. It was just her without words and she was right there with him, more present than anyone before her, meeting him at every turn, finding him one way and then another until it was very hard to say where one of them ended and the other began, and how many times can one say that about any one fucking thing? He was spent beyond caring in the wake of it, the taste of her still in his mouth, naked across the bed, in violation of the most basic tenet of his profession, as alive as he'd ever felt.

They might have dozed a little. It was hard to know. The point came when she rose to leave. 'You could stay,' he told her.

She smiled a little. She was standing at the side of his bed, naked, the muted light caressing her body. My God, he thought, there was no getting enough of her. 'I'm getting up early,' she told him. 'I have a ticket. I'm going up north for a bit to visit my daughter.'

'She's all right then? You know where she is?'

'Yes.'

'He told you then?'

'When I saw him in the hospital.'

The reference brought back all they had failed to discuss, the absoluteness of their little escape. 'This business about him handling things…'

'I think,' she said, and she took a long time doing it, 'it would probably be good for us not to see each other for a while.'

He just looked at her.

'I don't know what happened or what this will do to him. All I can say is, I know him well enough to know that he will be out for blood. You don't want to be in his way.'

He'd come to one elbow and lay there watching her dress. She did so without recourse to underwear, bra and panties being stuffed in her purse. Watching the jeans go up over her bare ass filled him with longing. He saw her glance in the direction of the cabinet that held his perfumes then look away, her eyes down. 'You know,' he said. 'We could try that again…'

She lifted her face. Her smile was from the bookstore in

Berkeley, sweet and smart, a little wicked. 'Try what?' she asked. 'Everything?'

'Yes. But what I meant was… we could try it again with the perfumes.'

She nodded.

'Would that be a yes or a no?'

'I don't know.'

'I didn't mean now, of course.'

'I didn't think I could be your patient.'

'You can't. But we can find someone else. We'll find the best there is.'

'He *is* getting out.'

What sounded like the music from a passing car found its way from the street, a shrill voice in Spanish backed by accordions.

'I don't know what he's going to do. I may never see you again.'

'Is that why you came?'

A moment passed. 'I wanted to,' she said. 'I've wanted to ever since that day we met in the café below your office.'

'I've wanted to ever since that day in Berkeley,' he told her. 'The day we met at the bookstore.'

She gave him a look. '*That* would have been forward.'

'I almost asked you out, to coffee or something.'

'What stopped you? Me being crazy?'

'My experience… the really crazy are rarely the ones who think of themselves as crazy, but in answer to your question, yes, that and the constraints of my profession.'

She smiled. 'Well… neither seemed to have stopped you tonight.'

'Placing me at your mercy.'

She continued with her dressing. 'I'm not sure we can stop,' she said.

'I'm not either but you're right… it *would* be best if we did, but only for a while, and it's not about him…'

'Who then?'

'You've been through an extended period of trauma. There

may have been other traumas before, things still hidden. There's lots of work to do. You have to be free to do it.'

She seemed about to respond then stopped, dropping to sit beside him, leaning forward, her fingers on his wrist and he saw that she had found him out because he had cut himself there once a long time ago and the scars were yet visible, old and faint but it must have been that the light was hitting them just so and suddenly she was tracing them with the tips of her fingers and when she had done that she turned her arm so that he might see other scars a good deal fresher than his own but he'd noticed those already, when she was beneath him, reaching out above her head, hands pressing into the wall, arms flexed and outstretched.

'My, my,' she said.

'It was a long time ago.'

'Still… we *might* not be so good for each other.'

'That would be very sad,' he told her, and at just that moment it seemed to *him* the saddest thing in the world. 'Could be it's still too soon to see that far ahead. You think?'

She wouldn't answer to that but it was while she was still there, leaning over him, that her eyes ticked to the book on the floor at the side of his bed. It was D's book *The Virtues of War*, and she picked it up and looked at it. 'I know this guy,' she said.

'Personally, or you know his work?'

'His work, smart-ass. One book anyway. He wrote one called *Gates of Fire*, about the battle of Thermopylae.'

'Right,' Chance said. 'And that one is about Alexander the Great – his confessions, you might say. I've only read about half. It was given to me by a friend.'

She put the book aside. She kissed him on the mouth and got to her feet. She took the leather jacket she had worn from one of his dining room chairs and put it on over the red Bob Marley T-shirt, effectively hiding the scars that crisscrossed the insides of her forearms like a junkie's tracks and putting his own modest efforts to shame.

'You do know your car's in the parking garage at my office?'

She stopped and looked at him. 'Oh my God,' she said. 'You're fucking right.' She waited while Chance got out of bed, covering his own arms with an old sports coat. 'Look at us,' she told him. 'The blind and the blind.'

They started playing on the drive over. He supposed it was her lack of underwear and him knowing about it that did the trick. They went at it one more time on the backseat of the Oldsmobile in the underground parking garage across the street from Chance's office, at that hour next to deserted. There was an attendant around somewhere – possibly even that old charlatan Jean-Baptiste – but Chance never saw him. Later he would find her footprints on the Oldsmobile's rear window as perfectly rendered as if she'd been called upon to make castings, spaced one to another at what might only be thought of as a provocative distance so that he would at times and in the days to come be drawn to them as if to moon rocks or the found artifacts of some lost world and be struck all over again with the wonder of it all.

She left him that night with a little something extra, gift or parting shot he would be a long time in trying to decide. 'That book you have on your floor,' she said. They were finished and she was buttoning her jeans once more. Her hair was mussed, a golden lock resting on the high plane of one cheek, her eyes still flushed with light. 'The one beside your bed? The guy who wrote it is Raymond's favorite author. It's why I noticed.'

'Ah…' Chance said after what was perhaps too long a beat.

'Strange, isn't it?' she asked.

'It's a hell of a planet,' he told her.

A monster's ball

H E SLEPT after that. It was the first time in days. Her scent lingered in the room, calling forth the warmth of her body. He shut off his cell phone, unplugged his landline, wrapped himself in all that she had left, and slept the sleep of the pure in heart. In time light appeared at the edges of his blinds. There were sounds in the streets, citizens of the city going about their day. Good things and bad things were no doubt transpiring, moments of fluid beauty alongside those of an unspeakable and rapid decline. There would be the wonderful first light on the waves of Ocean Beach. There would also be mutating cells and blind corners, scandalous and predacious behavior... new patients hatched at every turn. Some would even find their way to his door. He would do what he could and it would never be enough. The lights upon the narrow metal blinds waxed and waned. The sounds of the street came and went. The fat programmer argued and made love with his unseen companion. In the end, he believed that he might actually have spent an entire twenty-four-hour period in bed. For a time he was thinking this a first and was not displeased then remembered that he had spent long periods in bed at one other point in his life and at last began to worry that he might be here for the simple reason that he no longer had it in him to get up. Upon a closer examination it became clear that without his actually having been aware of it, he had assumed the fetal position. Over time worry gave way to a kind of panic. A good part of the problem lay in his inability to determine what exactly he would *do* when and if he *did* get out of bed.

He could not have said how long this period of inertia went

on before at last a task born of such necessity presented itself that he could not imagine what had prevented him from seeing it until now. In its wake he rose, lingered for some time in a hot shower, dressed, and went out. Not, however, before finding a little something she had left behind, an earring on the dresser, a bit of gold with a single amber stone. He left the apartment filled with a sudden and unexpected euphoria, this in concert with an unbearable longing, an understanding of the gross impossibility of things.

To reach his garage it was necessary to first go outside and he found the street alive with activity… all manner of people out and about as if the strange weather were some cause for celebration, oblivious beneath skies made thick with sludge. He took it for the day after the day after and was willing to cede the loss of one in between. He was pondering the very problem when his cell phone began to vibrate against the lining of his slacks.

It was Janice Silver wondering if he'd heard the news. He thought it best to play dumb. 'Where have you been hiding?' she asked. 'The thing made the papers. I've been trying to reach you for days.'

'What exactly are we talking about?'

'Raymond Blackstone. He was stabbed in back of a massage parlor. I was thinking that if you hadn't heard about it in any other way, she might have been in touch.'

'Not with me,' Chance said, uncertain as to why he was continuing to lie. There was no real reason for it. He might so easily be found out. Guilt's a funny thing, he concluded. It leads to ever more guilt. 'What about you?' he asked.

'Not a word.'

'What's the prognosis? Will he live?'

'Sadly yes. I suppose that's terrible to say.'

'An understandable sentiment. Anything about who did it?'

'Nothing in what I've seen.'

'And no leads?'

'Not that they're sharing. Why? What are you thinking?'

'Nothing,' Chance said. 'Not a thing. Just curious.'

'Well…' Janice said after a somewhat lengthy pause. 'Now you know at least. You may hear from her yet.'

'It's possible. If so I will keep you posted.'

'Please do,' Janice said. 'I know we've gone round some about her, but I'd like to know what happens. My offer to help locate someone willing to take her on still stands.'

Chance thanked her, extricated the Oldsmobile from his garage, and drove straightway to the old warehouse, as had been his intent on rising. Raymond Blackstone had said that he was going to handle things, that he knew what to do. Chance had yet to pass this on to Big D and in this he was no doubt remiss. It seemed to him quite possible that Blackstone's words were no more than bluff meant to rattle her cage. It seemed equally possible that sloth and poor judgment had already made him late for the dance. It was then, to his great dismay, that he arrived to find the place in an uncharacteristic state of disarray.

The front door was open to the sidewalk as usual but something was off. He sensed it walking in, even before finding Carl at the rear of the building where the door to D's quarters had been left ajar and the normally implacable old man pacing to and fro before it as if searching for something he'd lost. The old man looked as if he had not slept at any point in the recent past or if he had it was in the clothes he was wearing. There was gray stubble upon his cheeks, a haunted look in his deep-set black eyes. The nearby desk, normally so neat in its arrangement, was littered with paperwork. Peering through the doorway to D's room, Chance could see that one of the Eames chairs had been overturned. The bed was unmade and a number of books lay strewn across the floor. Even more disturbing was the plastic pill bottle at the foot of the bed, its cap fallen away, its contents scattered. 'My God,' Chance said, the starch draining from his legs. The old man himself appeared to sway, as though about to lose balance.

Chance led him to a chair from which Carl sat looking up, as might some cornered animal facing certain death. 'Where have you been?' he asked. The old man's voice was thin and wavering.

'Yes… I know, I'm sorry. I've been out of touch…'

'I tried calling.'

To which Chance could only nod. First the deposition, then Jaclyn, then sleep, his cell off the entire time. He could see how it had been.

'He's in the hospital. There was some kind of seizure…'

'The diabetes.'

Carl looked to the room. 'He was in there when I came. I always hear him at work on something.' The old man paused, seeking to control his voice, fighting off tears. 'If there's no work to be done for the studio, he'll be at work on his blades or his tomahawks. He doesn't sleep, you know. I've tried to tell him that's not good.' He looked to Chance. 'Why, each day they find out something new about how much we need sleep to stay healthy. You're not a superman, I tell him.' He paused once more to shake his head. 'He thinks he is you know. It's what he thinks. It's what he *had* to think, I suppose, when you stop to consider it.'

Chance was not altogether clear about what exactly he was being asked to consider but the old man went on without waiting comment. 'In the morning though… when I came in… I couldn't hear a thing. I gave it just a bit then knocked. Nothing, so I went inside. I found him on that bed in there but he was lying in a strange way and one arm was hanging off and on the floor…' The old man's voice cracked. He sought once more to collect himself. 'I couldn't get him to wake up,' he said. 'He was turning blue. I called the emergency.'

Fearing some impending medical crisis of his own, Chance found support upon the edge of the cluttered desk. He was very clear about what had happened. Having bested the massage parlor muscle and Detective Blackstone, having survived a stun gun, pepper spray, and a car accident, the big man had been undone by the great ice-cream hunt. 'What was his condition?' Chance asked. 'When the paramedics left with him, I mean. Was he awake?'

The old man moved his head. 'They took blood...'

'They would have to see if the coma was hypoglycemic or hyperglycemic. Did they give him a shot of something?'

'The needle was grotesque.'

'Hyperglycemic would be my guess. He was moving, though? Lucid at all?'

'I don't know,' Carl said. 'It was hard for me to see but they were talking to him when they carried him out.'

'That's good,' Chance said. 'Means the drug was working, that it hadn't been too long. Sounds to me as if it was a very good thing that you found him when you did.' He could see that the old man was verging once more on tears. 'I almost didn't,' Carl said. 'He likes his doughnuts in the mornings. Normally I bring some in from Bob's but the car was low on gas and I came straight here.' He wiped at an eye with the heel of his hand and shook his head. 'I've told him he ought to cut back. He doesn't always listen.'

'No,' Chance said. He was thinking of D's theory on the medicinal uses of salt. 'And that would have been what, two mornings ago?... Do you know where they've taken him?' He was surprised to find that the old man did not, which fact seemed only to distress him further. 'That's okay,' Chance said. 'I'll make some calls. Shouldn't be too hard to find out. My car is on the street. We'll go together, see how he's doing.'

Carl remained as he was.

'We've every reason to hope,' Chance said. 'What you've told me so far sounds promising. So long as there was no damage to the heart.' He took his cell phone from his pocket. 'I'm sure it's UCSF but we can call on the way. I know a good many of the doctors and nurses on staff.' He was already turning for the door but Carl seemed intent on holding his ground, the look of the cornered animal returning to his face. 'Is there a problem?' Chance asked.

'Certainly not on *my* end,' Carl told him, the sudden victim of as yet unspecified crimes.

Chance just looked at him. Carl exacted a wait. 'I am assuming *they* will be there,' he said at last.

'They?' Chance asked.

He had been envisioning the city's finest, the flash of golden shields amid a sea of blue but the old man was quick to set him straight. 'What passes for the poor boy's family,' he said, his voice having steadied to the point that he was able at last to abandon panic in favor of moral outrage. 'Monsters,' he added by way of clarification. 'Absolute monsters. More than one of them in one place at one time and it's a regular monster's ball.' He drew himself to his full height and took the measure of Chance by looking him squarely in the eye. 'And of course, they do *not,* as you might imagine, approve of yours truly. You'll have to go it alone.'

Darius the Mede

CHANCE WAS back outside and about to enter his car when the day's most striking omission occurred to him. So accustomed had he become to thinking of D as D, or Big D, or on occasion as Heavy D, it had, till just now, never occurred to him that even after all they had been through together, he did not actually *know* Big D's proper name, neither his first nor his last, salient information if he were to inquire after the big man's health and whereabouts from what might only be thought of as the *proper authorities*, an outfit from whom he had, over the course of the past weeks, become increasingly distant.

That the name could surprise should not, given every other thing, have really been all that surprising and yet Chance was surprised. 'Darius?' he asked. He was standing once more at the door of the warehouse where Carl had come to see him off. 'As in Darius the Mede?'

'As in,' Carl told him. 'The old man was some sort of college professor. Still is as far as I know. Darius Pringle. God knows best what that asshole was thinking.'

* * *

Darius Pringle had indeed been taken to Moffitt hospital at the UCSF medical center high atop Parnassus Avenue, a place in which Dr Eldon Chance was still listed as an associate clinical professor in the Department of Psychiatry at the UCSF School of Medicine. It was moreover a place in which he was still a respected member of the community and was greeted as such, admitted to staff parking even on the day in question where he donned the white lab coat with his name pinned to the breast, kept in the trunk of his car for just such moments, and where once inside he was greeted by several of the nurses and one young doctor in particular whose name he had long since forgotten but who had carried out a residency beneath his direction. He was greeted as Dr Chance and it occurred to him that it had been some time since so many had done so in such an agreeable fashion. Patients were encouraged to use his first name in the hopes of putting them at ease. Attorneys addressed him as Doctor but often managed to make it sound somehow slightly derogatory. These folk actually seemed to like and respect him. He might have wandered the halls for hours basking in such warmth, searching perhaps for the young man of promise it pleased him to believe he once had been, as if such a thing were no more than a valued but misplaced object. Little of course did any of his well-wishers know about why he was here just now or from whence he had come, of his walking about in the world, his going to and fro.

Having learned by phone of D's recent transfer from an ICU to a standard room, Chance went straightaway to the head nurse on the appropriate floor, a large-boned gray-haired woman of Irish descent with the unfortunate name of Gooley, who had worked at the hospital for many years, even before Chance's arrival, and with whom he was still on a first-name basis.

'And who are we here to see today?' she asked, as if Chance at her station were a more or less daily occurrence, though in point of fact he had not been there in months. He gave her the name and was rewarded with a chart. He read it with Gooley looking over his shoulder. It was as he had surmised. It was also worse than he had surmised with diabetes type 2 mellitus in concert with obesity, obstructive sleep apnea (severe), diabetic peripheral neuropathy (mild), and a mitral valve prolapse. A brief history indicated the patient had sustained a traumatic head injury and coma as a child as well as a compound fracture of the right femur and two other surgeries, also as a child. Much more was to come but this was what Chance saw at a glance, on the face page of the report. Current medications included Cymbalta, Valium, Provigil, Metformin, and Nexium.

'Is the gentleman a patient?' Gooley asked.

'I'm intending to see that he becomes one,' Chance told her, still aghast by what he was reading but trying not to let it show, then later in response to her look. 'The gentleman has done some work for me of late and I've come to think of him as a friend.'

'Well,' she said. 'The story is in the history on that one.'

Chance just looked at her.

'Someone asked for his records. I got a look.'

'From where?'

'Fort Miley and Napa State, to name two.'

Fort Miley was home to the San Francisco VA Hospital. Napa State was an exclusively inpatient mental health facility for the often criminally insane and did not qualify as good news. Chance hoped once more to disguise a level of apprehension bordering on out and out panic with what he hoped might be taken for a knowing nod. 'The patient was lucid then?' By which he meant to suggest that D had been responsive to questioning on the part of the ER doctors.

'I wouldn't know about that,' Gooley told him. 'The man's family has been in and out. It may have been them that asked for records to be forwarded. He's apparently been out of touch for some time and the old man is some mucky-muck from across the bay… is what I have been told.'

'What kind of mucky-muck?' Chance asked.

'UC–Berkeley, Livermore Lab… I believe he's a nuclear man, a physicist or something.'

'Ah,' Chance said. It was what he said when he couldn't think of anything more intelligent to say. He was saying it more of late and the habit was coming to irritate him. 'I'd like to take a look at all of that,' he told her. 'The medical history.' It was not strictly kosher, his asking to see records without first getting permission from either the attending physician or the patient himself but he and Gooley were close enough for him to ask and for her to deliver. 'Stop back when you're done,' she told him. 'I'll make you a copy. You just didn't get it from me.'

'Of course not. And are they still here, Mr Pringle's family?'

'Oh I think so, some of them anyway. Like I said, there have been comings and goings. You should have seen it on day one. It was like Grand Central Station around here.'

'Well,' Chance told her, 'you're used to that.'

Gooley nodded. 'You'll want a look at those records,' she told him. 'I've a feeling that's a young man who could use someone good on his side.' And couldn't we all, Chance thought, but remained silent on that score. For the day having scarcely begun was full already of such ominous tidings that in walking off down the long hallway with its disinfectant smells, polished floors, and open doorways he was certain beyond doubt that everything he had played at over the span of the past weeks was about to be found out on a grand scale, revealed for what it was and broken, a toy boat upon the rocks of an unyielding and pitiless reality.

And that was only the half of it. For the reality in question would surely prove so obvious, so absolutely visible even to the untrained eye, his missing it so far beyond the reach of reasonable explanation, that there would simply be no point in trying, and that the rest of his days, if not spent behind bars, would surely run their course in the engagement of some menial task, a meager salary garnered till time indefinite by some stern and unforgiving agent of a vast, impersonal, and criminally inept federal tax agency. So that finally it was the ghost of his own broken and long-suffering father who came in the end to provide company, if not succor, upon the occasion of his only son's ascent to the gallows, walking with him along these dark and gleaming halls with their bright lights and fecund odors, their open doorways that were each a little window upon the varieties of such shit as the world was composed and the old man just as Chance remembered him, stoop shouldered and silver haired, his voice low in Chance's ear. 'You can see how it is,' the old man told him in a familiar and authoritative tone, equal parts sadness and scorn. 'If He'd wanted you to fly He would have given you wings.'

He found the monster's ball Carl Allan had predicted a sorry enough affair. The illustrious father, having been last seen in person during the wee hours to further consult with staff, doctors, and assorted hospital officials, had since withdrawn to some stronghold across the bay. In the great man's absence, Chance was confronted by a faded beauty of indiscernible age, the obvious recipient of considerable surgical work. Her name was Norma Pringle and she lost no time in letting Chance know that the whale of a man now beached in the nearby bed was not of her loins but rather those of her husband, a fact in which she seemed to take such particular satisfaction Chance found it to border on the openly malicious.

There was a second man in the room as well, a rather listless youth of perhaps twenty with a style of dress and hair Chance had come to associate with the Goth movement of years past but which he was later informed had morphed into something new, its current name forever eluding him. As to the young man's identity, no mention was made. The youth did not rise to meet him or make any show of wishing to do so. Norma ignored him. Chance followed suit. There were no doctors present. Chance had hoped for a moment alone with D but saw rather quickly that this was not to be. It seemed to have something to do with the fact that, name badge and doctor's coat notwithstanding, he had yet to be properly vetted by the absent father, who to all intents and purposes had apparently taken over the show and was now running it from somewhere in the vicinity of the Lawrence Livermore Laboratory well east of the city.

'And you are?' was the question Norma seemed to have fixed upon with regard to Chance. It seemed to come at him from a variety of angles, sometimes prefaced by an overtly insincere and condescending apology for having already forgotten his previous answer to the same question. She couldn't get past it. Nor could he. A friend of a friend, a business associate, a concerned acquaintance – he tried them all and in various combinations till he'd pretty much exhausted the mathematical possibilities. 'But *not* one of his actual doctors?' was more or less the inevitable response. One might have thought the simple fact of his being both friend *and* an actual doctor would have been enough to tip the scales. It had been his experience that most people in the midst of crisis, the health of a loved one hanging in the balance, would have welcomed such personal and professional attention with open arms. Norma Pringle's arms were closed to any such business.

As for the big man himself, D appeared to have passed into a profound, possibly drug-induced sleep. He remained during the length and breadth of Chance's stay in his room inert and immobile on the bed, the recipient of an IV drip, attached to several monitoring devices including the black rubber mask covering much of his face for the purpose of forcing oxygen into his lungs, a countermeasure to the obstructive apnea Chance had noted upon the charts, and from which small lights would occasionally wink in the accompaniment of a faint mechanical whir and this the only sound in the room as Norma Pringle was an icy woman of few words and her gloomy companion one of even fewer, which pretty much meant none at all.

As to whether or not D's unconscious state was authentic or feigned, Chance could never get close enough to say. The determined and not unimpressive Mrs Pringle would not permit it. Chance was not on D's list of approved doctors. Her husband could not be reached for comment and she was intent on following his orders. It was as simple and as simply fucked up as all of that. And while this might change in time it was clearly not going to be without a fight and not anytime soon, leaving Chance few options save the tactical retreat, in the midst of which he paused just long enough at Gooley's nursing station to collect Big D's medical records before exiting the building. To his great dismay, if not surprise, he found the document only slightly smaller than a city directory.

He had at it while still in the building's underground parking lot, at times resting the pages against the car's steering wheel if only to steady his hand. To have done the document justice were he being called upon to render an opinion would have required hours and he supposed that in time he might get there on his own. For the moment, however, he was willing to settle for what one might euphemistically term the highlights and which might be summarized as follows, in the manner to which he had become accustomed, which is to say in the manner of his own reports:

Darius Pringle is a 32-year-old left-handed white male. He was born the younger of two children, having a brother three years his senior. His father is a PhD theoretical physicist. His mother, now deceased, was a classical violinist who toured and recorded extensively in both Europe and the United States. At the age of eight, Darius, along with his mother and older brother, was struck by a drunk driver while walking in a crosswalk in downtown San Francisco. His mother and brother died instantly. Darius sustained a coma lasting twelve days along with a compound fracture of his right femur. CT scans performed at that time reported a right frontal subdural hematoma. The patient spent a total of four weeks at San Francisco General Hospital. Upon release from the hospital, Darius was sent to live with his paternal grandmother, Ruth Morris, a retired English teacher, at that time, married to one James Morris, her third husband, a lay minister in the Church of the Infant Jesus. The reason for this living arrangement had to do with the devastating effect the loss of his wife and eldest son had on Sanford Pringle, Darius's father, who, unable to cope, left the country with no clear plans for returning and felt himself either unable, or unwilling, to see his surviving son.

Mrs Morris reports that from the time of Darius's release from the hospital, it was as if she and her husband had to 'raise him from infancy.' Specifically, he was unable to feed himself. His leg was in a cast. Poor balance made it necessary for him to wear a protective helmet. After several months with a cast, he began to walk with crutches and, very slowly, to recover a good deal of his memory and language function. It was around this time that James Morris brought two sons from a former marriage to live with their family in Oakland. It was shortly thereafter that Paul, the elder of James Morris's two sons, began to torture and sexually abuse Darius. The abuse continued for a period of roughly five years, at which point Sanford Pringle returned from abroad in the company of his new wife, Norma, twenty years his junior. At that time Darius was brought back into his father's home, though he continued to spend long stretches in the home of his grandmother whenever Sanford and Norma were out of town. During these stays, Darius stated, the abuse continued. He has further stated that his grandmother knew of the abuse but told Darius never to speak of it and would on occasion punish him by whipping and then binding him with electrical cords and locking him in a closet.

Darius reports that his father was kind to him on the rare occasions when they were together but was extremely preoccupied with both his career and his new family, Norma by now having given birth to a boy. On the single occasion when Darius tried to talk to his father about what happened it was 'as if his father was simply looking through him and was unable to hear a word that was said.' Afterward, his father continued to leave Darius at the home of his mother whenever he was out of town, often in the company of Norma and their new son.

By the age of fifteen Darius had begun to exhibit periods of what appeared to be mood disturbance with intermittent psychotic behavior. He also became preoccupied with books on warfare, the study of martial arts, and in particular a book entitled Unlocking Your Hidden Powers. *On several occasions, when left at his grandmother's house he became violent, to the point that on two separate occasions Ruth felt threatened enough to make 911 calls to the police. This behavior culminated with the beating of James Morris. Mr Morris was kept overnight in an Oakland hospital for observation in the wake of a concussion. He was also treated for a broken nose, four broken ribs, and a broken finger on his right hand. Darius was taken into custody by the Oakland Police and later transferred to the state mental hospital in Napa, where he remained for a period of three months, at the end of which he was released into his father's custody with plans for anger management classes and psychiatric treatment.*

None of these treatments were implemented, however, as within days of his returning home, Darius ran away. He was at this time sixteen years of age. For the next three years Darius lived on the streets, first in Oakland, where he found that he was able to make money as a 'street enforcer' for an Oakland crack dealer, and later in Palo Alto, where he was befriended by a number of returning military personnel. Many of these men were veterans of the wars in Iraq and Afghanistan. Some were themselves homeless. Others were in some way connected to the VA hospital in Palo Alto. A number of these men were addicted to drugs that Darius was able to procure through his connections with Oakland dealers.

It was during this period that Darius also began to use a wide variety of drugs, to the point that they, in his words, became a problem. He eventually attempted to find help from the VA hospital in San Francisco where, having managed to procure a fake military identification card, he was admitted by emergency services and was treated for

*chronic polysubstance abuse and intermittent psychotic
ideation and behavior before the ruse was discovered. He
was then turned over to the police, who contacted his family.*

   *Darius was transferred once more to the state mental
hospital in Napa and later to a privately owned institution
in Marin County, where, according to Darius, his father
moved to take complete control of his life. Exactly what is
meant by this phrase is unclear. Darius was by now nineteen
and therefore legally an adult. Darius states that he was kept
in a drugged state and asked to sign many legal documents.
Details relating to all of this are a bit sketchy and without
knowing more it is impossible to say what was entailed.
It may be that the elder Pringle was moving to excise his
son from any type of inheritance. It may also be, as Darius
has later speculated, that his father was attempting to get
Darius to agree to some type of permanent conservatorship
of person and estate, but this is speculative. Darius has said
that he signed some documents while refusing others and
that after a period of several weeks in this institution he was
able one day to simply 'walk out of the gate.' The particulars
of this remain unknown. What is known is that Darius
disappeared once more, eluding any and all attempts on
the part of the family to locate him until his present arrival
at the UCSF emergency room.*

It was here that Chance broke from his assimilation of the
report's biggest hits, resting the stack of pages on the seat
beside him. Was it his imagination, or did the fabric give
beneath the terrible weight of the thing? He was still in the
hospital parking structure and so able to watch an elderly
couple attempting to extract a morbidly obese blind woman
of no more than thirty from the rear of a badly oxidized
Dodge minivan. Through an aperture created by a break
between the great concrete platforms of which the structure
was formed he was treated to a brilliant sliver of sky across
which a number of frantic crows flew in pursuit of a lone
red-tailed hawk as from somewhere in the building a car

alarm began to sound. My God, thought Chance – and he was thinking now of one Darius Pringle, a.k.a. D, a.k.a. Big D, a.k.a. Heavy D – he's one of my very own.

Jane's addiction

HE WAS back at Allan's Antiques within the hour, having done little more than follow the car's hood ornament, the lumbering beast apparently knowing the way. All things considered, it was probably not the best of ideas. If one was looking for a level head in the midst of catastrophic decline, then Carl Allan was hardly your man. What the brief visit produced were complementary forms of paranoid ideation lapping up against one another like wavelets on a stony shore, each feeding off the intensity of the other.

'It's like the Kennedys,' the old man kept saying. 'They had that poor girl lobotomized.'

'Much more difficult to bring that off these days,' Chance assured him, the old practitioners having vanished into the mists of legend. He was thinking primarily of Walter J. Freeman, the last of the cowboy lobotomists. It was also true that a new crop of psychosurgeons many times more sophisticated were gathering in the wings but he kept this to himself.

It hardly mattered. Carl went right on as if Chance hadn't spoken. 'It was all because she liked to fuck black jazz musicians,' he said.

'I think we're safe on that score.'

'Speak for yourself on that score,' Carl told him. 'And you don't know the family.'

'Right,' Chance said. 'But I *have* seen his medical history. And I met some of them today, at the hospital.'

'Hovering like carrion fowl?'

'Hovering at least.' He was trying to imagine how best to

articulate his impressions of Norma Pringle and her strange son. In the end, he gave up, stating rather simply that it was the mother and some kid.

'Some kid indeed. Happy to see you, were they?'

'Not the first word that comes to mind.'

'Listen,' Carl said. He put a hand on Chance's arm. 'They'll try to pull something. They'll have him put away. We'll never see him again.' The old man's eyes were tearing up, his grip tightening.

'They can't,' Chance said. 'He's an adult.'

'What if they drug him, get him to sign something?'

'He can argue he was drugged.'

The old man appeared unconvinced. Chance sighed and tried again. 'It is almost impossible,' he said, as deliberately as he was able, 'in this day and age, to gain that kind of conservatorship over someone against his or her will…'

'You don't know the father. He's a wealthy and powerful man with friends in high places. And he hates his son.'

'That may be, but disinheriting him is one thing, putting him away is another.'

'You're a gift from the Almighty,' Carl said suddenly, his voice filled with conviction.

'I wouldn't know about that,' Chance said.

'Nonsense. You're a doctor. You know how the game is played. Imagine if it were just he and I.'

Chance was a moment in imagining it, Carl and D. Could it be they were actually a couple? Or was it simply that D was the son Carl never had and the reverse true for Heavy D? Could it possibly matter? Live and let live would be Chance's position, though he remained for a moment or two in the grip of the situation's seemingly limitless permutations, it being his experience that few things in the realm of human interaction ever qualified as simple.

'Hates him for what *he* did to him,' Carl said.

Chance took him as once more on the subject of D's father. 'Yes, or hates himself for having *allowed* it.'

'But takes it out on D either way.'

'Maybe, but I really don't think the old man is what we have to worry about just now.'

Carl lifted a brow.

'It's this business in Oakland,' Chance said. 'He didn't tell you?'

'He was out cold when I found him.'

'Right.'

'There was a hiccup, then, east of the bay?'

'One might say.' He proceeded to bring the old man up to speed on the exact nature and proportions of the hiccup in question. Carl received the news with a surprising measure of his old equanimity. 'You're worried that his being in some form of custody... he might be linked to events in the East Bay.'

'I'm worried the massage parlor may have surveillance cameras. I'm worried about digital images. There just aren't that many that would fit the description, if you catch my drift.'

Carl did and they stood with that. On a nearby stoop an emaciated woman of indeterminate age was attempting unsuccessfully to right herself.

'*Well,*' Carl said finally, 'I suppose if you're going to go *there*... there are any number of things he is in danger of being found out about.'

As to what exactly this might mean, Chance was not in a hurry to know. Nor did he feel inclined to comment on what Jaclyn had said, about how Blackstone was going to handle things himself. The old man had his hands full imagining dire moves on the part of D's family and Chance saw no point in burdening him further. This last was his to bear and bear it he did, in the dark confines of his apartment, in the still dark of one more not yet dawn as the din of the streets faded and the distant drumroll of the Ocean Beach surf rose to take its place. The old man had his worries. Chance had his.

There was, however, a place where Carl's fears of familial

machinations bumped up against the business in Oakland and before long he'd managed to find it. If someone were to tie D to the Oakland murder, and if what Carl believed was true, that the good professor really *did* want to put his son away, then possibly, if you wanted to get really paranoid about it, and why wouldn't you, to undermine any such charges as D might one day bring for child abuse and parental neglect… then D as a convicted killer might serve and a permanent home in the Napa State Hospital for the Criminally Insane not so far beyond the pale as Chance had at first surmised. And how then the clock did tick, with Blackstone convalescing, not only expected to recover but with minions to aid his revenge. To wait on him was to be again the receiver and it was not just Chance at risk, it was D and Carl and Jaclyn and maybe even his own daughter, and it was up to him to think for them all.

It was to this end that he took D's thumb drive from the dresser drawer where he'd hidden it away beneath his socks and looked at it for the first time since the night of its acquisition. In saying that he looked at it, it should be stipulated that the drive was not yet *in* his computer. He was not looking at its contents but rather at the drive itself, an absurdly small device when viewed in consideration of all that it had cost, a pale plastic obelisk, a retractable plug at one end, a tiny silver ring at the other.

The thought occurred while sitting there, the device in hand, the overwhelming desire really… that it might be good to speak with *her,* for any number of reasons, and he called her cell and it really was the first time he had done so since their night together, only to be greeted by a recorded message informing him that the number was no longer in service, a crushing enough turn though not entirely unexpected for reasons he thought it best not to dwell on at length. It was perhaps his desire to avoid doing just that which prompted at last the lifting of his own computer from its case, his opening it upon his kitchen table, his inserting of the device.

But even then he did not begin to read or even to open the files. Given the recent slant of things, who could say that by doing so he would not inadvertently send up a flare or some other thoroughly unexpected and fucked-up thing? Add to this the question of what he actually hoped to find. Incriminating data? Really? The guy was supposed to be smart for Christ's sake and the more Chance thought about it all, the more absurd it all became, yet more evidence of his own unsound judgment, as if further evidence were required.

Suffice it to say that a kind of paralysis set in. Time passed. Somewhere near dawn, however, a renewed sense of purpose fueled by a cheap cabernet having trumped inertia, Chance sat finally looking into the work of Raymond Blackstone himself, the man in his own words, in black and white.

Sirens had thus far not gone off. There were no red lights from the street or footsteps upon his stairs. In the downstairs apartment the programmer and his invisible lady friend had begun to fight. This was not unexpected. What *was* unexpected was the sense of intimacy the files provoked. They consisted almost entirely of reports, that is reports on crimes the detective had or was investigating and were in their way not unlike Chance's own reports, for he found in them the trajectories of the utterly clueless, the flat-out unlucky, and hopelessly fucked up.

There was the eighteen-year-old drug addict who kills a friend over a stolen sound system in a moment of drug-addled rage, is afterward unable to remember the incident but charged nonetheless with home invasion, armed robbery, and murder, charges which, if successfully prosecuted, and why wouldn't they be given the boy's certain reliance on public defenders, are bound to carry with them a mandatory sentence of life in prison. There was the troop of homeless heroin addicts who buried one of their own, dead from an overdose, then got to thinking about what they had done. Sensing a missed opportunity, they exhumed the body, removed the head with a tree saw stolen from a local Home Depot, and attempted to sell it to a number of equally homeless Satanists for thirty dollars. The Satanists were keen on the head but short on cash. A terrible fight ensued. There were injuries and one fatality when one of the head peddlers was stabbed through the eye with a screwdriver. The perpetrator of the crime, a twenty-seven-year-old homeless veteran of the war in Iraq, was now in custody.

It was the kind of stuff you couldn't make up and yet it was everywhere in every turning of the world and Raymond Blackstone had borne witness. And so had Chance. Their combined reports spoke to the absolute absurdity and utter frailty of things, to the shining truth that lay beneath what they were trying to sell and he wondered if the detective had ever been worn down by it or had wanted in some way of his own to strike through, to break free, to go under that he might rise above, before time and circumstance came for him as they will come for us all, never guessing, as people never do, that in a darkened alley behind the European Massage Parlor, yet one more of the walking wounded, skilled beyond reckoning in the art of the blade, was waiting to say hello.

It was not long upon the heels of this particular revelation, time-worn as it might appear, that he came upon the file that would claim his imagination in ways the others had not. The file detailed an investigation, or at least the beginning of one, into the death of a certain Gayland Parks:

... *Gayland Parks was found murdered inside of his condominium in a high-rise building overlooking the harbor in the city of Oakland. I, along with Homicide Team 1, responded to investigate the incident...*

There were a number of things about the case. The first was the date. While the other reports were more or less current, this was several years old. The file was incomplete in that there was a beginning but no apparent end. More current reports either were works in progress or were accompanied by arrest records and so told a little story complete with endings in which perpetrators were brought to justice, or at least to trial. In the Parks case there were but three interviews with two individuals of interest and that was it. There was no record of what would seem the obvious next step and no records of any arrests.

And then there was the case itself. Gayland Parks was a retired psychoanalyst from San Diego who, until the time of his murder, had been living in Oakland, where he'd opened a practice as a life coach. He died in the nude, handcuffed to his bed, shot full of heroin, and finally bludgeoned to death with a glass dildo that was found nearby. Clearly, Chance thought, it was a case possessed of all the right ingredients. How could a man in his own circumstances fail to relate? But that was only the beginning.

During the investigation of the above-listed crime, we discovered the decedent had a cellular phone that was believed to be missing or taken during the murder.

Parks's cellular phone number was determined to be an Oakland number. Detective Cesar Lopez researched the phone and discovered that calls were still being made on Parks's phone. I reviewed phone records and noticed that on May 8th six calls were made to another cellular phone and that this was a number with a San Diego prefix. Also, a phone call was made on the same date to a second San Diego number. Detective Lopez obtained warrants for both telephone numbers. The first number belonged to T-Mobile cellular service and the subscriber was described as Mari Hammond.

The second number was a Pacific Bell Telephone Company number belonging to the residence of Mari and Woody Hammond, located at 1345 Sixth Street in the city of Normal Heights, California.

Based on the numerous calls made to Mari Hammond's

cell phone and residence, it was believed Mr and Mrs Hammond were possibly involved in the crime or knew the person using the decedent's cell phone.

Using various Police Department computer systems, I conducted a records check on the Hammonds and their residences. I discovered the Hammonds did have contacts at 350 Green Street in San Diego. Furthermore, I noticed on one of the contacts that Mari Hammond worked for the Sunrise Travel Agency in San Diego, located at 3535 Camino de los Mares, Suite 400, in the city of San Diego where she was employed as a travel agent.

Further records checks of Mari Hammond revealed that she had recently received a traffic ticket. The ticket was issued by the San Diego Police Department. I noticed that Hammond was driving a ten-year-old tan Honda Civic. I believed this was possibly Mari Hammond's vehicle.

Detective Lopez and I obtained permission to travel to San Diego to investigate the Hammonds and their possible involvement in the murder of Gayland Parks. We left the following morning.

On that same afternoon I drove to 3535 Camino de los Mares to look for Hammond's vehicle. Parked in front of the building I noticed a tan Honda Civic. License plates revealed it to be Hammond's vehicle.

At 1600 hours I walked up to the Sunrise Travel Agency building located at 3535 Camino de los Mares, Suite 400. I asked the receptionist if Mari Hammond worked in the office. The receptionist told me Mari Hammond did, in fact, work in the office, and walked me to Mari Hammond's desk.

At approximately 1620 hours, I met Mari Hammond at her desk. I identified myself as an Oakland police officer and asked Hammond if I could speak with her. Hammond told me that she was just shutting down her computer and getting off of work. Hammond and I then stepped outside and spoke.

I explained to Mari Hammond that I needed to talk to

*her in reference to a homicide case. I asked Hammond if she
would voluntarily come to the police station and talk with
me. Hammond explained to me that she had to pick up
her three-year-old daughter at the day care center located
in Normal Heights. Mari Hammond told me that she had
no other family members or friends who could watch her
daughter. I asked Hammond if she would be willing to come
to the San Diego police station with her daughter after she
picked her up. Hammond and I agreed that I would follow
her to the day care center located at the intersection of
Blake and Ward streets in Normal Heights and then go to
the police station.*

*I followed Mari Hammond to Normal Heights, where she
picked up her daughter, Julie, at the day care. I then asked
Hammond if she and her daughter wished to eat prior
to going to the station. Mari told me that she had eaten
something at work but that her daughter had not eaten.
Hammond also stated that she did not have any money
to buy dinner. I provided Hammond with a twenty-dollar
bill and told her she could buy her daughter something to
eat on her way to the station. Hammond then drove to a
Burger King and bought her daughter dinner. Hammond
then followed me to headquarters.*

It was here Chance stopped short, as if by a shadow fallen
across the room, a sudden felt presence as palpable as his
own, that of Raymond Blackstone, the injured detective: 'I
provided Hammond with a twenty-dollar bill and told her
she could buy her daughter something to eat.'

The woman said she'd eaten, and yet without ever having
met her or been present at the time, Chance had the distinct
impression that this was a lie, and that, what was more, it was
an impression that Blackstone must have shared. She wanted
food for her daughter but Blackstone gave her a twenty, more
than enough for them both if the destination was to be a
Burger King. Now there might of course have been some
ulterior 'motus' in the detective's actions. One could always

hope for an ulterior 'motus.' It was Doc Billy's word but Chance had grown fond of using it at every available opportunity. Maybe this Mari had been a babe. Maybe Blackstone had been looking to score. The weird thing was, he couldn't quite get there. His head suggested the possibility. His gut held out for a different reading, the one in which she really was just a single mom down on her luck and the detective really was looking out for her just a little because... Well, because in the end, he was pretty much just like every other fucked-up specimen on the planet and there really were marks on both sides of the ledger – a discouraging enough proposition for a man in Chance's position.

The pursuit of Gayland Parks's assailant of course continued, Chance's reservations and Blackstone's humanity notwithstanding. Mari Hammond had stated that she had no idea who might have called either one of her two lines on a dead man's phone and that the name Gayland Parks did not ring a bell. She did, however, go on to state that while both lines were in her name, one line was used exclusively by her brother, a disabled veteran who also lived with her from time to time and might well have taken calls on one or both lines. Her brother's name was Woody Hammond. Woody, several years older than Mari, had served in the military at the time of the Gulf War and had not come whole from the experience. He had suffered serious burns over a good portion of his body, including his face. He suffered as well from long-standing post-traumatic stress disorder that he had sought to alleviate with alcohol and drugs. He was, however, and this according to his sister, now clean and sober, spending at least half his time in his own apartment, and had gone back to school in hopes of becoming a drug counselor. He received disability checks each month from the federal government. Detective Blackstone had gone in search of him.

On June 1, at approximately 1600 hours, I went to 320 Ocean Street in San Diego to locate Woody Hammond. I contacted the apartment manager for 320 Ocean Street. The apartment manager confirmed to me that Woody Hammond lived alone in apartment #6 and that he had seen Woody Hammond approximately two hours earlier. The apartment manager told me Woody Hammond was driving a green Ford Explorer and that Hammond was in parking space #6.

I located parking space #6 and saw a green Ford Explorer. I positioned myself in the parking lot, where I could surveil the vehicle.

At approximately 1645 hours, Woody Hammond got into the vehicle and left the apartment complex. I followed Hammond. Hammond drove to Northwestern College in San Diego. Hammond parked his vehicle and walked to the college campus. I continued to follow Hammond into the college to building #300.

Hammond turned around, looked at me, and greeted me. I could see at once the burn scars across much of his face that his sister had alluded to. Hammond told me he received a telephone call from his landlord telling him that a detective had been to the building to ask about him. I told Hammond that I was a detective with the Oakland Police Department. Hammond immediately told me the only 'bad' thing he does is meet with prostitutes in Tijuana, Mexico, and that it is the only bad thing he does. He told me he did not know why a homicide detective would want to talk to him.

I explained to Hammond that I wanted to question him at the headquarters of the San Diego Police Department and that I felt the college was not the appropriate place for an interview. I asked Hammond if he would voluntarily go to the SDPD headquarters building for an interview. Hammond told me he would. Hammond also told me he had no problem with taking a polygraph exam and that I could search his vehicle if I wanted.

At approximately 1830 hours Detective Lopez and I interviewed Hammond inside the SDPD Homicide *interview room. The described interview was video and audio recorded. This report is not intended to be a verbatim representation of his statement. This is an 'in essence' report.*

Detective Lopez explained to Hammond that he was not under arrest and was free to leave at any time. Paraphrasing, the following represents Hammond's statement in response to questions Detective Lopez and I asked him.

'I like Mexico. I go to Mexico once a week, sometimes more. I like to go to the racetrack at Agua Caliente and to the offtrack betting. I like going in the daytime because it is not so crowded. I go during the week. Sometimes I go to the red light district. I go to the Zona Norte. I go to The Alley in the red light district. The Alley is a club in the Zona Norte. I like The Alley because it seems clean and it is not too expensive.

'About six months ago, I met a girl in Tijuana. Her name is Jane. I met her in front of The Alley but, to be honest, I am not even sure if that was where she worked or not. I have been going to Tijuana for several years and had never seen her there before till that point. Her complexion is very fair. I always assumed that she was of mixed blood. We had drinks there once or twice but usually we would walk back across the border and go to my apartment. She had some kind of work visa and her English was better than mine. It has been a while since she called me, about a month. She would call me just to be friends. I have her phone number in my cell phone. Jane was nice. Some of the girls don't like to go with me so much, because of the scars. But this Jane didn't care about that. She was different from the other women I had met there. She is educated. She told me she was a teacher. I assumed she taught English in Mexico. But then once, when I was having trouble with this algebra class I had to pass for one of my breadth requirements, she helped with all of my math homework, to the point that I received an A-plus in the class.'

It began to blur a bit after that. The night ran to cold sweats and spasms, moments of lucidity bordering on the hallucinatory. Chance read on.

... I would pay her for sex and then a little more for helping me with my homework. I think it was about fifty dollars... for both things... She said she was doing what she was doing because she needed money to leave the country... She's strung out on heroin... She has a daughter who lives with her mother in Ensenada... She is about thirty years old... She is about 5'6"... She has light hair... and light-colored eyes... she has a nice figure... The last night that I saw her... we met at The Sports Book near the racetrack... We were going to cross... We were going to walk back to my apartment... She got scared... she became very paranoid... An incident had occurred... It was this kind of wild story... not sure how much to believe... but she was definitely scared and wanted to leave the country... She thought maybe my sister could help as I had told her that my sister is a travel agent. She said she had met this guy... he had money and was a doctor... he took her to somewhere in the Bay Area... an expensive place with a view of the water... some kind of doctor like I said and he was going to help her get off heroin but all he really wanted was a sex slave... he'd found something out on her... that there was a warrant in the state of Texas... She was pretty wired and it was pretty hard to understand... He wanted to tie her up but she talked him into letting her tie him up instead then busted him on the head and got away... That's all she told me and that's all I know. I am willing to cooperate... to help you in any way... to find Jane...

Blackstone's reports on the murder investigation of Gayland Parks ended there. A handful of newspaper articles found online, and Chance was at some pains to seek out as many as he could, had little to add. There were some salacious details concerning the psychotherapist-turned-life coach.

A stash of child pornography, mostly pictures of underage boys, had been found in his condominium along with what was described as a 'rather large collection of women's clothing.' Details regarding the detectives' trip to San Diego in search of the mysterious prostitute who was also good with math had apparently been kept from the press. A 'mentally disturbed' homeless man under investigation for the rape of two high school girls in the city of Oakland, according to the articles Chance found, was being considered as a suspect.

And that was pretty much it. As to whether or not detectives Blackstone and Lopez had ever escorted Woody Hammond across the border to look for Jane, there was no record of it in Blackstone's files. One could, Chance supposed, track down Woody Hammond and ask him. His address was after all right there in the report. Whether or not one could do this without rousing the kind of suspicion that might send Woody back to the police was another matter and Chance saw little point in risking it. Jaclyn Blackstone was now thirty-six. She was, according to Chance's own reports, exactly five and a half feet tall. She had a nice figure and light hair and light-colored eyes. She was good at math. Her English was not half bad either.

In certain of the literature on dissociative identity disorder it has been observed that nearly twenty percent of multiple-personality patients have worked as prostitutes. It is also the case that many prostitutes have dissociative disorders and that prostitutes *with* such disorders, who are also victims of childhood abuse, are often amnesic with regard to their prostitution. But that was in the literature and Chance felt no great need to go there. Sometimes you just knew a thing.

Live nude girls

TWENTY-FIVE HUNDRED dollars bought for him the Austrian-made Swarovski EL 10x50 SwaroVision binoculars. A Japanese salesperson of no more than twenty assured him they were the best his money could buy and that he would never need another, alternately referring to them as either bucket list or lifetime binoculars, to Chance's mind an unfortunate choice of words. He had presented himself as an avid bird-watcher and world traveler. Neither of course could have been further from the truth. The cash he placed upon the glass counter before him, a small portion of the ill-gotten gains from the recent sale of his furniture, was hardly his to keep as somewhere out there in the gloomy San Francisco morning an IRS agent was undoubtedly waiting, numbers in hand. And that was if things went well.

An hour later found him at the wheel of the Cutlass, parked in front of the Mongolian Grill at a long diagonal across a gutted parking lot from the European Massage Parlor where he had gone to case the joint. He was thinking of D's concerns regarding surveillance equipment, this in concert with what Jaclyn had said about Blackstone saying he would *handle things*. What did this mean? What did the man know? What had he seen? Perhaps, with the high-powered glasses, Chance would see something that D had missed in the poor light with the naked eye. If nothing else, it was a place to start and the best he had, save of course seeing patients, filing reports, preparing for his coming court appearance on behalf of the Doc Billy estate, meeting with attorneys to further his divorce proceedings, or sitting with the IRS to hear their number. The thing about all of that... it was too sedentary is what it was. It was *time*... to ponder the mystery of Big D and every other fucked-up thing that had gotten him here, time to think about Jane and Jaclyn and Jackie and the things he had read in Blackstone's files. And as of just now, he was running on empty, tapped dry by some weird type of information/sensory overload and sedentary was the last thing he needed. Movement was the thing, the engagement in something requiring his full attention, a high stakes distraction. It didn't help that Jaclyn was unavailable for comment.

He had no idea what Lucy must be thinking. They had not spoken in days. And then there was the matter of Carla's calls. Nicole was not doing well. She had missed another day of school then spent an entire weekend, in direct violation of Carla's orders, in the company of the new boyfriend Chance had yet to meet somewhere in West Marin, or so it was believed.

Chance invariably learned of such transgressions after the fact, sometimes long after, Carla calling at odd hours, clearly in the midst of some internal stew, suddenly deciding it was time for Chance to *do* something, yet never clear about what exactly this might be while at the same time rejecting any and all advice he was inclined to offer. At least this was how it *felt,* the full extent of his current involvement in his daughter's life.

In the beginning she had spent more time with him. Recent complications had served to make this less than desirable but that was about to change. He would find the place in Berkeley, a house perhaps where she might have her own room. He went so far as to envision the acquisition of a small pet. He would encourage her enrollment in the Berkeley school system. These things were not beyond the pale. It was within his power to make them happen and yet here he sat, with his expensive binoculars, looking for hidden surveillance cameras in the dredges of Oakland. He was racking focus on his new binoculars when Carla called for the second time in as many days.

'Where have you been?' she asked, the rancor evident in her voice.

Chance let the question go unanswered. Married, divorced, it was the same old song.

'Why aren't you at work?'

'Errands I needed to attend to.'

'For two days?'

Chance brought the shabby building into sharp relief, the Austrian glasses turning stucco walls to a landscape of cracks and crevices, craters worthy of the moon. 'Listen,' he said. 'Clearly this is a person she needs to stop seeing.' He had taken to searching beneath the eaves.

'Good luck with that.'

'Carla…'

'I'm not going to go around with her chained to my foot.'

'There's two kinds of pain in life,' Chance told her. 'The pain of discipline and the pain of remorse.' He was quoting Big D but only half there, lost in speculation on the mysteries of the human heart. Why had Blackstone kept those few reports in the dated file and why not anything at all of what had most certainly followed? Perhaps, he thought, there were other files on other hard drives – readily assembled should the need ever arise.

'You need to talk to her,' Carla said.

'I have, but yes, you're right, I will again. In the meantime you need to keep her close.'

'Have you heard anything I just said?'

'What I hear is this, you have a boyfriend and you don't want to be bothered.' It was, he supposed, a mean thing to say and only half true.

'You're an asshole,' she told him.

'Someone has to pay for it all,' Chance said.

'Right. And that's what you're doing, just now?'

Chance of course said nothing. He was thinking about

being an asshole and looking for cameras, but the lengthy pause was enough to push yet one more of Carla's many buttons. 'You don't want to hang up on me,' she said, apparently believing that he had hung up. 'Don't you even think about hanging up on me.'

Chance sighed, loudly enough for her to hear. He was about to speak. He was about to start in on his plans for the new place east of the bridge. He was about to sing the praises of the Berkeley public school system, the proximity of the UC campus, of lecture halls, of concerts beneath the trees, but then failed to do so, the words turning to ashes in his mouth. The problem was, having been here for not more than half an hour, he had just now spotted a woman with short dark hair but looking remarkably like Jaclyn Blackstone exiting the massage parlor in the company of what he could only imagine to be a john and a fair amount of oxygen had just been sucked from the air. 'We'll have to talk later,' Chance said, and ended the call.

The mystery woman's back was to him. Still, there was something in the curve of her hip and the way she carried herself, leaning upon the arm of the man at her side, even before showing Chance her profile and the high plane of a cheekbone giving her away, the short dark hair notwithstanding. Chance's heart strokes rattled in his ears. Music spilled from a passing car, a ghetto rumble above a baseline throb. She put the man into some sort of high-end, bloodred sports car parked before a liquor store at the far end of the lot and saw him off before starting back in the direction of the parlor.

Chance went to meet her, as if there were a choice in the matter, across pockmarked blacktop strewn with trash, the sun impossibly bright off such dead neon and stucco walls as bound them in on all sides, sorry storefronts in colors of the Mexican flag before flat asphalt roofs on which coolers the size of small foreign-built automobiles labored against the heat, the whole place smelling of car exhaust, garbage, and spice, ovens working overtime at the Mongolian Grill.

He came at her from an odd angle, quite certain he had not yet been made. She turned only when he called her name then stopped in her tracks, her mouth open, a series of expressions, or rather the possibilities of such, rippling across her features in the time it took to draw a breath. 'Oh my God.' Her first words, then once more with feeling, 'Oh... my... God...' as with the dawning recognition of some heretofore unimagined truth. At which point the curtain fell and she turned away as if nothing at all had just now passed between them. It was, in the shadowy realm of dissociative identity disorder, as remarkable a performance as one was likely to find. Her hair had been died to a blue black, cut short enough to suggest the androgynous and parted on the left. She was dressed in what he took to be the uniform of a Catholic schoolgirl.

Chance moved to block her passage. She squared off to face him. 'I don't know you, buddy,' is what she said. Her voice was loud and harsh and strange and very nearly put him off stride.

'I think you do,' he told her. He'd taken a position with regard to her affectations and was intent upon maintaining it.

'The fuck do you think you are?' she asked.

'I won't play this game with you, Jaclyn.' He spoke to her as if to a recalcitrant patient, in his finest authoritarian tone. He might have been wrong but it seemed to him that something flickered in the depths of her eyes, that she wavered momentarily before steeling herself once more. 'You need to leave,' she hissed. But the momentary hesitation had been enough. 'Got you,' he said.

She turned without saying more and started back in the direction of the parlor. Chance fell in beside her. 'I've no time for games,' he told her. 'Things have happened...'

It was as far as he got for she'd stopped short once more, suddenly shaking her hands as if trying to rid them of some unpleasant and possibly toxic substance, her face crumbling. It was a strange gesture bordering on the hysteric yet it touched him all the same, his bird with the broken wing. 'This isn't happening,' she said.

At which point Chance saw that a burly, dark-haired man in jeans, a black leather jacket over a white T-shirt with a gold chain around his neck, had walked from the front of the massage parlor to stand before it lighting a cigarette. What he felt next was Jaclyn Blackstone's hand on his wrist, a fearsome grip. 'For Christ's sake,' she said and pulled him into the doorway of the adult bookstore before which they had stopped, its interior all books, tapes, DVDs, and magazines, their lurid covers wrapped in plastic to discourage handling, shimmering in the fluorescent glare. 'Tell me something,' she asked. 'How insane are you?'

'I guess we know each other after all.'

'Listen,' she said. There was a heavyset Mexican man of perhaps fifty looking at them from behind the counter. When she gave him the finger he looked away. 'I don't know why you're here and I don't want to know. What I *do* know is this: You have to leave before someone sees you... they're watching everything right now... my God...' She paused for breath. 'What if *he* sees you?' He assumed her to be talking about the man in black who had exited the store and triggered this latest in what seemed a bottomless bag of tricks.

'And why would that matter?'

'Listen to me,' she said once more. 'You're a good person. I'm not.'

'Yes... you said something to that effect that night on the bridge.'

'What night was that?' she asked, but Chance wasn't buying. 'Something good has come into your life but you don't feel worthy, or are un*able* to feel worthy...' To which she produced a look of pained exasperation. 'Don't even go there,' she said, her voice suddenly distant, shot through with sad reservations. 'You don't know shit.'

'You could try telling me.'

Through the open doorway by which they had entered it was possible to see that the man in the leather jacket had begun to walk in their general direction. She took him by the arm once more. 'Pray he hasn't seen us,' she said, then something quick in perfect Spanish to the man behind the counter, the one she had just flipped off. The man nodded toward the back where they moved in a rush, single file, her reaching back to lead him by the hand, down a hallway made narrow by stacked boxes and into the alley where D had broken into Blackstone's car, where a man had died by way of a strange curved blade and broken neck, hooked through his ocular cavities. They hurried along behind the Dumpsters, hugging the walls of buildings then came up short near the mouth of the alley where it opened to the street, stopping just back in a small alcove formed by the walls of adjoining buildings where they paused to look back in the direction from which they had come, the alley empty as the moon.

'Who is he?' Chance asked.

Jaclyn shook her head.

'Talk to me, Jaclyn.' It seemed important to him to persevere in the use of her name, for both their sakes.

'You tell *me* something,' she said. 'Did you do it for me?'

There was scarcely time to formulate a response, as she was suddenly right up on him, her thigh pressing between his, once more the creature he'd met that night at the entrance to his own apartment. Jackie Black. He may even have spoken it aloud.

'You are crazy,' she told him.

He might of course have said the same, especially in light of the sudden revelation that she was possessed of a familiar scent, quite possibly the very one she had tried in his apartment then recoiled from to flee down the stairs. But there would, at just this moment, be no inquiring into that or anything else so obvious and nothing more in heaven or earth than just these two, meaning him and her and the promise of naked thighs beneath schoolgirl plaid, a desire beyond reason to lose himself once more in her magic.

'I have a car,' Chance whispered.

'I'll bet you do,' she answered.

He drove them to one of the many hotels that lined the
highway in approach to the Oakland airport. He had always
looked upon such establishments with disdain, corporate
and soulless on the high end, heartbreak seedy on the
low, buildings in whose sorry rooms one might expect to
find cigarette burns in the bedding, condom dispensers
in the bathrooms, a land meant for drug deals and cheap
assignations.

Deep into this particular blazing afternoon however,
they seemed to offer anonymity as well and so beckoned
with a new light. Little time was spent in the selection of
the one they arrived at. It featured a neon sign that included
a sleepwalking raccoon in cap and nightgown. There were
apparently live, nude girls at a club across the street, this
according to the marquee-type signage that fronted the road
leading almost directly to airport rental returns and long-
term parking. The lobby was all in shades of blue and orange
with potted rubber plants and large slabs of tinted plate glass.
The room they at last retired to featured views of telephone
poles and billboards with ads for cars and the racetrack at
Golden Gate Fields, a skimpy balcony from which one might
take in the Oakland airport while jet planes in traffic patterns
thundered overhead by the score and where, as the sun failed
and the darkness rose to take its place, a pale frosting might
be seen to appear in the far west that Chance was willing to
take for the lights of San Francisco. It was a room in which
he would spend the better part of two days before finding a
cigarette burn on one of the house blankets and where he
found even less in the way of food or sleep.

He really did think he might fuck the truth out of her and
that any such truth so arrived at would be his truth and not
some other, that the woman he had walked with that night
in the city and made love to in his apartment might be called

forth once more, conjured of hot desire and bodily fluids. But where she had once been so present there were now only shades and variations and places he couldn't reach. One of her was all about games with words. One wanted to try things, the cock ring in her leather bag… the loop of surgical tubing… a silver device hooked like a scimitar with attached ball and meant for the enhancement of male orgasm through stimulation of the prostate gland. One asked for permission to pee, inviting him to slap her. Another wept when he did so. One of their troubles, and the night and day that followed were filled with troubles, was that once she had gotten over on him with that routine in the alley… there was nowhere to go with it, not really, when all was said and done, and quite a lot really did get said and done.

They wore themselves out at it; he would give them that. Freud had famously said that he had come to regard any sexual act as one involving at least four people. Chance had no idea how many of them were there in the room, coming and going at all hours of the day and night, but between the two of them he imagined it was how it had been with the madman among the tombs, that their number was legion, far in excess at any rate of the number listed on the back of the door as the room's maximum occupancy.

'You see how it is,' she said during a break in the action. The truth of it was that he was in danger of losing sight, not only of how it was in the here and now, but of any larger picture in which the present might be contained or even made to give an accounting. It was not the first time he had traveled in such a land. He'd visited once before. It had ended in a psych ER in the town of Carefree, Arizona, where there had been a ride in an ambulance, hand restraints, and debilitating drugs, a suicide watch lasting the better part of a week.

'You should cop to everything,' Chance told her at one point. He was naked, standing at the foot of the bed, seemingly on his way to the bathroom when the thought occurred.

'What are you talking about?'

'I think you know,' he said. 'Come clean, plead self-defense in concert with diminished capacity. He won't survive that. You will. I'm a doctor who spends half his life in court and I see these kinds of things all the time and believe me you will do minimum time in either some minimum security prison or in a state hospital and yes that's a drag but you'll be free and I'll be waiting.'

She gave it a beat or two, studying the curtains that covered the door leading to their balcony, if one could actually call it that. When she looked back at him her eyes seemed to him as empty as those of a corpse. He found it an alarming observation. 'I'm not even going to ask what you're talking about,' she said. 'I just want to know if we're done.'

Chance just stood there.

'Go to the bathroom,' she told him.

He had no idea what caused him to look finally at the screen of his phone. He had gone to stand above the toilet bowl before a marbled mirror that was beginning to come apart at the edges where water had gotten in between the glass and the drywall. He imagined he had come in hopes of taking a leak, in itself a dicey proposition given what confronted him in the sorry glass, the damage done to his unit not to mention his poor prostate. One could only hope that none of his injuries would prove lasting.

The phone was on the countertop near the sink where he could not remember having left it. The sound had been turned off but the screen now blinked to life signaling the arrival of a text. As this happened, as the little screen lit up before him, he could see that it was in fact filled with messages that had arrived sometime during the past twenty-four hours or so. He could see that, and he could see something else as well. He could see that they were all from his soon-to-be ex-wife. Later he would see that there were also a number from Lucy and would find them bearers of the same sad news. But mainly what he knew, what he was given to understand over and against all else and even before he had read the messages, was that he was once more in possession of that larger present that had so recently threatened to desert him and that it was coming for him… right here and right now, very much as the beast in the jungle will come for its prey.

A shitty business

WALKING FROM the bathroom, he found her seated on the bed. Their clothes were strewn about the room, as were any number of hotel towels he could not now account for. The room's single chair had been overturned. She had opened the drapes to the balcony and the shabby world beyond it and was sitting there naked, braced upon a pillow. The morning light now filling the room was white and harsh and not doing her any favors, nor really was the dye job that had turned her hair to a spiky blue black so that her face seemed pale and drained by contrast and from which her darkened eyes were holding him with a look beyond despair. He was also naked and they were a moment in taking one another in, pilgrims along the road to perdition.

He needed of course to tell her the news. Now, however, that he was faced with actually saying it aloud, he found that he was not quite up to it. He tried once or twice but his throat seemed to knot up and the words wouldn't come. In their absence he remained in that no-man's-land between the bathroom door and the king-sized bed, naked in the unflattering light while a jet plane thundered and the poor, bare maroon carpeting vibrated beneath his feet.

She looked at him a good long while, and then finally, 'She's not coming back, buddy. What can I say?'

'It's my daughter,' he said and began to cry. Later he would wonder if it had been that way for his father too.

He finally got through to Carla on the room's phone, the battery having run down in his own. It was the dyslexic personal trainer that had found her, on the floor of her room, saliva running from one side of her mouth. Paramedics had been unable to revive her and she had been taken to the emergency room at UCSF, the same in which he had so recently gone in search of Big D. As she had not yet regained consciousness it was impossible to say on which of the several drugs found among her personal possessions she had actually overdosed. The prognosis was as yet uncertain. Her vital signs were within normal ranges. The lead doctor, a pulmonary specialist Chance had never heard of, had placed her on a tube to ensure her breathing, telling Carla that she would be kept sedated for the next several hours to prevent her fighting the tube then brought round when her stability was ensured. Till then she was being listed as 'stable but critical' and kept in the intensive care unit. Until she was able to regain consciousness, the whys and wherefores of it all would remain a mystery. Chance told Carla that he would be there as soon as he was able and hung up. He repeated it all to Jaclyn in fits and starts, working to master his voice.

'Oh my God…' she said. She was still in the bed, having drawn the sheet around her breasts and tucked it beneath her arms as one might a towel in a steam room, a stricken expression upon her face.

Chance sat beside her. He was still only half dressed, in T-shirt and boxers, one sock on, one as yet unaccounted for. She put a hand on his leg. 'Is there anything I can *do?*'

'Which one of you?' he asked.

'Don't be mean,' she said. The light had come back into her eyes and she pressed her head into his chest. 'I am so sorry…' she began, but her voice gave way and he was reminded of that first time she had crossed the bay to find him, of their talk in the little café near his office, the late light through low windows, the play of emotion across her face as he talked about his patients. A gentle soul, he'd thought then, and imagined for an instant she'd come back to him after all, that the sudden revelation of impending tragedy had called her forth. A second look into her face was enough to dissuade him. In another age of the world they would have burnt her for a witch. In some future age perhaps they would locate the faulty wiring, the chemical imbalance, they would know what to do. In the here and now he supposed that she would simply have to do as the rest of them, cowboy up and soldier on, hunting her way in a world without light. His reckless invitation of only minutes before seemed a lifetime away. He was back on planet Earth.

'You know he threatened her once,' Chance said. 'It was in the Thai joint that night in Berkeley.'

She nodded without meeting his eyes. '*You* need to go. Don't worry about me. I'll call a cab.'

'"A predatory species," is what he said.'

'Yeah, well… he would know.'

'She has a boyfriend. I've never met him, just heard about him. He sounds like a bad one. It could be that.'

'If that's what you think.'

'I don't know,' Chance said. 'I don't know what I think. If you do, now would be the time.' He rose off her silence and started once more with his dressing then found he was having a hard time with the buttons of his shirt. He seemed to have developed a moderate tremor in his right hand.

She got out of bed to help, the sheet falling way. 'Listen to me,' she said. 'When you get to that hospital… you need to stay with her. Just be there. When she gets better, maybe you should just take her and go away someplace…'

He took her by the wrist and looked at her. 'What are you saying?'

'I'm saying you need to be there.'

'Jesus Christ,' he said. 'This can't be happening.'

'I did tell you not to underestimate him.'

'You're saying what, this is him, or the boyfriend is some guy he's gotten to, someone on his payroll?'

'Let me tell you something about *him*,' she said. 'That massage parlor? That's his. He bought it with stolen drug money. He learned the racket from years of shutting them down when he was still in Vice. Now he uses his cop connections to keep out the competitors. He's partnered up with some Romanian mafioso types. They bring in girls from Eastern Europe, hook them on drugs, force them into prostitution, and those are the lucky ones. They have guys, Romanians mostly but not always, young handsome guys, and that's what they do, they troll for young girls and they're good at it. Not around here so much, mainly in Europe but he *knows* these kinds of guys. It's a shitty business. He's a shitty guy with shitty friends is what I'm trying to tell you and there's not much I wouldn't put past him.'

'Is there any way you could find out?'

'You think I should ask?'

'Clearly you have some connection to this place.'

'*I* have no connection to anything, except you. You'd have to ask *her* about that.'

'Give me a fucking break.'

'I'd like to,' she said. 'I really would.'

'And which *her* are we talking about, Jackie Black?'

'Listen to me,' she said. 'There's ones could swallow *her* with a glass of water.'

'Christ I'm tired of this,' he said finally. 'Aren't you?'

'The beat goes on.'

'Why were you there, Jaclyn? Why were you with that guy?'

'I told you,' she said.

'Right. So why was she there?'

'Let's just say we like to pilfer a john now and then.'

'Both of you?'

'She's a bad influence. What can I tell you? Drives *him* fucking nuts.'

'And how about Jaclyn? Is she in on it too?'

'Aw… your special lady friend.'

Chance was inclined to slap her but stayed his hand. There had been enough of that.

'Jaclyn can do the numbers. She's good at that.'

'And take a beating now and then.'

'Oh, we all take those.'

'And that guy we ran from?'

'One of the Romanians who brings in the girls. There used to be two of them but I'm guessing maybe you know *some*thing about that. I mean, if not, why were you even there?'

He declined the gambit, putting forth his own instead – now that they were back in the world with all of its unpleasantries. 'And how about Gayland Parks?' he asked, in what must have seemed to her as a bolt from the blue. 'What was he, a mark, a client, someone you pilfered?'

She stepped away as from an electrical shock. 'Whoa...' she said, 'look at you! Tou-fucking-ché!' She retrieved the sheet that had fallen, retreating to the bed, where she drew up her legs and rested her forehead upon her knees, a bit of the dramatic posturing that she was so good at.

Chance stood watching.

'That's what you meant... coming clean, doing time... and you at the place...'

Chance said nothing.

'The fuck, man?'

'I got to his computer. I saw some of his reports.'

She stared at him a good long while. 'You know what?' she said. 'You shouldn't even tell *me* that. Does *he* know?'

'I don't know. I don't think so. I don't know what he knows.'

'And you stand there asking if he's behind this other... Really?' Her voice trailed away. Chance waited. 'Well...' she said finally. 'You're fucked, is what I think.' She had begun to rock back and forth on the bed in the manner of a deranged street dweller. 'We're kind of both fucked,' she added, 'but he at least *likes* me.'

'Did he like Jane too? Did he fall in love? Did he bring her home? Maybe he found out she could do the numbers, or knew the business... And how about Myra Cohen, while we're on the subject?...'

'Stop it,' she said. She reached out suddenly to take him

by the wrist, surprising him once more with her strength
even after all they'd been through. 'We've been made, buddy.
Don't ask me how.'

'How?'

'That's rich. He's got fucking eyes, is how. He's hooked up.
I've told you he can get things done. Now you're seeing what
he can do.'

'Is he still in the hospital?'

'He was there for two nights and they sent him home but
I haven't seen him. He's called but I didn't return.' Chance
made to pull away but she held on tight. 'You are a good
person,' she said yet again. 'I can't imagine how you got to
his computer or what if anything you had to do with that
goat fuck in the alley…' She paused but kept hold of his arm
and for a moment was something like amused. 'I'm saying
that 'cause if I didn't you'd probably fucking tell me. Don't.
Never cop to anything and never talk to a cop. First rule, for
Christ's sake, and if you've got a magic rabbit someplace you
better go find him and you better hope he's still your pal. Is
this making sense? Am I getting through?'

'Help me find my sock,' Chance said.

She was still on the bed when he'd finished dressing. She'd
taken what he guessed to be the last of the beers from the
hotel minibar and was sipping from the can, staring out into
the unpleasant light, toward that place where the Oakland
airport shimmered in the distance.

'You'll be all right?' he asked.

'Would that be a joke?'

But he was still trying to process, to place everything she
had given him into some kind of real-world perspective,
given her state, given his, given every other fucking thing…

'Listen to me,' she said once more. 'If I *can* find anything
out I will and I will give you a call. But don't call me.'

'Righto.'

'I would go with you if I could.'

'Probably not the best of ideas.'

'You know what I mean,' she told him and he guessed that he did.

'Thanks anyway,' he said, then thought of something that had not occurred to him till just now, though well it might. 'I thought you had gone off to see your daughter,' he said. 'I thought that's where you were.'

'Really? And here *I* thought you were looking for *me*.'

'I was looking for cameras.'

'What did I just tell you?' she asked.

'And your daughter?'

'Let's not.'

'All right.'

'I'm sorry, buddy.'

'Two farmers meet on a road.' He'd stopped in the doorway and was looking back at her in the bad light. 'One farmer has a pig that he is holding up to eat the leaves of a tree. The second farmer takes this in, asks the first guy what he's doing. The first farmer says, "I'm feeding my pig." The second farmer says that must take a lot of time. The first farmer says, "What's time to a pig?"'

She gave him a long look. 'Would this be the kind of thing you generally charge your patients for?'

'To tell you the truth... I don't really see that many people, as patients.'

She gave it a beat. 'Wow. Let me think...'

'Yes, they scare the shit out of me.'

She said nothing to that.

'Think about the story.'

'And that's it?'

'It's all I've got,' he told her. 'The room is on my card. I'll tell them you're going to sign for it on your way out.'

'I really am sorry.'

'Me too.'

He closed the door behind him. Within minutes he had gained the freeway, heading north then west, the great span of the Bay Bridge groaning beneath the weight of midday traffic, cars stacked four abreast for as far as the eye could see, a harsh metallic rainbow run to the spires of the city it had so often pleased him to call his own.

Chance and the unimaginable thing

H E ARRIVED at the hospital shortly before the lunch hour, availing himself once more of staff parking but not bothering with the white coat. He was not feeling much like a doctor, or anything else for that matter, reduced by things as they were to little more than some bit of exposed nerve, passing like a shade through familiar corridors as if seeing them for the first time, returning straightway to the emergency care wing where he was just in time to find them spilling from one of the waiting rooms in varying states of rage and panic. They were all there, his soon-to-be ex-wife together with her support team, a small gaggle of soon-to-be ex-relatives and former friends, the dyslexic personal trainer among them. Chance, the only son of deceased parents, was quite alone in the face of their onslaught. If he had been hoping for a friendly face anywhere within hailing distance he was shit out of luck, having already been informed at the nurses' station by a Hispanic orderly of no more than twelve that it was Gooley's day off.

The source of their consternation, apart that is from the sudden appearance of Chance, apparently enough in and of itself to produce in his ex-wife an immediate and violent outburst, was the sudden disappearance of Chance's daughter. It seems that she was no longer in the building. Chance could only gape in wonder, to ask how such a thing had been allowed to happen. He might as well have stood upon the shoulder of the Great Highway at high noon to inquire of the wind.

'You're a fine one to ask,' Carla shouted at him, drawing stares from staff and passersby, a pat on the shoulder from her current flame. Chance just looked at her.

'About anything,' she cried, shaking off the boyfriend's hand. 'Why are you even here?' When he attempted to answer she turned away, burying her face on the shoulder of her mother, a faded glamour queen with heavily bleached hair Chance could scarcely recall ever having a single meaningful conversation with during the entire length and breadth of his marriage and who looked upon him now with the withering stare of a deep and lasting disapproval. He could only guess at his appearance.

In time certain things were made clear. Facts were established, emerging, it seemed to Chance, as might icebergs from a dense fog. At approximately ten fifteen that morning, the pulmonary doctor in charge of her case had decided that Nicole had been stable long enough to remove the breathing tube and to bring her back around. This had gone off more or less as planned and she had indeed regained consciousness, emerging from her long sleep in what was described to Chance as a rude and grumpy mood, wondering what the big deal was and wanting only to go home. 'She kept on asking for her cell phone,' the dyslexic personal trainer from Sausalito told him, his particular contribution to the unfolding narrative.

It was the first time that Chance had actually been in the same room with the man or spoken to him face-to-face. The guy was a head taller than Chance and in excellent shape. Chance declined to speak to him directly, preferring to address himself to Carla instead: 'And you let her have it?'

'How dare you,' she said. 'How dare you stumble in here after all this time and start making accusations…' She paused as if really taking him in for the first time. 'My *God*,' she said, 'you look like absolute shit.' In the aftermath of which she raced off to speak to a nurse. Her mother shot Chance a last hateful look before striking out in pursuit of her daughter. Other members of the support team withdrew in silence. Chance was left in the hallway, in the company of the trainer.

'Hey, man…' the trainer said to him. 'I'm really sorry about all of this. I really am. I can only imagine how you must be feeling.'

Chance nodded. The guy really was, it seems, the only person among the current support team willing to give him the time of day. 'We're not sure how she got the phone,' the trainer said. It occurred to Chance that in point of fact he could not recall the man's name. 'We're thinking it must have happened this morning, just after they took the tube out and removed the restraints. There was some kind of a break where one nurse went home and this other nurse came on… Looks like Carla must've left her purse in the room. She sat up in there with her all night. Anyway… Nicole must've seen this and seen she was alone and grabbed Carla's phone and made a call… There really wouldn't have been time for more than one.'

'Looks like maybe one was enough,' Chance told him. In light of the man's stab at some form of camaraderie, he was hoping to keep the rancor from his voice, or at least hold it to a minimum.

'It's fucked up,' the trainer agreed.

'And then what? It's not that easy to just walk out of here.'

'She said she wanted to use the bathroom. She would just have to have gotten to those stairs.' The man pointed to a doorway at the end of a short hall, a green exit sign above the door. 'It's only one floor down,' he added. 'If somebody was waiting right out there, with a car…'

'Have we looked at the phone… to see who she called?'

'She took the phone with her.'

'Right.'

'She's very enterprising.'

'Ah.'

'We've called the police.'

Chance was still trying to decide how he felt about this when the man went on once more. 'We're hoping they can get to the records from Carla's phone, get an address for whomever she called.'

'We're guessing it was the boyfriend?' Chance said.

The man nodded. They were guessing that it was.

'And do we know his name?'

'Tao.'

'That's it?'

'Nicole's never said much about him. Carla got what she did from one of her friend's mothers.' The man gave it a beat. 'I know it's a mess,' he added. 'But they *will* find her. She may even come to her senses and come home. She was together enough to walk out of here.'

Well, Chance thought, the guy was trying, however clumsily. Not trusting himself to speak, he simply nodded and looked down the hall, in the direction taken by his daughter while making good her escape. If the worst were true, the name probably wouldn't help much. It was doubtful Blackstone's boy toys went about using their Christian names.

Eventually Chance was able to speak with the pulmonary specialist who had treated his daughter and from whom he was given a list of the drugs the hospital had used in her care. It was all standard stuff, an antibiotic, a sedative… She would still, wherever she was, be a little groggy but all of her vital signs had been stable throughout the night. Shortly before making her escape she had admitted to the use of gamma-hydroxybutyric acid, one of the so-called date rape drugs currently so in vogue, known on the street as G. There had been, he was told, no signs of assault, sexual or otherwise. They had hoped to keep her another day.

The physician was interrupted by the arrival of an officer from the San Francisco Police Department whereupon Chance and Carla were whisked off to a private consultation in the course of which the officer proved himself professional and sympathetic if only a trifle detached, leaving Chance to wonder if it had ever been like that for certain of his patients, if he too had appeared professional and sympathetic and a trifle detached. Phone records, they were assured, would be obtained from Carla's provider. The appropriate number would be tracked. A missing persons report would be filed.

My God, thought Chance, in a refrain that was to run on a more or less continuous loop throughout the proceedings, it was all so absolutely sad, fucked up, and unimaginable that it had come to this, that he should now find himself at long last in the position of so many of his patients, the recipient of unthinkable news at the hands of a mild and sympathetic if only vaguely present professional. At which point the officer exerted a new claim on Chance's attention by announcing that a missing persons report would go out to all law enforcement personnel in the area, not only in San Francisco but throughout the region, including the cities of Berkeley and Oakland, east of the bay.

Chance in the wind

CHANCE REMAINED at the hospital just long enough for the police to contact Carla's provider. The number Nicole had dialed proved a dead end, a call-and-drop job, the kind favored by those types not eager to be found and was not, according to the detective who gave them the news, a promising sign and nothing for it in the here and now but to go home and wait... for a call... from someone from somewhere... for some news... to live in hope.

In the end, the missing persons report was filed and sent. Chance himself had shared in its completion. The dyslexic personal trainer had said they would be in touch. His wife, with whom he was apparently no longer speaking, had accordingly said nothing at all and they had begun to disperse, survivors of some unspeakable disaster, which is to say that while Carla and her support team made for the elevators and visitor parking, Chance used the stairs and went out alone. It should be noted that he did not do so without first inquiring after one Darius Pringle but the big man was gone with no forwarding address save for that of the family. Good luck in that quarter and Chance went on. He found it fitting that the stairs it was necessary to tread ran down instead of up and it was not only because he doubted his ability to climb. With each step along the descent his mind ran to an ever darker and more dreary place, to a world of systemic failure, of impotent restraining orders and missing children, of pedophiles and snuff flicks, of prostitution and drug addiction, of undue influence and bodies in shallow graves.

It was in just this mind-set that he came upon the flyer pinned beneath the windshield wiper of his car. It was an advertisement for the opening of a new restaurant somewhere in the city. The flyer's most salient feature was that the restaurant in question was not just any restaurant but one specializing in Thai cuisine.

He looked to see if other cars in the lot had also been left with such advertisements but found they had not. He looked about the great cavernous structure in which he had parked. He heard the distant screeching of tires upon a concrete ramp, the faraway hum of a car in retreat. The message was subtle and ambiguous to be sure but how else to interpret it other than as the work of Detective Raymond Blackstone, the same who had once threatened him by way of his daughter in that other restaurant specializing in Thai cuisine, east of the bay?

The claustrophobic solitude of his own quarters not even *about* to be borne, he made directly for the old warehouse in a state of profound dissociation, his thoughts moving by pathways both familiar and concentric, gaining exponentially with regard to speed, paranoid ideation, and general depravity. He simultaneously imagined the reach of Blackstone, bad boyfriends, broken marriages, a soul in torment... a girl in rebellion. Add to which the recitation without end of the sins of the father, in this case none but his own. He couldn't make it stop. He couldn't get over on it or under it or past it or around it. Nor could he imagine a move that did not end in some further catastrophe. He could not see beyond the frightful combination of impotence and rage, the certainty of knowing that in the event of some unspeakable ending it would always be his word against Blackstone's, and that if the latter was compromised so was he, the doctor who had slept with a patient, a woman suffering her own brand of dissociation, quite possibly possessed of multiple personalities to those willing to go there, a full-blown borderline to others, crazy as a shithouse bat to your average citizen, of whom pretty much any future selection of any twelve jurors was likely to be composed. Such was the sound track by which he ran at least two red lights, possibly more, narrowly missing at least one pedestrian in the person of a uniformed parking attendant in the act of posting a ticket. That he was able to do so with impunity seemed quite right and proper, suggesting to him a new way of being in the world.

As if on cue from what must surely have qualified as some demiurge among the lower levels of management, a call arrived from Jaclyn Blackstone. Chance was still en route to the Mission and stuck in traffic.

'The fuck were you even there?' she began.

He took her to mean the massage parlor, the very thing she had so recently warned him never to cop to. 'Why don't you just help me find my daughter?' he asked.

She gave it a long beat. 'I might have something.'

Chance had become one in a long line of cars in approach to a distant row of changing lights, his pulse quickening. 'Might or do?' he asked.

She chose to ignore the question. 'I saw him for the first time since he was in the hospital. He's gone completely off the rails. Some kind of near-death experience or some fucking thing.'

Chance gripped the wheel, breaking a sweat as the cause of the delay came into view, roadwork squeezing traffic into a single lane, Caltrans workers in orange vests and hard hats – what appeared to be three guys explaining the parts of a shovel to a fourth. The cars inched forward.

'All he can talk about is getting out. He wants to take early retirement. Go away someplace…'

'Getting out of what?'

'Everything. And he wants me to go with him.'

'I guess he would.'

'I'm serious.'

'So am I. You said you had something.'

'I just wanted you to know. I'm really scared. There would be nothing but me and him and him with nothing to do but keep me there.' She allowed a moment to pass. 'I'd rather take a beating,' she said, and then, 'I'm leaving. I don't know how yet but I am and I'm going to give you something. I want you to have something you can hold over his head, to use as leverage.'

'What?'

'It's just something. Where are you?'

'I'm in my car.'

'Where?'

'I'm in the city, stuck in traffic. You're not going to tell me?'

'It won't mean anything for me to tell you. It's something you need to have. How is she?'

'Gone. We think the boyfriend may have picked her up at the hospital. She got hold of my wife's phone.'

'God... Is there a place we can meet?'

'Why?'

'I told you,' she said.

'I need to know what we're talking about, Jaclyn.'

'You asked about Jane. I know what's in those files you saw. And I know what's not.'

'Ah.'

'Jane was good with numbers,' she told him.

'What does that mean, Jaclyn? You have his books? You're giving him up?'

'To you.'

'Why now? Why me?'

'I see your daughter.'

'Where are you?'

'There's a motel at the coast, up by Lands End. It's called the Blue Dolphin.'

He eased past the last of the construction, gathering speed, the city like bleached bones in the white light of a skittish sun.

'What are you telling me?'

'I'm telling you there's a place we can meet.'

'You said you could see my daughter.'

'I thought you would know what I meant.'

'Christ, Jaclyn. I can't do this.'

'Do what?'

Chance sighed. 'I need to talk to someone,' he told her.

'My God, you're going to the police.'

'Hardly.' He might well have mentioned that movements of extreme complexity were taking place he no longer felt competent to judge, that help was needed and not of the sort to be found between him and her, alone in yet one more grotesque motel. 'Where are you?' is what he asked instead. The place she had mentioned was in the opposite direction but not so far away as to rule out the half a chance he would turn around and go for it.

'I'm here.'

'In the motel?'

'In my apartment.'

Chance eased his grip on the wheel. 'And where is he?'

'I don't know.'

'Then you don't actually *know* that he is involved with my daughter. You don't know any more now than the last time we spoke.'

'You asked if there was anything I could do.'

'They may still find her,' he said, if for no other reason than to hear it spoken aloud, as if saying it might make it so and the world restored to its more recognizable assemblage of shadow and light, comedy and horror. 'The missing persons report has gone out. It's not like no one is looking.'

'Right.'

Time passed.

'Do you remember the name of the motel?'

'The Blue Dolphin, but like I said…'

'You have to talk to someone.'

'Will you call me when you get there?'

'I'm there, buddy. And then I'm gone.'

'I have to be smart about this,' he told her. And then, after a beat, 'I want us both to be smart.'

'I think it might be a little late for all of that.'

He found the old man in back of the warehouse where he appeared to be placing luggage into the trunk of the Starlight coupe. 'Thank God you're here,' he said. 'I'm just going.'

'You've found him, then?'

'Not exactly but I know where to look.'

'Should I drive?' Chance asked. But the old man was already behind the wheel of the coupe and in the end Chance joined him. It was, after all, the reason he'd come. He went heeding the advice of Jaclyn Blackstone, or at least of someone calling herself by that name, hoping against all reason that the magic rabbit was still among the living, neither institutionalized nor incarcerated, and above all still his friend.

In the Church of Big D

CARL FILLED him in as they drove, all about how D had been taken to the father's house in Berkeley, that they were trying to set up something... a transfer to some private facility... that D had gotten wind of it and left, even in the face of some apparent attempt to prevent his doing so.

Chance was a moment in trying to envision what that must have looked like before reminding the old man that Big D was in fact an adult, a subject upon which he was beginning to feel like a broken record.

'He's afraid of his father.'

'His father should be afraid of him.'

'I told him that was what you said but he may need to hear it from you.'

'And when exactly will he have the opportunity to do this?'

'Soon enough,' the old man told him. 'I'm just hoping we're not too late.'

'Meaning what?' Chance asked. They were by now leaving the city, headed south. The old man's shrugging motion was noncommittal and Chance was left to study the moneyed hills in approach to Palo Alto, their blue green tops lost to the great billowing banks of cloud that marked the coast and in whose canyons the Merry Pranksters had once partied with Hells Angels and the nineteen-sixties might be said to have begun. In time he closed his eyes, giving in to exhaustion, and even managed to doze, albeit fitfully. His dreams were in orange and blue, all nipple clamps and penis rings, a woman he couldn't find, all of it infused with the distant throbbing of unseen engines.

He woke in a place where the money ran out, where apartment buildings distinct for their resemblance to government-funded housing projects in close proximity to the 101 freeway running south to Los Angeles had taken its place. And then they were past even that, on a two-lane road now, and had come to some last vestige of what had once held sway here, long before the coming of the hippies or the yuppies that would rise from their ashes. It appeared in the form of a derelict avocado grove, its ruins commingling with those of citrus set to rows but long since overcome and in the midst of which the remains of an old Victorian half lost amid the brush and weeds and unkempt trees.

The old man veered from the pavement near the mouth of a long dirt drive leading toward the house, marked by two large stones and each of these the bearer of iron rings as might once have been used for the hitching of horses, and parked in the dirt on the side of the road. One of the rocks was painted red white and blue with an old-fashioned peace symbol sprayed over that in black paint. Opposite was a sign suggesting that much of the surrounding land had been recently sold and was now slated for development. It allowed for the imagining of shopping malls and industrial parks.

'That's too bad,' Chance said, by which he meant the sign and what it promised.

Carl took in their surroundings. 'My father used to pick out here,' he said. 'Only job he could find back in the day. Came out when I was a teenager. Family left Missouri, landed in Oregon. My dad started picking fruit, wound up following a harvest down the coast till we got to San Francisco.'

'That's something.'

'Yeah,' Carl said. He appeared to be watching a small, orange-throated bird at work at the top of a dying tree. 'He didn't like me much.'

Chance took this as a reference to the old man's father. 'Guess mine didn't like me much either,' he said, 'when you get right down to it.'

The old man watched as the bird flew away. 'Doctor. Thought that was supposed to be one of the good ones.'

'There were some bumps along the way.'

Carl nodded and lowered his window, their mad flight from the city having apparently come to this, a recounting of parental disappointment in the bucolic south. 'So...' Chance said, but the old man was suddenly mute as a stone and there was nothing but the hum of insects, the faintest trace of orangewood and sage on the dry and motionless air. Chance tried once more. 'So...' he said.

'I know what you're thinking,' Carl told him. 'But this is the best we can do. If he's here he'll know that we are too. He'll come or he won't.'

'And how long do we give it?' Chance asked. He found that he had joined the old man in looking toward the trees.

'That's a tough one,' Carl said.

In real time it was probably no more than five minutes before a sizable number of quail broke from the grass like a scattering of buckshot and the big man in their wake, moving out from some particularly dense thicket back up where the old house held sway among the trees then making his way down along the long drive, dressed as he had been the first time Chance laid eyes on him, in the old military jacket over a black T-shirt and cargo pants and combat boots with their laces flapping in the dust and he came up on Chance's side of the car where he wanted to know what was up. He posed the question as if nothing of consequence had passed since their last meeting.

Chance found himself more moved by the other's appearance than he might have imagined. 'How are *you* would be the question.'

There was a smudge of dirt on the big man's face. The cuffs

of the cargo pants were full of leaves and there were twigs in the laces of his boots. 'I'm good,' D said. They left it at that and Chance and Carl got out of the car and D led them back among the trees where Chance could see more clearly what had been a grand old Victorian such as the East Coast transplants had built when they'd first come west to escape their various and assorted histories, to grow their citrus and avocados, their almonds and walnuts. This one had fallen upon hard times with many of its doors and windows covered in plywood and a whole section of roof gone entirely yet managing even in the face of these insults to retain some air of stubborn dignity. It said something, Chance thought, about the people who'd built it, and he was reminded in just that moment of Jean-Baptiste's fierce and demented subjects, of the light in their eyes.

There had been, at some point in the tortured history of the place, a fire to go along with its other woes and the property rather obviously condemned, the final straw perhaps in prompting its sale to what had undoubtedly been just one of many hovering developers. The property was the last of its kind for miles around and certainly they must have circled, sharks drawn to the remains of a creature so much larger and grander than themselves.

From the looks of the place it had all been sitting like this for a good long while, with new brush, wildflowers, and the green shoots of trees spreading to hide a good deal of the charred and sorry wood. A small community of the homeless, of both sexes, had moved in. Some appeared to be occupying the old house while others had pitched makeshift tents among the trees. There was an old-fashioned carriage house off to one side of the big house and someone had painted WELCOME TO THE HOUSE OF SPACE AND TIME across one of the doors and ABANDON ALL HOPE, MOTHERFUCKER across another. A number of the men were dressed not unlike D in old military gear of one type or another and Chance was willing to take them for veterans of the fight, in flight from or perhaps part time denizens of the large VA hospital in Palo Alto, and knew it for one of the haunts described in the medical reports he'd read at the hospital.

Darius Pringle, Chance noted, his military service or lack thereof notwithstanding, was treated by the other members of the camp with great deference as they were shown somewhat ceremoniously to an old couch and recliner chair arranged about a battered coffee table someone had salvaged from what might well have been the city dump and placed far enough back among the trees to have been invisible from the street. A large canvas tarp in colored patterns of camouflage greens and browns had been strung overhead to form a makeshift roof and the setting was, as near as Chance could tell, based on the reaction of others, a meeting place of some distinction.

D dropped himself into the recliner. Chance and Carl took the couch. 'Talk to me,' D said.

Chance did.

'That's a crazy-ass story, Doc,' D said when Chance had finished. 'That's fucked up.' He looked to the old man as if for confirmation and the old man looked back and Chance sat there looking at the two of them. It occurred to him that the sun had moved to a place more directly overhead, thanks no doubt, at least in part, to the planet's rotation upon its axis. 'Well what isn't crazy?' he asked finally. He was possessed of the sudden urge to mount a defense. In truth, he felt at the verge of some hysteria, the light coming down preternaturally bright through a tear in the canvas and burning his neck, burning right through him is what it felt like, as if he weren't actually there or about not to be. 'How is it not crazy that there's something instead of nothing,' he railed, 'or that one day the mud stood up and began to walk or that the three of us are even sitting here right now? How fucked up is all of that?'

He had after all been days with very little in the way of food or sleep. His ass was on fire. It was not inconceivable that he was developing an infection, which would also account for his almost constant need to excuse himself for the purpose of making water amid the brush. Still he persevered. He was on to the odds of things now, of anything at all really, save some featureless void, and might even in time have worked his way round to Banach-Tarski and his particular take on their troublesome paradox had not someone at D's direction given him a slightly odorous plastic bottle filled with water from which to drink. That he accepted without further regard for the bottle's point of origin or even a good look at its contents, yet one more indicator of his precarious mental state.

'That's a goddamn interesting way of looking at things, Doc,' D said as Chance paused to drink. The bottle smelled even worse at close quarters.

'Fascinating,' Carl added.

Chance mopped at his brow. 'It's just that when you say a thing is crazy...' He was feeling the need for a second defense in defense of the first defense. 'The thing *I* want to say is... what isn't crazy? What is not against the odds? And who really thinks that we are rational beings? It's all such a goddamn joke.'

'We get all of that,' D assured him.

'The whore and the cop,' the old man added. 'My God... it's the stuff of song.'

'I'm good and lost,' Chance admitted. He might also have added that it felt as if a burning coal had found residence at a point just north of his perineum.

'Slow down,' the big man told him. 'Let's take a step back, see what this thing looks like piece by piece.'

'Amen to that,' Carl said.

The alpha and the omega

S HE REALLY *had* wanted help. Blackstone really had beaten her. And there *he* was… charging into Blackstone's deal with the universe. Forty-eight hours and there's an incident involving Chance's daughter. Ambiguous. Shit lands on Chance's computer. Not so ambiguous. Blackstone's come to play and he can't believe this won't work. 'You're a fucking doctor for Christ's sake,' D said. 'Big brain, tiny balls. Are we good so far?'

'Pretty much,' Chance told him. Piece by piece, the man had said.

'What he *doesn't* know about is me, and all of a sudden there's shit landing on *him*. He's on his back in the fucking hospital and he's thinking *this* is fucked up. I would just say welcome to my world, asshole, but that's another story. So he's trying to recover and he gets wind of her splitting with some guy in front of the massage parlor and it sounds a lot like you and this is starting to get serious. She's his frozen lake. He went way out on the ice to get her. If anything ever goes wrong she can hang him good. He could hang her too of course, but that's not what he wants and he's always figured as long as he can keep the plates spinning… But now you're fucking with that and he's tried scaring you. There's really only one thing left. But you want to be smart about that sort of thing. Fuck it up and it'll blow back all over you. Look at all this goat fuck in the Middle East.' This last drawing murmurs of approval from a small gallery of camp denizens who'd come for the sermon.

'But why make it look like an accident?' Chance asked. He saw no reason to drag the Middle East into it and the audience was making him nervous. 'If Blackstone is behind all of this with Nicole… if he's got these guys that troll for girls like she says… if one of them has gotten to my daughter… Why put her in the ICU then break her out?'

D nodded. 'I used to collect money,' he said. 'I had two rules. The person I was going to collect from had to have the money and they had to know they were trying to get away with something. That's very important, those two things. Okay. So now you're me and you're going to collect. You never just walk up to the guy and say so-and-so wants his money and if you don't pay I'm gonna break your legs. Threat's never that direct. In fact, what I liked to do was to be very nice. *That* freaks people out a little because I'd catch 'em someplace where we could be alone and they wouldn't know who I was. I'm this stranger and they see what I look like and they're a little spooked but there I am being nice to them and they can't quite figure it, at which point I say something like, why don't you give so-and-so a call. He'd really like to talk to you. And all of a sudden they know exactly what this is about, what kind of guy I am, and why I'm there and nine times in ten that would be all it took. They'd really like to keep being my pal. I would leave the alternative to their imaginations. But there's always some asshole thinks he's tough and maybe he is. What you do with a guy like that… you don't bother talking, you just grab him in a parking lot some night and you break his legs, break his hands too while you're at it. You break both a guy's hands he can't wipe his own ass. It's very humiliating. Then you wait till he's recovered, as much as he ever will, and that's when you go see him and it's the same deal. You get him someplace where you're alone and you just start bullshitting with him. Now if you did it right that night in the parking lot or wherever it was, and it was dark and you came at him fast and hard, it's going to be very difficult for him to remember much. It's a fucking blur. All he really knows is he got the living shit beat out of him. So there you are... and it's good if it's someplace like where he got mugged. He's still trying to recover from what happened, meals through a straw, some nurse wiping his ass, and at some point he starts getting nervous. He doesn't know you from Adam and yet there you are bullshitting with him about some completely banal thing with no sign of stopping anytime soon. He'd like to bolt but you're making it so he can't, but you can see he'd like to and that's when you say to him, maybe you ought to call so-and-so. And all of a sudden he knows. He knows what happened and he knows why. And most importantly, he knows you're the one. He knows what you're capable of and he knows that if he doesn't come through it's going to happen all over again and he picks up the phone and he makes the call and you've never said a direct word about it.

'Now you see where this is going. Blackstone hasn't *said* a direct word, but he's *shown* you what he's capable of, the overdose, the abduction... the menu on your car... very circumspect, very discreet and very ballsy. He's a worthy fucking opponent, this guy. He's my kind of guy if you want to know the truth. Too bad he's a douche bag. That menu shit... that's genius when you stop and think about it. Nothing you could point to that he couldn't deny. It's fucked up but you have to admire it.'

They were a moment in admiring it.

'And now?'

'Now we go at him,' D said, warming to the idea.

'And if he has my daughter?'

'You'd probably know it already.' He said this in an offhanded way as if to suggest everything with which he had just preceded it were pure speculation and quite possibly wrong.

'I thought we'd just concluded that he did.'

D went on without missing a beat. 'So let's *say* he has her.

That breaks two ways. He calls and says we need to talk. But he hasn't done that so we go to what's next. He lets you sweat, and maybe needs time to put his ducks in a row. However he works it, the endgame is the same, *him* telling *you* that the two of you need to talk. He's not going to tell you he has your daughter. Threat will never be that direct. He knows what you're thinking because that's how he's set it up, and he's counting on you to believe that if you can just talk to him and promise to be good it can still work out and he will think *you* will think that because that's the world you've always lived in, a place where educated people talk and work things out. But all this really is, this whole charade… It's all about setting you up. Your daughter's a means to an end – you in a meeting you don't come back from and that's the salient feature of this whole deal. It's you dead.

'He'll probably have it set up to look like a mugging or some fucking thing. He *may* not even be there. The bad boyfriend will bring your daughter back to wherever. Blackstone goes back to whatever sick deal he's got going with this woman you like. It's what they'd call in the Teams a perfect op; you're in, you do the job, and you're out. No one even knows you were there. You were invisible.

'But here's the rest of it. Let's say Blackstone doesn't have your girl. She's a kid acting out, making bad choices. She's got some shitbird boyfriend and that's who she's with. Where does that leave us with Blackstone?'

'I don't know.'

'Sure you do. Daughter, no daughter… This is all about frozen lakes, my brother, yours and his. In case you hadn't noticed, they're the same. You and her getting made outside that place… that was fucked up, Doc. That's the alpha and the omega right there.'

Chance entertained the fleeting impulse to deny it, to remind them all that he hadn't gone to *find* Jaclyn but to look for evidence of surveillance, an unnecessary step had D not been moved to break a man's neck by way of a karambit blade run through his ocular cavities. But then he supposed that was really just one piece. Had they not been tailing Blackstone, had he not gone to a man repairing furniture in the back of a warehouse for advice in extricating himself from his own ill-advised involvement in the life of a disturbed woman or, for that matter, when one went further in consideration of the simple fact that he would not have been at the warehouse in the first place had he not been hoping to alleviate the financial woes of a failed marriage by scoring on some fancy French furniture it had no doubt been foolish even to buy... and so on and so forth till the business of D's killing a man seemed but one layer of an onion best left unpeeled and the more appropriate question was: What next?

'Let's start with what's not next,' D said. 'I'm you... I don't wait for him to put his ducks in a row and I sure as hell don't go out to this fucking motel. I don't trust her to play middleman. I go right at him and I don't need her and whatever she's got or hasn't got or maybe just thinks she's got. I call him, on this.' He pulled a phone from his jacket and placed it on the table between them. 'What I took off that shitbird in the alley. You call him on this... it's a whole new day, my brother.'

'My God. You took his phone?'

The big man shrugged. 'Fell out of his pocket. I saw what it was. Why not take it?'

'But won't the cops be on this? Monitoring calls... whatever it is that they do?' He was thinking now of Blackstone's reports.

'No. It's a burner, a call-and-drop job. You buy X number of minutes, use a fake name, toss it when you're done. Check out the ghetto sometime. You can buy one on every corner.'

Chance felt no need for visual confirmation. He could

imagine it all well enough, a vast incipient system by which denizens of the underworld were in more or less constant communication in anticipation of the coming darkness.

'It's what I use, when I use one at all,' Big D said, and pulled one from his jacket identical to the one on the table. 'Cops won't be on it, but *he* will. He thinks you're trouble but he still thinks he's got the leverage. Call comes in on that…' D eyed the phone. 'And he finds out it's you… Buckle up is all I can say. Speed kills.'

Chance eyed the device with something akin to terror. 'The fuck would I say?' he asked.

'Tell him you want your daughter. Tell him *you* want to meet, you want to trade… you could burn him down but you'd rather negotiate.'

'For my daughter.'

'He'll never cop to having her. He'll probably just say something like we need to talk and you say fine… we'll talk as soon as I know she's safe and you give him a window. I don't hear from her in the next six hours, I'm taking everything I know and I'm going to the guys you work for. That's a bluff but it's a place to start.'

Time ground to a halt in the Church of Big D, dust motes like dwarf celestials in lazy circles beneath rent canvas. In the end, Chance took his wallet from his pocket and removed the card Detective Blackstone had given him. There was a photograph of his daughter in the wallet as well. It had been taken as she clung to a child's merry-go-round in a little park in Cambria where the family had once rented a house for the summer, at a happier time than the present, and he studied it for some indeterminate period before placing his own phone on the table between them and lifting the one belonging to the dead man. It was heavier than anything he might have imagined.

'It was what they told us at the hospital,' he said, holding the phone as if it were sharing time in homeroom and this were the thing he'd come with. 'About the number my daughter called... that it was one of these.'

The others sat watching.

'Nice,' D said.

Folie à deux

IT WAS just here, in the wake of all that had transpired, awash in the big man's logic, susceptible in other words to the undue influence of a highly intelligent and charismatic if mentally unstable individual, having dialed the number and Blackstone answering on the third ring in a voice with more air in it than Chance could recall, pitched perhaps at a higher octave, that a number of things happened at more or less the same time. One might envision it as the movement of certain types of objects toward the occupation of the same point in space and time, the act of coinciding as it were, the very thing he and the detective had once quarreled over at the Little Thai Hut, with Chance saying, 'I want my daughter...' and the words no sooner out of his mouth than a text message appeared on *his* phone, on the table at his knees – much, Chance suspected, as the writing on the wall had once affronted the Babylonian king. In Chance's case it was his soon-to-be ex-wife, Carla, saying simply, 'She's back.'

Blackstone didn't say anything but he didn't hang up either. Neither did Chance. Their connection seemed possessed of a particularly malevolent form of white noise, in the midst of which Chance elected for a kind of voluntary mutism while engaged in the forced review of what the *Diagnostic and Statistical Manual of Mental Disorders* has to say about shared psychotic disorder and this in concert with the rather jarring realization that Carl Allan had been right, that at the heart of the matter were the whore and cop and that everything else... everything that had led just now to his use of the dead man's phone... to his speaking in tongues in the Church of Big D ... might just as well be written off to Chance under the influence, caught between the twin magnetic poles of Heavy D and Jaclyn Blackstone.

He was very close to simply hanging up when Blackstone, sensing perhaps an existential crisis, began to speak. 'Listen to me, you twisted little prick. I don't have your daughter and I didn't hurt her, but I will now.'

The rank pronouncement was followed by a strange hissing Chance was willing to take for an oxygen tank. It was a sound he'd grown more or less accustomed to in the tiny kitchen of Doc Billy and he guessed that Blackstone, having suffered a collapsed lung, might well be in possession of one, at least temporarily. 'You don't want that to happen,' the detective said. 'You'd better drive straight to where I tell you to drive, and you'd better come alone. Now, I've got someone here that's just dying to talk to you and that's not a figure of speech.'

Chance was treated to the somewhat strangled voice of Jaclyn Blackstone. 'I'm so sorry, Eldon, I didn't know. He found out. He knows. Just do what he tells you to.' Her voice broke then came back. 'Please. He means what he says.'

Raymond followed. 'Here's the way it's going to be, *Eldon*. The three of us are going to talk and we're going to get straight on some things, and if you say and do the *right* things...' There was a pause, the faint whispering of the mechanism. 'Then maybe you can go back to being the type of shitbird who sleeps with his patients. You don't and I'm going to destroy you. I'm going to destroy you professionally and I'm going to destroy you privately. I'm going to destroy your family.' He let that one settle as Chance waited. 'We're in a motel. Do you know which one?'

Chance did.

'I thought you might. Now I'll tell you something else... that little incident that you were involved in, back in your days at med school and we both know what I'm talking about. I'm willing to bet you still have some paperwork attached to that... restraining order, court docs... You strike me as the anal-retentive type of asshole that would keep that sort of shit locked away somewhere. I want you to get that and I want you to bring it with you.' There was another pause on the line. 'You're going to want something to trade. Now where are you?'

'Palo Alto.'

'I'm giving you two hours. Now one more thing and this is very important. Be alone. I will know if you're not. You won't like what happens next.'

Chance asked for three.

'Three what?' D asked when Chance had returned the phone.

Chance repeated, as best he could, everything Raymond Blackstone had said to him in his new unpleasant voice.

'He really said all of that?' D asked.

Chance, hoping to avoid being sick, managed only to nod.

'That's far fucking out. What did I tell you? Calling him on that phone...'

'The subject of the phone never came up,' Chance said, cutting him short. 'He never mentioned it. It was like it wasn't even part of the equation.'

'Yeah, you kind of fucked up that part of it,' D said.

Chance snatched his phone from the table and turned it on, illuminating Carla's text once more. He passed the phone to Big D. 'This came,' he said. 'In case you didn't notice... just now... as I was calling Blackstone. She's back.'

D studied the small screen before returning the phone. He appeared unfazed. 'Her showing up is not proof he wasn't involved. Think it through.'

'The message is from my wife, D. My daughter is back. He never had her.'

'I think you're missing the larger point, Doc.'

'The larger point is my family is now in danger. They

weren't before. It was something we made up. All this guy wants is this woman.'

'And you as a loose end?'

Chance was silent.

'This is exactly what I said it would be, Doc, him getting you to a meeting you don't come back from.'

'That ignores *my* larger point that I just made, which is that all I wanted was for *my* daughter to be safe and now she's not. I just made sure of it. I'm not into doing what you and I did that night in the alley, D. I'm not into hunting the bad guys…'

'I thought you wanted to save this woman.'

'I've since come to a better understanding of just how fucked up it is between the two of them… and of why doctors in my line of work don't involve themselves with patients…'

'I'd say it's a little late for that.'

'Yes and thanks to that call on that phone, I'd say I'm pretty well fucked.'

'You're not fucked.'

'Yeah, I kind of am.'

'That's a poor attitude, man. Let me tell you a little story. Second tour in the Hindu Kush…'

'Darius,' Chance said. Rage, hopelessness, and a sense of impending doom had empowered him. 'With all due respect, my friend… I've read your medical files. You were never in the Hindu Kush. You were never in the Middle East. You were never in the military, Darius.'

It grew very quiet beneath the trees. Chance was vaguely aware of the old antiques dealer turning to a study of the ground between his feet, of even the insects having abandoned their song. 'Two things,' Big D told him, his eyes never leaving Chance's. 'These are emotions talking. You're scared. You're in the middle of an adrenaline dump. Enough time… I could teach you to deal with that, to think through it, but here's the other thing and you'll want to get straight on this... you ever call me Darius again I'm gonna punch you right in the face.'

'I feel you,' Chance said.

'Pull yourself together,' D said, and he told his story, something about the chance meeting of a Team on a mission with an old man and a boy. It was no doubt intended as some illustration of the battlefield's moral ambiguities coupled with irrevocable choice and ended badly, but Chance was barely listening. He was thinking about the irrevocable choices that had led him here, considering for what would most certainly be the last time the possibility of his going to the police, in this the eleventh hour, and of what that might look like... the unraveling of his career, the end of Jaclyn, his daughter in more or less permanent jeopardy. But he was thinking too of what Blackstone had only now told him... that if he would only say and do the right things and of how this in concert with what Jaclyn had said... that Blackstone was changed, talking early retirement, wanting out, and he was asking himself... Did not *all* of these things, when taken together, argue for some permanent stalemate between the two, Blackstone and himself, an ending in which further bloodletting might actually be avoided? He put the question to D when it appeared as if the story were at an end but the big man just wagged his head and the grotesque tattoo along with it.

'You know what *that* is?' D asked. 'You running out there with copies of some old incriminating shit that he's proven he already knows about? That's him doing two things. It's giving you hope that you can still weasel your way out of this. But what it really is, is you dead with old incriminating shit found at the scene. Cops find you like that, it will look like someone's been blackmailing you, or trying to, that the thing went south. And that's where they'll leave it.'

It was true, Chance thought, it would look like that, and he thought for the first time in a long time about Myra Cohen, her violent death consigned to the streets, forever unsolved.

'I just want to be smart,' is what he said. It was of course the same lame thing that he had said to Jaclyn.

'Be smart as you want but here's the deal. You either face this now or show him your ass and pray to God that you get lucky, that he backs off, that you can still go back to being who you were.'

Chance exhaled. He'd always thought that he knew who he was. Recent events had called him into question.

'My humble opinion…' D told him. 'It's a moot fucking point anyway. The man knows where you live. Good news is… you can still call the play…'

'He's already called it, D. It's me alone at the motel.'

'That ain't gonna happen.'

'He says he will know.'

'Listen to me… that call on that phone… that bought you some street cred brother, whether you know it or not. The time will come to spend it.'

'I call him now, he's gonna know I'm with someone. He's probably going to guess who, generically speaking.'

'And then what does he do, call a cop? Besides… you're not going to call from here. You're going to call when we get there. You're going to get him out of that room and then you're going to let me do my thing.' He slipped a flat, double-edged blade from inside the old military jacket and placed it on the table between them. 'Trust me, brother. As of right now, you are not the one in over his head. He is.' A final chorus of assent arose from the residents of the House of Space and Time, acolytes in the Church of Big D.

The essential feature of a shared psychotic disorder (folie à deux) is a delusion that develops in an otherwise healthy individual who is involved in a close relationship with another person (sometimes termed the 'inducer' or 'the primary case') who already has a psychotic disorder with prominent delusions and who, in general, is the dominant in the relationship and is thus able, over time, to gradually impose the delusional system on the more passive and initially healthy individual.

Chance looked at the knife.

'That's for you,' D told him, meaning the weapon. 'Me handling this fucker's not saying *you* won't get wet.'

The way of the blade

THE FOLKS at the House of Space and Time were not so far off the grid as to be off-line as in quick order two laptop computers appeared side by side on the old coffee table... all Google Earth and YouTube... aerial and street views of the Blue Dolphin Motel that was situated at the northern extremity of Ocean Beach where the Great Highway narrowed and turned into Point Lobos Avenue, winding uphill to the Golden Gate National Recreational Area with the park at Lands End and the blue Pacific in close proximity and Big D arranged before them, a great hairless Buddha in military fatigues, his fingers at play upon the keys, his small dark eyes darting between the screens.

'This is interesting over here,' someone said. D said, 'Copy that,' introducing the speaker as Gunnery Sergeant Hernandez, the latter now directing their attention to the coast very near the motel where the Cliff House restaurant and Camera Obscura backed by stairwells and concrete footpaths perched atop steep cliffs falling to the sea with the old city baths due north and these joined to the hiking trails in and around Lands End, as at the big man's direction a plan began to form.

* * *

It would begin with on-site reconnaissance on the parts of D and Carl with Chance following on his own and it would be all about getting Blackstone out of the motel to a place of D's choosing. It would be about selling the detective, not on détente, but on what Chance was willing to *believe* about détente. It was, at a certain level – his brashness in the use of a dead man's phone notwithstanding – about Chance selling his own naiveté regarding the world according to Raymond. And finally it was about a handful of shadowed angles and Big D waiting… silent as a stroke, serious as a heart attack.

It was Gunny who added this last bit, the poetic flourish. As to what Chance thought, no one bothered to ask. The thing had acquired its own momentum and Chance in its wake. Which is not to say that he had abandoned his most recent epiphany or hope for a more reasonable outcome. So that even as the Primary Case continued with his examination of angles the doctor was quietly at work on his own variation, the most salient feature of which had to do with Chance's luring Blackstone from the room. For D this was all about Chance selling his naiveté. For Chance it was a crack in the edifice, the place where the light got in, and naiveté had nothing to do with it but he was not about to share. Which was how he came to find himself in an open place beneath the trees, a blunted 'training blade' in his hand, face-to-face with Big D, an alarming spectacle even in play.

It was the last bit of D's planning, his preparation for the admittedly undesirable but not unthinkable, given the unfolding goat fuck of men at war, possibility that Chance might actually find himself in such close proximity to Blackstone, life and death in the balance and things gone sideways, that it would fall to *him* to deliver the fatal strike.

Their movements were based around a template of strikes, each aimed at a vital part of the body, each fatal. Chance was tasked with, if not the mastery, then at least some rudimentary grasp of three such strikes, *'three of nine,'* as D was wont to repeat, their two pairs of shoes scraping at the ground and Chance aware for the first time in his forty-nine years of his very own pyramid of power.

All three strikes were made with what D called a reverse grip – that is, with the hand made to a fist with the blade pointing down. It was, he said, a good grip by which to conceal the weapon. For when the hand was hanging at the side of the body, as when walking, the blade could very easily be made to lie along the inside of the wrist and forearm, all but invisible to an approaching target, a scenario by which the first of the three strikes could be particularly effective as it was delivered below the eye line, along the inguinal crease and into the high femoral artery. Off this strike came a second, with the hand lifting up into what D called the psycho position for one more quick strike down, this aimed for that soft area behind the subclavicle with the intention of piercing the aortic arch above the heart. While either of these strikes was capable of inflicting a fatal wound, they were particularly lethal as a one-two combination, ending life in a matter of seconds, the body bled out at both ends. And lastly there was what D called the money shot, a single fatal strike delivered to the chest at a point roughly even with the second button of a shirt and like the others it was also made with a reverse grip, a psycho strike in and down, aimed once more for the aortic arch.

There were, D said, a number of advantages to this strike, not the least of which was what he referred to as 'fluid management.' Severing a femoral artery was a messy business. When striking through the chest, however, and presumably as many as two shirts, under and outer, the blade might be counted upon to carry a certain amount of material into the wound. Now if in conjunction with this, one's strike has been true and one is able to hold the blade in place, for a two-count let's say, there will simply no longer be enough pressure left in the system to drive the blood any appreciable distance. The downside of this strike, particularly in the hands of a novice, was that it had to be made with sufficient force to break through the chest cavity and sufficient accuracy to find its target. Unlike the slash at a femoral, which even if not wholly accurate, was almost certain to result in a debilitating wound, the money shot, if not carried out with absolute precision and wholehearted commitment, was likely to prove a disaster.

* * *

And so it went... with the minutes going by and the sweat beading at Chance's brow and running down and Big D forever in front of him, patient as Job, amazingly quick with his hands and light on his feet, inviting, if one cared to go there, a renewed appreciation of what had transpired that night in the alley and how poor the chances of those would-be muggers had really been when matched against the size, speed, expertise, and power that was Big D in motion.

Aside from the fact that he could never imagine himself actually butchering another human by way of what the big man was trying to teach, Chance found that he rather enjoyed the workout. At first he had not wanted to get up, but once up he didn't want to sit down. He was coming to appreciate the utility of motion in holding thoughts at bay, not to mention reality, although at one point near what he took to be the end of their session he allowed his curiosity to get the better of him, to inquire about the odds... of *his* actually making any of this work, in real time in the real world, of his *actually* hitting the target.

'You've just hit it about a hundred times in a row.'

'Under *pressure,* would be my point. I mean, if you had to give a number.'

'Do you know Hamlet?' D asked. He really was no shortage of wonders.

Chance allowed that he did.

'Well,' D told him. 'There you have it. Time comes... trust your training. Do what you've been told. Worry it to death and you're fucked.'

When they were done, or at least as done as they were going to get and the big man geared up, the vest inside his coat hung with throwing blades, handgun clipped to a boot, collapsible baton hung from his waistband and Chance with his blade, a double-edged six-inch dagger that he would, at least in theory, know how to use – if that was really what it came to – when they were done with all of *that*, they set out from the House of Space and Time, Chance, Carl, and D, first to the warehouse and Chance's Olds and then on to Lands End, two cars now... rolling out from the alley behind the warehouse... into the last golden flaring of afternoon light, soldiers of the cross, loosed upon an unsuspecting metropolis.

Chance and the Camera Obscura

A s CARL and D made for the Blue Dolphin, Chance made for his apartment and the ancient paperwork. D had argued against his actually bringing it but Chance thought otherwise. He drove the streets of his city, at once familiar and unspeakably strange, struck through with a certain dumb wonder that it should come to this, that the artifacts of an aberration he had expended so much time and energy in trying to put behind him could, on this particular day, serve as the last bit of thread still binding him to any recognizable version of life on planet Earth, even as the flat, thin blade of Big D's razor-sharp dagger lay upon the seat at his side.

He collected the paperwork in a slim leather case with a zipper and a shoulder strap and returned to his car. He had not yet heard from Big D. The three hours he had promised Blackstone were only now about to be up as he turned onto the Great Highway. There were still, of course, his fellow citizens. He looked upon them as he had the streets, both familiar and strange. Most were in cars but there were still a few on foot, people out and about, surfers calling it a day, dog walkers, the last of the beachgoers, life going on… Might one say as usual? God only knew what sorts of fires, wrecks, and love nests lay beneath the apparently mundane or in what chambers of the heart men would in the end be brought to the dance, their steps in time from the day of their birth till that of their death the number by which they might one day be called before the Bar of Heaven. Or not. At which point a call arrived. 'It's looking good,' the big man told him. 'What's your twenty?'

Chance told him. 'Here's the deal,' D said and it was all pretty perfect. The motel was a little ways inland but close to that stuff they had looked at, the Cliff House and Camera Obscura, and he asked if Chance remembered and Chance said that he knew them well, that the Cliff House was just that, a building on a cliff with the sea below and the Camera Obscura just behind it – a smaller building shaped like a giant camera with a little red pyramid atop its roof – a trick done with the light wherein tourists might observe their surroundings in a somewhat altered form and D named it as the place, that he had checked angles and lines of sight, that there was plenty of parking along the street and that if Chance could get Blackstone to meet him there, and most specifically, to join him on the path leading from the sidewalk at the street to the Camera Obscura, at least as far as the first little turnout that would be obvious when he got there, it was a done deal and a sixty-foot fall to the water and rocks below.

Chance asked if he had seen them yet, one or both.

'Negative on that,' D said. 'But I've got eyes on and I can see the room and it's the number she gave you. Place is one of those old-fashioned motor courts. Separate room, no adjoining walls. They're on an end in the back. Curtains are all drawn but the Crown Vic is parked in front next to some other car that could be hers. There's a black Mercedes sedan parked around back and I saw some guy come out from the back door about ten minutes ago with a bucket to get ice. Looked like the twin of that fucker I sent away. Game's on, bro.'

Chance could feel the string going from the backs of his knees even as he drove. 'Plan's good though,' D told him. 'Weather's getting the whole place ass raped right on time so there aren't that many people out there by where you need to go but you can still pitch it as a public place. You make that happen, I can probably see his play. He won't come by himself but he'll try to make it look like that's what he's doing… maybe give me a moment alone with whatever asshole follows him out.'

The Cliff House rose in the distance, a pale edifice above seawater the color of asphalt.

'You copy?'

Chance did.

'Eyes in the back of your head, Doc. Wind shifts… don't wait to be the receiver. You good for the call?'

Chance said that he was, rolling up on Ocean Beach, the Pacific nothing but wind chop, salt spray blowing in as far as the highway, mixing with the fog, finding his windshield. He set his wipers to intermittent as the big man spoke once more. 'Roll the dice, brother.'

Chance got Blackstone on the phone. 'She's giving you up, pal.' Saying it and hearing himself say it and the voice he was hearing not altogether his own. 'There's no point in killing me 'cause that's just one more thing you'll do time for because believe me, you will do time.'

'The hell is this?' Blackstone asked.

'It's me,' Chance told him.

There was a moment of silence on the line. 'For Christ's sake,' Blackstone said. 'Are you insane?'

Chance went on. 'Only way out of this is for us *all* to walk and never look back.'

'Way out of what?'

'And that involves me giving you this shit you asked for and for you to give me whatever it is she has there with her.'

'Where are you?'

'I'm in front of the Cliff House.'

He could hear Blackstone breathing. 'You need to quit fucking around,' Blackstone said, and hung up.

Chance had made the call on the dead man's cell phone, his own resting on the seat beside him, both set to Speaker so that D might listen in. 'He hung up,' Chance said.

'You're doing great, now call the play.'

Chance got him back. 'I will meet you on the sidewalk in front of the restaurant.'

'And why would I do that?'

'Here's the deal,' Chance said. 'I'm not walking into that room and you should be smart enough to know that but what I will do is sit outside and call the cops and we can all burn 'cause as of right now my daughter is safe which is what I care about and this is what I'm willing to do.'

Blackstone said nothing.

'We settle this today, one way or another.'

'And where's your knife-throwing pal in all of this? Where's he on bringing in the law?'

'What friend?'

'Right.'

'It's just me and you,' Chance said.

'Tough guy.'

'It was all I could think of.'

He could hear Blackstone laughing. He laughed for a bit then coughed. Chance could hear the soft hiss of the tank. 'And why am *I* supposed to trust *you*, tough guy?'

'It's a public place. We meet in the open. We say what we have to say and we trade what we've got to trade. I've got what you wanted.'

'Yeah, you said that.'

'I can tell you right where I am. I'm on the sidewalk south of the restaurant, at exactly the place where the pathway starts that leads down to the Camera Obscura.'

This was followed by one more beat of silence. 'What I'd like to know is this,' Blackstone said at last. 'How has someone like you managed to live so long?' He did not wait for Chance to respond but ended the call once more.

Chance was unclear as to where they stood.

'That was fucking great,' D said.

'How do you know?'

'He'll be there. Trust me.'

Chance parked more or less where he had told Blackstone that he already was and got out. The wind hit him full in the face. It was sharp and cold and as D had predicted there were very few people around. It was getting on in the day with the sun low and the fog rolling in to mute even that. The air was damp and cold and you could hear the seals and sea lions going crazy out on the rocks amid the crashing of waves that were largely unseen amid the watery gloom, the shriek of gulls. He watched as a young couple bundled for caroling made their way into the restaurant and felt the cell phone vibrate inside his pocket.

'We're on,' D said. 'I'm at the motel. *Your* guy is getting into the Crown Vic and there are two other guys coming out and getting into the black Mercedes.' Chance asked if he could see her but he couldn't. 'It's just the guys,' D said. 'There's going to be some kind of play but I'm on it. Just get to your spot and stay there.'

'Copy that,' Chance said.

'Good man. I'm staying on the Mercedes because I think that's who'll make the move. Your guy's window dressing but I will tell you this… you get him alone anywhere along that path and you see a move, don't wait. Go first. Trust your training… land the money shot, help him over the railing, then circle out and head for the park at Lands End… Look for Carl.'

Really? Chance wanted to say but Big D was on again before he could. What D said was 'Hooya, Big Dog.' And what else *was* there to say to that? The big man was gone. Chance was alone. Time passed and precious little of it before the Crown Vic arrived on the scene. He watched as it pulled in and parked. He saw Raymond Blackstone getting out. It was really happening.

Now Chance had hoped to see Blackstone *with* something, a briefcase or satchel, anything by which to carry his own incriminating material, the stuff she claimed to have and Blackstone *had* said something about a trade… but there's nothing in his hands as he climbs from the car. There's no oxygen tank but Chance knows he might be past having to drag that with him everywhere he goes. The thought occurs that he might have something in his pocket… that the stuff she had spoken of might be stored electronically. There are times when one needs to believe in something. It's standard advice for the terminally ill.

Chance has his stuff, of course, the old paperwork in the leather case D told him he should only pretend to bring but this is *his* plan now, the unspoken one forged in hope, so that he's not really pretending about anything. He doesn't know where D is and he doesn't see any black Mercedes. He supposes that any deviation from the plan agreed upon might well upset his friend but knows too that this is his time. He imagines the triumph of reason, a path to understanding.

He's still where he said he would be with maybe fifty yards between himself and Blackstone and his heart beating so loudly he can barely hear the sea. There's some construction equipment nearby, a backhoe and some kind of small cement mixer where they are doing repairs to the wall that runs along the sidewalk to keep pedestrians from falling off and the stuff is situated about halfway between Chance and Blackstone. The machinery is using up a number of parking spaces. Chance had taken a spot near the restaurant but Blackstone has parked farther down, south of the equipment, and the weird thing is… he's still there, still standing at the side of his car. He's where he began except he hasn't begun. Is he waiting for Chance to come to him? Does he even know Chance is there? Chance considers waving but this seems absurd given the circumstances so he continues to stand with the leather case hung from his shoulder and D's double-edged blade in the pocket of his slacks that D has rigged for him with one of those little sheaths like what he fixed for Carl with the wires on it so that when and if Chance reaches into his pocket to draw the blade, the wires will catch on the pocket's lining and the blade will come free but he has no real intention of ever doing it.

And then, finally, it appears that Blackstone has spotted him and has begun to walk uphill in Chance's direction. And maybe this is all it took… the sight of Blackstone moving toward him like some inexorable moment of truth because very suddenly and out of nowhere the oddest thing happens and Chance loses his nerve. Just like that and it's gone. In its place there's a pain in his arm and sweat coming out his ass. He may not be able to feel his feet but of this he is not altogether certain. In accordance with plan A he was supposed to have stayed put. In accordance with plan B, which is his own, he was, at the appropriate moment, to have gone rogue, to have moved from his assigned location, to meet Blackstone in a place where *neither* would be ambushed, where the detective would see that he was for real and a meeting of the minds take place. By one plan he was to have trusted in D. By another he was to have trusted in himself and the great god of reason but it's all starting to feel like trusting in transubstantiation or resurrection of the dead and Chance is losing his religion along with his nerve, not to mention the feeling in his lower extremities and he is suddenly moving away from the designated spot and *not* to meet Blackstone, but in the opposite direction, where he soon finds himself on a concrete stairway behind the restaurant lashed by the wind. It occurs to him that he is running away, but the insight does little to slacken his pace. He comes within sight of parking spaces on the north side of the restaurant where he sees that a black Mercedes sedan is parked in a no-parking zone very near the sidewalk. He assumes it to be the car from the motel although there can be no way of knowing this for certain. The car's windows are heavily tinted. It sits at a distance in the poor light. He can't see who's inside. He can see some people walking up near the ruins maybe half a mile away but it is far too far and the Mercedes is blocking his path. If D is out there somewhere Chance can't find him. The wind sings in his ears. The sky has darkened dramatically. He can see lights coming on inside the restaurant. He's too low to see the people at their tables but he knows they're there. He thinks about joining them but does not quite see how to make that work. He ducks back behind the restaurant, back to the stairs, and takes out his cell phone only to discover the battery has run out of juice. It becomes clear that events are conspiring against him and that he has lost his way. He hears someone walking in approach to the stairwell from what he takes to be the parking lot. It is the sound of hard-soled shoes on concrete and he imagines they are coming for him. He does not wait to find out but flees from the restaurant altogether.

The absurdity of all this is not lost on him but there's nothing in that to lift the spirits. He's going south again now past parked cars at the edge of the street and is able to look back down the sidewalk he's on and see that Blackstone has stopped at a point still south of the construction equipment, possibly because Chance had vanished, but when he sees Chance walking toward him he too begins to move, albeit slowly, and Chance is a little surprised by how far apart they are, at how much distance he has managed to cover in so short a time and wonders if in fact he had begun to run which would account for the dramatic amount of perspiration on his back and face. He's headed downhill and still moving at a pretty good clip, past his car and the path to the Camera Obscura where they were supposed to have gone and Blackstone is just now coming up on the construction equipment so that it is really going to be just the two of them... out in the open as Chance had imagined it and there is something in this that he actually finds calming, so he goes with that and he begins to think it through, to reason it out… to say to himself… okay… I really *do* have the stuff this guy asked for… we are *going* to talk… this *might* actually work. And he can see Blackstone more clearly now and this helps too because Blackstone is really not looking all that great and certainly not all that ominous, thinner than Chance remembers, in slacks and a sports coat, a pale blue dress shirt with no tie worn open at the top in spite of the cold, his black hair looking wet and slicked back and the wind tugging at the cuffs of his slacks and in a weird way Chance almost feels sorry for him until he realizes there's a car somewhere just in back of him and when he looks over his shoulder he sees that it's the black Mercedes. It's close enough now and the light is hitting it at a different angle and he can see that there are two men in the front seat, and he knows it's the same car he saw on the north side of the restaurant and he knows that it's there for him. This certainty is reinforced by the fact that the car is neither accelerating into the street, nor is it parking, even though there are spaces available, but continues in the lot that skirts the sidewalk, that is little more than a broad shoulder of the road, clearly shadowing him as Blackstone approaches from the opposite direction and the thing lands on him like a brick. A blind man could see the future. The Mercedes is going to wait until he and Blackstone draw even, which is going to happen at their present pace on the north side of the construction equipment but very close to it, whereupon someone… Blackstone… a Romanian… perhaps several acting in concert, will force Chance into the car and further than that he does not care to think… only that D was right and that plan A was certainly the better of the two plans but Chance has already blown plan A six ways from Sunday and D is nowhere to be seen and maybe never will be again and the pain he felt earlier returns to his arm and the air grows thin. At which point, and out of this darkness, he sees something else… he sees a bright yellow Starlight coupe rounding a bend in the road, heading his way.

There is a moment that sometimes arrives on certain days in the city at this time of year and it has gotten to be that moment, the sun about to descend, finding some bit of space between cloud and sea and so able for just that moment, and it will only last for a very short period of time, to pierce even the fog and so manage these last long slivers of light as if the gates of heaven had come slightly ajar. The life expectancy of this beauty will be figured in seconds and with its passing it will be all but dark but it is the light by which he sees these things occurring. The coupe has got a good hundred yards to cover and it is unclear what will happen first. Chance throws a look back and can see that the Mercedes has already edged over, getting as close as it can get to where he walks. Blackstone is twenty feet away. So, he thinks, is the Mercedes. But the coupe is coming fast, gaining speed, until finally the old man is visible through the windshield. He appears to be in there alone with that little hat he likes set well back on his head, his hands atop the wheel, closing at quite a clip, as very quickly, in less than a heartbeat, really, Chance can and with absolute clarity see how it will be and what will happen and when and where and why... like a chess master seeing the board and it's the pure geometry of the thing that dazzles, the heretofore unimagined figure suddenly obvious as a sphere and just as elegant and he wonders only briefly that if by seeing it he has not already abandoned any such free will by which his own part in its completion might yet be withheld or that if by seeing it he has not already called forth its inevitability. And so it begins... the old man blowing past... the ensuing explosion of breaking glass and ruptured metal... what can only be the Starlight coupe taking the Mercedes head-on. There does not seem to be anyone else around but if there is... *this* is what he or she will see. Blackstone is *definitely* seeing it and Chance knows this because what he is seeing is Blackstone, or... to put an even finer point on it... the second button on the pale blue dress shirt that Blackstone wears open at the collar because Chance knows that the crash was for him and that for just this moment *he* is the still point in a turning world, all but hidden in a wrinkle of time, all but invisible, his right hand dipping to his pocket to draw the blade, lifting it to the psycho position, his balance shifting with his gait in accordance with his pyramid of power, his weight lending force to the blow...

Just as there is the occasional moment of magic light, there is also the sound a blade makes as it breaks through bone. The human heart, capable of pumping blood by way of a severed artery in excess of thirty feet, may lose the ability to do so in a matter of seconds if the blade has indeed carried enough cloth into the wound and if the aortic arch has indeed been pierced. That's the end of days right there and he was certainly intent on making that happen and making the count and believed himself to have done so, but it was just here, in midstride, that the light seemed to fail and memory with it. He had come to envision the fatal strike and his moving past it with such clarity, his escape into the park, that he was some time in accepting the slowly revealed truth of a new and heretofore unimaginable present, that in point of fact he was no longer in a parking lot nor anywhere near the Cliff House restaurant nor for that matter the Camera Obscura in which light was projected upon a metal plate to the delight of children, but rather in a kind of room that felt almost to be in motion – strapped to a board, his head in a metal cage.

He was far from alone. There were others with him. The person nearest him, a capable-looking young man in the uniform of a paramedic with a closely trimmed goatee and shorn head, was cutting away his sweater with a pair of scissors. He saw this well enough but was determined to reject it outright. He was determined to believe that he had struck with both force and precision and that in the aftermath Blackstone had tumbled to the sea and Chance had passed on, to the anonymity of the park and from there had found his way back to his apartment where he no doubt was just now… asleep in his own bed where at any moment he might expect to be treated to some disturbance on the part of his downstairs neighbors, fighting or fucking, it scarcely mattered, and that this state, this unpleasantness involving men in blue and the loss of a favored and valuable sweater, could be little more than some admittedly unusual stop along the road to a more full awakening.

When, over time, this failed to happen of its own accord, he set about trying to *make* it happen by force of will. The struggle seemed to go on for a good long while until finally, exhausted, he was forced to accept, as had so many before him, that however inexplicable, this was not a dream, that in some extremely opaque and fucked-up way the unacceptable had in fact occurred, certainly without his consent, without even his knowledge, until finally there was nothing for it but to humble himself as the others had humbled *them*selves, to look up into the face of the young man with the scissors, admitting by dint of his own words to his utter helplessness and dependency upon the kindness of strangers and to ask as so many others had asked before him, 'What happened and where am I?'

'You're in an ambulance, Dr Chance,' the young man said. 'You've had quite a bad fall and we're taking you to the hospital.'

He might have asked for more but he didn't. He went straight for the pact with God. He knew the routine. It was common as dirt. He promised God that if he could move his fingers and toes he would never want for more. When that was done and he had waited for what seemed a respectable amount of time, he tried and found that he could indeed move his fingers and toes. God had come through. He guessed that he could live with the rest of it but then he guessed too that they'd probably by now shot him full of morphine and the fact was... now that his business with the universe was out of the way, he was not really feeling all that bad, all things considered.

Chance and the limit experience

THE LIMIT experience (generally imagined as an interrogation of limits by way of transgression) is a type of action or experience that approaches the edge of living in terms of its intensity and seeming impossibility, and is therefore capable, at least in theory, of breaking the subject from itself – and from which the subject may emerge transfigured, as from some mystical encounter.

He spent the night in a room in a hospital, the same in which he tried unsuccessfully to visit both Big D and his daughter. When they asked him if there was someone they should call, he gave them the name of his receptionist, Lucy Brown. From time to time a nurse came to ask him things. They were especially interested in knowing the month, the day, and the year. He knew the drill. At some point Nurse Gooley arrived. It was, as nearly as he could tell, sometime around dawn of the following day.

'You should just move in here,' she told him. 'How's your daughter?'

'At home, with her mother. Thanks for asking. And thank God you're here. They keep asking me to name the president.'

'And what did you tell them?'

'I told them it didn't matter. I told them history is coming for the empire.'

'I bet they liked that.'

'They told me on the way over that I'd had a fall.'

'You fell off a goddamn cliff.'

'Do you think,' Chance asked her, 'that we could get them to add just a dash of the intravenous Valium?' He was looking at the spout in his arm.

'I don't know why not. You're the doctor.'

Chance had seen several doctors since his admission into the trauma center. He'd been scanned, X-rayed, pumped full of a radioactive dying agent proven to damage the thyroid, and scanned again. His pupils had remained somewhat dilated with no evidence of subarachnoid bleeding, intracerebral hematoma, or any shift to the right or left of intracranial content. Still, his concussion had been relatively severe. He was missing time, certainly an hour or more.

'How long do you have to be out,' Nurse Gooley wanted to know, 'before they break down and call it a coma?' She was, as nearly as he could judge, only half kidding but picked it up again before he could decide on an answer. 'You had this with you in the ambulance,' she said.

Chance saw that she was holding the satchel he'd carried to Lands End. It was still zipped tight and seemed little the worse for wear. 'I thought it was something you might want, so I tucked it away when I heard the police were asking for your clothes.'

'The police?' Chance said. He was not so drugged up as to avoid the first stirrings of panic.

'Yes. There was apparently someone else hurt out there or something and they wanted your clothes. Don't ask me why. They said it was routine.'

Was it his imagination or was she giving him a bit of a look? She placed the satchel on the rolling table at his bedside. 'Did I do good?' she asked.

'Yes,' Chance said. 'Yes, you did. I would very much prefer to have this with me, thank you.'

She patted him on the leg. 'I imagine someone will be around.'

By someone, he assumed her to mean the police. He felt certain that she had winked at him on her way out and waited a full ten seconds to be sure she was not stepping back in before opening the case. It was all there, the old shit, that and a few grains of sand that had mysteriously found their way inside. When he had assured himself of its contents, he shoved it beneath the blankets and dozed with it there beside him, growing warm beneath the back of a thigh.

He woke hours later to the play of sunlight through the room's single window to find that a man had appeared in his doorway. The man was probably no older than forty with a broad, suntanned face beneath short blond hair neatly trimmed. He wore a dark gray suit with a white shirt and burgundy tie, and Chance took him at once for what he was, the someone Nurse Gooley had predicted.

He introduced himself as Detective Newsome of the San Francisco Police Department and proved, if nothing else, a fountain of information. Chance it seems had managed to make contact with the pedestrian safety wall above Ocean Beach at just that point where the top portion had been removed as part of a general renovation. The sidewalk had been cordoned off with yellow tape but that was hardly enough to prevent Chance, distracted no doubt by the traffic accident that had occurred almost right on top of him, from stumbling into the site and over, some forty feet, to the sand below.

If not for the work, such a fall would have been all but impossible. It was equally true that on any other day the fall would, in all probability, have proven fatal. What saved him was the very work that had allowed for the accident's possibility, which is to say the large mound of imported sand piled against the cliff face just below the wall as part of the city's ongoing war with beach erosion. The sand had both shortened and cushioned his fall. There was also the day of the week to be considered. Chance had fallen on a Sunday. This had been revealed to him only at the hospital, for up until then, given the events of the past days and the run to

Lands End, he had pretty much lost all sense of time. On any day of the week *save* Sunday, workers would have been present, preventing access to the site. And finally there was the hour. Chance had fallen on the lowest possible tide, a minus six feet, meaning that a good deal more of the beach was exposed than might normally be expected. Had he fallen on a higher tide, he might well have rolled off the temporary dune and into the water, where he almost certainly would have drowned before help could arrive.

'You see where I'm going with this,' Newsome told him. The man had a pleasant enough manner.

'I got lucky.'

'Yes, but only after you were unlucky.'

Chance could've made an entire meal out of that one but Detective Newsome was hardly the guy to share it with. 'Tell me about the accident,' he said finally. 'With the cars.'

'A very old man lost control of his very old Studebaker, ran head-on into a new Mercedes.'

'Was anyone hurt?'

'There's a whole story there,' Newsome said. 'Guys in the Mercedes took off. Ran over a girl on a skateboard trying to get back on the road, then abandoned their car in Golden Gate Park, where contraband was found inside the vehicle.'

Chance didn't ask about the contraband and Newsome didn't say. He asked about the girl instead.

'Girl's going to make it. But that's only one piece of it. There was a homicide in progress with multiple victims at very nearly the same time and only blocks away. A dirty cop was involved so of course the media's all over it. Front-page news as of today so I'm not telling you anything you won't read in the papers.'

Chance was aware of certain physiological changes taking place, a distant, high-pitched ringing, a prickly sensation at his hairline. He wondered aloud about the men in the Mercedes.

'Still at large,' Newsome said. 'But yeah… we'd love to

find 'em. Witnesses made them as foreign looking. The dead cop had Romanian mob ties, but like I said, you can read all about it. Papers probably know more than I do at this point.'

Chance doubted it. He was beginning to doubt the detective's conviviality as well. Surely, he thought, it was a trick on hoopleheads, a trap waiting to spring. He inquired after the old man.

'Nothing serious. Probably just too old to be driving... couple of onlookers said it was his fault.'

'How did they find me?'

'Some guy on the beach walking his dog. At least that's what he said. He didn't stick around. When we tried to trace the call, we hit a dead end. Phone was a burner. Do you know what those are?'

Chance said that he did.

'Doctors told me you weren't remembering much about the incident. I'm wondering if you remember why you were there?'

'I enjoy the walk up to the old baths and I needed to clear my head,' Chance told him. 'We've been having some trouble with my daughter...' This is how it begins, he thought, the cat and mouse of it.

'I understand there was a missing persons report filed but that now she's back.'

'Still some things there we need to address, but yes, it was a great relief. The last thing I remember is getting out of my car, putting my keys in my pocket.'

'That would have been by the Cliff House.'

Chance nodded but he was thinking about his pockets and what else might be there... a little sheath with wires on it.

'You're a doctor, they tell me.'

'Neuropsychiatry.'

'Interesting stuff,' Detective Newsome said. 'Does the name Raymond Blackstone mean anything to you?'

Chance said that it did not, but pretended to deep

reflection. 'Of course, I've seen many patients over the years, but the name does not stand out.'

'Well,' Newsome told him. 'He's the cop I was telling you about, but he was also one of the victims. He was found nearby but witnesses have also placed him near the Cliff House. Do you recall seeing anyone else anywhere near you before you fell?'

'The answer to that is no. My amnesia for the event is quite complete. It's my guess that I'm missing about an hour altogether.'

'Weird how that works, isn't it? But then I'd guess you'd know more about it than most.'

'We are continually in the business of laying down memory,' Chance told him, only too happy for the opportunity. 'With an injury… such as mine… that physiological process inside the brain gets interrupted. But as to *exactly* how or why the retrograde component can vary so wildly… why there are people whose memory loss may be a matter of minutes while others may lose months or even years…'

'And it's not just the severity of the injury?'

'That's of course a factor, but there may also be psychological factors… psychogenic amnesia… We tell ourselves stories to make sense of who we are. Certain types of highly charged, highly traumatic events are simply too terrible to fit into the narrative we have created. So we block them out. You find this in soldiers, others with post-traumatic stress…'

'Cops.' Newsome was smiling at him.

'Police officers are certainly in a position to have those kinds of experiences.' He supposed it was time to rein it in.

'And what are the chances that any of this comes back?'

'That too varies. Some people, over time, will remember everything. Others never do.'

Detective Newsome produced a card. 'You get any of it back, call me.' He placed his card on the table at Chance's side. 'You're an interesting guy. I'd enjoy talking some more, when you're up to it.'

'The nurse said you'd taken my clothes.'

'Yeah, sorry. We want to look them over, see if maybe you and Blackstone came into contact or were victims of the same perp.'

'Really?'

Newsome shrugged. 'We're still trying to determine where exactly Blackstone was injured. Like I said, he was seen at Ocean Beach. Same location the guys in the Mercedes were trying to get away from, in a hurry. And here you are... a doctor. Maybe you saw something out there, tried to help. Lab may tell us more... fibers, hairs, blood... Let me put it like this. I'm not a big believer in coincidence. Goes with the job, is what my wife tells me.' He smiled once more.

With Newsome gone, Chance rang for additional morphine and a copy of the day's paper.

The detective had been right of course. It was all there, the obvious stuff anyway. Raymond Blackstone had been found dead in a room at the Blue Dolphin Motel. Incriminating evidence had been found at the scene linking the former homicide detective to a prostitution and human trafficking ring with ties to a Romanian mob based in Oakland. As to whether or not the body had been moved, as Newsome had suggested, the papers weren't saying. A second body had also been found in the motel, a Romanian male with ties to the same Oakland-based mob. Two more men, also believed to be Romanians, had been seen fleeing the scene of an accident at nearby Ocean Beach. These men were also wanted for a second hit-and-run incident involving a pedestrian and finally there was mention of the San Francisco–based doctor, name withheld, who had fallen from a cliff at very nearly the same time and place as the two hit and runs.

There was a good deal of speculation as to how all of these things had occurred in such close proximity to one another and what if any were the connections between them but little in the way of fact. Additional witnesses had yet to come forward and authorities were still looking for the men in the Mercedes. Anyone with information was being asked to contact the police.

Chance stayed where he was and willed himself to remember, to little avail. It occurred to him that Jean-Baptiste had for a time trafficked in hypnosis and was supposed to have been quite effective. A phone call to the building, however, informed him that Jean-Baptiste's condition had worsened suddenly. He was in the building but had withdrawn to his apartment and was declining calls.

In the absence of verifiable fact there was little for it but to work with what he had. Certainly he and Blackstone had come within reach. The Starlight coupe had collided with the Mercedes. Horns had sounded, but here already he was into the realm of conjecture. Horns *would* have sounded. Metal *would* have screamed and given way. Glass *would* have broken. Anyone even remotely near the scene would have turned to look. Chance would have taken the opportunity to plunge his blade into Blackstone's chest at a point more or less even with the second button of the pale blue dress shirt the detective had worn... And all of this *seemed* to have happened... the bloodred blossoming across another's chest... the rhythms of a heart in cardiac arrest felt even by way of steel run to the aortic arch...

But then he might just as well, with an equal or even greater clarity, remember other things too. He might, for instance, and in great detail, recall the bungalow with its horrid shades of yellows and browns, Formica beneath paisley prints, louvered blinds on rusted metal – the Blue Dolphin, after all, dating to the sixties, the decade of his birth. One might've thought they would have refurbished the place between then and now but that would have required some heave of the will it was clearly not theirs to command. The room smelled rather of stale cigarettes and Pine-Sol with its sorry set of house rules even now affixed to the inside of the door that disallowed smoking, loud music, and dancing but omitted outright murder. As with what he knew of those events in the parking lot, he could, and with very little effort, build it out from there…

He would have found *her*… seated on the bed… eyes round as a deer's in the headlights and known right then that he was fucked, that Big D had been right, that the point in Blackstone's inviting him to talk was no more than Chance dead in a tawdry motel and this old incriminating shit right there with him and what *else* would there ever be, but to think that someone was shaking him down, the skivvy doctor, and the thing gone sideways? As for what Blackstone had planned for her, it was more difficult to say. Would they have found her dead there as well, or in some other corner of the world, or not at all? It scarcely mattered now. Still… Raymond Blackstone must have felt himself at the very brink of pulling it off, of ridding himself of at least one if not both of them, close enough to taste it when the wrench lands in the gears… Big D blowing through the doors, perhaps… Or maybe it was *him*? Maybe it was *here* that Chance had drawn his blade and if not, why else would he remember it so just now… right down to the last detail of the sorry blood-soaked room? What he *can't* logic is how, in the aftermath of *this* horror, he also comes to be on the sand at Ocean Beach. Would it not be true that the beach and room are mutually exclusive propositions? On the other hand, and this is where it got *really* messy, if it was also true and he knew it to be, particularly in such cases as those described by him to Detective Newsome, that in certain instances involving *both* amnesia and post-traumatic stress, a patient's *most* vivid, detailed congruent memories might also be complete fabrications and if every last part of it anyway, at both beach and motel was, in *any* configuration or even combination thereof, when judged by all previously acceptable standards, already so far beyond the pale as to be more the stuff of fever dream and confabulation than any heretofore recognizable reality… well then, at the end of the day, why *not* indulge oneself? Why not mix and match, as if these shards of memory were no more than the bits of colored glass in a child's kaleidoscope and thereby subject to rearrangement on a moment's whim with a flick of the wrist?

Suffice it to say the head injury had brought him to a place that no longer felt like home. He was there and then he wasn't. The only experience he could even remotely liken it to was that of being prepped for surgery – drugs run to the main line, counting backward into the void as the present vanished. But in that there was context. In this there was none. In its absence, his sense of the present had grown fragile as a robin's egg. Perhaps he was only imagining that he could still move his fingers. Who could say that at any moment his present sense of space and time would not dissolve once more, admitting him to a different and even more terrible reality? The prospect was enough to induce sweats and palpitations, yet he indulged it tirelessly. The room and the beach were but two possibilities. How could there not be a version of things in which Blackstone or one of the Romanians had bested him? Perhaps *he* was dead and this was what it was like. Perhaps he was strapped to a bed in a psych ward in a county jail. He was not so far gone that he could not recall patients having described similar states or the sorry-ass justice he had done them in his endless and dreary reports…

Eldon Chance is a 49-year-old right-handed neuropsychiatrist who is now 36 hours post cerebral concussion suffered in a fall from a cliff at Ocean Beach in San Francisco in which he also sustained fractures of the T-3 and T-4 vertebrae as well as fractures of the 8th, 9th, and 10th ribs on his left side and two broken fingers on his left hand. He has no clear memory of the fall or of events immediately following or preceding it. He reports memories that are in fact mutually exclusive, but experiences them with the intensity of hallucinations. After an initial sensation of relief at finding himself alive, he admits to trouble in dealing with his current mental state, which he finds to be muddied and unstable. He believes that this is not who he is but is uncertain as to a more definite and recognizable identity. He worries that everything he has done with his life thus far has been little more than a banal series of empty and futile gestures. He recalls with clarity the people in his life but believes himself to have failed them on many fronts, as husband, father, and physician, and that in the days leading up to his accident he may have done bad things that have been pushed below the level of conscious thought and that he may be, in his own words, 'some kind of asshole.' Uncertain as to the events in his most immediate past, he is also uncertain about his future. He feels that he has lost the ability to judge what he is or is not capable of and worries that he may in some way bring harm to himself or others. He is aware of certain disturbing urges in this regard and worries about his ability to hold them at bay. He is also fearful of a second loss of consciousness from which he will emerge into even more undesirable circumstances and of his learning of even more bad things that he has done. When pressed to reveal more about his 'certain disturbing urges' he admits to having entertained the drinking of household cleaning products, of wishing to acquire a pet rat together with a handgun, and of a desire to begin reading all printed matter backward, that is from right to left across the page and from the bottom of the page to the top. He recognizes in these urges certain pathologies he has treated others for over the years but fears that in the absence of a more concrete and recognizable version of himself, he may be inclined to adopt these and as a consequence of which will, over time, be no more than a walking repository of the thousand and one mental illnesses he's been forced to deal with throughout his twenty-odd years of medical practice, and that this may be only the beginning...

A happy man in every crowd

FROM TIME to time figures appeared. Chance took them as visitors, asking only that they treat him as he did them – players in a dream.

'I'll do nothing of the sort,' Janice Silver told him. 'What the hell anyway?'

'You knew my daughter was in the hospital?'

'I do now.'

'I had gone for a walk.'

'I'm so sorry. And how is your daughter?'

'She's better,' Chance said. 'I am too.'

'And you *know* about Blackstone.' She had already seen the paper on the little cart by his bed. 'Guess we weren't the only ones that didn't like him.'

'It's a dangerous gig even for the good cops,' Chance said, repeating what Big D had once said to him and taking some amount of pleasure in it.

'You were right there, for Christ's sake.'

Chance said nothing.

'Have you said anything?'

'To whom?'

'They're asking people to come forward.'

'They're asking for people with information to come forward and anyway *they* were already here.'

'And?'

'And nothing, Janice. I went for a walk. I fell.'

She gave him a long look then waited a bit before saying more. 'And have we heard anything… from her?'

'We have not,' Chance answered.

When they'd sat with this one for a while and he had told her that he was sorry, that he needed to sleep, she leaned over to squeeze his arm. 'All right,' she said. 'This thing is over. You're alive and thank God. If you ever want to talk, you know where to find me.'

Chance thanked her and he meant it.

There were more visitors. Carla came, as did his daughter.

'I don't know what's to become of you,' Carla said. It was after she had studied him for a good while before withdrawing to leave him alone with Nicole.

'I'm really sorry, Daddy,' his daughter's first words. Without being entirely clear about what all she was sorry *for*, Chance said that he was sorry too. He assumed they were talking about everything. They held hands. She wept. He thought at first that it was over him and maybe it was, though what he came to learn in short order was that the bad boyfriend had broken her heart. It was her first foray into *that* bleak land and he hoped it would be her last. The boyfriend, an exchange student from Italy, studying for a degree in environmental law at UC-Berkeley and ten years her senior, had, on the very afternoon that he'd helped spring her from the hospital, been found in the company of another woman, in a compromising position.

Chance had no idea what to make of this or of how to place it in the secret history of things. He had, at just that moment, been busy doing battle with an intrusive memory, possibly false, of the blade in his hand, of Blackstone's face and strangled cry, yet still doing his best to console and cajole. In the end she sighed and rested her head on his chest. A merciful silence descended. The intrusive memories, either real or imagined, came and went along with recurrent glimpses of the thing's geometric shape... of which even this was perhaps a part. If he could only be more certain of what, precisely, the *this* was, by which he meant the here and now.

But the thing kept running before him like a shadow: *You're not in it now... you're not in it now...* Perhaps, he thought, one need simply embrace the infamous axiom, that what in the end it all came down to was a matter of choice. After still more time had passed and his daughter had gone, Jean-Baptiste walked in.

'Thank God,' Chance said. 'I've been at the end of my rope. They told me you were sick.'

Jean-Baptiste dismissed this with a wave of the hand and took a chair. 'Talk to me,' he said.

Chance did. He confessed to everything. He wondered aloud for the first time to a discerning ear at how more had not been clear to him from the start... that he should have strayed so far from the path that it should have come to this. Jean-Baptiste, in his inimitable style, would only say that while there was no doubt he might have been a tad more prescient, his *failure* to stray so far from the path would certainly have made for a less interesting story. As far as its being the road to ruin, he was more inclined to find in it the Nietzschean path of going under to get over.

On the subject of what, exactly, Chance had gotten over to, his friend was less forthcoming but also unconcerned. 'I wouldn't worry about any of that,' Jean-Baptiste told him. 'This funk you're in is not at all uncommon in the wake of a serious concussion, as *you* well know. As to this other... Do not despair. You will find it.'

'You don't think the whole idea is a reach?'

'Everything's a reach, brother. You have no idea how this kind of thing lifts me up. And you, of all people.'

'You know,' Chance said, 'now that it's over... and I think about her... I think about the Laocoön.' He could guess that Jean-Baptiste would know the piece, the father and sons locked in doomed struggle with monsters from the depths. 'And I think that must be what it's like for her, that there's this huge thing in the past she can't get clear of... that keeps dragging her back...'

'Against which her strategy is to spin *possibilities* of escape in the form of new identities.'

'Did I tell you one of her was a Romanian hooker adept in the language?'

Jean-Baptiste stifled a laugh.

'You think that's funny? Let me tell you, it was scary as shit is what it was. I had to turn on the lights to make sure it was her.'

'How's the gland by the way?'

'They've given me an anti-inflammatory and antibiotics. You'll never know what a relief it is to be pissing again.'

'Ah. But from what you've told me, these identities of hers have little in the way of duration.'

'That's right. They break apart. The monster pulls her back.'

'Much as I admire the old Nietzsche I've always thought he was full of shit on the what doesn't kill you makes you stronger routine.'

'Yes, Pollyanna-ish and glib.'

'There *is* maimed for life.'

'Chemical deviations...'

'Shit we're not yet equipped to see.'

'Yet something heroic in the struggle.'

'And how might *her* struggle be defined, do you think? The predator hunting predators, finding one man to trap another...'

'Maybe even aiding and abetting the trapped man in*to* some type of predatory behavior, making him into the very thing she needs to destroy.'

'That's dark.'

'Her special gift.'

'But always as part of this unconscious need to free herself... doing unto others what was done to her in some past life we know nothing of but at which we can guess? Is that her deal with the universe, the most authentic version of the self she can manage? *Or...* was it her *believing* that your daughter was in mortal danger that generated her play at the end, her crossing him and calling you? It wouldn't mean that at certain points along the way she wasn't playing you, only that we must also consider the possibility of the child in danger as the thing that in the end called forth her most authentic self.'

They sat with this.

'And wouldn't it be fun to ask? Some final reckoning in the wake of everything, one last reading of the old ledger.'

'If ever there is such a thing.'

'Yes, well… there *is* that. Still… we don't suppose that we will ever hear from her again?'

'I wouldn't imagine it. The way it ended… I would imagine her long gone and nothing here to bring her back.'

A mechanical device at Chance's side began to emit a soft humming sound. 'You really did like her though,' Jean-Baptiste said, more or less out of the blue, 'that one you found?' The idea seemed to please him.

'That would be one way of putting it.'

'And that *is* the saving grace in all of this,' he said. 'Whether you know it or not. You've read your Kierkegaard: *Purity of Heart Is to Will One Thing.*'

This time it was Chance who laughed.

'Go ahead,' Jean-Baptiste told him. 'But I'm telling you there is something in that, and that it *is* necessary to remind oneself almost constantly that many among us will die without ever knowing they were alive, save only in the most rudimentary ways, of course, but don't get me started.'

'No, we wouldn't want to do that.'

More time passed. The device ceased its humming. It had been delivering drugs, the old morphine drip among them. Jean-Baptiste got up to inspect the plastic bag on the rack at Chance's bedside. He often did volunteer work at state hospitals and rest homes in search of his pictures and knew his way around a room. 'You gotta get off the sauce,' he said. 'It'll fuck with your head. And stop rummaging in this grab bag of possibilities. It seems plain enough to me that you were never in that room. You were on the sidewalk and then you were on the beach and then you were here. Stop running.'

Chance said nothing but watched as Jean-Baptiste sat back down. He looked awfully tired, Chance thought, and was quite moved by the generosity of spirit with which his old friend had undertaken the journey to see him. Given Jean-Baptiste's enthusiasm for things, the reach of his mind, you sometimes had to remind yourself that he was dying.

'And what about him?' Jean-Baptiste asked.

'Him?' Chance had been thinking about his friend.

'This Blackstone. Final thoughts?'

Chance gave it a moment. 'I think he was like me,' he said finally. 'I think he loved that whore.'

'I want you to have my photographs,' Jean-Baptiste told him.

'I'd like that,' Chance said. 'I'd like that very much.'

It was only later that he would learn Jean-Baptiste had died on the very day Chance had fallen, that someone in the office had thought it best to withhold the information, perhaps until he was stronger. But he would never quite be able to believe that they had not by some means communicated or that Jean-Baptiste had not by some means beyond his reckoning been there with him in the room, so that when Lucy Brown finally did come in with the news, it was *he* who told *her* about having inherited the collection. 'He was here, then?' she asked. 'With you, in the room?'

'How else would I have known?'

Lucy said nothing for a good long while but advised him on her way out to journey safely among the spheres.

Of his last visitor there was less doubt as to his actual physicality but no relief from the surreal. The man was built like a spark plug, a personal injury attorney with the dress and manner of a strip club barker. Having read in the papers of Chance's fall he had already been out to Lands End to visit the spot. *'I want you to listen to me,'* the guy told him. *'I took a ride out there and I saw that sight. It's a joke. Tape where there ought to have been some form of barricade... It was their job to protect people and they failed. You're a doctor with a head injury. Your entire livelihood is at stake.'* He went on to wonder if anyone from the city had perhaps been by, *'looking to settle,'* and was relieved to find that they had not. *'That's a good thing,'* he said. *'Fuzzy state you're in, you might have signed something and then where would you be? Now on, anyone wants to talk to you, they talk to me instead.'* As apropos of very little save his prowess to wrest great sums from large, impersonal institutions, he went on to tell of a former client who, while attempting to draw money from an ATM, had been struck by a drunken driver, losing both legs from the knees down. The bank had offered a million dollars. The attorney had gotten him ten. 'You know what he does now?' the attorney asked.

'I can't imagine,'Chance said.

'He pulls a rickshaw in Chinatown on prosthetic limbs, ten million in the bank. Go figure.'

Chance saw that the guy was not so different from himself, or for that matter from the late detective. They had all spent a good deal of time prowling among the ruins. In time he would learn that the man had offices on the Great Highway with a view of the beach. On each step of the stairway leading upward was an old surfboard. Inside there were photographs of the waves of Ocean Beach and Chance would find that he liked looking at them. *'These fuckers are liable and they're going to pay,'* the suffering attorney told him before leaving the hospital. 'I need two hundred and fifty thousand dollars,' Chance said. The guy just laughed, told him *'the Big Guy'* upstairs must've heard already and to start adding zeros. *'And you should get in the water sometime,'* he added, apropos of almost nothing. *'It's good for the head.'* Chance, who had not yet been to the man's offices or seen his pictures, had no idea what he was talking about but he was no longer paying much attention either. He was thinking about the big guy and not necessarily the one upstairs. He was thinking that between Jean-Baptiste, the cop, and the surfing attorney he was ready for yet one more go at the old kaleidoscope, one more turn of the wrist.

It would have begun, would *had* to have begun, with D and Carl trailing the Mercedes from the motel to the restaurant where D would have gotten out, eyes on the men, waiting for them to make their move, to come at Chance from behind and the whole thing set to play out more or less when and where and even how the big man had said it would. But Chance throwing the block into *those* gears with his dead phone and headless chicken act, that must have left them *all* guessing. Then Blackstone gets a visual and everybody is set to improvising… the Romanians coming by car now, but still slow enough for D to shadow in the failing light, and the big man seeing it like Chance had seen it, and calling in what might pass for air support in the person of Carl Allan and his Starlight coupe – the great diversion beneath which Chance makes his play… It was only everything else that continued to elude him. Blackstone stabbed by the beach but found in the room? And why no murder weapon? The best he could come up with was something like… D arriving at the scene to find Blackstone already dead, the knife still in his chest, and not only removing the blade but guessing it was Chance who'd gone over the wall, and calling it in, just in case, anonymously of course, as a man and his dog… and then goes even further and stuffs Blackstone into the Crown Vic (the keys would have been on Blackstone's body) and drives him back to the Blue Dolphin, trying to make it look like it all happened there, and kills the Romanian who'd been left to guard her and the two of them walk out, him and her, and disappear… back into the cool gray city of love… Was that all too much, or was it like the old man thought, and Big D a kind of ongoing magic act? Maybe it had something to do with that book his grandmother had mentioned – *Unlocking Your Hidden Powers*. But when at last an opportunity presented itself and he'd limped with the aid of a walker to a pay phone in the lobby and gotten D on his burner and asked how he'd managed it, in truth that is, and had she mentioned his name? D would say no more than, 'Managed what?' adding only that he was happy that Chance was happy… it all having worked out so well with his furniture and all, because when you got right down to it… these things were, in point of fact, never an exact science and happy endings a long way from written in the stars and there was little for it but for Chance to agree that yes, timing was indeed everything, and to return to his room where for the first time in a good long time, he actually stopped to consider the possibility of his being happy and of what that might look like, the war in his prostate notwithstanding.

Chance and the bleeding heart

THE BETTER part of a week and his doctors were ready to discharge him. He was brought by a male nurse to the front of the building in a wheelchair, dressed in the baggy gray sweat suit Lucy had picked out and delivered to his room along with the pair of red felt house slippers he was also wearing that she had declared to be cool and a real find. Romeos, she had called them. Any remainders of the clothes he had come with were apparently languishing in a police lab in some quarter of the city and there still had been no word regarding what if anything had been found in his pockets. His shoes on the other hand had been inexplicably returned and rode now in his lap along with his overnight bag and a magazine promoting men's health, the promise of six-pack abs in thirty days.

The gland and broken fingers were in pretty good shape but the ribs and vertebrae still hurt like a bastard when the pain meds wore down and he was still subject to the odd moment of vertigo. Lucy had gotten the Cutlass out of compound and ordered a hospital bed installed in his apartment. She was proving invaluable and he was expecting her there to pick him up when he noticed a woman he didn't recognize entering the main waiting room and walking in his direction. The woman had what looked to be very short, strawberry blond hair beneath a bright turquoise scarf and oversized dark glasses like something Jacqueline Onassis might have worn. He was expecting her to turn to one side or the other and was surprised to find her walking directly to him. 'Look at you,' she said, in a voice at once strange and familiar and he saw that it was Jaclyn Blackstone.

There are times when it is good to be seated, if even in a wheelchair and this was one of them. Jaclyn told the nurse she would 'take it from here.' And from there rolled him into the harsh light of what he took to be midday. 'I like your slippers,' she said.

'Lucy picked them out,' he told her, but it was like talking at altitude where they were stingy with their oxygen.

She pushed him to the street where the Oldsmobile was waiting and asked if he needed help getting in but Chance told her that he could manage. She next wondered if he would need the wheels to get into his apartment. He reminded her of the stairs then waited in the passenger side of the front seat while she returned the chair and came back to the car.

'How is this possible?' he asked finally. They'd ridden for half a mile in stone silence during which time his pulse had returned to a somewhat more normal count.

'I'm not sure what you mean,' she said.

'Well,' he said, 'this for starters,' meaning her and his car.

'Your assistant and I reached an agreement,' she said.

'Should I ask about what?'

'Probably not.'

'And what about the rest?' he asked at length. 'Should we talk about that?'

She didn't say anything at all for another city block and then she did. 'I remember some of it,' she told him. 'He came back after he'd left to find you… and there was a knife sticking out of his chest… I could see it moving in time to his heart… I was still cuffed to the bed but the guy he'd left to watch me walked over and looked at it, and when he bent down, Raymond pulled out this special gun he carries and shot him with it, under his chin. It wasn't that loud, really, but you could see part of his head come off. And then…

before he could say or do anything else… the knife stopped and he was dead.'

'My God.'

'How does something like that even happen?'

'The heart's a muscle,' he said after a good long beat. 'It could do that… knot up around the blade. But the heart rests inside this membranous sack called the pericardium. The sack would fill with blood, constricting the heart. Imagine a small bird gripped in a hand, trying to spread its wings.'

They were both, he supposed, a moment in trying to imagine it.

'The condition is called cardiac tamponade – obviously fatal if left untreated. The severity of the bleeding, the speed at which the pericardium fills would determine how much time one has,' is what he said. *This was me…* is what he thought. He had missed the money shot, by which death would have come in a hurry, and hit the heart. There remained the question of why Blackstone had driven back to the motel and not tried for a hospital, or called for paramedics.

'I don't know,' she said. 'The guy he left there was supposed to have killed me if no one came back.'

Chance stared between the buildings that flanked them to a sliver of pale blue sky the color of Blackstone's shirt.

'He always *said* he would protect me.'

'And you were still on the bed.'

'That's when this big guy with a spider on his head showed up. He took the knife and he let me go. I asked if it was you but he gave me a look and I shut up. He's a little scary. Where did you find him?'

'He fixed my furniture,' Chance told her.

'Right. But that's a good answer. How is your daughter?'

'A little older, a little wiser, but otherwise whole. How is yours?'

Her hand moved to make some minor adjustment to her

glasses before returning to the wheel. 'She's good. He never had her, you know.'

'Who?'

'Your daughter.'

'Are you certain of that?'

She appeared to give this one some thought. 'I know it's strange… you look at everything else… but he was never much of a liar.'

Chance thought about that and what if anything there was to even say about it. The subject felt exhausted somehow and he fell to watching her instead. She had a funny way of holding herself as she drove, tilting her head up as if she were too short to see across the car's hood, which of course she was not. She was five foot six and a half for Christ's sake, with a good figure… and a bit tentative behind the wheel, which was somehow unexpected given every other thing he knew about her. She was, among other things, slow from red lights and got herself honked at on three separate occasions between the hospital and Chance's apartment by which time he had stopped counting, lost in a study of her profile, the bones of her wrists as her hands opened and closed atop the wheel, the sunlight on her skin and he was trying to decide which one she was – not exactly the shyly flirtatious one from the Berkeley bookstore, but not the broken one from that first day in his office either, and certainly not Jackie Black. 'Are you coming up?' he asked.

She all but laughed at him but it was good-natured enough, a little flirtatious even. 'Really?' she asked. 'You haven't had enough excitement for one day?'

Two hours ago, a nurse carting away his bedpan, he could not have imagined that he would so soon be so dizzy with wanting… in spite of… because of… He supposed it written all over him.

She smiled again but it turned a little sad as she looked to the entrance of his apartment and Lucy seated on the stairs in front of the metal door where he and Jackie Black had once vied for his member. 'You're the best friend I've ever had,' she told him, and got out.

Chance opened the door and using it for leverage managed to stand, first in the gutter then on the sidewalk, still bracing himself upon the car. There was a good breeze blowing in off the breakers at Ocean Beach where perhaps his very own surfing attorney was even now at play in the fields of the Lord and he could feel it stirring the hair on the top of his head where it had begun to thin and imagined that he must look very much like how he felt, a scarecrow in Romeos and baggy sweats. As she came around to his side of the car he saw that there was a manila envelope in her hands and that she wanted him to have it. 'I decided this was something you should see,' she said. 'It's the least I can do.'

He wanted to ask if he would see her again but she had removed the dark glasses and the answer to that was written in her eyes as very suddenly she pulled him close, pressed herself against him, and was gone, fixing her glasses and walking briskly toward the coast before rounding a corner at the end of the block, and then she was really gone and there was only the sunlight pooling where she had been and then even that lost to the first traces of what he knew in very short order would turn to a dense and impenetrable fog. He might still have run after her, had it not been all he could do to remain vertical. And then there was Lucy to help him inside. 'Don't even ask,' she said.

Chance waited until she had gone before opening the manila envelope, alone now in the room where they had once been together, recognizing at once the work of Raymond Blackstone...

On May 5, Gayland Parks was found murdered inside his apartment in the city of Oakland. I, along with Homicide Team 1, responded to investigate the incident.

Phone records obtained at the time suggested that Parks's cellular phone was still in use and that calls were being made to parties in San Diego, California. Detective Lopez and I obtained permission to travel to San Diego to question the parties involved.

During the initial investigation, it was also learned that the victim, Gayland Parks, was a collector of Empire State Buildings. The buildings were made from a variety of materials, including paper. Many were quite elaborate and worth considerable money. Many of these collectibles were still in the original boxes or in plastic display cases.

After two days in San Diego Detective Lopez returned to Oakland in response to a family emergency. I traveled alone to Tijuana, Mexico, to meet with Detective Raul Moreno of the Mexican State Police. Detective Moreno was familiar with the case and informed me that Jane, whose real name was Jo Ann Patterson, had been picked up on the previous day in the Zona Norte region of the city and brought to police headquarters, where she had confessed to the murder of Gayland Parks but stated that it was in self-defense. She further stated that she had stolen several of the collectible Empire State Buildings from the Parks condominium and taken them to her mother's address in Ensenada, Baja California, and that her mother's name was Gladys Patterson. According to Patterson, her mother lived at 1416 Calle Nuevo in Ensenada, Mexico. (See Jo Ann Patterson Arrest Report and Interview of Jo Ann Patterson.)

Detective Moreno and I spoke to Gladys Patterson shortly thereafter and obtained permission to search her residence in Ensenada. According to Mrs Patterson, the collectibles were in Jo Ann Patterson's daughter Sky's bedroom at that location.

The same day, at approximately 1530 hours, Detective Moreno and I met with Mrs Patterson at her residence in Ensenada. Mrs Patterson directed us to a bedroom where items belonging to Gayland Parks were recovered.

It should be stated that these items were no longer in their original condition but had been cut apart, reassembled, and joined with additional materials to make what appeared to be a dollhouse of elaborate proportions. The work, while of interest in and of itself, effectively destroyed the value of Parks's original collection.

Mrs Patterson informed us that Jo Ann often brought gifts to the room and in fact the room was filled with all manner of items, everything from dolls and dollhouses to jewelry and children's clothes. When I inquired after Mrs Patterson's granddaughter, Sky, I was further informed that Sky had died at birth some eleven years prior to our visit to Ensenada.

Mrs Patterson broke down at this point and began to cry. She told me that her daughter would have been a good mother but that drug addiction had ruined her life, then went on to give us further details regarding her daughter.

Jo Ann's father, now deceased, had served in the Foreign Service for the United States government and had spent considerable time in Central and South America. Mrs Patterson stated that she and her daughter often accompanied Mr Patterson and that at the age of thirteen, while living in Lima, Peru, Jo Ann had been kidnapped by a guerrilla faction of the Shining Path and held for nearly a month, during which time she was subjected to torture and rape. Her father later committed suicide. As a teenager Jo Ann became promiscuous, having at least two abortions for which she later felt guilty. Her first husband was a musician. Both Jo Ann and her husband became addicted to drugs. He died of an overdose. She had a daughter she named Sky who was born addicted to drugs and who died in the hospital… Her mother says that in her opinion, her daughter was never the same after the kidnapping and that there were instances of cutting and other 'strange' behavior.

During the conversation I asked Mrs Patterson to explain to me when and how the various items were brought to her *granddaughter's bedroom. Mrs Patterson essentially told me the following:*

My daughter, Jo Ann, has, over the years, come here from time to time to live. I made her her own front apartment unit attached to the house. She sometimes works in Tijuana and comes and goes. As far as I know, Jo told me she is on her feet a lot and that she works for a flooring company.

I did notice that my daughter wears gloves whenever she comes to the house. She told me that she wears the gloves because she is always cold. I noticed she has been very fidgety lately and nervous. I suspected she might be using drugs again. I really didn't want to know what was going on. Jo Ann spent about a year in a drug rehab center in New Mexico prior to this.

I'm not sure exactly when Jo Ann brought all the items to Sky's room. I think it was about a month or a month and a half ago. She showed up with two duffel bags. She told me someone owed her some money and gave her what was inside instead of the money. She put the items in Sky's room then spent considerable time constructing the dollhouse, which I thought was kind of strange but I also have gotten used to her doing strange things, and I guess I just did not want to know any more about it.

When, at one point, I asked Mrs Patterson if, in the wake of Jo Ann's childhood ordeals, any psychiatric help or evaluation had ever been sought, Mrs Patterson informed me that this was something she did not wish to discuss further.

This concluded Gladys Patterson's statement.

At exactly 0800 hours on the following morning, I drove to the headquarters of the Mexican State Police for the purpose of taking custody of Jo Ann Patterson. What I found there was a scene of considerable commotion and confusion. Federal soldiers had been called in and were present. A shooting had occurred hours before my visit. The shooting had taken place on the grounds of the headquarters and was believed to have been carried out by a newly formed splinter unit of the Tijuana Cartel. Three officers of the state police had been murdered. The station house was in a very chaotic state. I was informed that Detective Moreno was one of the officers who had been shot and that Jo Ann Patterson was no longer on the premises. It was unknown what had become of her. It was unknown if she had been hurt. It was unknown whether she had been abducted, or had simply found a way to walk away at the height of the confusion.

I spent one more day in Tijuana, but as the state police were occupied in dealing with the aftermath of the gun battle, and as Jo Ann Patterson was now very much aware of her situation and probably already gone from the city, there seemed little point in remaining. I returned to San Diego.

It was difficult, Chance thought, to know where the truthfulness of Blackstone's final report ended and began, why he had kept it, whether or not it had ever been filed or really, when one thought about it, if he was even its author. She was after all handy with both language and math. But even *if* one were to take the report at face value, there remained the matter of the detective's final hours in Tijuana and Blackstone's claiming them as *uneventful* – most certainly the beginning of the great long lie that would one day do him in. For if it was true that Jo Ann Patterson had vanished into Mexico, it was equally true that Jackie Black had come home with Raymond Blackstone and Chance was at least thirty seconds in trying to imagine what all of that must have looked like before abandoning it in favor of sleep. What did it matter now, the thing that had taken place between them, the cop and the whore? Already, he felt it slipping away – one more bit of chicanery, of which the planet was already filled to overflowing.

A few good men, and hard to find

Recovery was a slow boat to a questionable port. Some days were better than others. All were spent in his apartment. Some were spent beneath the covers. Some were spent in fashioning small sheaths of heavy paper with staples passing for wires, practicing with a kitchen knife... how many times the sheath stays in his pocket versus how many times it falls out, or comes out partway, so that it might come out the rest of the way later on... in a forty-foot tumble say, to the sands of Ocean Beach. Hours were spent in worrying about the men in the Mercedes and what if anything they would ever say if they were ever caught. Additional hours were spent worrying about the blood but there was something D had said to him once... that even as he was being struck, a man might turn from the blow, that a blade might catch on bone or otherwise be made to miss its mark, and before long Chance is beginning to feel it like that... striking and falling and Blackstone spun, so that any blood spray is going away from Chance and not toward him. And then of course there was that other bit, Blackstone's bit – the thirty downhill feet it had been necessary for the detective to traverse before reaching his car, the very long city block he'd had to drive, then managing by some force of will Chance can only imagine to get to the room and then to a chair and finally to kill the man who would have killed her and Chance thinking that at least one of his hallucinatory memories was at least partially correct, that seen in a particular light, Blackstone really *had*, when all was said and done, gotten the better of him – if only there had been someone to stab him through the heart every day that he lived.

As for anything more concrete, which is to say anything that might have passed for recovered memory with regard to things as they had actually transpired on the cliffs above Ocean Beach... *that* room was bare and continued so... as the days passed, as Detective Newsome failed to come, which was not, of course, to say that he never would, but in the end, one can only worry about such things for so long. Blackstone was dead and Chance was alive, as in the city beyond his windows the long hot summer was grinding finally to an end and the Doc Billy case was coming at last to trial.

It was Lucy who at last helped him down the stairs of his building and into the street. He was equipped with a walking stick and temporary back brace. 'You know,' she said, 'you really don't have to do this.'

'*Au contraire*,' Chance told her, adding that he was called upon to act, if only as a soldier of the heart.

'Are you *sure* you're all right?'

'It's the least I can do.'

'I asked if you were all right?'

Chance nodded. There was a longer answer to that question but it would have to wait, time being of the essence.

She drove him to the main courthouse near City Hall in downtown San Francisco. At question was Dr William Fry's overall mental health, both neurological and psychiatric, but most particularly his susceptibility to undue influence and how all of these factors when taken together might or might not impact upon his testamentary capacity, which would in turn affect his Mexican lover's ability to keep the considerable amount of money he'd given her, or for that matter, whether or not the two might continue united, a restraining order on the part of attorneys for the Oregonians having prevented this from the date of Chance's original reports. If the court were to rule in favor of the plaintiff, for whom Chance was being called, Doc Billy would no longer continue as the master of his fortune, pecuniary and otherwise. His Mexican lover would, in all probability, be facing either jail time or deportation as she had been living in the country on a temporary work visa.

They were all there of course, Mr Berg and Mr Green, the relative from Oregon Chance had only spoken to once or twice on the phone and whom he liked even less in person. The questions he was asked while seated on the stand were very much like the questions he had been asked at the time of his deposition. He was asked to read from notes made prior to his deposition and asked if those notes generally expressed the opinions he was ready to testify to under oath. He was only too happy to lie copiously on behalf of the star-crossed lovers, at times going so far as to blatantly contradict some of his earlier findings, saying simply that upon reflection this and upon further reflection that. He demurred and deflected, hedged and equivocated. He was at times vague, at others intentionally opaque, to the point that Mr Berg, acting on behalf of the plaintiffs, appeared upon the brink of some cerebrovascular event.

Chance did all of this without fear of repercussions or reprisals. If pressed at some later date in some later proceeding… he was positioned, he thought, quite nicely to blame events in his *own* recent past for any failure of memory or even mental acuity. It might of course be a good long while, once word had spread, before anyone in need of an expert witness came knocking but then he was pretty certain that he was pretty much done with all of that.

He could, from time to time, see Doc Billy grinning at him like an ape from a corner of the room and at one point even suffered the momentary fear that perhaps the old man was already lost to dementia. In the end, he chose to interpret the grin as more sly than apelike, conspiratorial as opposed to simply deranged and went so far as to imagine for the first time just what the doctor's last stand might look like. He was thinking Mexico, the lovers' mad flight… He was, after all, at just this moment, buying them a bit of time and it wasn't like they were short on cash. He had begun to think of a song. He imagined Chet Baker singing 'Let's Get Lost' as the couple streaked for the border. The exercise lifted his spirits, higher really than they had been in quite some time, so much so that when the attorneys had at last had their way with him and he had been asked, somewhat unceremoniously, to leave the stand and perhaps the country, he suggested to Lucy, waiting for him at the back of the room with an odd expression on her face, that they should drive just up the street to their old offices, that it was a terrific-looking day and he was curious to see if any of Jean-Baptiste's infamous death-defying photographs might yet have been delivered.

Captain America

MORE THAN two hundred of the gems had in fact arrived. Some had been mounted and framed and these individually packaged. Many more had been stored in the particular type of large brown envelopes Chance had seen the art students use in transporting their drawings. Each of these contained dozens of photographs separated by sheets of newsprint. 'I know you liked the guy,' Lucy said at one point. 'But… we get up and running again… I would recommend keeping the ones we hang to a minimum.'

'I've learned how to look at them,' he told her. 'It's all about the light in their eyes.' He waved to the old man in the diaper, Captain America. 'Check out that fucker. No surrender there.'

'Umm. I would still suggest limiting the number.'

'Yes, well… Moderation in all things, I suppose.' He was taking this to include the amount of truth people might be asked to confront at any one sitting then moved on to something else that had been on his mind of late, the subject of his French furniture, the Printz collection.

'That old stuff you sold?'

'I've been thinking a lot about that lately. It's been kind of eating at me if you want to know the truth and now I'm thinking it might look good in the office.'

'I thought you couldn't wait to get rid of it.'

'I needed money,' he told her. 'I cheated a bit on the sale.'

Lucy pursed her lips.

'It's a bit complicated but what I would like to do is contact the current owner, make him an offer to buy it back.'

'And tell him he was cheated?'

'I intend the offer as generous to the point of being ridiculous. Is that good enough, do you think?'

Lucy shrugged but he was willing to take it as a yes.

'The other thing I'd like to do... There was a girl on a skateboard that got hit the day I fell. I'd like to find out who she is and how she's doing.' He was at the point of asking her to look into it when he became aware that a fashionably dressed woman of perhaps forty had come to occupy the doorway that separated the waiting room of his office from the hallway beyond. The woman had very black hair and very white skin and seemed to tilt slightly to one side.

Her name, she said, was Veronica Woods and she was recently of the Unit for the Victims of Violent Crimes at San Francisco General where she had spent the better part of the summer. He could see that she'd had some manner of reconstructive work done on one side of her face, the net effect of which was to render her both gaunt and striking, a damaged bit of fine art. Like Chance, she carried a cane and walked with a slight limp. Unlike Chance, her condition was, she said, permanent. There was a story that came with her of course. It involved failed restraining orders and threats of violence, a cultish religious group she'd somehow managed to run afoul of. The story appeared to involve the attempted extraction of a family member together with a car bomb and would require a good deal more attention than Chance was just now prepared to give for the picture to become complete.

Someone on the ward had mentioned Chance by name, one of the volunteer orderlies, she thought now. She'd heard that he had been in some kind of accident and was sorry to intrude unannounced but had not known what else to do or where to turn. 'These people are still out there,' she told him, by which he took her to mean the perpetrators of the violent crimes that had landed her among the victims of such. She had rarely been out of her apartment since leaving the hospital. Her life was in shambles, to say nothing of her career. Her medical insurance was no longer. 'My life's a thing of the past,' she told him and began to cry. He could not help noticing that the part of her face where the work had been done remained quite rigid. 'I was a chef,' she said finally. 'But now, since all of this…' She lifted a hand to her face. 'I've lost the ability to smell… I was told this was an area in which you have some expertise…'

Chance said that he was sorry and he was but he had begun to think about this place she had named and to think about it in a particular light. The phrase *mutilés de guerre* came to mind. The French had coined it for those mutilated in war but *life and love* might do as well and he was somewhat taken aback that he had not heard of it until now, this abode for the Victims of Violence, and thinking too that he needed to get out more while at the same time experiencing some difficulty in mastering his own bit of vertigo, attributable no doubt to the sudden, simultaneous rush of so many large ideas.

They had moved to Chance's office where he was now half seated and half standing, braced on the edge of his desk near a partially open window and so able to take the full measure of the day, unlike the poor creature before him. The air at last was full of the season he wanted to tell her, the coming of winter – all white light and seas the color of naked pearl. At which point the woman alerted him once more to her presence. 'Should I go?' she asked.

The words stopped him in his tracks. It was what J… he had started thinking of her only as J… had once said to him in very nearly the same way and place and hadn't he caught some rhythm in her voice, some trace of the familiar like a scent left upon the room and was there not too some certain slant to the line of her jaw, the height of her cheek… impossible to conceal even by the work that had been done or the dark glasses she'd chosen to hide behind? Surely this was impossible, for any number of reasons but what he understands as by the flash of a strobe is that *every* woman in distress would from this point forward not only look like J but in a very particular way *be* J and the thing is… he's *kind* of all right with that. And then he knows something else too, that one day it just might be. There was after all an address in what she left, a place she visits now and again in Baja California. One might even go bearing gifts. The drive, though a good deal farther than Mariella Franko's apartment in Palo Alto, no longer seemed so constrained by the workings of the world. What after all was any of that to him, or the caged heart any but his own? But as of now there was this new creature before him, this victim of violent crime. One might just as well have said manna from heaven but he could see that he was making her nervous, twisting one chafed hand inside another, nails bitten to the quick so that he was moved to place his own upon her shoulder. 'It's okay,' he told her. 'Really. I'm a bit preoccupied and I'm sorry but I'm thinking I'd like to help.' He took her tears as those of joy or at least relief and when she had gone he phoned Big D by way of Allan's Antiques. It was the first they'd spoken since the day Chance had called from the hospital lobby.

'What's up, buddy?' D asked. He put the question to him as if they had spoken only yesterday and then about the weather.

'I may have something,' Chance said.

ACKNOWLEDGMENTS

I would like to thank Tom Kier, Ronald Newquist, and Jonathan Mueller, MD, for their incredible generosity of both time and spirit. Also… mention is made of Steven Pressfield and Hugh MacLeod, excellent writers who don't know me from Adam and should not be held responsible.

A CONVERSATION
WITH KEM NUNN

Most of your books have been set in Southern California. What made you want to head north and place *Chance* in San Francisco?

I lived just north of San Francisco for about eight years and spent a fair amount of time in the city. Later, when I landed on the idea of writing about this doctor, Dr Eldon Chance, the doctor I most relied upon for my research is based in San Francisco, which led to my spending more time there. And I could see it was going to be this noirish kind of tale and the city felt right for that. We often associate noir with Los Angeles, but there have been some classics set in San Francisco as well. I'm a particular fan of the old Robert Mitchum movie *Out of the Past*. And it is, after all, the cool, gray city, at the edge of a particularly turbulent sea, with its ever-shifting winds and fogs – a useful enough metaphor in a story about secrets and hidden agendas.

Are there certain themes in *Chance* carried over from your previous books?

I like to think so. I have often written about characters that begin in some place of isolation. I don't mean physical isolation necessarily. It's more a function of what they believe about themselves, of how they see themselves in relation to others. Then the story kicks in and eventually they are forced to action, and by that action are drawn back into the world, back into some sense of community – however small or esoteric that community might be. And I do believe that is where we find the truest expression of our humanity, in community. I have always admired Dietrich Bonhoeffer's line 'I only know God in the company of my brothers.'

Dr Eldon Chance makes a series of bad decisions – one to forge artwork on an antique and another to sleep with his emotionally unstable married patient. Why was I still cheering for him?

Possibly because you need years and years of therapy. Okay, seriously… I would hope it's because that even in his brokenness, you also get that he is not such a bad guy. It's a function of what fiction can do – we see some character that is really screwing up, not out of malice but just out of being human and confused and fucked up, which I would argue go hand in hand with being human, and they're absolutely blowing it – in a kind of larger than life way. Their screw-ups are so obvious and on such a scale that it winds up making for a kind of dark comedy. But if the thing is firing on all cylinders, we are not just laughing at the character, we are laughing at ourselves. We are finding some reflection of our own failings and foibles, so we're laughing a little, and cringing a little, but we're pulling for the guy too, because we realize that at some very fundamental level, he's just like me. It's a gamble that as a writer or filmmaker or whatever you can create a plot that will in some way reflect the general 'human condition,' for lack of a better term. And that your audience will at some level get that, and have some fun with it.

Your characters get beat up a lot, even the women.

There's a phrase that finds its way into the book – *mutilés de guerre* – coined by the French for those mutilated in war. The phrase pops into Chance's head when he is talking to a patient who has come to him from a unit for the victims of violent crimes, and he thinks of its much broader application – that life and love might just as well suffice. I even thought, once upon a time, that the book could be called *Victims of Violent Crimes*, as the term pretty much applies to everyone in the book in one way or another. D is the story's principal purveyor of violence and it seemed important to make what he is capable of seem real, so that it's not just fantasy violence; it's raw and ugly the way violence really is. And when he shows that to Chance, in a Tenderloin alley, it's a very visceral way of saying this is how the world works and if you're going to survive this thing you've gotten yourself into, then you need to get hip to it. And for all that to work, that particular scene needed to be just that – raw and ugly and maybe a little shocking – so that the reader can be shocked in the same way that Chance is shocked. It also needed to be like that so that it could stand in contrast to D's very detached and analytical attitude about violence: his belief there are no victims, just volunteers.

Did you set out to write a psychological thriller? What do you think of that term?

I don't really like to think in terms of genre. I understand that others have to, that books have to be marketed in certain ways and all of that, but I don't really care about it, and don't think about it when I write. I think – and I would guess this is probably true for anyone who wants to work well – that what one is really after, in whatever medium, is to arrive at some particular way of rendering the world that feels authentic to one's self. I really think that is the goal. And you know it when you find it. It's the thing that makes great writers great, in my opinion. I think the first writer I ever really discovered that in... I was about sixteen or so and I read *The Metamorphosis* by Kafka and was just bowled over. It was such a voice, such a way of seeing, unlike anything else I had read at the time. It's all about finding your voice. And whatever helps you get there... If certain tropes from certain genres play a part... well then, all is fair game. There's more than one road to Jerusalem.

You've written for the HBO series _Deadwood_, developed _John from Cincinnati_ with David Milch, and are currently writing and producing for the FX series _Sons of Anarchy_. How does writing for television differ from writing your novels? Do you prefer one to the other?

Prose allows for a certain kind of narrative voice that is simply unavailable to you as a scriptwriter. Prose was my first love and I still like to think I'm better at it. That said... I do love the movies. I also think there is some pretty interesting writing and storytelling going on in cable television right now and it has been my privilege to work on shows with David Milch and Kurt Sutter. They are different men and different writers but they are both out there doing their thing in their chosen medium, finding ways to express their vision, making their voices heard, and I admire both of them for that.

Working with David Milch as my introduction to television was a kind of revelation. David comes out of the Iowa Writers' Workshop, where he was a tutorial assistant to Robert Penn Warren. He comes to his scriptwriting out of a real love and understanding of literature, and seeing that, and working with that on a daily basis for the better part of three years, kind of changed my perspective on the two modalities. At some very fundamental level, it really is all writing, that what you're aiming for in a script is not so different from what you're aiming for in a book. You may be using different tools but the goal is essentially the same. It gets you back to that earlier article of faith – that there is more than one road to Jerusalem.

What other writers and books do you recommend?

All writers create their own canons, the books they return to for inspiration, etc. I doubt mine is so unique. It would include the likes of Kafka, Beckett, James, Melville, Conrad, Flannery O'Connor. Those are some that pop to mind. Among more contemporary writers, I have always admired Robert Stone. I like Cormac McCarthy. I recently read a book called *This River* by James Brown that I liked a lot. I read a fair amount of nonfiction, especially literary biographies. I liked Robert Richardson's book on William James, Carol Sklenicka on Raymond Carver, D. T. Max on David Foster Wallace, to name three.

Are you working on another book now?

Does in my head count?

About Us

In addition to No Exit Press, Oldcastle Books has a number of other imprints, including Kamera Books, Creative Essentials, Pulp! The Classics, Pocket Essentials and High Stakes Publishing > oldcastlebooks.com

For more information about Crime Books > crimetime.co.uk

Check out the kamera film salon for independent, arthouse and world cinema > kamera.co.uk

For more information, media enquiries and review copies please contact > marketing@oldcastlebooks.com